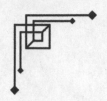

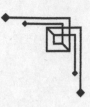

MARKETING CAMPAIGN

- Social Media Advertising

- National Radio and Podcast Interviews

- National Print and Online Media Coverage

- Bookstagram/BookTok Influencer Campaign

- Influencer Outreach

- Features in the *Harper Voyager* Newsletter

- Targeted E-mail Marketing Based on Consumer
Browsing and Category Interests

- Features on the Harper Voyager Social Media Platform

- Social Media Video Shorts

- Dedicated Audio Marketing Campaign

- National Distribution of Advance Reader's Editions

- Digital Galley Available on Edelweiss and NetGalley

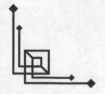

BINDLE PUNK BRUJA

BINDLE PUNK
BRUJA

A NOVEL

DESIDERIA MESA

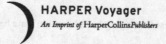

HARPER Voyager
An Imprint of HarperCollinsPublishers

BINDLE PUNK BRUJA. Copyright © 2022 by Desideria Mesa. All rights reserved. Printed in the United States of America. No part of this book may be used or reproduced in any manner whatsoever without written permission except in the case of brief quotations embodied in critical articles and reviews. For information, address HarperCollins Publishers, 195 Broadway, New York, NY 10007.

HarperCollins books may be purchased for educational, business, or sales promotional use. For information, please email the Special Markets Department at SPsales@harpercollins.com.

Harper Voyager and design are trademarks of HarperCollins Publishers LLC.

FIRST EDITION

Designed by Angela Boutin
Map designed by Jeffrey L. Ward
Title page illustration © tartila/stock.adobe.com
Chapter opener illustration © bewalrus/stock.adobe.com

Library of Congress Cataloging-in-Publication Data has been applied for.

ISBN 978-0-06-305608-4

22 23 24 25 26 LSC 10 9 8 7 6 5 4 3 2 1

*My daddy sat me down when I was five years old, getting down on his
knees so he could look me in the eye. His dark eyes shone with tenderness
and laughter as he told me who we are.*

*"Hey, Desi!" He grinned. "Did you know that you're a Mexican?"
My lip quivered. My eyes got all watery. I thought he was calling me a
name. I burst into tears, crying, "I don't wanna be a Mexicaaaaaan!"*

He laughed.

I wailed.

And so began the journey of figuring out who I am.

*To my family and friends, whom I love dearly—you lifted me up when
I needed it most. To Kenneth, who always believes in me. And to my
children, my three blessings on earth, who have celebrated every moment
of this project with me—I also write this story to remind us of who we are
and where we came from. If not for the bravery of our abuelas and the
abuelas before them, we would not be here to share their amazing stories.*

And I thank God for the skills and courage to tell them.

To adventure.

To unfailing love.

To pirates and poetry.

BIN-DƏL PUNK, NOUN

An early twentieth-century term to describe one who carries his clothing or bedding in a bundle, usually derogatory in nature. Also used to classify a hobo, wanderer, migrant worker, tramp, or one who has no home.

BROO-HA, NOUN

A woman thought to have magical powers, also known as a witch.

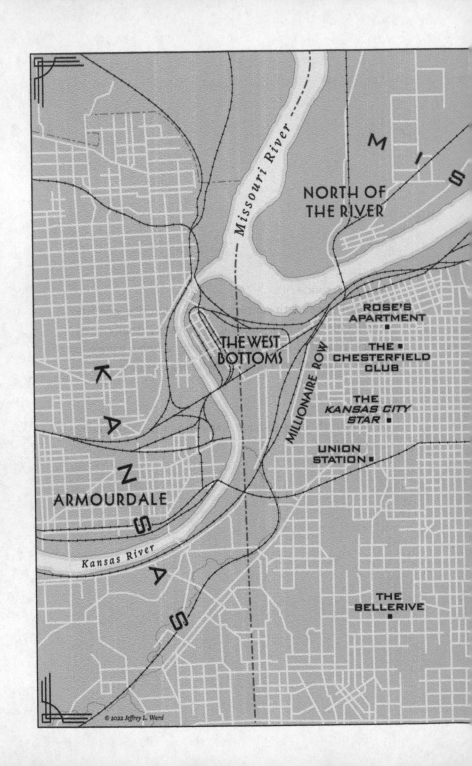

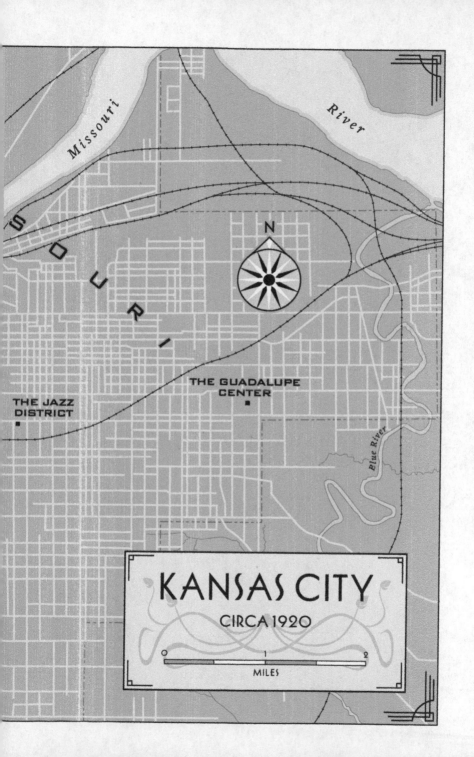

BINDLE PUNK BRUJA

1

I AM WHO I SAY I AM.

The family spell book stares back at me from the black cushions of my Model T. Rough limbs twist around the tree on the front cover, splitting off into three branches of magic—my reminder of everything I'll never be. I practiced for nearly an hour after I left the newspaper office, but I don't know why I try anymore. Time never stills and the stars won't speak to me. All practicing ever does is solidify the fact that I'll never fit into my family, that my father's Anglo blood is mucking up my abilities even though I carry around his physical features that help hide that I'm the daughter of an immigrant. So there's at least that.

But it's not like I'm gonna thank the classless man who left my mother out of shame, either.

Ugh. Just the thought of my biological father makes the side of my nose wrinkle as I tuck the useless book under my arm. Pretending to check the crimson on my lips in the rearview mirror, I make sure the dirt road is clear of anyone who might recognize me. My hands are already dampening at the thought of someone seeing me anywhere near the river community. Not because I'm embarrassed by my family. I wish every day that I could claim them. But my mother worked too hard to erase any ties I had to them long ago—can't let all that go to waste just because I got careless.

"¡Bruja falsa! ¡Bruja falsa!"

Oh no.

Instinct slides my body down the cloth seat, my heart and head ducking below the door panel before I hear the tiny, annoying cackles over my gasping. Righting myself with as much dignity as I can muster, I smooth the front of my blouse with leveled eyes at the two barefoot ragamuffins who are bent in half with laughter at the front of my car. My breathing calms back into submission at the relieving sight of the only kids near the tracks who are brave enough to mess with me.

"Step closer if you wanna see how real my magic is!" I snap, cracking the front window open.

"¿Síííí?" The little boy without a shirt flashes me a gap-toothed sneer while the tiny one reaches up to play with the metal headlamp. "Mi mamá says you're a night owl."

Shorty stands on his toes to shout over his brother. "¡No puedes hablar español!"

"An-an-an she says you're a gold dig—"

I jerk the driver's-side door open with a challenging glare in their direction, the two grubby darlings hopping backward with amused, curious eyes.

Not quite the intimidation I was hoping for.

"Well then!" I call out with twitching lips as brown water splashes their legs from a grassy puddle. "You tell your mother that my business is none of hers. And if you ever bother me again, I'll come and walk around in your brains while you're sleeping! ¡Fuera de aquí!"

The muddied boys shriek with fearful giggles, grabbing each

other as they sprint toward the riverbank's line of oak trees. Out of sight, I finally let free a bursting laugh, rolling my eyes at the newest gossip. *Can't speak Spanish. What a racket.* Of course I can . . .

I just hope my mother didn't hear it.

My eyes dart at a passing Roadster, its nickel grill catching my breath as I think of the tales she used to tell of greedy men who would come after us if I didn't hide my heritage to play the part of an anonymous citizen. Presenting as anything but white would strip me of everything my mother and I have worked for. There's no real opportunity for immigrants and their kids, even without our witchery. But what they would do to a bruja like me is a whole other realm of danger. Though most people don't know our magic exists, the risk of visiting home is still very real—as real as the lump in my throat as I hold the book tightly to my chest at the thought of something happening to the people I love if I get careless.

Luckily, my mixed ethnicity has helped keep me from being found out . . . and arrested, since non-whites can't rent in most parts of the city. Not to mention the risk of having even a little bruja blood. The goons I work with would sell me out in a hot second if they ever discovered who I really am or what (little) I can do. Of course, independent women have to use what they've got. I mean, I know I *shouldn't* charm them. But . . . it helps me get what I want. What I *need.*

Besides, those guys are too busy looking at my legs to be suspicious about childhood fairy tales of witches on the west side.

Swallowing my angst, I grab the hand brake with a cringing glance up the hill toward the *house.* A family of four living in a boxcar near the decimated Union Depot is unappealing enough. That it's my family, the one I'm supposed to be hiding from even while I'm supposed to visit them (because no sane person tells their abuela they're not stopping by because they're "white" now), makes it even tougher to make myself move toward it.

The humid sunset thickens the marinade. As my automobile

idles in the rail yard, the breeze rushes through the open windows, sharing the pungent cattle sweat and ash from the nearby steel factory and stockyards, adding to my dismal mood. The more time passes between visits, the more I feel like a stranger in my own family. It's not their fault I was born different, though. It's all a risk, but it's all for family, so it's worth it.

With another nervous glance around me, I pull the hand brake with dread of soot-stained mud that's sure to cling to the bottom of my heeled shoes.

Okay—mostly worth it.

I cling to my handbag with a groan as I step out onto the damp earth, soaked by spring rains carrying the river from its banks. Heavy, sticky steps push me toward the shoddy double boxcar with crude windows cut beside the retractable door. Like the many others around it, green ivy and honeysuckle vines cover a good portion of the dilapidated wood panels. The connecting front porches are filled with hanging plants to make the community more livable for the wives and children. Not that there are many families out here anymore. Most rail workers have moved on since the Great Flood of 1913. Earth magic is stronger by the river, but we can still use it anywhere. Why my family insists on staying in the industrialized flood zone after twelve years, I'll never know.

I wave to a few passing neighbors coming home from their long day in the factories, who return a curt nod as I climb up the splintered steps of the boxcar at the end of the row. My community has never been a big supporter of my endeavors, but they're too afraid of my abuela to say so. Before my hand even reaches the long iron handle, the door slides open.

"Well, well. Luna has decided to bless us with a visit," the young man in front of me says, his saucy tone unmasked. "Did you mean to travel to the River Bottoms, hermanita, or have you lost your way to your boulevard apartment?"

Flattening my eyes at his smug countenance, I wait for him to step aside. My older brother's sarcasm has been less than subtle lately, his former humor no longer glinting behind his espresso eyes. Javier could be counted as handsome if not for the dirt sticking to the sweat on his dark skin, caking his coveralls and intense eyebrows beneath his straw hat. Or maybe that's just me saying that because he's such a nuisance. A nuisance that I love like no other. As if knowing his effect on me, he suddenly breaks into a pleased smile, making the dimple in his chin more prominent. It's an exact match to my own, the only feature we share from our mother.

"Stop standing in the doorway, niño!" her voice lectures from somewhere inside. "You'll let the flies in!"

"Yes, Mamá," he calls over his shoulder before turning an ornery gaze back to me, smile gone once more. "You better get in here before someone sees an ivory spinster like you hanging around our little village."

My eyebrow arches as I pull a pamphlet from my bag, holding it in front of his nose. "If they do, I'll just tell them I'm proselytizing you."

He lets out an exaggerated gasp that makes me laugh, snatching the paper from my hand and stuffing it into his back pocket with a glance behind him. "Don't let Mama Sunday see that. She's in a mood today, and I need a remedy."

"Shoulder again?" I ask, pushing past him into the warm living area, sliding the spell book onto an end table. He nods, stretching his arm in circles as he nudges the door closed with his toes. Removing my cloche hat, I hang my bag on the coatrack, a wistful smile crossing my lips as I take in the scene before me. I would never admit it out loud—especially to my family, who has sacrificed so much to give me the opportunities that I now have—but I miss these simpler times. My mother bustles in the corner, tending to the night's meal in front of the cookstove, its white enamel chipping near the cast-iron burners. The savory aroma of chili verde and browning tortillas transforms the boxcar into the place I once knew so well, though time has taken its toll. The flowers on the orange upholstery of the small couch and chair in the living area are fading. Yet the oak trim shows great care, shining with polish. Javier is a man of many talents, with only his woodworking skills rivaling his sarcasm. The handcrafted kitchen table and chairs are arranged in the corner by the cutout doorway that leads to the other boxcar—the rest of the house. The furniture and small cactus are stuffed into a space not meant for it all, but it smells like home. It sounds like home.

My mother's low, melodic voice sings a mysterious tune about enchanted riverbeds as she flips soft flatbread from the skillet onto a ceramic plate. Though her graying raven hair is pulled back into a debonair crown about her head, a few strands float around her face from her laborious day at the bakery. The tiny crinkles around her eyes and mouth have deepened. But she is still beautiful, perhaps even more so seeing how content she looks right now.

"Aye, aye, aye, Mamá," I say, planting my hands on the high waist of my trousers. "You cook for an army."

She whirls around, shaking her wooden spoon at me, the salsa verde splashing on her stained apron. All sense of contentment is gone. "What did I tell you about speaking Spanish? The world won't accept you if you catch an accent."

I nearly smile at the irony. Her accent is unhinged. But her dialect doesn't rouse suspicion the way mine would if I let myself slip anywhere else. I understand the reasons. My smiles are hard to force these days. Still, my heart pricks at what I'm forced to hide.

"Don't worry, Mamá," Javier says with a teasing grin as he plunges his sooty arms into a water-filled basin on the wooden counter. "No one's gonna find out she's related to a bunch of witches. The tax surveyors visit more often than she does."

My nose flares at his insinuation. He knows I can't just drop by anytime I feel like it. Even if I wasn't hiding from cops and heisters, I'm a twenty-five-year-old single woman with two jobs and a healthy social life, and I intend to keep it that way for a long, long while. Yes, I miss my family. But I'd miss my freedom even more.

"I've been . . . busy," I reply with all the innocence I can muster. "It's hard enough holding a job at the *Star* as a woman, but running the club at night—I hardly have time to myself."

The statement is kind of true. I have to hobnob in a city like this one to keep my customers coming back. Javier laughs in a grunting sort of way, scrubbing his face before taking the hand towel from our mother's shoulder. "You write a serial fiction column part-time for that newspaper, and I believe I do the heavy lifting at that speakeasy, hermanita. Nice try, though."

"Fine," I say, leaning forward with attitude since I can't make myself as tall as him. "You carry boxes and pour the whiskey, but I have to keep a bunch of drunk jerks entertained and keep their hands off me at the same time. And make sure that whiskey is there in the first place. They hardly look at you, so what are you complaining about?"

"Oh, por favor, without that light complexion, you wouldn't have it as easy as you do! Your father's only good contribution to your life."

I force my terse face to relax with a deep breath through the nose. My damn complexion isn't enough to save me from a man's world and he knows it. At least he should. I won't get drawn into another sparring match, even though I want to tell him how his snarky comments make me want to curse his feet to itch all night. *Damn curses.* Or curses be damned, because they never work anyway.

My silence knocks the smirk off Javier's face just as a wooden spoon knocks the hat from his head. "I've told you to take that off in the house!" Gloria Alvarado is such a prim woman in her pressed calf-length dresses, with pride to rival any person of a higher station. "And how many times do I have to tell you, that lawyer is no longer Luna's father. My José would have never treated us in such a way. White men and their privileges, deciding when and where to plant their flag—"

"Dios, Mamá," my brother groans. "We're about to eat."

The wooden spoon wags inches from his nose. "Don't you take the Lord's name in vain, niño! Your father would roll over in his grave. God rest his soul." She touches her fingers to her forehead, chest, and shoulders, a religious sign of the cross meant to shy away bad luck, I assume. "But to see a daughter of mine, living in the fancy part of town, owning her own business—he would be so proud!"

"Sí," Javier says, carrying a pot of pork-filled stew to the table. He winces as he sets it down. "She flaunts her Anglo face and our abuela's money around with those powers of persuasion. That's a real accomplishment, Luna."

My ears start to burn. "Javi, if you think for a second that I haven't had to work for what I have—"

"Hey, if all I had to do to move up in this world was kiss a few of the right fellas, then paint my pretty lips, hermanita."

Heat simmers from somewhere beneath my rib cage. I'm used to the anger I feel. But I'll never get used to the shame. "The magic doesn't work like that, and you know it. I can't convince anyone to do anything." And I can't. Not like our abuela, anyway. Maybe not ever, since I can't get the stupid spells to work. My brother's got it all wrong—just like so many of the men in my life.

"No?" His jaw is setting in the way it does when his joking has turned serious, and my hands clench on their own. "You just toy with their minds and call their bluffs. I get it, sis. Wish I had the gift, but don't complain to me until you've had to work twelve-hour shifts in the bitter cold for fifteen cents an hour while your white betters make double in half the time!"

And there it is. As if the privileged gringo and struggling Latina inside me aren't always at odds with each other, my brother has to join in the fray too. ¿Quién sabe? He's got his vantage point and I've got mine. I'll never know a life with dark skin any more than he knows the life of a woman.

"Stop treating me like I'm the enemy, Javi," I say, holding in a hiss.

"Then stop acting like it."

My narrowed eyes pop open. *¿Oh sí?* "Don't act like you don't know exactly how many times I've had to slap a guy because I was too flustered to charm him."

"Fine, but don't act like you know what it's like for me."

"Don't act like you know what it's like for me!"

A plate of steaming tortillas bangs against the table, our mother's mouth tight with warning. My brother and I share a silent glare as we take our seats across from each other, bitterness creeping up my neck and across my tongue. It's not a new argument. It's certainly hitting harder than usual right now, our relationship straining like the days we're apart. As the colorful glass bowls make their way around the table, I force my back straight and shoulders square. I won't let Javier's words get to me. He's just tired, the worn look in his eyes betraying his youth—only three years older than me. His life hasn't been easy, being brought to a strange country from his home in Mexico as a young boy, his father dying on the journey.

Being Mexican in America, period.

I, at least, was born here, my immigrant blood mingling with the blood of an upper-class gentleman who refuses to acknowledge me. But it's those very features that were passed on to me that allow me the privilege that Javier resents. My mother said it was a gift, my chestnut-brown hair and blue eyes, with a body and skin like Clara Bow—and the men at the gin mill tell me the same thing, but for different reasons. I rather like the comparison—a famous flapper, "the It Girl" who broke out of poverty and brought sexiness to the moving pictures and slapped her boss for trying to kiss her. Labeled as a husband-stealer and a rebel against social norms, she's become my hero.

So maybe it was a gift. But, more often than not, it felt like a loan—one that could come due any minute.

"Luna . . ." My brother's hardness is gone from his face as he pokes his fork around his bowl. "I know it's not exactly easy for you. But if you saw the world through my eyes, through my skin, you would understand. And honestly, I wouldn't wish that on anyone, especially you, dear sister. I'm glad you've found favor, making a life for yourself."

My bitterness melts away as he takes a quick bite, avoiding my eyes. He doesn't quite apologize. I'm not certain he's said anything wrong. It's how he feels. If my mother hadn't sent me to the Guadalupe Center to learn of white culture as a young girl, things might have turned out differently for me as well, even with my light skin. Gloria had forethought, though. And Abuela's funds. Not all immigrants come to America poor and desperate. There's just a lack of opportunity to invest. My mother quickly realized the advantages of having a Caucasian daughter, taking me home and hiring a private tutor to continue my training to assimilate into American culture, and through the years, the affluent women at the center forgot about me. So when I eventually stepped out into city society as a white woman from north of the river, no one was any wiser. The ruse took, and now Luna is gone . . . except when I come home.

"Speaking of making your life," my mother starts, my head dropping with a groan. My hair tickles beneath my chin, the marcelled waves losing their hold in the humidity of the room. "Don't you think it's time to walk away from such a dangerous profession? Selling alcohol, working at night—you're breaking two laws at once. Marry a nice businessman and let him deal with these things."

Javier tilts his head, his playfulness returning. "Which suitor, Mamá?"

"¡Niño!" Gloria turns her attention back to me, her flashing eyes softening. "Luna, those men you rent your bar from can't protect you forever. I just don't trust mixing with gangsters. Who's going to protect you from them, eh?"

"Mamá, por favor, those gangsters are some of my best patrons, and you know my goal is to own a place soon."

At least, that's the plan. I've been saving for a long time, but if this is going to happen "soon," I'm going to have to borrow. Bitterness swirls in my stomach at the thought. As advantageous as my position in the world seems—at least, as advantageous as Javier seems to *think* it seems—I'm going to need a male cosigner for a loan . . . or a husband.

Ew. May the fates have a kinder plan for me than ending up as some guy's frau.

"Well," my mother continues, handing me two tortillas even though I only ever eat one, "they're your best patrons only because they don't know who you are, chiquita. If you think for a second that they would still protect you if they knew you were an earth bruja—a mixed one at that! And stop with the Spanish, yes? You'll catch an accent!"

I shake my head at the five hundred different things she's saying at once, tearing a small piece of the warm bread and dipping it into my stew. The flavor is robust and salty, kind of like the pride in this family that clashes with the undertone of shame. Shame of being who we are. My brother hates that I'm white while my mother whitewashes me in name and culture to fit me into society . . . even the underbelly. I mean, I'm barely middle class, for goodness' sake. And it's not like they're destitute—my abuela's money could get them a decent enough bungalow with what she's got left. But renters in better parts of town refuse them. Still, there are other places than the train tracks. Yet I do know why they stay here. Principle. Principle and pride.

Javier's comical voice breaks into my musings. "Don't worry, Mamá. She might be only half devil, but it's enough to drown out that accent and half her magic, too."

"Half bruja is still bruja!" an old voice lectures from the cutout doorway. I turn as my brother jumps up to hold our abuela's arm while she leans on a cane, her thin gray hair pulled into a tight bun. She shuffles across the creaking floor, her flowery dress hanging around her ankles where her stockings have slipped. As he lowers her into her seat beside me, she tsks her tongue, snatching the pamphlet from Javi's back pocket before cracking him on the behind with her cane. "I tell you I'm not going to those Mexican reservations."

My eyes roll. I can't help it. The Hispanic community finally has parts of the city to call their own, a nice neighborhood just to the east of here with their own shops and a church, but Mama Sunday won't go. It's not that she wants to live among the whites on the west side of Troost Avenue; she just doesn't like how the minorities were forced to the east side of the cement dividing line by zoning ordinances and shifty title restrictions. Again, principle and pride. I get it.

But this boxcar's literally starting to rot.

The heavy cane whacks me on the shoulder, a light bump that kind of hurts. "Keep your eyes ahead, niña. I travel on foot and sneak on trains to get here, nearly die of thirst on the way, lose my son, and I won't be told where to spend my own money." I rub my shoulder, my heart aching more as she reaches out a withered dark hand. "Ven aquí, give me your hand."

I try not to roll my eyes again. I really try.

The old woman slaps my knuckles. "No disrespect earth magic, niña!" From the pocket on the side of her homemade dress, she raises a fist, hovering it over my opened hand. Rich, wet dirt sprinkles onto my palm. "Some tales nearly lost, only a whisper left behind."

The granules don't look like dried insects and tobacco with a dash of river sand, but a cringe threatens the sides of my face anyway. If I wash my hand now, she'll get upset, so I stay still as she hums a haunting melody before speaking. "Some deserve their fate, but are blessed anyway. The earth hears, cries, drinks our blood and tears, and sometimes"—she claps her hand over mine, her diminished brown eyes nearly glowing—"grants us what we do not understand. But the *earth* understands. Luna Alvarado, you not half anything. You whole. And everything you put your hands to shall prosper."

As the weight of cutting criticisms in my head lift their burden at her blessing, I blink back the misting in my eyes, wondering how she does this to me every time. Her elixirs could bring an army to its knees. But she simply soothes broken hearts instead. Her gaze sharpens at Javier, who hangs his head.

"Lo siento, Abuela," he says. "I was only playing with her."

"Your playing is no playful."

"Sí, señora." He nods, throwing a twinkling glance at me. "My shoulder is making me a little cranky, I think."

"Yes, Mama Sunday," I say, taking up his cause. "He mentioned it earlier."

The old woman purses her lips, her wrinkles gathering around her mouth. "Then why you not heal him?"

"Abuela—"

"English, niña!" my mother pleads.

My abuela lifts a defiant index finger to interject. "Español."

"Madre," my mother says, "ella debe hablar inglés—"

"*Español.*"

Javier and I exchange amused glances as the two matriarchs bicker until my stew grows cold. "Grandma," I start again, pushing away my bowl. "It's not my talent."

I wouldn't call the ability I do have a talent, but I don't tell her that. *Charm.* The branch of magic I tinker with is actually amazing . . . if I could get it to work properly. I could have been born a healer or with the power to call down curses from the sky. Or all three abilities, like my abuela. But I am grateful for what little I do possess. It's better than nothing.

"Aye, aye, aye," the old witch says, turning to Javier with another handful of wet dirt. "Your only talent is doubt, niña." She smashes the black earth into my brother's shoulder with a firm grip that makes him grimace, rubbing it into the fabric of his shirt with a knotted hand. "Fear kills magic. What makes it grow? Depends on magic. But no hope means no magic."

The small crackling fire from the stove silences. My neck prickles as the little hairs rise. Like I'm plunging into water, the air grows thicker around me somehow, time standing still outside these slatted walls. My brother lifts a slow gaze to me, but it's like he doesn't see me—or our abuela's eyes. Just around the irises, the dark brown begins to shift and change like branches blowing in the wind. Mama Sunday looks to the ceiling with a gasp. "From dust you came. To dust you shall return." As the air releases, she slumps onto the table, Javier jumping up to gather her into his arms.

"I should not have asked that of you, Abuela," he says with a strain in his throat. "I know it's harder for you now."

"Ah, my niño, I no let you suffer." She turns her head from his chest, smiling at me with those swirling brown eyes swallowing her pupils as they always do after an incantation. She looks majestic . . . and exhausted. "You will learn, Luna. You must go now."

"But . . . but, Abuela—"

"No, really," my mother says, stuffing another tortilla into my hand. "You're going to be late for work."

The sun's golden light nearly reaches the top of the couch.

Rats!

I bolt from my chair, offering my brother a ride before leaving my family in a flurry of kisses.

IT'S TAKEN ME A YEAR, BUT I MANAGED TO SAVE THE $230 TO BUY my Ford Model T coupe. It's used, but I'm proud of it because it's mine. One day I'll get the sedan with the retractable roof—red, with a back seat and all the bells and whistles. But for now, this will do.

Inside the tiny cabin, my brother raises the front window to annoy me. The breeze assaults my hair and whips my face, but the Missouri weather's not too hot, even for April. At least it airs out the sharp scent of his hair pomade; I don't want that manly smell sticking to me. He cleans up nicely, though, in his crisp white shirt and pressed apron. The drive smooths out once we reach the boulevards, passing the bustling white businesses and neighborhoods, heading deeper into the city toward Eighteenth and Vine.

My excitement grows as the fancier neighborhoods give way to chains of tall brick buildings with signs lighting up in the dusk to show incoming nightlifers where the hotels and billiard halls are. Being a Friday night, the streets are already rumbling with butter-yellow Tatras and three-liter Super Sports automobiles with their tops down and caps on, parking along the curbs and honking at each other. I adjust the hand throttle and drive down an alleyway to the back of my little slice of underbelly heaven, parking by a few cars belonging to the other club owners.

The River Rose is nestled in the cellar beneath a grocery store, between the basement of a watch repair shop that stores inventory for my gin joint and a gambling parlor that fronts as a hats and hosiery store during the day. Though the back entrance is almost hidden by overgrown rosebushes and ferns, none of us in the jazz district are truly hiding anything. And why should we? The city officials frequent these places more than the blue-collars do—though they're starting to set up their own nicer juke joints in the better parts of town. Things could get dicey then. But it's okay, because they're all going right where I aim to be someday with my own fine jazz club, offering all the things gentlemen are willing to pay for with a bit more refinement than what I have right now. As long as the bigwigs keep coming, a place like that is going to shine.

Kansas City seems to wipe its behind with mundane things like laws and prohibitions.

As I pull the hand brake, shutting off the car engine, my brother grabs my keys and jumps out before I can say anything. He's been quiet the whole ride. From beneath the curve of my bell-shaped hat, I shoot a coy look to the fellas waiting outside, all donned in their boxy single-breasted suits, adjusting their lapels and tipping their fedoras and gambler hats as I pass by their vehicles. An inward groan seems to have set up residence in the back of my throat, but then again, I've chosen to associate with brutes like these. *The cost of dreams, I guess.* Ahead of me, Javier opens up the back entrance of the club and ducks inside.

"Hey, Rose!" the guy with the hard middle part says, pressing a cigarette to his lips. "You gotta stop givin' that riffraff a ride in your car." The other fellas laugh, nudging each other at my deadpan expression. "You'll never get the smell out!"

My frown deepens. Our businesses work hand in hand and I hate that I need these John Ds at all, but I'm Rose Lane, a middle-class spinster who doesn't take guff from anybody. And I can be this way because I'm not a half-immigrant bruja wanderer from the River Bottoms. It didn't take magic to pull one over on most people—I realized a long time ago, I can be whoever I want to be. And right now I ready my perfected Margaret Young impression, a little bit of New York with a side of vamp from Savannah, and twist my crimson lips. "'Ey, he's the best bartender in town, and you can't have him no matter how hard you beg."

The middle-part's smooth grin does nothing for his awkward nose over his tiny mouth. Guys like him turn from swells to hoods once they're half-seas over, so I'll have to watch my humor as the night wears on. I can handle him for the time being, though.

"Yeah, don't go gettin' in a lather, baby. You know I'm just givin' you static," he says, smoke rolling from his nose. "I got no problem with immigrants, 'cept he needs to trim that jungle you got growin' around the place."

My flat stare holds. "The plants were a gift, they hide the back door, and it's my business. Besides, Javi's no gardener."

"They're all gardeners, baby."

The big six towering next to him knits his brown eyebrows, sticking his bulky finger under his hat to scratch his head. "Hey, ain't we immigrants, Giuseppe?"

The owner of the gambling club rolls his eyes, looking up at the muscle-bound henchman with an exasperated sneer. "Nicky, would ya quit usin' my full name? Jeepers creepers! And no, we ain't the same kinda immigrants, ya goof. We been here since we was babies, our families makin' a respectable livin' with our, uh, community establishments." He points the glowing end of his cigarette in my direction, my ears slowly heating for the second time today. "But I gotta tell ya, Rose is onto somethin'. We don't gotta pay those border-hoppin' bindle punks the same wages as the rest'a ya. They don't know the difference and don't know half'a what you're sayin' anyways. Smart girl, this one."

"Gus is right, Rosie," another man pipes up. "I can't hawdly unda'stand what they're sayin'. Why you gotta guy workin' here if he don't talk good English?"

I adjust the thin beaded strap of my bag over my blouse, their ignorance choking me more than their cheap colognes. "I assure you, gentlemen, my employee understands every word that I say, and if you'd ever bother talking to him, you'd know he speaks better than the lot of you."

"Aww, Rose," Gus says, cocking his head. "You're cute as hell, you know that? All learned and shit. Hey, why won't you lemme be your sheik? I'll take care'a these clubs for ya. Take you for a ride in my breezer, unless you'd rather neck in that flivver you call a car." The company of testosterone laughs and elbow-jabs him as their eyes travel down my body. These guys are nothing more than big mouths with little spines, but the way they regard anyone in heels still sends acid up my throat. I'm glad women's trousers are so stylish these days.

The henchman with the big guns and the conflicting adorable face scrunches his eyebrows again. "Didn't she already turn ya down, Gus?"

"Shut the hell up, Nick!" Gus flicks his cigarette away, pressing his hand to his chest as he turns back to me. "Rose, you can't go kissin' a guy durin' a poker game and leave him cold and dry like that after. I can't get that night outta my head."

The acid continues climbing. *Here we go again.* My daily round on the greaseball carousel.

"Yeah, well, that was two years ago," I state, glancing behind me as Javier swings the back door open again, beelining for our row of metal garbage cans against the brick walls. "And I was just tryin' to look at your cards." Mostly true. I also wanted to know his intentions. Turns out, he was cheating me out of money in the game *and* with his cut of our shared patrons. It was worth the short, slimy kiss that I've worked hard to forget.

I turn away, but Gus wraps a sweaty hand around my wrist. "Hey, baby, you can look at my cards anytime. Give ya the tour of Italy. I gotta taste that mouth again."

"Thanks," I say among the snickering. "That's real sweet of you, but I don't date dewdroppers." His buddies guffaw at my icy mitt and throw their hats at him as I shake off his hand and the nasty intentions that shot through my arm when he touched me. Heading toward the budding rosebushes, my heels crunch over dirt and gravel. His nasally voice calls after me.

"Aww, c'mon, Rosie!" He laughs. "I work hard for what I got! I'm the king'a the underground, baby!"

Javier and I share our matching eye rolls as I lift one of the smaller boxes from his arms, heavy glasses clinking from within. He casts a squinty-eyed glare in Giuseppe's direction. "You don't have to take their bushwa."

"I can handle it, Javi."

"If he even tries to touch these plants—"

"I said I've got it," I insist. "Plus, I don't need my only bartender getting locked up or worse."

My brother's signature grumble serenades our stare-down, which lasts as long as it takes for me to jerk open the club entrance before entering my haven of spirits.

THIS IS WHERE I CALL THE SHOTS. MY WORLD. MY SAFE PLACE, which is ironic because it's frequented by gangsters from all walks of life in a less patrolled part of town. But, much like the rail yard neighborhood of my upbringing, this feels like home—Rose's home, the caramel whiskeys and sweet rums wetting the air with their fragrance. Smooth cigar and cigarette smoke haze under the warm sconces around the bar and wooden tables. The laughter's as loud as the swearing and I'm not sure whether patrons are playing or fighting until one of them is pushing up against another, but I've got Nicky to deal with those blottos. The gambling house's bouncer works the late shift at my club as the winning cardplayers gather their stashes from Gus's place and bring them here to spend the night celebrating and harassing anything with a skirt until Nicky gets ahold of them. He's not alone in his efforts, though. My abuela's blessed wall of shrubbery outside helps keep tempers from simmering too hot.

After ten, it really picks up, wall to wall with rambunctious men who cackle in a roar of clinking tumblers and shouts that can barely be heard over the brassy trumpets and heart-pounding floor toms from our house band, led by the world's best saxophone player. Charlie "Clip Lip" Williams might not be known anywhere else, but here he's a legend.

His new pianist, however, is a nameless torpedo who's already on my nerves with the way he keeps giving me the eye. I make a mental note to find out what the hell his game is later, but I don't have time to mess with him right now. My customers love talking to the skirt club owner, kissing my cheek and asking me to dance to try to chance a quick grab. I'm being waved down in every direction, removing those roaming hands as I push through the hot crowd of white shirts and striped ties, their suit jackets long since abandoned with their scruples and inhibitions.

I'm no prude; touch is just my game. But the guys in my club make some pretty sketchy playmates even if some of them are lookers. On one hand, they're a few classes below what I normally prefer. On the other hand, their physicality plays into how my limited magic works. Direct contact gives them the satisfaction they're looking for, but it also gives me so much more—it allows me inside their heads, just with a simple kiss like I did with Gus the Greaseball. I like them distracted and I like them happy.

Happy customers have looser wallets.

Now *that's* magic.

While my gift doesn't tell me much that isn't already evident in this crass joint, every man's thoughts seem the same and their intentions start to blur as the night wears on, soaking into my skin with every grope and peck. People don't often think in complete sentences, so deciphering phrases and feelings turns into a game after a while. Some are angry about their jobs while others are fed up with their nagging wives. One guy is thinking about proposing to his girlfriend but isn't sure what her father will say. Out loud, he tells his friends that she's a cuddler he wouldn't handcuff himself to since he's getting the cake for free, but he's goofy for her. His unspoken words tell me so. On and on, their musings spin, growing foggy as the amber liquids flow, soon turning their inner desires toward me and the other girls. Taking a breather from that kind of attention at the moment, I decide to clean up some spills by the bar.

"Hey, baby! Come sit with us!" some men call out from a crowded table. *Not a chance.* They're way too sauced. The protection spells cast on my indoor plants don't necessarily keep these guys from getting out of hand, but they do make them more agreeable to Nickels's interventions. I move a potted cactus across the bar top and pretend I can't hear their jeering.

"Rosie! Quit workin' so hard, will ya?"

"Sweetheart, I gotta place you can rest right here!"

I send my rosy-cheeked waitresses out to collect empty glasses for Javier to refill as I lean up against the shining black bar top, wiping my damp neck with one of his hand towels. My employed flappers laugh as the men pinch the hems of their shimmery dresses, patting their silky head wraps with flashing smiles. At their request, I've given permission for some of the girls to earn a buck by sitting on men's laps; they walk away with several dollars stuffed into their rolled-down stockings just below the knees, a promise for later. It's none of my business as long as I get a cut.

From the looks of it, it's going to be a good night for the house.

By a quarter after three in the morning, the crowd has dissipated and my feet are screaming for relief. I want to take my shoes off so badly, but the band is still packing up for the night, and that shifty-eyed piano player's still looking at me. My ears buzz at the emptiness and the brush of Javier's broom as it scrapes across the oak floors.

"You don't gotta wait up for me, señorita," he says, picking up a chair with one hand and turning it over onto a tabletop. "Clip said he'd give me a ride home."

"Charlie lives on the other side of town, Javi."

He holds up a hand to my protest. "Go, Miss Rose. I still gotta sprinkle the perimeter, and let's face it. You're no help to me in those shoes, yes?" His soft smile lets me know that he's all right, that his earlier mood was just that—a mood. I stumble over to hug him and he kisses my temple and whispers, "It was good seeing Luna today. Tell her that her crabby brother misses her."

I tell him that I will before waddling out to my car. I should help him spread our abuela's dirt around the rosebushes. They're the only things keeping the harmony in a venue that's normally crawling with lowlifes everywhere else. The blessed plants give my club a warm and comfortable feeling once our clientele passes the threshold. They're less likely to fight. *And more likely to spend.* I can't help but smirk.

My triumph fades to worry gnawing at my conscience. The spells are becoming more difficult for my abuela; I wonder how long we should let her continue to prepare the mixtures. My heart is both warm and broken, and I suddenly remember why I don't visit home more often. In those fleeting moments in my brother's embrace and the floral breezes from my abuela's roses, I just want to run away from this fabricated world I've built and curl up in bed beside our mother. But when I'm there, I lose sight of Rose, and when I'm Rose, I lose sight of Luna.

I am who I say I am.

But right now I don't know what to say.

2

"OH, ROSE!"

The man beneath me reaches above his head and grips the dark teal iron bars of my bedpost that keeps knocking against the wall. I close my eyes to his scent of lumberyards and earthy tobacco, the burn of our forgotten cigarettes in the ashtray beside us. Bracing against his shoulder, I reach down for a fistful of my lover's black curls. The pitch in his voice rises a few octaves. "It's like you're in my head, baby—di mi!"

I tease him with a biting smile. It's like I'm in his head because I am. My *gift*. My allure—it still tingles on my lips. The charm spell I placed on his desperate mouth travels to his hooded eyes that transform in a way that only I can see. Black pupils fade into a night sky with shooting stars and purple galaxies. *It's working.* He would do almost anything for me right now . . . if I could ever master this damn wonderful branch of magic. But being able to charm these suitors to come crawling back for more is satisfying enough. For now. Plus, allure is a hell of a lot easier to use when the guy's got a body that makes me wanna throw my T-straps over his shoulders.

All of last night's stress melts away in this flowered bedroom. Confidence lifts my chin and drives my body against his. Soft sheets soothe my knees. Everywhere our skin touches reverberates with his pleasure, turning into my own, coursing through my bones like the sound waves of a standup bass. The heat scaling up my waist demands my hips to quicken the rhythm. Drawn out by my charm, his wild thoughts soak into me as well, a cacophony of desires met by my ability to hear each one of them. And with each silent request he doesn't know he's sending me, I return with steady thrusts exactly where he wants them to the reward of my lover's swears. His breath hastens with mine as my thighs tense around him. Hidden magic. Heartless passion.

It's better than a bruja love elixir.

He arches his back with a final groan, moist beads clinging to the coarse hairs on his chest. I let out my own satisfied sigh as I collapse on top of him in a carefree heap, our sweat mingling. The light breeze through my open windows flutters the layered floral curtains, awarding my damp arms and neck with cool relief as the late-morning sun blankets the rosy wallpaper and matching rugs. My visitor's chest rises and falls as he lifts up strands of my hair with his fingers, letting them drop away from my face. He's breathless inside and out, wanting more but too depleted, just how I like leaving them. I can feel his devotion and awe rising, his inner conflict emanating from his body like it does every time I take him to bed. My body is fuzzy and glad, but I can't linger here. It worsens their desire for me.

And right now I want him just on that edge.

I push against his shoulders to move away, but he grabs my arms with a wicked yearning in his sultry brown eyes. "I'm stuck on you, Rosie. You know that, don't you?"

Edward doesn't know what it is about me, and I'm sure to never tell him. Not that I feel guilty. My little infusion of allure isn't all that powerful, and he's really attracted to me on his own. I hardly ever have to use impartation, which is a good thing since it takes more concentration than I want to expend in the bedroom. That charm spell is about as tricky as getting out of this tedious conversation.

"Edward, I don't have time—"

"Look, I memorized a poem for you and everything," he says, ignoring my flat stare, "so just lemme get this out . . ."

Gross. His romantic plight is getting precariously close to going over the edge, and he's practically begging to be put out of his misery. Closing my eyes like I'm actually listening to his nonsense, I relax to ready myself for the impartation I've eventually had to use on every other joker I've brought home. Poetry is where I draw the line . . . unless it's sexy, and the sonnet Edward is spewing is crashing my libido harder than a bad stock on selling day.

Impartations aren't easy, though. Unlike the reading spell, I can introduce thoughts and feelings, but this one's a lot harder to control. And it's not like I can make a guy just believe them whole cloth. Just like any other thought that pops into a man's head, these guys have to accept my impartations as their own for my charms to work, like a Trojan horse, but not nearly as powerful. That's where my brother gets the wrong idea about my half-blood abilities.

I really only half know what I'm doing.

How fitting.

Leaning down to stop this train wreck my lover is headed toward, I press my lips to his waiting mouth, the floral melody of impartation swirling past my tongue. The taste might just be the best part of this. *You don't love her,* I send to him with a tremor I know only I can feel. He doesn't actually love me—thank the fates. I'm just reminding him because my allure has him revved up like a six-cylinder. "Big-timer," I say with a smile, "you'll say anything when you're under me."

"You got that right, baby." He grins with a wink, slapping my thighs. "When you got these gams wrapped around me, tastin' the way you do, it makes me want things I never wanted before." He leans up on his arms, nearing my mouth, but I hold him back like I'm being coy. His curls tilt with his head. "I'll be your sugar daddy, Rosie. I'll be so good to ya—someone as airtight as you."

He means it at the time he says it, but the thought of a long-term commitment pricks him almost as soon as the words leave his mouth. I've got to find a way to let Edward down easy without wounding his pride. He's so damn good-looking, and I'd hate to take him off my roster. He bought me my telephone and my favorite armoire. I could have bought them myself, but why would I? I'm the one getting the cake for free. Thing is, even if he doesn't really want a girlfriend, he won't like being rejected. Most guys don't.

"The only thing airtight I've got is my schedule, Edward," I say, kissing his forehead with a farewell vibration that has me fighting a yawn. Meager as the impartation spell is, it still drains me a bit. Not a bad trade-off for making good whoopee. Throwing back my patchwork quilt, I ignore his huff before skipping to the bathroom. He follows me, his handsome face frowning back at me as I close the door, his sigh resounding on the other side. I tap my fingers on the dark frame. "Oh, don't be sore. We can always talk about it when our blood's not rushing to one place."

His silence answers back like the big baby he is, but I've got another appointment to get to—one that sends a flash of angst to my chest. I've gotta stay sharp today. In a flurry, I grab my botanical soap bar and soak a hand towel in my pedestal—the scent of a carpenter can linger. After a cold scrub that also helps fight the fatigue, I snatch my dusting puff and pat a cloud of antiperspirant powder over my entire body before tugging on my clothes, my stockings sliding over the sea-foam green tiles the entire time. Pausing in front of the beveled mirror, I admire the gold trim and apply a thin layer of face powder from my compact tin before smearing a fresh application of rouge to my cheekbones with damp cotton.

I think about drawing in my lips with my favorite scarlet color, but decide against it. No eye work, either. The business I need to tend to today won't be as kindly received if I show up looking like a flapper girl. I might very well be one, but those mouthpiece suits only do business with upstanding ladies. *Yeah, sure.* If I were a man, my lifestyle wouldn't make a difference. But different jobs demand different hats, and catching men's eyes is the last thing I want to do today.

With one last approving look, I ease open the door. Edward is still standing there in all his glory.

"I'm gonna be late, Edward." My apartment is small, and I'm glad for it because I'm soon making my way through the art deco living room with my own davenport couch and chair. The fringe bottoms brush over a large rug the man at the furniture store insisted I take for half price after we mugged on a fainting chaise. It wasn't even a long kiss, just a little tongue and his eyes started that twinkling starlight like they always do. I didn't do it on purpose. Well, not entirely. He wanted me *before* I kissed him . . . and he was cute and really laying on the applesauce.

Edward clears his throat like I'm supposed to say something else. I drop my long, slender cigarette holder into my bag by the front door as his jaw sets, his hand on his bare hip bone. "I'm not askin' you to make me dinner every night, sweetheart," he says. "Hell, I'll even let ya keep all these damn plants if ya like 'em so much."

He sweeps his arm toward my collection of small ferns and basil in colorful pots around the patio door, my eyes flattening at his proud posture. Tall cats always hate the hanging hibiscus. I smooth my hair, donning my blue beret. "How thoughtful of you."

He grabs my elbow, jerking me backward. "I don't see the other guys, but I know they're there. And face it, baby. A woman runnin' a juice joint for workin'-class bad eggs like me—you're askin' for trouble."

My smug mood starts to spoil. Why are all the brainless potatoes so fantastic between the sheets? *I don't have time for this.* I pull my arm away, thrusting open the door with my mother's prim glare.

"C'mon, Rosie," he pleads with an unattractive whine, his eyebrows knitted together so fetchingly, I almost forgive him. "When we're together, you do somethin' to me. You got me by the heart, baby."

I let my eyes fall to his most prominent feature. "It's not your heart I've got."

"Well, I . . . We . . ." Edward looks like I've asked him to tell me our state capital, his confusion consistent with the impartation and the allure fighting it out inside him. The magic will wear off, eventually. But I don't have time to wait for it. *Pity.* Sounds like the end for Edward.

"Okay, fine, Rosie. You're right," he says as I breeze away. "Call me when you can?"

I wave my fingers at the potato from the stairwell, making him smile. *That was a close one.* I've probably got one more ride on that Ferris wheel, which I don't hate the thought of.

"Water the fennel on the patio before you leave, won't you?"

My heels click over the smooth pine-and-coral tiles as I scale down three flights of stairs, sailing out the entrance of my apartment building. I stop in my tracks with a sharp inhale through the nose. A young sandy-haired man is kneeling on the front stoop, his trembling hand holding a large diamond ring in the air. I look to my left in a panic, the rows of colonnade apartments along the boulevard awaiting my testimony like a courtroom of redbrick judges, their white trimmings and large pillars ready to sentence me to permanent public shame. This guy was *definitely* not my fault. *¡No mames!* I don't have time for this.

While this suitor rambles, my eyes roll as the memory hits me of our single night's rumble after we met at a jewelry store. *What?*

I argue with myself. *He needed help picking a ring.* The same stupid one he's now holding. I should've never brought a first-timer back to my place, and I most definitely should have cleaned up my own mess. So maybe it's a *little* bit my fault. But it was late when he left, and I'd had a little too much gin to do a proper impartation to counter the allure.

Poor sap.

The kneeling man produces a large bouquet of fragrant lilacs, holding them out to me as a declaration itself. "I'll do anything, sweetheart. I'll work double shifts. I'll give you the damn world. Just say yes."

I peer up at my third-floor balcony to make sure Edward hasn't decided to see me off. That would be awkward, considering his currently nude state, among other factors. Letting out a long exhale, I lift my chin and turn back to my present suitor as my hand hits my hip. "Is your fiancée okay with you being engaged to two women?"

"Not at all," he says, his hopeful face faltering. "I mean, I haven't told her, but I'll do it today if you take this ring."

"Henry—"

"Please, baby. I'm nuts without you. I . . . I . . . I'll paint the sky with your name on it. I'll travel to the center of the earth and bring you back your weight in diamonds. If you ask me for the stars, I'll fly to the moon with a galactic fishing pole and fill up a bag for ya, Rosie. Can't you see that I'm desperate for ya?"

"Get off the ground, Henry. You're making a scene." I gust past him, my pace quickening across the green lawn as I head to the street where my car is parked.

"Is that a no?"

I pause with a slight cringe. *Ugh, I really don't have time for this.* I know he's probably still kneeling there, so I turn. He is.

"Look, I promise you'll feel differently by morning," I say, pursing my sympathetic lips. His allure hangover should be gone by nightfall, but I don't want to chance it. "Go back to your fiancée and catch her some stars." He tries to protest, but I shake my head. "I don't want my name in the sky, and I can buy my own diamonds. I'm not that kind of dame. I don't do flowers and rings, you get me? Don't confuse a tumble with love."

I leave him there mumbling something about romance and devotion—all fallout from the magic. He doesn't understand it's all baloney. Even if a man were capable of such a thing, I could never trust it—not with my charms. Love's not for everyone and that's more than okay with me.

Some people's lives just don't have room for it.

HUNDREDS OF STRIPED AND HERRINGBONE SUITS GRIP THEIR briefcases and lead their families in and out of the grand archways of the city's new train depot. Eight hundred and fifty thousand square feet of French neoclassical architecture provide a transitional reception for traveling merchants, vacationers, city officials, and a whole slew of questionable types on unofficial "business." I can't keep the small grin from twisting up the side of my face. This place makes me think of some exotic courtyard in Europe, a place I can only dream of visiting. I've seen pictures, though. It'd be amazing to see the real thing, but at least we've got a spot in Kansas City that comes close enough.

My eyes travel the loud, bustling corridors like a gaping kid at the county fair as I stroll along the shining marble floors. Slick-haired men make their way to the barbershop, lighting cigars from the store next door. Their wives pick through an array of shops, their knee-length pleated skirts fluttering over silk stockings as they saunter. Railroad offices are calling out the next train due to depart while a pearl-draped mother snags her screaming toddler from climbing up the stone walls. Slowing my pace, I gaze upward past the golden wall sconces to the massive chandeliers that are attached to the painted ceilings with intricate moldings and designs of beige leaves and blue skies nearly one hundred feet above me. Union Station is the most enchanting building in the entire city.

I stop by the rows of wooden benches of passengers, my heart pinching with envy. So many on their way to new adventures. I'm sure they don't see it that way. Their lives seem mundane. But at least they're safe. With a cold thump in my chest, I stand on the toes of my cross-strapped court shoes, peering over the tweed and lace shoulders that push past me in haste. My goal is just ahead, a man surrounded by a company of well-dressed oilcans—a balding fellow with spectacles, a bird-faced suit, and a blond appetizer of a man with a dashing smile. I think of my desperate suitor on his knees outside my apartment and decide I should finish what's on my plate first.

"Rose? Yoo-hoo! *Rose*, is that you, darling?"

My eyelids slide closed, my stomach throwing a groan upward. I'd know my coworker's singsongy fabricated greeting from anywhere. I was hoping to get this done and give her the slip before she got here. Sharing a desk with her at the office is an irritating penance for needing a day job; having to conduct such a stressful interview with her blabbery mouth is nearly intolerable. I paste on what I hope is an amiable smile and turn to the Brooksy who's already barreling toward me, her hands outstretched like she's going to hug me. I'm forced to accept her friendly embrace so as not to offend her, and count to three as the floral scent I liken to decaying petals assaults my nose from her hanging cardigan.

"I've looked everywhere for you!" she declares, pushing me back by the shoulders. "And aren't you just lovely in that blouse and trousers. I wish I could be so cosmopolitan, but men like dresses, you know! We don't all have your figure." I start to respond, but she's giggling like she's said something clever, grabbing the curved ends of her gray hat, which molds over cropped hair that's more orange than a sunset. "Isn't this kippy? I hope it's not too daring. I think it's perfect with this dress, don't you?"

The last thing in the world I want to do is talk fashion with a woman who is most definitely not a flapper, but I give her a once-over. The most boring frock I've ever seen hugs her tall, lanky body in all the wrong places, complete with a belt on her hips to make sure her cardigan doesn't fall open and show even more frock. The pasty color is a difficult pairing with her matching skin. She needs some rouge on her lips. It's not that she's ugly; she's just trying too hard to be something she's not. Something that makes her uncomfortable to even think about too much.

At least, that's what I gleaned from the hug when her cheek brushed mine.

She juts out her hip, tilting her head at me. I ready myself for whatever nonsense will surely come spilling out of her pale mouth. "Rose," she says with a coy squeak at the end of my name. "You're not nervous now, *are* you?"

I ignore the twinkle in her eye, turning back to my destination. Her excitement about interviewing henchmen has my stomach wound up tight. I'm the one with everything to lose, not her. This newspaper gig as a front for my nocturnal career was a perfect setup until today. When I asked our boss for new assignments, confronting the very men who could bring down my nightclub wasn't exactly what I had in mind. These guys are no joke. I just want to get in and get out as fast as I can.

"Just stick to the script, Margaret," I mumble, searching the thick crowd. She stands on her toes beside me, although she doesn't need to, craning her head around with a thrilled squeal. The throng of passengers parts just enough, my palms dampening in anticipation. A prominent, well-fed man stands near the exit booth with the small entourage of other suits I saw earlier, who shake his hand and offer to carry his bags.

Margaret whirls around, her green eyes rounding. "Are you thinking what I'm thinking?"

"Stick to the *script*, Margaret."

"This is our chance at real news, Rose."

"You can't be serious." My stomach somersaults as she aims for the towering politician, my unsettled nerves driving me forward. "Do you have any idea how dangerous this is?"

Of course she doesn't. She's got her daddy's money and nothing to hide—both things I've never had.

My coworker is tugging my sleeve and in my ear. "Rose, he's the chairman of the Jackson County Democratic Club, former chair to the city council—"

"Yes, exactly," I say, letting her drag me along to the death of both my careers.

"So we're just going to ask him fluff questions?"

"Mr. Roberts will sentence us both to line editing for the rest of our days if we screw this up, even if you are his niece."

And that former councilman will send my underground business packing if I cross him the wrong way. Not that he would even know who a small juke-joint owner like me is, but I can't take that chance.

Margaret excuses herself far too many times as we slip in between small groups of travelers. "So you're just going to ignore this . . . excuse me . . . ignore this amazing political story . . . beg your pardon . . . fraud, extortion, payoffs—and you're going to ask him about his holiday?" She's not such a Dumb Dora after all. I give her a look that says so. She huffs more dramatically than I thought possible. "*Rose.*"

"Look," I say, pushing past her with a hiss over my shoulder, "you've got your way of fighting the chauvinistic bureaucracy and I've got mine. Don't screw this up for me."

"If my uncle cuts your pay, I'll make up for it."

"Keep your privilege and leave me out of it."

"Oh, don't be such a wallflower, Rose."

I've made it farther than I realize because when I turn my deadpan stare from Margaret's objecting face, I'm nose-to-black-tie with the most crooked politician in Kansas City. I nearly choke trying to swallow.

"Whoa there, toots," he says. His crew casts curious, amused eyes over me. "No need to rush around." He leans down with the look of a man who knows how powerful he is, his brown hair greased back like the others. "There's always another train."

I do my best to recover myself, smoothing the front of my blouse before fumbling in my handbag for a notepad. "Thomas Pendergast, I presume?"

He laughs heartily, nudging the scowling man next to him. "Why the formalities, little miss? I'm always happy to autograph for a fan."

As I flip the spiraled page to our list of preapproved questions, Margaret lifts her rounded chin. "Mr. Pendergast, we are not *fans*. We're journalists from the *Kansas City Star*."

"Aw geez," he says with a big sigh, nodding to his team of yesmen. "I count on you fellas to take care of this shit. I'd beg your pardon for my language, but I don't apologize to witch-hunting news reporters." A few grumbling chuckles follow as he starts to walk away.

Great. Of course he's not taking a couple of skirts seriously. Oh well. No interview is better than a disastrous one.

"Then how about you apologize to the voters you bamboozled into establishing a city-manager based government instead of a chamber of councils?" Margaret asks, my body freezing. I may as well be dead. The looming powerhouse pauses, keeping his broad back to us. I shoot my obtuse coworker a warning glare, but she presses on. "Doesn't that setup make it easier for the Pendergast machine and its goat followers to control the political arena in Kansas City, opening our doors to the likes of Al Cap—"

I reach for her hand with a hard squeeze. "Margaret."

The blush in her face is a brilliant pink. Her thoughts are running a thousand miles an hour through her heated palms. She feels like she's gone too far, but doesn't know how to turn back. Her words were harsher than she intended, but there really is no easy way to sugarcoat this level of corruption. No votes. No debating councils. Just one Pendergast puppet running the city however he's told. I almost admire Margaret. They're all valid questions. But that's not how this game is played. Mr. Roberts figured two dames would have a better chance getting close to Pendergast to get a fluff quote. And then, *maybe*, it would set Pendergast up for future discussions.

That seems shot to hell now.

And as much as that disconcerts me, I have a more pressing issue. The political giant in front of us governs the entire night scene, and therefore, my world. But of course Margaret doesn't know that. And I can only hope to God he doesn't ask me anything.

I'm kind of hoping he just keeps on walking.

His slow turn is filled with promise, a threat even, his dark eyes leveled at her in a way that fights his side smile. "Look, toots." The men laugh again as he places an innocent hand to his chest. "I run a little Democratic club down on Main Street. What kinda power could I possibly have?"

"Oh?" My coworker scoffs, yanking her hand from mine. I'd impart a few choice thoughts to her right now if kissing her was legal. My lips tingle with my nerves. There goes that idea. Charm magic is tricky enough in the protective calm of my bedroom. *Close your head, Margaret!* My heart starts racing as she nods to the spectacled balding man next to the former councilman. "And *he's* just an investor, right?" His mouth drops open as Pendergast's jaw hardens. "Mr. Nichols, is it true that you've purposefully restricted property titles to only white owners in neighborhoods surrounding the Country Club Plaza district to keep minorities from mucking up your shiny new metropolis?"

The city developer begins stuttering, but Pendergast clears his throat, shutting him up. I give a considerable amount of effort to stand tall as his determined eyes land on mine. "What's your name, toots?"

Aw hell. "Rose." He lowers his chin, lifting his eyebrows with considerable expectancy that keeps me mumbling, "Rose . . . ah . . . ah . . . Lang . . . ley. Rose Langley." I look around for my paling coworker, who has already begun fading back into the bustling masses. Brave enough to ask the hard questions, but not so hardy to wait for the answers.

Thanks, Margaret.

The former city councilman rolls his big eyes and lights a cigar before strolling away with the bald man in tow.

My heart and breath somehow find their rhythm again. Copyediting's not so bad.

"Lane. You're Rose Lane."

As I whirl around, my eyes narrow to cover my panic. The bird-faced goon I'd forgotten was there is sticking his pointy chin and nose toward me like he's looking for the chinks in my armor. Next to him, the well-plated blond offers me a sympathetic doe-eyed smile that irritates me.

"And you are?" I ask the bird, squaring my shoulders.

He gives a short, tight laugh with a brief scan of my neckline. "Your salvation. So I would drop the Amelia Bloomer act and listen very carefully." His hands tent below his chin, the condescension in his face making my neck prickle with heat. "I just so happen to work in the permits and fundin' department. You should know who I am because your application for your *community business* just crossed my desk, and I know who *you* are because I haven't signed it yet."

My eyes drop at his outstretched hand. *Damn.* I should have just kissed Margaret. If anything, it would have changed the topic real quick with these fellas. To hell with the newspaper. I can't lose my club. With my hot ears doing their thing at his expectant grin, I take his offering for a quick scan. *No surprise here.* These jerks' thoughts are all the same. He likes a lot of leg and a lot of sass, but

I've only got one of those handy right now. I cock my head with a shrug that tightens his smile. "I submitted that paperwork months ago. How the hell should I know whose desk it lands on?"

He lets out an impressed grunt, shoving his hands into his pockets. "I'm Leone Salvatore, sweetheart."

As my dry mouth tries to drop open, I will myself to shut it. I should have figured the thirtysomething hotshot henchman was working in public service, his attempt at a cosmopolitan dialect mostly covering his Italian accent. The city hands out public money for clubs and joints tagged as community improvements like candy at a parade. I knew trying to secure that kind of green glorious to purchase my own place was a long shot. This guy's big trouble—trouble that has nothing to do with my loan. While Pendergast paves the way for the underground, Salvatore's night-shift boss has been building a small kingdom under him. If I'd known the city's liaison to a nefarious mobster was also the community funding co-ordinator, I never would have applied. I might be in a dangerous business, but that doesn't mean I want to make deals with the devil.

Honestly, at this point, I just want to get the hell away from here.

"Well," I breathe, forcing what I know is a frightened smile. "Thank you for your consideration, anyway. I'll just send our interview questions to your office for Mr. Pendergast to review at his convenience, and please thank him for his time. I know you're all very busy."

"Just a minute there, sweetheart." Salvatore's face softens, almost making me believe he might have a soul. He looks to the frozen blond man, who has yet to say a word. "Whaddya think, Heck? Should we take her out for a drink? You need a tour of our humble metropolis anyway, but if you expect me to take ya to get German food, you're on your own."

"Oh, I really *do* appreciate the city's warm reception," Heck says with a slight bow, "but I must meet my lawyer to secure my apartment."

"Hey, Pendergast insists on entertaining new money in our city. I might be bein' paid to brownnose, but you're not gonna turn down free gin, are ya?"

"Oh, very *well*." Heck's chiseled jaw rises into an earth-shattering smile that does nothing for me as he slides a thumb into his pin-striped pocket. "That is, if Miss Lane is willing to accompany."

His cerulean eyes would normally hold me prisoner, but I'm not in the mood for Cops and Robbers today. "Well . . ." I shift on my heels, exploring the possibilities. After almost losing two jobs in one day, gaining an audience with Salvatore might be a strike of gold. He could turn my dreams into more than just something I lie awake at night thinking about. I just don't know what he wants. The good thing about having no real connections in the city is that my hands are clean of these higher-up goons; the risk is low.

This might change all that—hopefully for the better.

Salvatore sighs at his wristwatch. "It's just a drink, honey."

"I've got a paper to turn in by four."

I don't. I plan to fake a toothache and take a nap until sundown. Maybe Mr. Roberts will have cooled down by tomorrow.

"Aw, quit workin' so hard. I'll get your interview questions answered. Fluff only, though." He points his hand toward the exit. "You comin' or not?"

Everything you put your hands to shall prosper. My abuela's words have never been so comforting. These moments are where dreams die or fly.

"All right then, gentlemen," I reply, crossing my arms, "it's never too early for hooch."

AS I WALK PAST ANDERSON'S RESTAURANT, MY HEART SKIPS A beat. Coming to a stop beneath the glowing lettering of the Chesterfield Club's hanging sign, I immediately regret agreeing to come to one of Pendergast's many establishments. I've done a fine job sticking to the shadows to avoid the eye of the mobsters that run these places . . . until now. Feels like climbing into the devil's bed without Vaseline ointment. The upscale gentlemen's club offers the trinity of nightlife vices—booze, gambling, and floor shows—all one block down from the courthouse as a reminder of who really runs Kansas City.

Salvatore holds open the glass door that's set between many other storefronts like it. I don't have to wonder how the hell I got in this pickle. My ambitions make way too many decisions. As I stare down the threshold of a place I aim to rival someday, my apprehension answers back with a stomach-twisting warning. I'm in way over my head.

But haven't I always been?

"You comin' or not?" the mobster asks with a challenging grin. I keep my chin high and press forward across the tan tile floors, the silent tourist I know only as Heck following close behind. Slowing my pace, the thrill of my surroundings stun me for the second time today. What I'd always known as a sleazy jazz club is everything I imagined and more. Thirty or so empty round tables surround a wooden dance floor that shines from the hanging lights in a dropped ceiling that's painted with gold and green vines. At the far end of the dance floor, a raised stage holds a variety of drums, sleek microphones, and an upright piano with curved moldings.

Wowie.

Heck's less than subtle awe captures my attention, his throat clearing with discomfort. I follow his inquisitive gaze to the mural walls where men and women cling to each other's nude bodies as they partake in pieces of dripping fruit from lush trees.

"The Garden of Eden," Salvatore explains, startling us both. Heck is still gawking as he offers me his arm, leading me away to one of the tables near the bar at the back of the room. While my nerves are thankful to be escorted by this man whose name sounds like a lovely swear word I wouldn't mind crying out over his shoulder, I can't stand being led around. Makes me look weak in front of Bird-Face.

"Hey there, Heck," Salvatore says, giving him a slight nudge toward the bar, "we got some dancers that have been dyin' to meet you."

Heck flushes an impressive shade of red. "Oh, I'm already running late—"

"They're in the back." The mobster claps him hard on the shoulder. "They been waitin' all day. Don't disappoint them."

"Oh, for heaven's— Very well." Straightening his tailored jacket with a huff, the ruffled tourist walks toward the bar like a man on death row, which is fine with me. I don't need him in my business.

I spin back toward Salvatore with my hands on my hips as he snorts something about upper-class babysitting. *What's this guy's game anyway?* As he scoots back an oak chair, offering me a seat, I decide to ask. "Mr. Salvatore, what do you want from me, exactly?"

He pulls a package of Old Golds from his pocket. "Smoke?"

He's testing me, keeping control of the pace and avoiding questions like every other man in town. I fish my gold-plated cigarette holder from my bag with a tight lip before flouncing into the chair. *Fine.* Joke's on him. Tobacco strengthens the charm should I get an opportunity for a read. I take my time removing my beret and securing the offered cigarette to the small trumpeted end of the holder. Leaning down, he presses the large button on his banjo lighter, his eyes on me as I suck on the long, dainty filter. The relieving burn of warm tobacco fills my lungs with a calming familiarity as he circles the table, taking a seat across from me.

"I gotta say, I've got real respect for you, Rose," Salvatore finally says, tucking the yellow package back into his breast pocket. "The way you kept your head today—I would'a never known by lookin' at you that you was a snake charmer, a pretty little thing like you runnin' a gin joint next to a gambling den. Reporter by day. Vamp by night. I think I'd like to know more about you, Miss Lane." He settles back, taking a long drag while my heart nearly stops. "See, I'm aiming to invest more time into my boss's tenants."

What?

Confusion adds its unwelcome presence into my nervousness, buckling my eyebrows together as I blow a delicate line of smoke into the air. The Chesterfield is Pendergast's club. He owns all the high-class establishments in town. So what's he got to do with my place? *Besides making the underground run smooth?* As I take another drag, it dawns on me like the haze clearing between me and Salvatore. He isn't talking about Pendergast—that guy's a swell compared to his real boss: Frank "Icepick" Moretti.

Landlord to the River Rose? I don't think so.

"I think you've misunderstood somewhere, Mr. Salvatore," I say. "Giuseppe is my landlord. Not Mr. Moretti." Just saying the notorious mobster's name gives me shivers. I'll take dealings with Gus over these guys any day. Salvatore cocks his head, his eyes shining like he's holding all the cards. And he really is. I'm not even sure I know what's in my own hand yet.

"Damn, you're cute," he observes, effectively raising my disgust. "Gus is just another checker on the board. You think he owns anything?"

Not even the tobacco can drown out the bitterness climbing across my tongue.

"Who do you think that slum-bucket rents those stone basements from?" Salvatore's smile breaks out at my shocked silence, dread building around my teeth. "That's right, baby. I'm surprised a smart reporter like you hasn't done some investigating." He laughs, clearly pleased with himself. "If you had, you'd know Mr. Moretti owns half the jazz district, and it's my job to make sure those businesses stay profitable—not that I'm sayin' you're doin' a bad job. Gus's reports show your payments are prompt. Patrons are faithful, and I can see why they keep comin' back."

His victorious eyes slide down my flushing neck and back up again, stopping at my mouth. I press the filter end of my holder to my lips, filling my lungs with a sneer and hoping it keeps down the bile. "They come back because I run a good business. This is our best year."

"And *that* is why you've got our attention, sweetheart." Salvatore sets his dincher into a glass tray and intertwines his long fingers. "That slimeball Gus is in love with you. Charges you hardly nothin' other than a nice cut of your earnings. So tell me, baby. After you pay my crews for rum-runnin' to keep your stock of devil juice in supply, Gus's thugs for protection—discounting your little band and flapper girls' wages, keepin' the lights and water on—how much do you bring home?"

His *crews*?

I always run my orders through Giuseppe, never thinking about who he's dealing with or who might actually own the buildings. Never thought I had to until now. I thought I'd lucked out with Gus. He's easy to control and nothing ever indicated I might need to consider a silent partner—one who isn't so silent now.

I'm a damn sap.

My head is spinning, but this jerk is looking at me like he wants an answer, and something tells me he usually gets what he wants. Not that I'm sure what that is yet. I'm in a jam, no question, but it may not be as sticky as I think. I can't let this goon rattle me before I know the rules to his game.

Selective truth is the best strategy.

I straighten my back, flicking my wrist like I don't give a damn. "After expenses, I clear two hundred a week, split that with Gus, plus what he pays for your shipments. I walk away with fifteen dollars a week, easy." Not counting the tips that get kicked back to me from my girls. It seems like a lot when I say it out loud, but after sending half of it home each month, it's not quite as glamorous as it sounds.

Salvatore is not impressed, lazy smoke drifting from the tray to his scrunching face. "Two hundred—what, are you chargin' beans for drinks down there?"

"They're working-class men who just want to have a good time," I snip back. "I make enough."

"Yeah, so much you gotta write fairy tales for the papers."

A huff escapes my lips, shooing away my earlier apprehension. *Get to the point, Salvatore.* I didn't plan to spend my morning as some henchman's entertainment. Then again, Margaret ruined any plans I had for this morning with that yap of hers.

"Is this conversation going anywhere? I've got places to be." I want to scratch the smug smile off his face, but I raise my holder instead. I'm glad he favors scrappy women. I don't have to do much pretending with him.

"I like you, Rose," he says as I tap my ashes into a glass bowl. "I think you got potential, so here's what we're offering. We wanna combine the gamblin' club and the juke joint, and turn that basement storage into a proper brothel. I know you use it for cuddlin' clientele anyway. The kicker is we want *you* to run it all on a lease to own, splittin' the house eighty-twenty until your contract is fulfilled." My eyebrows arch, making his grin wider. "Obviously, you're gonna have to raise those prices and implement a cover charge to meet our payment increases. And you'll deal directly with me for shipments from now on, with the added benefit of our protection from competition and snoopin' cops."

A lease to own?

I hear all he's saying, but that's what makes me sit up a little straighter. The prospect of owning my own place stirs my bedded excitement and quenches my resolve to be patient. I can't get a loan without a male cosigner—that's just a fact. This could be a great way around that. But reason sinks through me like lead because there's another fact: This is Moretti's money . . . and the prying eyes of his henchmen on me all the time. One hiccup, one late payment, could end my club or worse. They could own everything I have. They could find out who I *am*.

Even with all that, I can't believe I'm considering it.

"I like my setup with Gus the way it is," I force out of my mouth. "Why would I change that?"

"Because a woman like you could make a killing." I must be staring pretty dumbly because he laughs. "Quit thinkin' so hard, baby. You can still pay Gus to run the gamblin' for ya. You applied for fundin' to buy your own joint. We're offerin' you a way to do that. I thought that's what you wanted."

"It is," I say, trying to recover my stupefied face. "I just don't understand why you're offering this deal to me instead of him or one of the other club owners. I'm barely two years in the business."

"How many ways do I gotta explain it? You're a young, hot skirt runnin' a speakeasy." Salvatore shrugs with a patronizing chuckle. "Ice is intrigued and so am I." And there it is. Salvatore's use of his employer's nickname is no accident. If he thinks I'm looking away, I'm not. I refuse, regardless of how much my insides are squirming. His tongue rolls across his exposed canine tooth. "If you didn't want that kind of attention, then you picked the wrong basement—and the wrong profession, baby."

I pull another small drag from my holder to steady my nerves against his expectant stare. Part of me wants to ask him where to sign, but eagerness is a bad quality in this business. "I'll think about it." My legs cross to offset the staring contest we're having, smoke rolling from his flaring nose. I haven't agreed to anything, but I already feel bent over for this guy—and not in the good way.

"You have till tonight, sweetheart."

My dangling heel hits the floor. "That's not enough time."

"It's exactly the right amount of time when it's the only decision."

"But what if it's not?" Probably not the smartest comeback.

All traces of amusement leave Salvatore's face, his nose pointed at me like he's got me in a bull's-eye. The last thing I wanted was to become a target. This is the reason why nobody wants to go into business with these sleazeballs. I worked hard to retain my choices in life. It's just too risky. Unfortunately, turning down Icepick's offer could be just as dicey.

But if I was intimidated by every man who threatened me, I'd have melted away a long time ago. I'm not melting yet.

Salvatore can surely see that. The glaring mobster's assistant leans forward with a frigid smile. "The only reason we don't railroad you right now is 'cause you doubled the patrons in that rat-hole. But these are hard times for businesses that make stupid moves."

His meaning is anything but cloudy.

Light giggling from the back room grabs his hardened eyes, leaving me stunned at the prospect that my club plays a major role in feeding Moretti's network. Worse, that he wants a bigger bite. *But hang on.* Salvatore gave away something—I don't know what he means by "hard times," but I've got more leverage than I thought. Which only makes me realize I want out of Moretti's network altogether. This gangster might say I only have one choice, but games like these are full of bluffs and I'm not ready to fold just yet. My silence makes Salvatore look like he wants to either ravish me or strangle me.

I give him the dissatisfaction of a short shrug. "I said I'll think about it."

"You know what?" he says, lifting a nonchalant hand in the air like he's celebrating a victory. "I never got you that drink." As he shoots out a high whistle, the click-clack of chunky heels sounds behind me, accompanied by the sexiest voice I've ever heard outside of a gramophone, singing a popular jazz tune about misbehaving. Heck, who appears at my side, sliding into his seat like he's late for court, gives us a sheepish nod before I turn to see what he's blushing about. I was right about the shoes coming in our direction—red with sparkling sequins, the only article of clothing the bountiful waitress is wearing besides her cellophane apron. Her hair is lighter than Heck's, nearly white, and from the view of her lower extremity, is most definitely natural.

Heck swivels his golden head around. "I don't think this is an appropriate place for a woman like Miss Lane."

"How do you mean?" I ask dryly, scanning the nude attendants waving to us from the back doorway. "This place is *full* of women."

"Hey, I pay ya to serve drinks, not sing," Salvatore says, slapping the waitress's behind as she sets small tumblers on the white tablecloth from her tray.

Her full lips stick out, her eyes pouting like a sparkling jade pond. "But, Leo, I'm a good singa'."

"I know you can sing, but I need your other talents, baby." He pinches her backside, sending her away before turning his attention back to me. "I got a guy that sings. Doris, there, makes more money on the floor. It's business. I'll teach ya everything you need to know, Rose, starting with not chasin' down my clientele at train stations."

"It's my job," I say, staring at the muddy liquid. "My other job, that is." As I sip, the bitterness makes me cringe. I expected better quality from this club.

Salvatore laughs at me—and Heck, who's making a similar face. "What, you don't like the house specialty? That's real moonshine, ya sissies. I got some toothless appleknockers in the hills that make it for pennies, and nobody here gives a damn. They just want their wheels greased and their ladies dancin'." His glass rises in the air. "That's how you make the money. Stick with me, baby. I'll show you all the tricks you'll need to be able to leave that joke of a day job."

I slide my half-empty tumbler away with a proud grimace. I don't want to show a guy like him my hand. He doesn't need to know my club is my everything. Gives him too much power. "I happen to write because I like it. Just like I enjoy running the River Rose."

"Very respectable," he says with a nod before downing his drink. The return of his friendly demeanor doesn't make him seem like the sordid criminal from earlier, smiling and offering me my dreams with a side of moonshine . . . and a chaser of a threat. And while I've heard threats before, I need to know how real his are. I need to test his intentions. But the last thing I want to do right now is touch him just to get a read. A guy like him might get the wrong idea. I peer at the frowning blond man, who looks like he's trying to keep up with the situation.

"Miss Lane," he says, "why would someone as lovely as you need to work at all?"

It takes all my power not to roll my eyes. Another potato rears its stupid handsome head. If his cosmopolitan accent wasn't there, I'd hate him already.

"Aw, Kessler," Salvatore snorts, reaching across the table to take my glass, "this ain't St. Louie. KC women are commercial, you know. Progressive and all that jazz."

That's it. My ears can't take anymore bombshells. The growing scorn on my face begins to melt Heck's beaming smile. "*Kessler?*" I ask, my eyes narrowing. "As in, the nephew of the man whose boulevards and park systems displaced over seventy minority families from the city's bluffs to make room for million-dollar houses?"

The chiseled man doesn't seem to know what to say, his forehead wrinkling all innocent-like.

Yeah, mi mamá told me all about you.

It may have been over twenty years since the City Beautiful movement came to reform our city, raising land values and changing the landscape, but the price of such an improvement was paid in both money and tears, displacing those who couldn't afford to stay in the new neighborhoods—not that they would have been allowed to anyway.

And it all started with a Kessler.

Clearly this man doesn't see it that way. "I beg your *pardon?*"

Heck replies, his face reddening and alive with an impressive amount of indignation. "You would not have a city if not for my great-uncle. He transformed this town from a trading outpost to a major metropolis. He meant no harm to anyone."

"Tell that to the families on the east side of Troost Avenue," I spout, standing to my feet in a hurry, grabbing up my hat. I needed an excuse to get out of this quicksand anyway. "Are you part of Nichols's upper-class-only establishment too?"

"I . . . I've just moved here. I'm not a part of anything."

"Yeah, I bet you live in Midtown."

"Where do *you* live, Miss Suffrage?"

"Somewhere I actually earned," I snap back.

Salvatore's laugh barely breaks through the thickness as he twirls the glass in his hand. "Geez, sweetheart! Whaddya, a walking history book? I thought I told you to stop harassing my clients!"

Heck's baby blues are searing back at me, but he can throw away his indignation with this club's moonshine.

Salvatore's still talking. "Besides, his uncle passed a couple of years ago. What's this kid got to do with it, huh?"

Maybe he's right. *Or* maybe Heck's a brainless root vegetable like the rest of them. Time and magic could tell, but I've got bigger potatoes to fry. Salvatore's coming for my answer tonight. "Thank you for the drink," I say, adjusting my bag on my shoulder. "I have to be off."

I try to shake away the unease of his offer along with the bitter taste of that drink. I've got enough people trying to control my life. It's not like I can sneeze at the offer either. I've got to think, and I've got to think fast.

There's got to be another way to scale this mountain.

The mobster's cocksure laugh is still sounding behind me as I storm for the glass door like escaping from a cave with collapsing walls.

"We'll talk soon, baby!"

3

CHIPPED BRICK WALLS, WORN RUSTIC FLOORS, AND TARNISHED
bronze wall sconces have become my oasis as I settle into my weekend routine, picking up filthy glasses from calloused hands that
reach out to kiss my ring finger in a hundred tipsy proposals. Trumpets squeal as the drumming rain outside spatters near the open
entrance, airing the room of its cheap cigars and gin-soaked laughter. The humidity clings to my skin, running down my neck and the
front of my cream blouse, giving the patrons a decent show of my
underthings, but I don't mind too much as long as my heavier eye
work isn't running. We're all sticky from the damp night and the
stuffy room, rolling up our sleeves and fanning ourselves with our
hats. But it's not all bad—my flapper girls use their glistening skin
to their advantage, holding ice cubes to their necks and shoulders
along with the eyes of the patrons.

"Split's got a real handle on the band tonight!" I yell to my
brother over the edgy, foot-hopping number "Doctor Jazz." Charlie's dynamic saxophone and roaring, bluesy vocals bring the house

to its feet, serving as another reminder of why I love this place. For these few hours, skin tone and backgrounds don't exist. We're in some other place and some other time, scrubbing our racial and economic barriers with thick-tongued camaraderie.

We are who we say we are.

"¡Sí!" Javier agrees, rubbing the growing stubble above his lip as he leans on the shining bar. "Gio was a good pick, I think. Seems to be keepin' up." My eyes squint through the smoky haze toward the corner of the room where the house band is playing, their heads bobbing and fingers flying. The new piano player's charcoal hair hangs over one eye, his shoulders hunched over the faded ivory keys of our upright piano. I'd nearly forgotten about him in the hustle and stress of the day. I'm not sure what Charlie saw in him when he interviewed the traveler a few weeks ago, the odd variety of black tattoos spread across his bare forearms. The only guys I've ever known with marked-up skin spent some considerable time behind bars. I don't like the idea of a hardened criminal working in my club, but I do trust my lead musician's judgment. And Gio does sound incredible. I'd make him roll his sleeves down, but it's hot as a bearcat's temper in here. Either way, he better keep his eyes and hands where I can see them. My club's the perfect balance of riffraff meets classy, and I don't need internal drama.

Like a thumbed nose to my harmonious atmosphere, the back door greets a group of raucous men in fine suits as they strip themselves of their jackets and hats. The stomach-wrenching moment I've been distracting myself from all night has finally arrived in threads fancier than normally step into my joint. I would offer to hang their accessories on our coatracks, but I'd hate to make them feel welcome.

Not that it stops them. Salvatore's greedy eyes and pointed chin have already found me. I circle around the bar, joining my brother in pouring clouded drinks before the small entourage slides onto our barstools—casually, and sometimes not so casually, taking seats that were already occupied—with obtuse grins, rolling up their crisp white sleeves. As the band switches to a syncopated "Rhythm Club Stomp," chairs and tables scrape across the floor to the edges of the packed club to make room for a makeshift dance floor.

"What can I get you, Mr. Salvatore?" I ask, loading a tumbler with frozen cubes from our icebox, avoiding his eye like I'm too busy for his nonsense; it's his offer I'm really avoiding. We both know it. I want that money more than almost anything. We both know that, too. But these mid-level mobsters surely want something more from me than some rent checks and higher profit cuts, and I can't figure out the angle.

Is my joint really that popular?

"Aw, Rose," he says, leaning forward like a falcon perched above its prey. "Why the formalities, huh? After all we been through?" I shoot him my best flat look, stirring up a few chuckles from his goons as Javier plucks up the glasses, filling them from unlabeled bottles. "C'mon, baby. Lighten up, will ya? Let's get half cut and make a night of it. Whaddya say?"

"I'm working."

"Not if I say you're not." His pleased smirk makes my eyes roll. "Picture this. You and me, runnin' Troost Avenue, takin' you home every night of the week with pockets full of green. You'll be safe, cared for. In fact . . . I won't let you outta my sight."

His gaze falls to my clinging dress, solidifying my apprehensions. Just what I thought. This guy plans to be all over my professional *and* personal life. All I can picture is him driving me around while I have to taste his seedy mouth in impartation spells just to keep his hands off me. That's way too close for comfort and definitely not worth risking him finding out about my family for money I could earn on my own. Eventually.

Maybe.

I grab Javier's wet rag, running it across the countertop with purpose. "Yeah, well, I don't need a sugar daddy."

Salvatore lets out a bitter laugh, reaching over the bar. Whatever it is about guys and wrists, it makes for an easy read. His fingertips grip me as much as his amused rejection. He's still playing a game with me . . . and he plans to win. "Don't be like that, sweetheart."

"Excuse me, Miss Lane, would you care for a dance?"

Salvatore whirls around, snorting at the slick-haired blond in the pin-striped vest. Heck Kessler represents everything my family loathes, but his subtle wink is unmistakable. He thinks he's saving me. But his less than necessary hero act is interrupting my read. Ignoring my deadpan stare, he throws a wide grin my way, lifting a beckoning hand in the air.

My chest tightens. "You want me to *dance*?"

"Don't tell me you're not a hopper," Heck calls out over Salvatore's irritated head. "I can't believe I've met the only flapper who doesn't dance." From behind me, my brother joins in the laughter, shaking his head as I turn to glare at him.

"Come on, kitten," Heck goads. "Put that rag down and get out here."

Javier's fingers poke my back, nudging me from the counter. I answer with a subtle scowl before sauntering around to the smiling aristocrat. I hate dancing almost as much as I hate pet names. Salvatore's smirk returns, laughing into his tumbler at my lack of enthusiasm and throwing out loud jokes about kittens having claws.

Drink up, Salvatore. I hope you choke on it.

Heck seems to be enjoying my torment as well, amusement glinting in the sea of blue around his irises. Same threat goes for him. I'll take this as far as he wants to go.

Keep messing with me. I'll break your heart, pretty boy.

The giggling cohort at the counter reaches out, clapping him on the back as I pause in front of him, determined to profit from this somehow.

"I'm afraid we got off on the wrong foot, Miss Lane," he says, offering me his hand with a slight bow. "I'd like to think most people are more than what they seem."

My throat grumbles with annoyance as I glance at his manicured hand. *That, they are, Mr. Kessler.* I slide my palm over his, my reception strengthening on its own. *Tell me all about yourself.*

It's hard to have the upper hand, though, when it's being used to swing me onto the dance floor. I squeal as he tugs on my arm, dragging me to the center of the club. While the floor toms and trumpets hit their heart-thumping solos, Heck transforms into a billboard of a man, flashing his dazzling smile and—I have to admit—rather unrivaled dance skills as he kicks his feet and spins me until I'm dizzy. His excitement reverberates through my forearms, his thoughts on his next steps, which helps me follow him, giving me an impressive edge as a dance partner. He grips my hands, Charleston-style, and I try to listen to his palms over my own heavy breath while working to make my feet do what his are doing.

A strange thought passes from his skin to mine. Behind that smile, he's angry. And sad. He can't keep doing this . . . whatever *that* means. I tighten my grip, but he spins me, letting me go before pulling me close against him in a twirling flurry. Shrill whistles float through the air as I grasp his taut arms to keep from falling, his hands secured around my waist and the back of my head. My damp hair falls back as he hovers over me, our chests heaving.

His eyes search my face, his mouth nearing mine in the clamoring room. "Are you going to keep giving me the absent treatment?"

"I'm not shy, Mr. Kessler. I'm just cautious."

"You're too young to be so paranoid. Are you afraid of falling in love with me?"

I attempt to stifle my own smile. "That's never a fear of mine."

He bites his plump lower lip with a sultry grunt. "Then we are made for each other, I think."

The crude crew at the counter jeers and hollers for him to kiss me, sending Heck's eyebrows wiggling. Something is off, steadying my racing heart as his fingers brush against my scalp. His mind is pleading for his friends to stop. *Huh?* He's giving me all the signs of a man who wants a woman, his wanton look, his forward flirtations. But his fingertips tell a different tale. He wants to let me go. He wants to be home.

He definitely does *not* want to kiss me.

I must be frowning because he frowns. "Only if you want me to."

"I would," I reply, recovering my irritated smile, "if this whole display wasn't about impressing your friends."

He leans around me, his mouth near my ear, invoking a new round of hooting and hollering from the crowds. "They are not my friends . . . but I *am* new in town. It would be terribly embarrassing to get turned down after dancing so well."

"So this *is* for your ego?"

"Isn't it always?"

I pat him on the chest with a tight-lipped smile. He's handsome, but obviously not interested in me, and I'm not interested in a show—I pay the band for that. "Thanks for the dance," I say. "Save your kisses for when it matters."

He stands me up with an obliging grin, bidding me farewell with another bow before I walk back to the bar. The room yells sympathy to the young gander who has already moved on, dancing to the next brisk number. I laugh with the crowd as he spins one of my girls, dipping and pressing his mouth to hers in what appears to be an earth-shattering kiss. Their eyes close and the room ignites with congratulations and rum-induced encouragement. Soon every unaffiliated flapper is grabbing his sculpted jaw, pressing their painted lips to his, stirring up the rowdy room even more.

Even Salvatore has stopped pouting, joining the fray of the laughing crowd, leading a few guys to a small poker table.

"Is that Heck guy a creep or what?" Javier whispers as I rejoin him behind the bar.

I cross my arms, my own ego assaulting me. "No."

"¿Pues?" My brother places a few whiskeys on a waitress's tray, waiting for her to walk away before asking, "Aren't rich, handsome goats your game, or have your qualifications changed since yesterday?"

I shrug, turning my lips down in nonchalance.

"Okay, well, what about that goon who grabbed you earlier?"

"Oh, who knows what men want these days?" I mumble, avoiding his squint. Javier isn't kippy about anyone being involved in our business.

"Fine, you don't wanna talk." His fingers encircle a potted saguaro as he arches a black eyebrow. "Perhaps the cactus knows your secrets."

"Protection plants don't gossip." And if they did, I'd want them to tell me what the hell just happened with Heck.

"Oh, it tells me everything," my brother whispers, his overly wicked smile making me laugh. "Like how it wants you to do the dishes while I lock up tonight."

His dimple deepens at my obliging groan. As we set back to work, I can't help but wish the earth would connect to me like it does to our abuela. Her blessed dirt has fed the wild greenery around the building since the first day I planted it here, her enchantments to grant it a good dose of luck and favor nearly draining her for a week.

The spells are especially useful on a night like tonight, keeping jerks like Salvatore more lackadaisical than he probably usually is . . . as long as he's inside, anyway. I wish I had expanded the rosebushes around the parking lot. But my abuela is getting too old for such a major project. Maybe one day my powers will grow. Maybe never. But for tonight I'll use what I've got.

A TINY FLINT MATCH DROPS AT MY FEET, MY FINGERS PINCHING the long-awaited cigarette outside the nearly empty speakeasy. The last few patrons are helping each other into their raincoats and hats inside, though the storm clouds have finally passed. My lungs accept the roasted burn, pushing out the white smoke into the night sky as I lean my head back against the splintered rear door. The tinkling of glass bottles echoing in the alleyway between the storage basement and my club jerks my head down, the cigarette freezing near my mouth. Some drunk hiphound has probably lost his way to his car around front. The half-moon lights my path like a silent horror film as I step over a few puddles, careful to keep my heels off the ground. My heart's as deadpan as my face as I round the corner.

"You call that locking up?" I ask, pressing the Camel to my lips. My brother and my best flapper jump apart, nearly knocking over a metal can that we use to transport my best hooch.

He clears his throat, smoothing his slicked-back hair. "Miss Lane . . . me and Penny . . . we didn't see you."

"Yeah, well, if the wrong person sees *you*, you're both in trouble."

"Aww, Miss Lane—"

"I'm not saying you two can't have fun. I'm saying maybe a public driveway isn't the best place for it?"

"Yes, Miss Lane," Penny says, skipping backward toward the street side of the building. "Call me, Jav!" He nods with a wave, fastening the collar button of his bartender's shirt.

I sidle up to my brother with my hands on my hips. "You don't have a telephone."

"I use your joint's phone. She doesn't know I live in a box."

"Well, I'm not sure I'm comfortable with you seeing one of my girls."

He snorts, turning his aloof eyes on me. "I'm not sure it's any of your business."

"Javi," I insist, lowering my voice with my chin. "It's dangerous for you both."

"You *just* said—"

"I said that to *her*." The truth is, though, that they'd both pay the consequences if they got caught. I honestly don't care who my brother necks. But if the wrong cop sees a black woman schmoozing outside a basement gin joint in these parts, they'd lock her up—my brother, too, since only white men get a pass.

"*Everything* I do is dangerous," he hisses back. "Dios, I'm still a man." He purses his lips, his rounded nostrils flaring. "But since you must know, I'm not seeing her . . . just *seeing* her." I cringe at the thought of my brother barneymugging, but I can't blame him. We work in a sexually charged environment and he spends his spare time working with steel and caring for our family. It's not the first time I've stumbled on his back-alley meetups anyway. I know he's lonely. And we're used to skirting the law. It's easy to think we won't get caught, especially with bruja magic giving us an edge. But that doesn't mean we can afford to become complacent.

I think about the proposal on my doorstep this morning and cringe.

"Look," I say to my brother, avoiding his gaze as much as he's avoiding mine. "She knows to take her highjohns to the repair shop. I'll talk to her."

Javier's head shoots up, his eyes wide. "Don't you dare, hermanita. You think I *pay* her?" He steps closer, his eyes darting around. "I know it's hard for you to understand this, but those of us on the bottom of everyone else's privileged shoes like to have a good time too."

"I . . . I know, Javi." My heart sinks at his forlorn expression. "I'm sorry. I just don't want anything to happen to you."

He sighs, leaning back against the brick wall. "I know, Rosie." He looks back up the alley, a small smile crossing his lips. "You know, you could have interrupted a few minutes later. I'm crabbier than usual—"

"Oh geez! Stop right there," I say, shutting my eyes with my hands in the air. His laughter is warming me for the second time tonight. He doesn't do it often enough anymore. "Just . . . discretion, Javi. I don't want any heat on you or on Penny or on the club. Okay?"

His smile softens as he nods. "Okay."

I stand on my tiptoes, hooking my arm around his shoulders with a mischievous grin. "At least it was a woman this time."

"Aye, aye, aye." I know he's blushing because of his swift walk to the back door. I teeter across the gravel to my little black automobile, smirking at my own cleverness.

"You wanna lemme in on da joke?"

My cigarette butt drops to the ground as I spin around with a gasp. Salvatore's laugh mingles with the club door slamming shut. I take a deep breath to calm my startled heart. "Geez! I didn't see you there, Leo."

With an exaggerated eye roll, he saunters toward me. I know he's tanked before he's close enough for me to smell the liquor on his breath. His movements are less suave than earlier, his speech thickening. "I'm glad we're past the formalities, my little delicate Rose." His fingers fumble up and down my sleeves, my stomach flipping at the empty alleyway. My eyes shoot to the vine-covered building with longing. I'm outside the barrier. Hell, even if I had the potted cactus, the best I could do is hurl it at his face. I can't strengthen a protection spell, much less perform one.

Maldita sea. The fates couldn't give me something better than a magic kiss? A resigning sigh rumbles in my throat. Charm is a last resort and I'm used to handling business without it. I've dealt with handsy rats before.

"Good night, Mr. Salvatore. Take a cab," I say, leaning away.

"What, are ya streetin' me, baby?"

He leans closer. My back hits the door of my car, but I keep my tone steady. "Hey, stay as long as you like. But I'm calling it a night."

"You need a ten-cent box, too?"

"I've got a car."

Salvatore's persistent hands glide up my sleeves to my shoulders. "Why'd you turn him down?" I squint in the dark, my forehead wrinkling. "Kessler. He's a good-lookin' fella'."

My eyes follow his hand, which brushes over to my collar and back down to my elbow. *Damn.* If he touches my face, I can read him without having to take this any further. I'm desperate to find out his real intentions—about me, my club, his interest in me and Kessler—but I don't want to set him off with the wrong idea, either.

"I just wasn't interested," I reply.

He cocks his head, catching my gaze with his own. "Ah, I see. What *are* you interested in, baby? Hm?" His nose inches closer to mine. "Not dancin'. Not kissin'. You gonna turn me down too?"

I let out a slow breath, treading carefully. "A kiss or the business offer?"

His lip twitches. "Both."

As his eyes fall to my mouth, I have to make a decision. Reading him now isn't my favorite idea. But given his sway and slurring speech, it's the best chance I've got. He might even accept the kiss as a down payment on the answer to his question later, giving me more time. If I'm lucky, he might not even remember this in the morning. Besides, if he tries something, all I have to do is poke him in the chest and he'd fall over.

"You sure you wanna do that?" I ask. His lips lift into a light, impish grin as they brush against mine, a spark of a thought pushing through to my cheeks. He wants me. Now. And he can't think straight. *How shocking.* But that's all I'm getting, and now his heated grunt tenses my body down to the bones. I've got to stop this. I'm getting too nervous. This is going too far, and this jerk's too dangerous for this game.

I try to pull back, but it's too late. I can feel it climbing with my alarm. Like a floating flower petal on a light breeze, the tiniest bit of allure leaves my lips without my permission. His breath picks up speed. *Rats.*

Definitely a bad idea.

I start to say something about forgetting my hat inside when his mouth pushes deeper, his gin-laden breath heavy and strong. As much as I hate it, at least I'm starting to read something from him beyond just desire. His twisting tongue tells mine that his boss wants me for more than my business skills. Salvatore's just glad to be the middleman. His thoughts soon turn back to their carnal vibrations, though, sending me no other clues. He needs to feel comfortable talking since this is getting me nowhere but trouble.

I form a thought, an easy one that I can manage under pressure. *Tell her.* Lavender and hibiscus ready behind my teeth, their perfumed taste the first sign that the spell is beginning. Pushing the impartation through my lips, he groans, rearing back with his sweating forehead against mine.

"Damn, baby," he breathes, closing his eyes. "I ain't neva' met a Sheba like you." I smile like that's the first time I've ever heard that applesauce. His mind is a jumble of all the things he wants to do to me. *Tell her,* his thought echoes back through my skin. He's taken the impartation as his own. He swears again, stepping back and running his suit sleeve across his brow. "My boss . . ."

Salvatore swallows, rubbing his eyes with his fingers before throwing his hand down, his mouth setting. "My boss told me to keep my mouth off'a you. Did you know that?" His eyes narrow as he lurches toward me, pressing my body against the car. He's stronger than he looks, my own fury settling into my burning ears, but his hands have clamped around the back of my trousers. I'd shove this slimeball away if I didn't need to hear what he has to say. "Ice said that women that run gin joints can't be trusted—that they're full of mischief. And maybe he's right." His fingers start sliding upward, inching my blouse from my waistband. My heart thumps behind my temples. I'm going to have to hurt him. "But I don't need to trust ya to get what I want outta ya, do I?"

"Look, you're a little drunk and I'm lot tired." Adrenaline fights the spell's fatigue as I brace my leg, readying my knee for impact.

"You been teasin' me all night, sweetheart," Salvatore growls, shoving his hands up my blouse, his thoughts sending shivers across my skin. "Me and all those otha' guys."

He's not going to take no for an answer—my powers aren't needed to decipher that much. *Such an animal.* If I wasn't so enraged, I'd ready every horrible, sickening, terrifying thought I could muster and load them at my lips. But imparting takes some serious concentration, and while I've been in tight spots, this is different. I've got too much to lose to be tangling with monsters. I'm as flustered as an anti-suffragette in a brothel. My hands manage to grab his forearms, stopping him from going any further. "I was doing my job, Salvatore."

"Your job is to not piss me off!"

"Get your filthy hands off me!"

As he fumbles for the car handle behind me, he gives me the room I need to stomp my chunky heel down onto his loafer, shoving him backward. He stumbles and curses, nearly toppling over before righting himself. Lifting a menacing finger in the air, he favors his smarting foot and gasps, "Now, that was real stupid, Rose."

No doubt. But stupid gives me more time. Time is the opportunity to think.

Time also means the back door to my club swings open again, a group of musicians and staff filing out with a few drunk patrons, helping them to the alleyway to find their automobiles. Javier lingers, stacking what I know are empty boxes near the entrance. I shove my loose hem back into my waistband with trembling hands.

"You comin', Javi?" one man yells from the group ambling up the hill toward the street.

My brother lifts a hand, shaking his head. "No gracias. Miss Lane offered to take me home." We both know that I didn't, but he's pretty keen on reading a room, and there's not nearly enough space between me and Salvatore right now. The thug's wavering eyes glare at us both before he lets out a snorting laugh.

"I heard you let those damn bindle punks in your car," he says, limping toward me. "Where else you let them in?" His sneer seems to be trying for amusement. "Maybe my little Rosie ain't as sweet as I thought, runnin' with River Bottom immigrants."

I glance at my brother's clenched fists around his apron, and hope he understands my pleading look in the dark. *You can't fight this guy, Javi.* Even if he wins, he'll lose. It's not tough to tell why he's so angry. His mouth presses into a hard line, but seems to heed my warning look.

The back door to the gambling club next door squeals shut, the owner strolling to his blue Sunbeam beside my car. "Hey, Rose! Ain't it past your bedtime, baby? What are you all doin' out here anyway—"

"Don't you got somewhere to be, Giuseppe?" Salvatore snaps, trying to stand on both feet.

"Yeah, I'm the last one out now that Rosie's an unda'ground star," Gus replies with a silly grin, opening his car door. The air is still, cooling from the earlier storms that drenched the parking lot with soaking apprehension. I've got to hope that means this is over—at least for tonight.

Salvatore buttons his jacket, taking his keys from his pocket and pointing them at me. "I got respect for you, baby. You're fearless, lettin' one of those homeless drifters check your car for ghosts, if you know what I mean." He turns, careening up the alleyway, his laughter bouncing off the brick walls. "No tellin' what kinda diseases you could get from their juju! So be careful, huh?"

Ugh, what a rummy. With a relieved sigh, I turn back to Gus, who has already cranked his rumbling car to life. He slides into his seat, leaning his arm on the door, his tiny mouth pressed together. "Rose . . . you all right?"

"I'm fine. I can handle myself."

"Ain't nothin' wrong with askin' for help."

"Yeah, well, you two parking lot gladiators won't be there every time." I rip open my car door, flopping onto the broadcloth while my brother waits near the front headlights, his hand on the curved crank. Ignoring Gus's concerned face, I open the throttle, the coils buzzing as I turn the key.

"Baby, one'a these days you're gonna realize this scene ain't for you," he says. "Icepick's got a sudden interest in our places, both of us. You keep lippin' like that, he'll raise rent . . . or worse. I told you, if you wanna go in on a loan togetha', we can buy our own joint and get out from unda' their thumbs." My rumbling car engine shakes the steering wheel. "Freedom's more powerful than love, baby."

His taillights make the alleyway glow red as my brother settles into the passenger seat beside me. I don't understand the mob boss's interest, either. That doesn't mean I'm going to tuck tail and run to another greaseball to save me. Gus is all right for a racist scavenger, but I'm not joining forces with him if I don't have to.

It's the thing none of these guys understand: I don't *want* a partner—in life, in love, and definitely not in business. That's just not who I am.

My mind is numb with tension as I put the car in gear, soon gliding along the boulevard.

"Hermanita . . . I'm sorry—"

"I was taking care of it."

"Not from what I saw."

"Oh, you know," I say, pushing up the throttle. "Just gotta learn to kiss the right fellas. It's easy, right?"

Bitterness swirls in my heart. I know I'm being snarky, but my life isn't cupcakes and love spells, and I resent my brother for pretending I think otherwise. Does he think I *like* being pressed on by every fella I come across? Or that I got to where I am without knowing how to protect myself? Tonight was messy, sure, but I was handling it.

Gus, Javi, Salvatore—they all think they know what's best for me. And if I didn't want to deal with them, I know it *would* be easier if I just married a decent, boring man.

But who the hell wants that?

"Luna, I should not have said that to you."

"I don't feel like talking about it, Javi."

And I don't. So we don't.

MY FEET PROTEST LOUDLY WITH EACH STEP AS I MAKE MY WAY under the dim stairwell sconces to the third floor of my apartment building. I drag myself up the final step, leaning on the wall to un-buckle the straps around my ankles. My front door may be only six feet away, but I can't take it anymore. The tiles beneath my thin stockings cool my soles, the arches in my feet relaxing with thanks-giving. With my heels in hand, I trudge to my apartment as the door across the hall creaks open. An irritatingly familiar shade of ceru-lean stares back at me with a jarring look that matches how I feel.

"Mr. Kessler," I say, too exhausted to keep my attitude and sur-prise at bay. "Don't tell me that you've moved into my building."

"Miss Lane. You run a speakeasy, write columns for the paper," he replies, leaning his arm on the doorpost. "And now you own an *entire* apartment building?"

I let out what I'm certain is an unattractive snort, turning my doorknob. "Good night, Mr. Kessler."

"Wait." His bare feet shuffle across the floor, his loose shirt hanging over what I imagine is his unbelted trousers. Aggrava-tion from our embrace-less dance stirs my foul mood, helping me keep my eyes where they belong—on his smooth, frowning face. "Rose . . . may I call you that?"

Since he looks like he might become emotional, I shrug. "Sure . . . Heck."

"That's great, Rose," he says, shoving his hands into his pockets. Definitely no belt. "See, I think I just keep messing up with you, and I really was hoping we could connect."

Stop right there, cowboy. I've just finished this chapter of aroused drunks for the night, and I'm not adding someone to my roster I have to see across the hall every evening. *No way.* Unless that isn't what he wants. Thing is, I really don't *care* what he or any other joker wants from me. I don't want to give my freedoms away to a slimy gangster. I don't want a business partner or a boyfriend, and I don't want to dance. And right now I'm dead tired, so if this cosmopolitan wants a broken heart, I'm happy to oblige.

He must have expected a faster answer, because his face is turning red.

"Geez, Rose. I'm not really a drinker, and those guys kept giving me that piss water." The glassy-eyed man in front of me looks as empty as I feel. I could walk into my apartment right now, and he wouldn't stop me. I didn't feel any vileness from him on the dance floor . . . other than his rejection. He didn't want me. Yet here he is, and he wants . . . something. Heck sticks his fingers into his hair, shaking it loose from its pomade, adding to his choice disheveled appearance. "Liquor takes me from silly to sad, and then I have a hard time being alone." His eyes grab ahold of mine, pulling me into a sea of melancholy. "Do you ever have a hard time being alone?"

Oh hell. It's been an ugly night. At least he's pretty.

"Kiss me, Heck," my reckless, overworked, violated mouth says. It's a stupid idea, but I'd rather end the night tasting my new annoying neighbor than remembering Salvatore's filthy tongue-assault. Heck's forlorn face draws closer, his feet padding forward as he frees his hands from his pockets, sliding them to my face. When his soft lips meet mine, his mouth is everything I imagined, bold and commanding, with his tongue joining my fervor. My knees would have buckled if not for the angst his palms and lips share. He's despairing about who he is. Fearful, even. I must have been too hard on him. He can't help who his uncle was.

I pull away, my breath quickening. "Heck, I may have misjudged you."

"People often do." His mouth is against mine again, and I nearly lose myself in his passion and heavy breath. But as my hands slide down his fit chest, terror spikes through his lips into my face. I move my hands down farther. It flares again. As I press my hips up against him, I notice his lack of excitement, his apprehension like a shrill alarm. My allure could help if he's having a tough go. Wouldn't be the first time I've had to help a half-seas joker with a poorly timed whiskey limp. But that doesn't seem to be Heck's problem.

Is this what he really wants?

I step back, taking his hands from my cheeks.

"Are you all right?" I ask. His eyes are wide with confusion, but his hands tell me he's afraid I'll find out. *But what?* With his nerves louder than his thoughts, I can't get a clear read. But he's definitely got a secret.

It's gnawing on him too. "Wh-what? What do you mean?"

"Heck, you just seem nervous."

His laugh is forced, his scarlet cheeks and telling hands giving him away. "Why would I be nervous?" Before I can respond or read him further, he steps back, holding one elbow like he's been caught in the candy dish.

"Look," I say, "if this is your first time, just say so."

He leans forward with that same laugh, a little shock thrown in. "My first time? Just because you've kissed half the men I've met so far doesn't make you an expert."

My hardening jaw keeps my mouth from tumbling open. Doesn't stop my response from pushing through clenched teeth. "*Excuse* me?"

"Yes, Salvatore told me all about you."

"I'm sure he did," I snap, my neck blazing. "And I'm sure that's why you came after me, you gink. Rose runs a gin joint and thinks marriage is baloney. She must be easy!" I turn toward my door. "Well, I'll tell you exactly what I told him: Take a cab!"

"You *told* me to kiss you!"

"Because I thought you were a nice guy who was actually interested in me," I shoot back. "Obviously, you are neither!"

Heck flips his hand in the air, his perfect nose flaring. "Hey, I'm not the one who stopped us."

"Oh please. I can't stop something that never got started."

"What's that supposed to mean?" he asks, his chin lowering. Raising an eyebrow, I glance at his trousers. He gasps, his eyes wide with indignation. "And I suppose that's *my* fault?"

"It sure isn't mine!" *Pendejo.* Nothing is *ever* a man's fault.

With a cavalier huff, he spins on his bare heel, storming for his door and throwing it open before turning back to glower. "Women shove their room keys into my pockets in every city I visit. This one's no exception. I saw the way you looked at me at the train station. The way they all look at me." Heck backs into his dark apartment, gripping the door. In the shadows, I can swear his eyes are misting. "This was not my *first* time. And if it didn't go the way you hoped, then it *is* your own fault!"

I'm left staring at my new neighbor's closed door, wondering if I should be disappointed or relieved. Between Salvatore's threatening kisses and Heck's failure to keep his car in gear, my aggravation rushes me through my apartment. I've had my fill of his gender and their games for one night. Heading straight to my bed, I flop down on my quilt with all of my clothes still on.

Men are so dramatic.

4

"'THE THIRTEEN OPALS,' BY LAURA KIRKWOOD," I MUMBLE, HIT-
ting the last few weighted keys on my Underwood typewriter. The
only thing saving me from death-by-desk-job is living vicariously
through my pseudonym, who travels the world over in search of
lost treasure. Funny thing is, I'd never want to be my heroine—I'm
not dying for more adventure than I've got right now. But as soon
as I'm running a fancy club of my own with no strings attached, the
first train I'm headed on is to the ocean—don't care which one, as
long as it's got a port and a ship and I can get the hell out of here for
a while. Right after I thumb my nose at this office.

The ocean's got its other appeals too. My abuela says the waves
make the most majestic sound, whispering secrets under the moonlight. Of course, she says that about the river, too. And as much as
water supposedly loves a bruja, it's never had a word to say to me.

But the river can be that way, I'm told. Perhaps the ocean will
be more chatty.

My eyes begin to melt in my head as I turn to a thick stack

of line edits, beginning with an advertisement for Folger's Coffee that I landed when a businessman from San Francisco decided he needed to wet his beak at my joint, but of course that was never acknowledged. Didn't help that he called Mr. Roberts to set up the ad the next day instead of me.

I can't be too sore about it, though. The last thing I need is to explain to the bigwigs how what's supposed to be a glorified typist landed a big-money ad.

A day job is the perfect place for anonymity as a woman.

I blink hard, stretching my fingers and peering around the bustling newspaper office, the ticking of typewriters and subtle flirtations filling the room. Men in plain suits weave around the demure secretaries, stopping to sit on their steel desks, allowing the ladies to adjust their crooked ties and suspenders. Gotta keep those real reporters looking sharp.

Around here, if you want to make friends, as they say, you've gotta present yourself as friendly. Nobody bothers coming to my desk. Romance and kinship have no place at work for me . . . or anywhere else for that matter.

The boss must be in because everyone's acting like they're in a big hurry, and his frosted-glass door is closed. I'm crammed at the desk I share with Margaret, our boss's niece and full-time office snoop, who doubles as his secretary when she's not busy writing fluff ad copy and wrecking my career. She'd be a damn good reporter—except for her bad knack for asking the hard questions and then running away—but like me, she's got the wrong body parts, sentenced to organizing cleaning product ads for the housewives of America. I flinch as my tall, gangly desk-mate plunks down next to my typewriter, adjusting her turquoise dress to cover her knees with the lace embellishments.

"If Mr. Roberts didn't turn you over his knee for what you did at the train station, then I'm going to," I say, ignoring the copy Margaret's holding in front of her chest with the ends of her orange hair pointed at her proud grin. "And I swear, if I get fired because of you—"

Her U-shaped smile falters. "No one is getting fired. We got the interview."

"I mean, you *left* me there, Margaret. You . . . What?"

"Rose," she says like I did something wrong. "The interview questions were hand-delivered yesterday afternoon with a small quote about the financial benefits of a city with title restrictions." Her proud look is back. "I mean, it's still all baloney, but we got Pendergast to *comment* on it. Can you believe it?"

I almost can't. Salvatore said he'd send over the interview questions, but I didn't expect him to keep his word. Even before I nearly broke his pinkie toe with my chunky heels. Maybe he was too drunk to remember that interaction. *Probably not.* No wonder he acted like he deserved a favor last night. *Gross.*

Somewhere between furious with Margaret and thrilled that I've still got a job, I ask, "So Mr. Roberts isn't about to can us both?"

"Oh no, he's definitely angry, but my uncle is a toothless old bear!" she gushes. "Plus, I told him I had the dropsy yesterday. Now look at my front cover idea!" In a half-hearted attempt to seem interested, I lift my gaze to this week's Sunday edition.

"'Cocktail dresses for the modern woman,'" I read aloud as she wiggles with self-satisfaction. "Margaret, it's 1925. We're throwing our corsets and cautions to the wind. I'm surprised a woman who confronted Pendergast is satisfied pushing a fashion fluff piece."

"I can't know what you even mean," she replies, smoothing her outfit with an innocent pout. "I may voice concerns, but like my uncle said, I was way out of line. Though women do tend to get overheated during ovulation. Thankfully, I have the weekend to recover."

I lower my chin. I don't know why I'm shocked. She's always hiding her progressiveness behind a conservative skirt. We're all hiding something, I guess. Doesn't mean I don't like poking her hornet's nest from time to time. It's something to do before lunch.

"You know, Margaret," I say, folding my hands on the desk, "Tennessee just passed a law prohibiting the teaching of Darwin's theories in their public schools, like they're afraid their children can't think for themselves."

Her emerald eyes roll. "Also none of my business."

"And there isn't a single city official who can explain why whites can't legally marry a person of African descent."

"Oh, Rose." Margaret crosses her cardiganed arms. "Do you have any idea how dangerous that is? You could get arrested for fornication, even after marrying." Her eyes widen, darting around the room as she leans down. "Don't tell me you're considering such a risky thing."

A smirk crosses my mouth. "Oh, dear, if I ever narrow down my suitors enough to talk about marriage, I'll let you know."

"Ugh. Rose." Margaret suddenly perks up, gripping the edge of the desk. "Speaking of marriage, did you see the bridal announcements on page three?" My smirk falls flat. "Carolyn Wheeler is engaged to that insurance salesman. *Carolyn Wheeler!*" A few heads pop up from the surrounding desks. Margaret leans closer with a secretive sneer. "You want something to investigate? Find out how a bug-eyed Betty like that can snag such a man."

"I think I'll stick to line editing."

"Oh," she says, laying a tender hand on my shoulder, "I told my uncle we would never let anything like yesterday's gaff happen again."

"*We?*"

From behind me, the telltale sound of the editor in chief's glass door rattles open. I think it best to keep my eyes on my desk. "Lane!" I flinch at his gruff voice. "In my office right now!"

Amid the sympathetic faces, and even a few looks of delighted curiosity, I push back my chair and enter the brick-walled office with my head held high. Mr. Roberts's wispy hair sticks out in its typical mess on the sides, likely from years of pulling at it in a con-niption. His rounded belly hits the desk as he leans over it with his face down, scraping at a meat sauce stain on the blue fabric of his shirt. He's probably eaten cold spaghetti for breakfast again. I inch the door shut like I'm trying not to wake up my father from his nap.

"I consider myself progressive," Mr. Roberts begins, my stom-ach undulating like the upward climb of a Coney Island roller coaster. "I send a couple'a women to conduct a scripted interview for our very prestigious newspaper, and they go off like Sherlock Holmes to interrogate a city councilman as he's getting off the train." He lifts his head, his eyes lighting. "His ratty assistant was here yesterday for God's sake, askin' about you. Are you tryin' to get me shut down?"

I can't hide my shock, the coaster car in free fall. *Salvatore*. He was here. I thought he'd send a carrier. That's way too close to home for me. I'm used to the small-time thugs who frequent my bar, but that's all they are—low-rent fellas without the juice to get me in a jam. But Salvatore's connected to more than just phony moonshine. He's connected to his very real employer, who comes with more than a sip of danger, Moretti . . .

Icepick.

Goosebumps rise on my arms with my pulsing heart. I don't want anywhere near a mobster like that, allure or no allure. Hell, my magic would likely spasm in a fit of nerves if I got in a room with him. I'd hate to know how he got that name.

And I hate that he's sending his crony down to my legit day job. I don't like mixing my lives up. It's too damn messy, and this proves it. The salt in the wound is that none of this is my fault. I glance down at Mr. Roberts, who's still scrubbing at that stain on his tie.

"What am I gonna do with you girls, Rosie?"

"She just wanted to write a real story."

"I didn't approve that interview!"

I bite the corner of my tongue to keep my underworld persona at bay. Rose Lane in the daytime is a loyal employee who doesn't make too many waves. She's an accommodating cog who doesn't talk back.

I hate Daytime Rose.

"Did you even try to stop that dippy girl?"

I begin answering by noting how Margaret is a foot taller than me and twice as loud, but the chief editor lets out a growling sigh before I can say anything, throwing his hands in the air as he ramps up the conversation he's clearly having with himself. "I ought to put you on the choppin' block right now, but I know how my niece can be. Geez Louise! How many times do I gotta tell her, huh? She's gotta work her way up in this business, like Cliff or Gerald. I took you *both* on when you had no experience. I gave you girls a chance, and you treat me like a goon."

As much as I want to point out Margaret was the loose cannon here, I'm not sure Mr. Roberts is interested in the minutes of yesterday's disaster. Besides, it's clear from his tone that my job is safe. I shift on my heels, a silent breath sliding from my nose. And he's finally stewing quietly, so I guess that means I can talk now. "Mr. Roberts," I say carefully, "she's only ever wanted to write something that matters."

"What are ya talkin' about, Rose? Her ads are very popular with the ladies," he says, his chair creaking as he drops down to the padded cushion. If he wasn't my boss, I'd protest that's not the same thing, but he's on another roll that doesn't involve my participation anyway. "But the truth is, men in this city don't wanna read a shakedown of their beloved city councilmen, especially if it's written by another angry woman. We just got through that damn suffrage. You got the right to vote. What more do you birds want?"

Daytime Rose. Daytime Rose. Shut up, Luna. Daytime Rose . . .

I repeat my current role as an inward mantra, rejecting the fire in my ears. I am a loyal employee. I don't make waves. I am who I say—

"We want to make what Cliff makes."

Dios mio, Luna!

My boss's eyebrows shoot up like two bushy caterpillars arching away from a fire. "After that stunt you just pulled, *now* you're askin' for a raise?" His finger shakes at me, the redness in his face brightening. "You got a lotta nerve, kid! I brought you in here to dock ya two weeks. Five dollars, and if you give me any more lip, I'll take three more. Don't make me do it, Rose."

My penance for being a woman. Half of my month's pay because Margaret couldn't stick to the script. Five dollars gone, leaving me a dollar short on my rent. If I didn't have the River Rose, I'd be done for. *Does he know that?* I doubt it.

He sits up at his desk, twisting his spectacles around his face. Looks like we're done. His caterpillars point at me as I turn to leave. "Cozy mysteries, you get me? No more interviews."

"Yes, sir," I reply, leaving the office before my mouth betrays me again.

THERE'S HARDLY A BETTER FEELING THAN THAT FIRST DRAG OF A cigarette, the mild Camel tobacco giving me the appreciation I deserve. It doesn't care who I am and never changes when it meets my lips. I blow out the chalky smoke in a slender stream above my head like the disdain from my day is sailing into the air with it.

Tossing the last of my edits onto my desk, I pass by the break room door, pausing at the muffled whispers from the other side. A strange hiccupy gasp cringes my nose. *Aw geez. Is someone crying?* Office drama is the worst.

Before I can make a break for it, the door swings open. "Rose Lane. I *thought* I heard those size sevens clunking down the hallway. Get in here!"

"Oh, um, I really—" A wiry hand drags me over the threshold into a gang of button-down sweaters and mid-heeled oxfords in a sea of tans that match the walls. Margaret's felt hat is smashed down over her bobbed hair as she tsks her tongue toward the center table, where her secretary colleagues are huddled around a red-nosed woman, handing her handkerchiefs and patting her back. I lift my cigarette to my mouth. "So, uh . . . what's Beth so grummy about?"

The bawling grows louder, the huddle closing in on what looks like an impending group hug. Glancing at my strap watch, I inch back toward the door as a few ladies stroke the sobbing woman's hair. Her head shoots up from her damp hanky, her red-rimmed eyes lighting.

"I'm in love!" she wails before collapsing onto the table. Several disapproving frowns shoot my way as I lower my chin, letting the absurdity cross my face. Hell, I'd cry too if I let myself get that heart-strung over someone.

"You know," I say to Margaret, my hand fumbling behind me for the doorknob, "last time I checked, most girls are happy about that."

She turns her back to the flock with one of her secretive glances. "Oh, they are. Usually." Her hand grips my elbow, tugging me to the corner of the room by the slotted mailboxes and far from my escape of the door. "He's an immigrant. And not just any immigrant, Rose. The man is an *Oriental*. I told her to leave that guy alone because of the risk of being arrested, but no. She thought he was the duck's quack—"

"No one wants to hear your stupid advice right now, you ninny!" Beth cries, falling to her friend's chest. "You don't even have a man!"

Margaret turns back to me with a sigh, shaking her head. My dumbfoundedness must be all over my face, because she rolls her eyes. "She'll lose her citizenship if she marries him, Rose."

Lose what? Di mi. I rear my head. "I thought they did away with that law decades ago."

"They did," Margaret says with a wry smile that doesn't reach her eyes. "For men."

My heart softens and hardens at the same time. While Beth's decision to join her life to one man is silly, she should have the freedom to make that choice. Yet she doesn't. I don't know why I'm surprised to hear the law is a one-way street. Our world is run by men who think they're kings who think they're gods. And my enchantments are powerless to change it.

Mr. Roberts—this is what us "birds" want. Women's suffrage is definitely not over.

"Are you really that surprised?" Margaret says with a wave of her hand. "Well, what can we really do about it? Boycott men?" Margaret's clever laugh distills the grim atmosphere as I look down at the ashes that are growing on the end of my cigarette. *Damn.* The one thing that had been good about today, and it's turning into a dincher. Before I can bring it to my lips, Margaret grabs my wrist, her eyes twinkling. "Speaking of which, I happen to have a prospect."

I'm too disinterested to feign even a modicum of attention at this point. Marriage is for the desperate, lonely birds, and while I am a strong advocate for an engaging dating life, I can't fathom how Margaret's pursuit will end in anything but a break room disaster. I think it's her height that intimidates most of the middle-class men she's gone after. That, and her bossy personality. And the fact that she lost me half my wages for the month—although the last part isn't really about her dating life. I just want to keep reminding myself of it.

Of course, I don't plan on telling her any of that. She'll figure it out . . . hopefully.

Her grip on my wrist tightens, flooding my arm with nervous excitement mixed with mild apprehension that kind of tingles. "Rose! Aren't you even going to ask me about him? Well, I'll tell you anyway." She pinches her lips, her curved nose flaring. "He's kind of an airdale, but he's a splendid dresser, which he *can* be because he's—get this—a *lawyer*. And he's two inches taller than I am! We're going to the moving pictures."

Movie houses are one of my favorite dating locations—dim lighting and loud music to cover my purring. But sometimes I go alone for less lascivious reasons. Greta Garbo and Bridget Helms dominate their leading roles, becoming whoever they want to be. But that's me. I can only imagine someone like Margaret on a date like that, talking too much and ruining a perfectly good opportunity for necking.

My expression may be permanently flattening. "So you're telling me that he's not good-looking, but he's a tall Joe Brooks with a lot of kale?" I can see that I'm popping her balloon, so I sidle past her, making my way back to the door. Margaret's on my heels as usual.

"Hold on, there," she hisses into my ear. "You date darbs all the time!"

I spin around, tossing my waves with a squinting smirk. "Exactly, Margaret. I *date* them. But they're not the marrying kind."

"I'll have you know he's been a perfect gentleman."

Her hardened expression is giving way to a nervous bite of her lower lip, making me feel for her a little. "I'm sure he is," I say, tapping my ashes to the floor with a simple smile. "Just don't put up with any bushwa, okay?"

"Rose! Language!" Her lips curl into an almost grin as I let myself out, smoking what's left of my cigarette on my way through the building.

From the street, I gaze back up at the break room window where real women struggle against the shackles laid on them by male society, and I can understand why they get so excited about silly fluff pieces about modern women and hair products. Real life's far less beguiling.

"WE'RE THREE SHORT THIS WEEK, MISS ROSE. THERE WAS NOTHIN' we could do."

Of course my weekend has flown by, leaving me oddly grateful for my part-time hours at the newspaper. I don't know how I'd handle the stresses of my club's inventory day otherwise. I shove my exasperated sigh back into my chest, feeling the inside of my handbag for my box of Camels, only to find it empty. I'm short too.

Isn't this swell?

I can't be too hard on Nickels. As sharp as his metal-knuckled fists are, he doesn't know how to take reprimand from me. I don't know if it's because he finds me intimidating or attractive, but his skittishness would only get worse if I ever tried to find out. What matters is, he's been a good worker for me and Gus's parlor and has given me no cause not to trust him so far.

"That's okay, Nicky," I say. "Just stack them in the back room for now."

"Yes, ma'am." The gap in my hired henchman's front teeth shows as he flashes a compliant smile, lifting two hefty crates in his bulky arms, glasses clinking from the inside. As his sandy hair rounds a wooden partition that makes up the rooms in our makeshift storage facility, I step away from the dirty stone walls, kicking the door open farther. This room needs more sunlight. The single bulb hanging from the exposed ceiling may provide the right mood for our patrons and paid flappers, but it's a real pain on inventory day.

Javier sidles in with another crate, followed by the brooding piano player, who could use a haircut and a shave. "Hey," I hiss, pinching my brother's suspenders as Gio heads in Nickels's direction. "What's he doing here?"

Javier's eyes flick to the ceiling. "Dios, even with the cops taking their share, we could still use the muscle on Mondays, *Miss Lane.* He offered. I accepted." My brother looks at me too square in the eye when he's holding something back. I slide my hand up to his collar, pretending to adjust the cream lapel. He ducks away, his eyebrows lowering. "Don't."

I know he hates it when I try to read him. But I don't appreciate him bringing a man I hardly know into my storage facility. "What are you not telling me?" I whisper, glancing back at the storage room, where Nickels's belly laugh rings off the walls.

Javier pinches his mouth together, following my gaze with a long inhale. "Rose . . . I've been talking to Gio, and . . . he's got some ideas." His careful eyes travel back to meet the scowl that I have waiting for him.

"Ideas."

He tightens his arms around the crate with a smiling shrug. "Ideas."

"Uh-huh." *About what?*

Before I can ask, Nickels's stomping loafers jaunt back into the room, his arm hooked around Gio's shoulder as he finishes telling some joke I've heard a thousand times. "But anyway, I gotta go see a man about a dawg. Unless you need anythin' else, Miss Rose."

"No, that's it for now, Nicky. Thanks," I say, my polite smile melting as I turn back to the two men with their gray newsboy caps. My brother's expectant grin is searing my patience. He shouldn't be talking to this stranger about *my* business, especially with Gio's background. It doesn't take a genius to surmise that the man has spent some time up the river, with his disrespectful posture, the exposed tats, and the small jagged scars around his left eyebrow. "So you two lovebirds gonna keep sizing me up, or are you gonna tell me what this is all about?"

Javier clears his throat, setting down the crate and crossing his arms. "Miss Lane, Gio here has experience in the import business. Chicago, Philadelphia, New York—you name it."

"I'm sure he does. But I'm doing just fine, Mr. Alvarado." My deadpan gaze doesn't leave my brother. I resent being cornered by a guy who's obviously using Javier to get to me. Ugh. My brother's smarter than this.

"At least hear him out, señorita." Javier's hands find his hips, his jaw setting. "It's not like you gotta say yes."

Wondering if snapping his suspenders against his chest would be considered unprofessional, I resurrect that sigh from earlier, matching my brother's posture. "I've got someplace to be." I let my eyes roll to my right, where the bootlegging pianist is flipping his metal lighter open and closed with a subtle smirk, a cigarette dangling from his mouth and another in his hand. "So make it quick, Mr. Cattaneo."

Gio holds the Lucky Strike out to me. "I heard you got an offer from Ice."

Great. Another criminal with *connections.*

With a crisp look, I take the offering. "Word gets around, it seems."

"That it does," he says, holding a flame to his cigarette before tossing me the lighter. I catch it midair, avoiding my brother's twinkling eye, bedding down my annoyance—a decent man would have lit my Lucky. I'm not shocked, though—I expect nothing but deplorable manners from this hood anyway. Gio takes a long drag, tossing his dark hair from his eyes. "So, you gonna get involved with those creeps, or what?"

"Well, I'm already involved, apparently. Through Giuseppe," I say, letting the burn wrap around my lungs. "Not that it's any of your business, but it'll take me years to save up enough for my own place, and dealing with these guys has been all right so far."

"That's 'cause you got a middleman right now. But just between you and me, Gus's had his nose broken a few times messin' with Ice." This might be news to me, but the piano player doesn't need to know that. For one, it's embarrassing, and for another, it's disturbing. The orneriness in Gio's face disappears, smoke rolling out of his nose. "I ain't you. But if I was, I'd find some otha' way than makin' a deal with that devil."

I open my mental notebook, turning to the page where I jot down suggestions from random men about how to run my life.

"I never said I was making deals with anybody," I say with an irritated tilt of my head. "I already turned down Salvatore and I sure ain't picking up a drifting pianist with an attitude problem."

"Well, Miss Smarty-Pants, I may not be the shiniest employee, but I got a hell of a lot of experience that could help you. Like, how to make a real profit sellin' the real stuff. Not Ice's lake watta'." The man has the nerve to roll his eyes at my bewildered expression. "He's sellin' ya watta'd-down piss made outta corn and chemicals. You do know that, right? Most'a your gin's made from medical alcohol. It's makin' people blind and shit."

"I *do* know that. And I know it's not happening here."

"Not yet, anyway. Not till some drunk farma' gets the measurements wrong. But hey, it's cheap." Gio's lips press around his orange filter with an airy shrug that begins to redden my neck. This guy just doesn't get it. I can't afford the real stuff and save, too. He throws me a grumbling huff. "Look, I can get real good deals off the Canada shipments. It'll cost you a hundred and fifty dolla's a case. Maybe less if you got the capital to buy in bulk."

My face freezes between a scowl and complete shock. *He's off his nuts!* "That's fifty more than I pay now!"

Javier's hand is on my shoulder. "Señorita, let the man explain—"

"Explain what? There's no *way*."

"A billion-dolla' business, doll!" Gio snaps, pointing his cigarette at me like I'm not his boss. I start to respond but he steps forward, his sable eyes determined. "Rum-runnin' is a billion-dolla' business. And the stuff I can get you is the real deal, Rose. Do you have any idea how much people will pay for a Scotch whisky or an authentic cordial?"

I blink, shaking my head at this hooey. "Not my customers. They're just working-class people."

"Yeah, well, it ain't workin'-class people I'm talkin' about." Gio's face turns all business, like he's calculating the books in his head, sucking on the last of his dincher. "You start by drawin' in new customa's. Schmooze with that clientele you're gonna hafta have for that nice jazz joint you're wantin'. In the meantime, it ain't like you can't sell both. It's up to you, but if you're wantin' to bank some real green glorious to get the hell outta here fasta', that's how I'd do it."

Of course that's how he'd do it—it's all real easy when it's not your money. I'm already biting off more than I can chew in this business. Now some guy comes in with more ink on his arms than I've got in my typewriter, offering me a way around the local gangsters who want more from me than they're letting on. To be fair, all men want more from me, and that gets me thinking. I jerk my head up in a quick nod, pressing my cigarette to my mouth. "So what do you get out of all this, Mr. Cattaneo?"

"Ten percent. Earnings only on real liquor." He smiles, shaking his head at my suspicious squint. "What? Ain't nothin' wrong with ridin' your coattails to fame and glory. I never liked bein' in charge anyway."

Smart. Not sure I believe it, but smart.

"It's certainly something to think about," I say, stretching out my hand in farewell. He smiles, taking my hand and the bait as my reception picks up on its own. I love it when my magic does what it's supposed to do. I turn to my brother. "Mr. Alvarado, would you bring the car around? It's getting late." My brother shifts on his feet with a tight-lipped nod. I know I've made him mad again, but I'm miffed with him, too.

As soon as he ambles from the basement, I turn my best stony face in Gio's direction, tightening my grip. "Why are you involving my bartender?"

"Whoa, geez," he says, his other hand flying up in defense as he lets out a light laugh. "He carries your inventory every week.

Thought he'd be the guy to talk to, and you ain't exactly easy to approach." His fingertips convey honesty to my knuckles. I sense no ill will. Which is more than a little surprising.

"Okay, tell me about this business of yours."

"It ain't mine." Gio's eyes dart to our hands. Being a bruja has its perks. I now can feel he finds me curious . . . and amusing, which pokes at my ire. I'm not letting go, though—not yet. "I just have contacts. They tell me when and where to pick up. That's it. The partnership fee is a thousand dolla's. Pays for the lawya's pockets and protection from the syndicate."

"Syndicate?"

"Think of it like a memba'ship."

"To an organization I'll never see."

"You'll see the results. And they take care'a their own."

"I already have protection."

"Who? Nickels? That Giuseppe goon?" Gio snorts, shaking his head. "They gonna protect you from Ice takin' all your profits and blackin' our eyes? With the syndicate, you could net fifty dolla's a case if you price 'em right and Salvatore won't be able to mess with you anymore."

His lack of malice or condescension when he says it means he doesn't think I'm some dummy, which again makes me curious. My eyes search his calloused fingers, desperate to use my powers to hear any hidden details he can give about this syndicate. Or maybe this is just another setup from Salvatore to snag me into a partnership. *That's why Gio's been watching me!* I hold tight to his hand, but the whole conversation is starting to fluster me. The read that started off so naturally is now all out of joint and I can't hear a thing.

"Look," Gio says, interrupting my concentration further, "if you're the gold digga' folks say you are, then that's gotta rev your engines, right?"

My head shoots up with a gasp—now, *that* I heard. "Wwwhat

did you call me?"

The scars crinkle in his eyebrow when he grins. "You're way too easy to ruffle, doll."

"*Miss Lane.*"

"Whatever you say, boss." His crinkle smooths out, the determination back in his face. "But we both know a woman runnin' a place like this can't be easy. You gotta be smooth, but not too smooth. Crimson lips, but just enough leg. Smart, but not cocky, or it'll piss off the roosters who think they own everything, including you. I see you walk a line that gets harder to see the more this place fills up with glassy-eyed jerks. But you're *doin'* it, and I respect that. I could be a part'a somethin' like that."

I hate my heart for warming at his kind words. He can't mean them, but this suspended handshake tells me he does. *Damn.*

A strange, comical smirk crosses his lips. "You gonna read my palm or somethin'?"

I rip my hand away, my cheeks burning. "Of course not."

"Yeah, well"—he bends his arm, showing me a top hat drawn near his elbow—"I know a few tricks myself."

"I'm sure you do," I say, fighting a smile of my own. I don't want to be familiar with him just yet—not when I'm still not comfortable about using him. "So that's it? That's all you want? The only man with no ambitions."

"I guess I'm just lookin' for somethin' simple for once."

"Yeah, I bet prison was a little too much adventure, huh?"

The comedy leaves his face as he rubs his stubbled chin. "If that's what you choose to believe, sure. Why not?"

Guilt worms its way around the confident upper hand I thought I had. He hasn't done anything but try to help me so far, but it's not like I haven't had my share of run-ins with nice guys who weren't nice at all. Not that Gio deserves my bitterness until he's earned it. I'm sure he will with his gender's track record. "Look." I sigh, dropping my stub to the ground before crushing it with my shoe. "I

BINDLE PUNK BRUJA • 85

don't even know you."

"No, you don't," he snips, stepping into the sunlight in the doorway. "But I'm used to it. I'll keep my sleeves rolled down if it offends you. And if you'd ratha' deal with those gangstas, by all means. Go right ahead."

"I didn't say that. But I'm not just going to dive in because a piano player says the water's nice. How do I know *you're* not with them?"

"Why? Because I'm Italian?"

"No . . . that's not what I meant. I just—" I feel the hypocrisy of my own bigotry rising in my throat.

"Yeah, well, it ain't like we're all friends." Gio gives me another snorting headshake, mouthing a second Lucky Strike. "Some guy sure must'a done a numba' on you. But we're not all animals. Even in the unda'world."

5

THE CAR RIDE TO THE RIVER BOTTOMS WAS A QUIET ONE. AS MY tires crunch over the dirt and gravel, my headlights beam over the faded lettering on the wooden boxcar in front of us, nearly drowning the flickering lights in the windows. My brother looks to me in the twilight, his mouth pinched and his fingers on the door handle. "So? Did he pass the test or what?"

I push my lips up with a high-pitched grunt.

"Is that a yes?"

"I guess so. For now."

Javier's widening eyes shine in the growing darkness. "So . . . we're doing it?"

"Probably," I say, my brother's excitement falling at my hesitance. "Look, there's something about him that bothers me. He's on the lam or something."

"Dios, Clip would know if he was running from the police. Plus, you *read* him, Luna."

"I didn't get a lot of time. But there's something he's hiding."

"Well, he's handsome enough, so why don't you make some time?"

I gasp at my brother's twitching lips. "Very funny."

"No, you wanna know what's bothering you?" Javier says, clicking open the passenger door.

"You're what's bothering—"

"He didn't offer to light your cigarette."

"*What?* I am more than capable, Javi."

"You know what I mean, hermanita. He wasn't flirting with you and that lit your fire."

Javier just has to be *so* damn aware. Big hermanos and their big noses. I fly out of the car after my laughing brother, who's bolting for the front door. "I get attention everywhere I go, Javi! As if I need another doting admirer who thinks I owe him something."

"Whatever you have to tell yourself." He chuckles, pushing past the potted plants in the living room to the washbasin on the wooden counter. The smell of steaming masa and savory pork waters my mouth. My mother's singing and Mama Sunday's welcoming hug stir my affection, calming my earlier angst as our family sets the table. Over tamales and tomatoed rice, I fill them in on my conversation with Gio, my brother interjecting his silly opinion every two minutes. But overall, it's a nice discussion that pulls at my yearning to be home again. My abuela's toothless smile makes me smile as my mother smooths her crowned raven hair, telling the tale of a customer at the bakery who tried to cheat her out of four cents.

"He thought I wasn't watching," Gloria says, her shining fork straight in the air. "But I assured him that women and immigrants can count! Gringos. And I'd recognize his Rolex watch from anywhere. He's one of those Pendergast puppets, probably working on Nichols's title abominations, hailing from Millionaire Row. Four cents!" She shakes her head fiercely. "If I read one more homage to George Kessler in the papers for revitalizing our city—and now his nephew has moved here. What's *he* planning to do, hm? Move us into the river itself? Aye, aye, aye."

The red-and-gold cloth napkin in Mama Sunday's dark wrinkled hand waves in the air. "You upset yourself, hija."

"Aye. You're right, Mamá. Let's have a nice dinner—" A timid knock sounds at the door like small raindrops, but the cloudless sky blinks with brilliant stars through the two cutout windows on either side.

"I'll get it," I offer, swishing the sweet, warm rice milk around in my mouth. "It's probably those bratty kids again." I saunter to the door, rapping my knuckles against the grainy wood with a jaunty smile. The neighbor children tend to be afraid of my family and the other earth brujas, except for the two urchins who accosted me the last time I came out here. Gripping the door handle, I give it a violent shake before easing it open with a mysterious tone. "¡Oye! ¿Qué te pasa? We're trying to have dinner! If you don't leave our house at once, my mother will add you to our stew!"

"Luna!" Gloria exclaims with a chastising look on her face that sends me giggling. Her disapproval hardens to a fearful disdain as she looks past me, raising the hairs on my arms. With a slow turn back to the open door, I find myself face-to-face with a pair of stunned eyes and a matching blue tie.

"Ahm . . . haaaa . . . y-you . . ." I'm not sure what words are anymore.

"Miss Lane?"

My presence of mind comes back just enough to offer the unexpected visitor a blinking glare. "Did you *follow* me here?"

"Of course not!" he hisses, glancing behind him like he's now worried someone followed him. "I'm just . . . looking for someone, and I'm clearly in the wrong place."

"What's *he* doing here, Luna?" Javi barks.

"Niña, who is this man?"

Mama Sunday's chair scrapes across the wooden planks, her

shuffling sandals nearing the front door that I'm stuck holding, my mouth still dangling open. "¡Caramba!" she scolds, pushing me from the doorway with her cane. "You excuse our manners, Mr. Kessler. Por favor, come in."

Heck's eyes stay glued to mine as my abuela tugs him to the corner of the boxcar, pulling him to the floral cushions of the couch. I grab my elbow in a nervous rush, seating myself in the armchair around the coffee table. I've got to come up with some kind of story as to why I'm here. A man like him can't know about me. Ever.

"Mr. Kessler," I say, straightening my posture to force confidence into my voice. "I thought this was my adoptive family. Surely, the Guadalupe Center hasn't assigned us to the same one. Aren't they endearing—"

"Luna." My abuela's kind smile turns to the frozen suit on the couch, his fair hair shining under the moonlight spilling into the room. The flickering stove and the candles around the boxcar lick the remaining darkness with what could be considered an eerie ambiance if I weren't used to it. Heck tilts back as Mama Sunday grabs both his hands, peering up into his face. "Mr. Kessler no believe you anyway."

His eyes round even more, an ocean of wonder and terror. "Echt jetzt! Er, uh, excuse me. I just . . . How did you know my name? You really are a . . . sorceress?"

"I no sorcery!" she exclaims, making Heck jilt, his eyes darting between me and my brother, who sinks down on the arm of the chair beside me. "I am bruja. Magic from earth, not hell."

"I see." Heck swallows, staring down at their hands. "Well, that's a relief."

Javi and I trade a look of both amazement and unease. We've seen the occasional drifter from the railroad crews come in for bruja magic. But someone as prestigious as Heck hasn't visited the River Bottoms since my father met my mother, the rumors of witchery buried shortly thereafter. My mother told me he was trying to protect us from being found out. But I think shame was the leading factor in his abandonment. That still doesn't explain how Heck found us. And if he can find us, so can anyone.

My abuela continues her hard stare. "You come here for a reading, yes?"

"Y-yes, I was hoping . . ." He avoids every eye, his cheeks blushing as he stammers. "Could we talk in private? You see—"

My abuela lifts a soft cotton bag from her flowered pocket, taking a fistful of the earthy contents within. Dropping the dried tobacco leaves into his palm, she mumbles a Spanish limerick before grabbing a melting candlestick from the coffee table.

Heck pales in the twilight. "No! Wait!"

His incoherent swears fill the room as much as the fermented cigar smoke that creeps up to his frightened eyes, stopping there to examine him like a ghost without form. The flame in his hand dances higher, glowing a myriad of colors until it brightens like a magenta camera flash, making him gasp. Javi and I used to love this game as children, letting the cool fire dance on our hands as our abuela entertained us. Heck doesn't seem to be enjoying it as much as we did.

Mama Sunday begins to hum, rocking back and forth, her eyes shutting. Even in the firelight, the man's tension is all over his face and posture. The humming comes to a sudden halt, her graying eyes shooting open as she claps her hand down over his, quenching the flame. "Your caretaker."

Heck takes a big gulp of nothing. "Wh-what about her?"

"She tell your mother. About your secret."

Heck lets out a grunting exhale, his eyes brimming. "She . . . found out. Yes."

"They try to cure you," Mama Sunday says. Heck's head falls forward as he presses his face into his shaking shoulder, away from us. "Did not go well. Doctors hurt you. Electrocution. Starvation. Exorcism."

"They—they were trying to help me in their own way." Heck lifts his blotchy face, sniffling with desperate eyes. "Can you help me? I'll pay you anything."

"No pay." My abuela reaches into her ivory pockets, turning his palms upward as the moistened dirt sprinkles down over them. "Can help."

I lean close to my brother, whispering, "Help with what, exactly?"

Heck's head snaps toward us, his breath hitching. "Rose, or whoever the hell you are, I'm . . . well, I'm . . ." His lip trembles. "I can't even say it."

"Luna," Javier says as though I'm being rude. "He's wearing a mask." My lowering chin makes my brother huff. "Hermanita, you didn't notice anything *queer* about him when you danced? I know you touched him."

Heck scoffs, blowing his nose into a handkerchief. "Touched me. Kissed me. Insulted me. Like all women do when they find out I can't be what they want me to be!"

I'm sure the firelight isn't hiding the shocking realization across my face. The underground has its share of misfits, like my brother's alleyway tussles and my own archive of undisclosed lovers, but a man whose shoes cost more than my Model T . . . His reputation is front-page. Even the working class doesn't broadcast their unconventional bedroom romps. Hell, Javier and I agreed long ago that it was better not to even talk about it. But here we all are, blushing around this man, whose tears are as discomforting as his confession. Or maybe I'm the one blushing. While the rest of my family glares at my lack of grace, my abuela taps ashes on Heck's soaked cheek with a loving smile.

"All right, geez," I say, folding my arms across my middle. "I knew you were hiding something, but it was hard to tell. The way you carried on at the club—I had no idea you were . . . gay."

"Is *that* what they call it now?" he sobs, his face scrunching.

"Because I've never been more miserable!"

My brother and I look to each other with wide eyes and wrinkled foreheads, unsure of how to comfort such a blubbering man. Gloria would knock us over the head for carrying on like this. Our shock doubles as our prim, stern-faced mother stands behind him, laying a tender hand on his shoulder. "There now, Señor Kessler. All will be well."

My suspicious squint makes a cameo, Javier's shrug mirroring my curiosity. Earth magic only heals broken things. The only thing broken on Heck is his poor, rejected heart. But the old bruja knows what she's doing. Her loving hand is often what most people need, and his beautiful soul will realize it at the right time. He'll accept himself soon enough.

Hopefully he'll stop crying much sooner.

"Are . . . So you're going to use magic?" he sniffles over his shoulder before looking back at my humming abuela. "Does it take the both of you? Should Rose help? What do I do?"

Gloria breathes a tiny laugh, patting him on the back like a poor drifter who needs a sandwich. "No, niño. The gift skipped over me, and my Luna is still training." *That's* an understatement, but I don't care to explain. "Mama Sunday will tend to you. Just relax."

"It's done!" the old woman chirps, leaning on her cane to push herself up. Javier scoots to his feet, grabbing her elbow to help her from the room.

"Oh!" Heck calls after her, his handkerchief staining black as he runs it across his cheek. "Is that it? No more magic?"

Mama Sunday shuffles to a stop outside her doorway, turning with her dancing old eyes. "Hope is magic, Señor Kessler. You full of hope."

While I'm happy my abuela is speaking such affirmations into Heck's life, my heart sinks a little. She's never said that particular thing to me.

"I see." His smiling nod melts back into a frown. "But . . . I don't feel any different."

"You want to set other hand on fire?"

Our ash-stained visitor folds his hands in his lap in a hurry. "No, thank you."

"Muy bueno. Truest love will set you free in two months' time." The old mage giggles, her gums shining as Javier helps her hobble from the room, her crackled voice singing.

My mother scurries to the kitchen once again, joining the earth melody with her back to us, leaving Heck emptying his nose into a silk handkerchief, oblivious to my family's exchanged winks during their exits. While I think the promise of truest love in any form sounds more like a curse than a blessing, I can't help but be happy for him as the angst leaves his red-spotted face. My abuela's readings always come to pass—not like a fortune-telling huckster at a fair. She tells the truth. And she never leaves a hollow heart without some solace and a kind word.

The rest is up to the other person. Just like me with my struggles, Heck needs to believe. As interactive as the magic show my abuela gave him was, the tobacco flames only allowed her to see inside him more deeply. She always says that most people need to see magic manifest even before it manifests—that the real magic is within those who seek it. Sounds easy enough.

If only.

If only I could tap into all parts of myself, fully.

If only I could be who I say I am and not just say it.

Heck's delighted face makes me more forlorn as my mother hands him some flatbread. I don't need to shake his hand to find out that he believes every word my abuela spoke over him—he *will* find love. I hope it works for him. Hell, it might even give me some hope. She's told me countless times that I *will* come into my magic, and it just hasn't happened yet. I wish I could be as green and full of faith as our sniffling visitor. He's definitely one worth watching. If this surprisingly sweet-natured darb can come to terms with who he is, then maybe I can too.

"SO TONIGHT EXPLAINS A LOT," I SAY, EVOKING A LIGHT SMILE from Heck as I hand him a glass mug. I don't know if it's the secrets we've shared in the past hour or the cool spring evening, but the front steps of this run-down boxcar are playing a comforting host to our conversation, the frogs and cicadas adding their discourse. He and I are like old friends, with his tie loosened and his jacket slung between us. I'm nervous to be talking so openly about myself, but I'm sure he is too.

Heck blows the steam from his mug, his elbows on his knees. "Yes, well, it seems we're both good at hiding." His cup lifts in the air. "To cowardice and lonely nights."

"I will not drink to that." I laugh, pushing his mug from his lips. "Do you know you're breaking the law just by seeking out mystics?"

"My whole adult life is breaking the law, being who I am. So why not add some witchcraft?"

"Shh—don't let Mama Sunday hear you call it that!" *Bruja* may translate to "witch," but my abuela is more than that.

"Don't you worry, Miss Lane," Heck says. "I've had plenty of practice at keeping quiet."

"Oh?"

"I've spent two years searching for real magic." He rests his cheek on an ashy palm. "Just follow the children's stories of the underground. The ones that no one believes."

"Or that everyone believes, but they're too afraid to venture."

"The places society forgets about."

"The loathsome side of the train tracks."

He nods.

"That's not cowardice," I say. "That's tough as hell."

He sips the rim with a pleased smirk. "I've broken a lot of laws, Miss Lane."

My neck flushes in the dark. The laws against sodomy *are* rather harsh, even in this roaring decade of sexual exploration. Flappers like me aren't exactly respected, but I don't get arrested for all the men who have left my apartment.

"Yeah, well, I ain't seen nothin'!" I insist. Heck laughs, nearly spitting out his coffee. "If anyone asks, I'll tell them you're just an Ethel with an eye for fashion."

"Ah yes, just the label I need." He spreads his hand against the starlit sky like he's painting the words. "Effeminate sharpshooter. That'll bring the ladies in."

"You are a sharpshooter, I'll give ya that. I've never seen anyone dance so well."

"Well, dancing isn't going to save my inheritance if I don't straighten this out." Heck's face sinks again as he stares down into his mug. "My accounts were supposed to be released to me when I turned eighteen. Then twenty-one. Now I'm nearly twenty-four and I wonder if I'll ever be a man."

My eyebrows pinch together. "Wait. They can't keep your inheritance from you, can they? Your mother and great-uncle have both passed. It should all be yours."

"It's in my contract," he says, bringing his misty eyes back to me. "Like a title restriction for life. I have to marry. And no basketeering."

"Basketeering? Do I want to know what that means?"

"I do beg your pardon, but my time in New York has educated me quite a bit on queer subculture," Heck explains, the amusement back in his face. "Your city has some freedoms if you know how to speak the code. For example, we liken eggs to a certain part of the male anatomy—"

"Is that right?"

"And as you know, you must assess a basket of eggs at the grocer before buying them—"

"All right! I get it." My face is burning.

"I mean, you assessed *mine*—"

"Aw geez!" Our laughter decompresses the heaviness of the subject matter as my hand slaps his shoulder.

"Which I will allow you to do again, once I'm cured with truest love like your grandmother said."

Oh, Heck. I wipe tears on the arm of my blouse, trying to stifle my guffawing as my initially carnal interest in him gives way to a growing compassion. He needs a real friend in the midst of his self-loathing until he's cured. Cured of thinking he needs a cure. Fighting another giggle, I swallow a snort. "No way. I don't think we're meant for each other."

"But why?" Heck whines, his eyebrows knitting. "I could trust you. We seem to get along. And you're obviously attracted to me."

"Well, aside from your proposal knocking me off my feet with romance," I say, making us both chuckle, "I don't want to marry anyone. Ever."

He wags his head back and forth, coming to a grumbling agreement. "Fine. Then we must always be friends. Those are hard to come by. But you'll be sorry when I am able to please a woman. I plan to be extraordinary about it."

"I'm sure you're extraordinary at everything."

The thing is, once he realizes what Mama Sunday really meant, he won't want to change. I take a big gulp of my rice milk while Heck swats away a mosquito like he's never seen one before. The night and his company are as warm as the mug in my hands. Oddly enough, I'm not ready to go home.

"So, next question, Rose Luna Alvarado Lane," he says, setting down his mug on the steps. "While I find your powers of persuasion to be fascinating, how did this all happen? And does Javi have the gift?"

"Well, no." My eyes drift to the shadowed riverbanks in the far distance. "Only the women, and don't ask me why. I have no idea. Our origins are strange, just a whisper of a tale, really."

"Oh, I've lived on whispers for the last few years. Now I must know!"

I giggle at his glowing face. The man really is handsome and innocent, somehow.

"Sometime in the sixteenth century, while New Spain was being established and conquered, an earth bruja was discovered in a native village. She was forced to marry a viceroy, who sold her spells in royal lotteries."

"He sounds deplorable."

"He was. So one day he received an anonymous bid for a large shipment of blessed soil. Being the greedy bastard he was, he put his wife to work day and night in her palace quarters."

Fireflies blink around the small porch, lighting Heck's creased brow. "The bidder wanted *dirt*?"

"Oh, the earth is very powerful," I say, letting mystery creep into my voice. "Depending on the ingredients, some mixtures can be used to read past and future. Others can be sprinkled into potions for spells of ardent lust. Some even heal wounds down to the bone." My audience's breath is silent as he hangs on my every word. "But this bidder wanted the most coveted mixture of all—a spell that increases prosperity. The dirt was worth more than the jeweled boxes that carried it."

Curiosity and wonder spread across Heck's face like he's calculating his stock portfolio. "So you're a family of dirt witches, then?"

"*Earth* witches, to be exact." I rub my hands together, squinting. "A full bruja like my abuela can connect to nature in ways most can't even fathom. They can even grow plants that increase protection and luck or"—I give him a pointed look—"even love."

"Sounds wondrous."

"Yes," I say, the humor leaving my voice. I peer behind me at the wooden door to the boxcar, the hanging pots beside it rocking in the breeze. "It can be, but the spells take energy. Sometimes all the strength one has, so it's also dangerous. The stories say she drained her own life, cursing the dirt instead of blessing it. War and sickness came, many villagers escaping and moving northward from Mexico. They say only a few brujas survived."

"Like your grandmother."

"Yes."

"And you?"

I laugh at the incredulity in his question. "What, I'm not magical enough for ya?"

"It's not that. It's just . . . I guess I haven't seen you do anything."

"And now that I know your proclivities, you probably never will."

He blushes. "Well, lucky for you, my curiosity won't be reined in by my discomfort. Spill it."

Hesitation warms my own face. I couldn't be more exposed if I were in my bloomers. I've hidden this for so long—like so many other things—I'm not about to start singing because a seemingly nice man asks me. And yet . . . his secret is as dangerous as mine. And Mama Sunday doesn't let just anybody in. So, with more struggle than I thought possible, I take a deep breath and take a chance on trusting him. "I can read people. Charm them, even, if I get close enough." I touch his lips, and his eyes widen before a laugh shoots through both our noses.

"So I take it the spell your grandmother just did isn't your specialty."

"It's one of many I don't have in me," I say. I nod to a large maple in the distance. "Our magic is like three branches—healing, curses, and charm." As a growing amount of excitement ramps up in my chest, it occurs to me how much I actually know about my magic—and how much I've honestly always wanted to talk about it without fear or judgment. And it feels nice to share with someone other than my family. More than nice. My words flow freely for the first time ever. "And those three branches, they each have several limbs of their own with different ways to use them. Mine is more like, I don't know, a twig on the charm branch, while Mama Sunday is the whole tree."

"She's that powerful? Then why stay here?" he asks, as if he can't imagine what other reasons might keep a family of Mexican immigrants tucked out of sight. *Aye, gringos.*

"Magic has limits, even for her. Everything has rules—games, society. Hell, even romance. Magic is no exception."

Heck nods again, somber, but perks up just as quickly. "Good God—what about this branch of curses? What *kind* of curses?"

"Oh, our book has so many," I say, leaning in like someone's listening. A child couldn't be more captivated than he is right now. "Not that I've ever seen my abuela use them. It's one of the reasons she's still here, instead of living a swanky life on Millionaire Row."

He lets out a long breath. "Right. Well, that's good." I give him a hard look. "I mean, it's not *good* she has to live here, but—"

"It's okay," I say with a shrugging sigh. A man like Heck could never fully understand the riches of the River Bottoms. I'm having a hard enough time with it myself. "Honestly, my abuela is happiest when she's caring for others—our community, Javi, me . . . and you, apparently." Between that thought and Heck's awe, a smile crosses my face. "Does she make you nervous?"

"A little earlier, but I'm starting to relax." A cricket chirps beneath the steps, making him jump. "It's just that I've never known a sorcer—um, a witch—a bruja before. Do you always have to use dirt?"

Now we're both grinning like idiots.

"We have to make connection to something from the earth." I hold my palm in the air. Heck's suspicious smirk matches his tentative hand as he lines his fingers up with mine. He's thoroughly enjoying this. "Dried plants and herbs, soil, and water are best for more powerful spells, but I only know how to connect to people."

"Because you're half witch or because you don't practice?"

"Oh, Heck, who knows?"

"Well, if it's any consolation"—he intertwines his fingers through mine—"I think you're a pretty fantastic bird."

"Look at you, sounding all manly and offensive."

"Thank you. I think your grandmother's dirt is working."

A snort shoots through my nose as his thoughts flicker to Javier's dimpled chin. "It's not."

"Damn."

We share another laugh, turning back to the slivered moon I was named after.

I SHOOT HECK A WARM SMILE AS HE LETS HIMSELF INTO HIS apartment with a wave. As his door shuts, I jump to the snap of a lighting match. Whirling around with my heart in my throat, I gasp at the tiny flame that lights up a pointy face in the shadows. An Old Gold cigarette pinches between sneering lips. *Oh no.*

"What are you doing here?" My voice comes out as a weak rasp.

Once again, I find myself outside my abuela's protective barrier with this creep, my ferns and cloves beyond my apartment door. Salvatore slinks up the short stairwell, the glowing wall sconces providing a view of his hardened eyes lingering on Heck's door. "So that's where you been all night, huh? He's kippy enough, I guess." Salvatore's darkened gaze trails back to me. "A little weak for someone like you, but maybe that's how you like 'em."

"It's not really any of your business," I say, tensing my shoulders. This gangster has violated my workplace, my gin joint, and my mouth. I can't let this dog smell my fear. "But Heck happens to be a devilish lover."

Bird-Face's jaw twists in amused irritation, his tongue pushing against his cheek. "Not my business, eh?" He rubs his chin in a light laugh, looking around like he's trying to find his words before pointing a finger at me. "Lemme tell you something, baby. You *are* my business."

"Not yet, I'm not."

"Oh really? So you're runnin' that joint on your own, huh? Without any help from Ice?" Salvatore steps closer, forcing my back to the hallway wall. "Your writing job, your filthy little watering hole—it's all in our hands, and so are you." His eyes float down to the top of my blouse that I've left unbuttoned from the humidity at the river. "A sexy, stubborn woman like you fallin' on hard times. The things you would have to do."

"Don't make me hurt you again, Salvatore."

A small, wicked smile curls on his lips as he lifts his cigarette to his mouth. "God, I want you so bad. Do you know that?"

"I got that impression when you were slobbering all over me by my car."

"Those weren't my best manners, I admit."

"I suppose you're gonna blame that tonic you call gin."

Salvatore rears back, leaning his hand on the wall as he takes a drag. "Whaddya mean, baby? My shit's the best they got around here."

"Yeah, well, maybe I'm lookin' elsewhere."

His other hand seizes my jaw. Shocked at his audacity to touch me, harm me right outside my damn door, all I can do is glare at him as smoke lifts from the glowing cherry of the cigarette between his fingers. "You're a smart woman. Sell what you want. But don't even *think* about cuttin' us out."

I hold his challenging gaze, grimacing in disgust at the pinch of his hand and the desire in his thoughts. "What's so wrong with wanting to sell quality product? I'm trying to make a living here, not friends."

"Thing is, you need friends to make that livin', baby," Salvatore says, relenting my chin to tend to his smoke. Even in that brief vise grip, I heard the threat—*To keep livin'.* It's the words that people don't say that carry the most weight. Anxiousness climbs up my arms like pins and needles.

"Besides," he continues as if he hasn't just threatened my livelihood and life in an offhand utterance, "ain't nothin' wrong with what I provide. The most important thing is to make your customers believe they're gettin' the real thing. They ain't had real hooch in years. Those jerks don't know the difference."

"They'll know soon enough."

I know I shouldn't have said anything. But I finally got to be both Rose *and* Luna in the same place tonight, and neither one of them can stand this clown. Rose wants to charm him and send him away looking goofy and stupid, but Luna . . . the seething anger she feels almost scares me. All I know is, for now, one of them needs to stand down, because the look on this guy's face is growing more concerning.

Salvatore's lips press together as he pushes away from the wall with a frustrated growl, his eyebrows and dincher pointed at me. "Look, I don't know what I gotta do to convince you that I would take care'a you. I work for the city *and* your precious gin market. Me and Ice are gonna be bigger than Luciano or Torrio. Bigger than Capone. Hell, Pendergast'll be answerin' to *us* soon. I'd make sure no one ever messed with you again."

"You're the only one messing with me, Leon."

Aaaand there goes my mouth again.

"You know what, you got some nerve," the glaring mobster says. "You betta' think about how to treat a fella—I don't like my offers tossed aside like garbage." His eyes seem to blacken as his voice continues to grit through clenched teeth. "You ain't nobody, sweetheart."

Salvatore throws his cigarette to my feet, leaving a trail of smoke behind him as he storms down the stairwell. Soon my living room greets me like a hidden fortress, the door slamming before I lean my beaded forehead against it. I don't need enchanted tobacco fire to know how far Icepick's man is willing to go to gain my compliance. The amount of charm I'd need to temper him is way out of my league, and curses are too dangerous for my abuela these days. Besides, bruja magic is what's drawing these goons to my club in the first place. Damn prosperity spells. I've gotta climb my way out of this one the old-fashioned way—a little smarts and a lot of green glorious. Slow and steady isn't working anymore. I told him about the new hooch to shine him on, but now I'm giving it serious thought.

Because he's wrong: I'm definitely somebody. *I am who I say I am.*

And *I* am not about to have my life run for me.

I slide the locks on my door with an indignant sneer. Looks like Rose and Luna have run into some common ground for once. Which means it's time to change strategies.

Time to change my club.

6

"ROSE, YOU REALLY DIDN'T *HAVE* TO MAKE ME BREAKFAST." MY morning visitor feigns a polite smile as he lifts a steaming blueberry to his mouth. I've never seen anyone eat a muffin with a fork. His tepid chewing is followed by a struggling swallow that presses my lips together.

"You don't have to eat it, Heck."

"Oh, thank God," he says, shoving his plate across the iron tabletop and pressing his handkerchief against his mouth. With a scoffing laugh, I stick an orange filter between my lips, covering the match flame with my hand to shield it against the damp breeze. The overcast sky is a great trade-off for a cool meal on the patio. Heck's checkered ensemble is making me hot just looking at it.

I blow a long stream into the air, leaning back as the first blessed cigarette of the day rushes through me. "I'm not much of a cook."

"Nor a host," he huffs. "You're barely dressed for company, and now you're going to bathe me in soot."

"It's my balcony . . . and what do you mean?" As I scan my best wide-legged pants and matching blouse, he breaks into a laugh, leaning forward with dancing eyes.

"For someone who loves men as much as I do"—he pulls an Old Gold dincher from his breast pocket—"you certainly seem to be scaring them off lately."

I snatch the cigarette butt from his hand, tossing it over my shoulder. It bounces off a white pillar, landing in a potted rosebush, its harmonious magic giving a subtle warmth to the atmosphere. "He wasn't courting me. He was threatening me."

"In the middle of the *night*? Rose, why didn't you yell for me?"

I have to choke back a giggle with a slight cough. This man is afraid of mosquitos. I'm fairly certain even small-time mobsters require more than a good verbal thrashing. When Salvatore wants to dance, he's using his fists, not his feet. Besides, it's like I told my brother: There's not always going to be a man to come to my side when I yell. I've known that forever. My shoulder lifts in a shrug. "I can handle Salvatore."

"For how long?"

"Long enough to get away from him," I say. After tapping my ashes into the air, I take another burning drag, letting it out slowly to gather my words. This handsome cosmopolitan is the last person on earth I ever thought I'd be asking for help. But my lone wolf approach to business is getting me nowhere. I don't want to risk an ounce of independence; however, he might just be the key to keeping it. "Heck . . . that's why I asked you here."

"Just say the word. I can have you and your family in Chicago by morning."

"No, no, no. It's nothing like that." Discomfort heats my cheeks. "I've just gotta move my plans along. Higher-class club. Higher-class booze. I'm raising my prices a little to pay for the extras. The only thing I need is someone who's familiar with . . . well, higher class."

Settling back in his chair, Heck crosses his legs, brushing lint from his trousers with a sly smile. "I see."

"I've got a supplier and a bar manager," I continue, flicking my Camel over the balcony. I'm too anxious to even smoke. "But I'd like you to work with me on presentation and marketing."

"You want my name."

"And experience."

"No need to butter me up after what your grandmother did for me," he says, pushing his mug of coffee away like it's full of vinegar. "I'm happy to help . . . on one small condition."

"Give it to me straight."

"Agree to marry me."

I spring to the edge of my seat, my chair tilting. If it weren't for the table between us, he'd have a red hand mark across his face. "That's one *hell* of a thank-you."

"You don't have to follow through with it," he pleads, matching my posture. "Don't you see? I just need the agreement so I can have the first installment of my inheritance. I'll even water that jungle in your apartment!"

"Heck! No!"

A guttural sound rushes from his throat. Men who throw pouting tantrums are the embodiment of romantic repulsion. *Ugh.* Soon, Heck's head falls into his arms as he lays them across the table. His suit sleeves could wrinkle. This is serious.

My first smile of the day.

"Rose," he grumbles into his sleeve before his head shoots back up. "Rose! How long will your price increases take you to raise the money you need to get out?"

I lose my smile to a wary squint. "Longer than I'd like. Why?"

"I won't get much, but if you agree to be my fiancée, it *would* be enough," he says. His words are like a speeding train. "I can invest in talent, decor—even a down payment for a new place. Rose, you need an investor and I need a woman to wear my ring. Our trust was forged by a night of magic for more reasons than salvaging my love life. We can *help* each other."

Sincerity emanates from his eyes. *I . . . No way.* Just no way. Heck and his baby blues cannot ask this of me.

"Come now, Rose, how is this a bad thing?"

I start to answer, but catch myself in curious wonder at his hopeful face. Even the midmorning birds sing in the grass below like an unwelcome agreement. Since the first day I met the man, he's finally starting to make sense. It wasn't my plan—I originally just thought he might be a fun ride around the block—but a ring on my finger, one that doesn't mean anything, to get what I want . . .

"It's still my club." I point a warning finger at his gushing grin. "This isn't a favor."

He shakes his head. "Not at all."

"It's business."

"Business and friendship."

"Mostly business!"

"Whatever you say, my dear flower."

"CLIP, YOU'RE SURE ABOUT THESE GUYS?"

I peer over at the nervous huddle of jovial applicants, the guys in their white button-downs and tweed slacks, the gals all dolled up in silky head wraps and lacy beaded dresses accented by long strings of pearls. My band leader gives me a side grin. His teeth shine against his dark skin as he presses his mouth to the lip of his saxophone, giving it a bleating test. Charlie and his musicians practice every night, rain or shine, his dedication to this hole-in-the-wall joint bewildering to anyone who doesn't know how the potted lavender behind the bar draws in people with sincere hearts. Kindness and trust are such commodities these days. The wooden stool beneath him creaks as he settles back on the small stage, his team tinkering on their instruments behind him.

"Miss Rose," he says in that deep, thick tone of his. "You asked for entertainers, and I got 'em."

That's all he has to say. I hold in my huff, sticking my hands on my hips as he turns away from me. *Guess that's my cue.* It's time to hold these interviews whether I'm ready or not. My apprehension is more due to not knowing what I'm doing rather than Charlie's ability to locate new talent. He's always been good at that. *Keep moving forward*, I tell myself. This is something I've got to do.

"All right," I announce, pointing my hand at a group of ladies in silver dresses. "Let's start with you three."

They giggle as my head waitress brushes against my arm, laying her bronze chin on my shoulder. "Look at 'em, Miss Rose. Those jokers'll go nuts over 'em."

"I suppose, Penny," I say, easing away from her. I don't mind that she's touchy—with others. She's a strong, kippy woman. She'd make a great friend. But I'm her boss, and even more importantly, I've never wanted that kind of friend. Trust is hard even though her emotions read that she's trustworthy. "Let's see if they can move first."

She lifts a pencil-thin eyebrow, smirking toward the stage as the ladies line up, their brilliant smiles nearly blinding me. *Perfect.* But if they can't cut a rug, it won't matter, so I'll wait for Penny's assessment. She knows if a lady's got what it takes.

"All right, Clip, give 'em all you got!" my best flapper shouts, her manicured hand by her ruby mouth that matches her wig. The band's deep floor toms and thumping bass drive the heartbeat of a Jelly Roll Morton number, the brassy saxophones and trumpets ricocheting around the empty club. The flapper triplets shake their shoulders, kicking their knees and strappy heels in syncopated rhythm, their garments twisting and shining under the wall sconces and hanging bulbs. Their white stockings stay in place, rolled just below the knees during their impressive kick routine that stills my brother's duties behind the counter. I shoot him a warning look that he returns mockingly before turning back to the shimmying triplets, his lower lip between his teeth.

"Well, it looks like they know what they're doin', huh?" I yell to a smiling Penny.

"They sure do, Miss Rose—Clip!" Charlie folds his hand into a fist, and the band quits playing. "Let's see if they got pipes, too." At Penny's eyelinered wink, he nods to Gio, who cracks his knuckles before playing a skipping number about a woman who knows how to use what she's got to get what she wants. The dancers jaunt to center stage, crowding around the silver oblong microphone. As they begin to sing, Clip's rugged eyebrows hit the ceiling with the rest of the band, Gio's fingers flying as he maintains his tight-lipped smile. Penny's got her lips pushed out, squinting like she's tasted something horrible. Heck must have arrived during the painful serenade because he's standing on my other side with the same look, his fingers pinched in the air.

I lift my hand, stopping the madness. "That's quite enough, I think. We'll definitely give you a call."

Heck leans close, sending them a friendly wave as they sashay through the exit before turning back to me with a lip-curled sneer. "Is it just me or were their voices almost as horrible as those frocks?"

"Well, they're good dancers," Penny points out, smoothing her lace dress. "And they're willin' to work the underbelly."

That's a big point in their favor. Our after-hours services make almost as much money as the booze, and it isn't always easy finding talented flappers who will work here. Now, if I could just find a lead singer besides the bass player—his voice is nice enough, but no one is going out of their way to hear him sing. This place is home to male patrons. And there are few simple things that draw them—a doll with pipes would be a whole new kind of magic in this place.

"True," Heck says, scanning his fingernails. "But they'll need a ton of work."

Penny tilts her ginger head with a curious smile, her wig never out of place. "I agree, Mr. Kessler. You know . . . if it's not too much trouble, you wouldn't mind givin' me an eye to get them ready for showtime, would ya?"

Heck startles, blinking with a light laugh. "Ah well, sure. I guess that would be all right."

"Great!"

"If I can make time, that is."

"Of course," she says. "Be here tomorrow at ten."

My new, conflicted friend starts to stammer, but my grinning shrug makes him shake his head. Might as well make himself useful if he's going to be here.

After several more auditions—some with real potential and others leaving me questioning what the hell it is I'm doing—I plop down on a barstool with a sigh. Penny hands me a blessed hope chest and I light up faster than my brother's eyes when he saw those flappers. The burn tells me everything is going to be all right.

"Am I too late?"

All heads crane to the open doorway where a long-legged blonde stands on chunky heels, the lace of her dress at a questionable length near her mid-thigh. The fabric barely holds in her curvy frame. I glance back at Javier, and sure enough, his eyes have fallen to the garter straps that are keeping up her nude stockings. Her curly hair is piled around her head, a silky headband sunk into the center. She looks to me with pouting smoky eyes. "I'm not too late, am I?"

"No, but—" My heart stops dead in its tracks. I know this billboard.

Heck shakes my shoulder. "Rose. It's her."

"I know. And no, Mr. Kessler. Can't do it."

"But, Rose . . . she can *sing*."

"I know that, too. But—"

"Oh, gimme a chance, Miss Lane!" the billboard exclaims, her hands clasping in front of her.

"No," I insist, shaking my head as the room grumbles their disagreements.

"Aww, at least hear her out."

I whirl around to find my club's muscle gawping at this newcomer like he's struck gold.

"It's not your business, Nicky. She belongs to Salvatore."

The blonde marches to the stage, her face reddening like a cherry tomato as she straightens her back, lifting her chin. "I ain't *nobody's*."

I cross my arms, recalling the mobster's threatening eyes in the hallway of my building. "He'll come after you. You know he will."

"Maybe," she says, gripping the slender microphone stand with a raised eyebrow. "But it ain't the first time. I can take a black eye. I can't take not singin'." My lips part as the band shifts, readying to play like I'm not even there. "Besides, all I gotta do is send my cousin in Philly a letta' if he gets too sideways. You boys gonna play or not?"

Gio peers around the piano. "What song, miss?"

"Shock me."

His hands move across the ivory keys, tinkling out the provocative song from earlier. The woman opens her crimson mouth, wetting the atmosphere with a voice that grips my soul—a sultry husk like Sophie Tucker.

> I confess that I possess
> The sweetest gams in town
> And unless I miss my guess
> The boys all follow me around
> I could make a music master drop his fiddle
> Make a bald-headed man part his hair in the middle
> Cuz I'm a red-hot mama
> Red-hot mama
> But I'll have to turn my temper down

Her enchantments fill the room better than bruja magic, her beckoning green eyes almost as beguiling as Heck's. I'm absolutely certain I only prefer men, but moments like this can make anyone question their inclinations. When the song ends, I scan the silent room, blowing out a plume of white smoke with a roll of my eyes. "All right, so what else can you do?"

She fluffs her curls with an innocent blink. "Sing. That's it. I'm done with the rest of it."

"I'm fine with that," Charlie grumbles, pursing his lips.

Gio leans to the side as she bends to adjust her garter, tipping his piano bench. "Sounds good to me."

As the other players call out their agreements, I turn to my drooling bartender, who quickly snatches up a glass, wiping the inside with his towel. "How 'bout you, Javi? You got an opinion too?" He flicks his raven eyebrows with a tiny smile before turning back to his duties.

Aw hell. I like her too. But I'm not thrilled at giving Salvatore more ammunition to hate me. Not that anyone here cares. The staff is already falling all over themselves to make this woman feel welcome. I know Split's happy to have a voice like that on his team. I get it—she's gonna have the darbs fighting their way in. It's just the one in particular I'm worried about—the one who'll bring a gun to a shoving match.

Heck's strong arm drapes around my shoulders, giving them an encouraging shake. "Look, no one's going to blame you if you back out. This is a tough road to walk, Rose."

I sigh with an unattractive groan. "I know. But I've pursued this life to get out from under men's thumbs. To make the life *I* wanted, so . . . I guess I'm not about to keep another girl from doing the same."

"So . . . we keep going?"

"We keep going."

"Great!" Heck's movie star grin spreads across his face. "Because I may have already pulled a few strings and gotten you an interview to tour a new location. The price is unbeatable."

I can't help but smile back. This all seems so unreal. "Well, I guess it doesn't hurt to take a look," I say, lifting my forgotten cigarette to my mouth. I don't know how long it will take to save enough, but the new product from Gio will help. New booze, new place, new talent . . . I'm afraid to feel excited, but my palms dampen, a small shiver running through me anyway.

"Good," Heck says, giving my shoulders a final squeeze. "Now, let me see about this new girl. Her dress is about two sizes too small, and it's apparent she doesn't know how to snap a garter." He turns to the chattering blonde on the stage where Nickels stands, lighting her cigarette. "You there! What's your name, miss?"

She pops a puff of smoke into the air with a wink. "Doris Fenton. But my friends call me Bearcat."

Heck whirls around, his excited eyebrow arched.

"Bearcat?" I repeat, my expression flattening. "You got a temper problem?"

"Yeah," Doris giggles, waving her hand. "Don't we all?"

Great. That doesn't sound problematic at all. Yet Heck's grin remains as he whisks her away with Nickels in tow to convene with Penny. "Don't mind me," I call out, tapping my ashes to the floor. "I'll just be over here worrying about everything." The room bustles around me like I don't cut their paychecks as they prepare for another night of revelry.

"You know, because I'm the boss and all."

WORRIES OF THE MORNING FADE TO THE GIDDINESS OF THE EVEning as another successful, hustling night at the River Rose has me smiling like a ninny as I help my brother fill drink orders. Gio's stash is selling faster than Heck's hopping feet as he spins ladies around the dance floor to the stomping jazz music. One of the new hires fills in on the keys for my new rum-runner during his break as he leads me through the smoky, sweating crowd toward the back door. The cool night air hits my face, blessing me with the soothing quiet of the parking lot. A lanky man in a rounded black hat waits for us beside his Buick coupe.

"How you doin'?" Gio says, shaking his hand before gesturing to me. "This is my employer, Rose Lane."

I reach my hand out. "How do you do, sir?"

The man's eyes drop to my salutation, his long face cemented into an expressionless stare. "I understand you're interested in the syndicate. How are you liking our products so far?"

"I . . . They're selling really well," I say, crossing my arms. "Our earnings are through the roof tonight."

"We thought they might be. Once word gets out, you're going to need more." The man's long fingers curl around the silver door handle, opening the back seat. "You can purchase these ten cases, but if you want real inventory, you'll have to sign the agreement."

Gio lifts the leather seats, revealing several wooden cases all labeled with various brands of soap. "Look here, boss," he says, holding one up with a grin. "Ivory is Scotch. Octagon is gin. All the good stuff, straight from the Brooklyn warehouses."

My heart flutters with the adventure of enterprise. "Well, where do I sign?"

"I need to ask you a few questions first," the man says, folding his hands in front of him. "When do you plan to move?"

"Move?"

"Yes, you can't stay in Frank Moretti's territory. There are rules."

"Rules?"

Gio lifts his hand in the air as though bedding down my apprehension. "Boss, local mobstas like Ice are still respected by the syndicate. He's a nobody, but they won't step on his toes just for the fun of it. You gotta get away from him if you want their protection.

Can't get remarried until you sign the divorce pape-uz, you know what I mean?"

"So I can't sell your products until I'm outta here?" I ask, my heart sinking. "How am I gonna earn enough to do that without the syndicate?"

The man shakes his head. "Not to worry—you can pay the membership fee and sell our products on a limited basis. But if you owe Moretti rent, payments for inventory—anything at all—we won't get involved if he comes after you to pay up while you're still here. That being said, if anyone messes with you outside of that, then they're messing with our profits, and we *will* settle it."

I take a deep breath, my fingers gripping the ledge of freedom. *So close.* Too close to give up now. I squeeze my hips, pressing my lips together with a tight nod. "All right, gentlemen. I'm in if you'll have me. I'm looking at a new place next week."

"Very good," the man says, climbing into the front seat. I suppose our conversation is done. Heading back inside, I send Nickels to help Gio carry the new products to the bar, sending my brother a knowing smile. He claps me on the back, tending to more refills and engaging in light banter with a few of the new girls I've hired to work the floor. Heck and Penny have done a fantastic job dressing them up in glittery frocks, their painted lips stretching with smiles and laughter as they strut around the tables with drink trays in their hands and dollar bills stuffed into their stockings. Things are definitely picking up around here, the newness in the atmosphere felt by the clientele and charging my own mood. Even Gio interacts with the patrons a little more, astonishing them with a few card tricks and using a man's fedora to make his drink disappear.

The guys guffaw and continue their card games well into the night, the joviality hacking away at my defenses as I hug my brother at closing time, telling him to take off. I don't mind locking up for one night. I'm too excited to sleep anyway. Not with my dreams within reach. I take a small swig from an unmarked glass bottle, the smooth liquor—the real stuff—gliding down my throat. It tastes like victory.

And victory tastes like gin.

NICKELS'S SANDY HAIR IS A LITTLE ASKEW FROM THE BOISTEROUS night, though he only had to break up two fights. He checks the stairwell door that leads to the upstairs grocery, wiggling it to make sure it's dead-bolted. "Miss Rose, I'm gonna do the outside walk and then I'll come take ya to yer car."

I start to tell him it's not necessary, but I let him walk out anyway. He's just trying to help. Throwing the last dirty bar towel in a wicker basket, I lift the handles and waddle to the back exit. As the stairwell door clicks behind me, I spin around, the basket clattering to the floor. *Nicky doesn't come in that way.* The door rattles before creaking open, my heart squeezing in my chest as four suited men file into the room. The familiar goon with the pointed face shuts the door, turning the dead bolt before strolling toward me.

"Miss Rose? Did Heck have someone dig up the ferns?" Nickels's panicked voice closes in, the door slamming and locking against his banging hand on the other side. "Hey! Who's in there? You better open up right now or I'll bust this door down!"

His swears are drowned out by the thumping in my ears, cold sweat flashing across my neck. The invisible fence around my building . . . it's gone.

Do they know about me? Can't be. There's no way. *Maldita sea.* This can't be happening now. It's just not possible.

"Calm down, Nick," Salvatore says, leaning his shoulder against the wood. "Ice just wants ta chat with your employer, and since it's none'a ya damn business, why don't you get the hell outta here?"

"I . . ." My words come out in a choking jumble. "What've you got against my plants, Salvatore?"

He flicks his thumb against his nose with a sniff. "How about everything? We been tellin' Gus to get you into compliance for months, but you don't listen to nobody."

"Compliance?" The spinning in my head halts at the memory of Giuseppe jeering about the shrubbery around my club's entrance. I didn't think he was serious. And I certainly didn't suspect low-class mobsters being behind the request. I didn't know shrubs were so offensive. *They're not* that *messy.*

"Your days of doin' whatever you want are over."

"So you cut down my *ferns*?"

"Principle, baby!" Salvatore's face is as red as a cardinal during mating season. "You were told to clean that shit up around our building. You didn't comply, so we came and did it for you. So next time we tell ya to do somethin'"—the goon pinches his fingers in front of his face—"don't be shocked when we bring another guiding hand down on you."

"Oh, you're going to *force* me to sign with Moretti?"

"This is not the time for that mouth, sweetheart!"

"Rose!" Another heavy fist pounds on the door, my stomach twisting in knots as I turn my attention to the three silent gentlemen who've been assessing me like predators before a kill. I could use Abuela's magic about now—the kind that stills a room or lights their brains on fire. Hell, I'd take an apprentice spell, forcing them to sneeze uncontrollably, but I've never been able to muster up even such a childish curse. All I've got is charm.

And I'm sure not using my lips on these jokers.

The gangster in the middle stands out with his myriad rings and a fierce countenance that complements his bent nose. He glances at his golden watch before sliding it back into his breast pocket. His empty eyes study me from toe to head, a small sneer crossing his upper lip.

"So," he says, his deep, scratchy voice sending goosebumps across my skin. "You're the charmer my associate's all goofy for. Wouldn't be the first time he's let his pistol get in the way of business." I back up as he steps closer, my back hitting a barstool. "So here I am, doing what he couldn't. I want to make you another offer, Miss Lane."

I summon my courage, forcing what I hope is a confident answer from my mouth. "Yeah? What's that?"

His sneer deepens into a loathing scowl. "I'm going to help you pay for your new club. Get you out of this place. Clean you up. You'll make us both a fortune."

Clean me up? I narrow my eyes at this jerk. "Thank you, but like I told Salvatore, I'd rather earn my way. I don't like the idea of owing anyone."

Ice's smooth face erupts into an eerie smile as he nudges his chuckling goons next to him before nodding to Salvatore. "She doesn't like that idea." Bird-Face storms away from the door, his hand stinging across my cheek before I even see it. I double over with a high-pitched grunt, grabbing my searing face as Ice's shining shoes near me.

"You're too cocky for a woman," Moretti says. "Too sure of yourself. The world is a dangerous place for someone like you."

"The world is a dangerous place *because* of men like you," I say, forcing myself upright. Salvatore's hand flies again, my loud cry sending Nickels's fists and threats pounding against the door once more.

"The world keeps on spinning because of men like me," Ice says, leading his two goons to the stairwell door. "You'd do well to remember that." He keeps his back to me as they unlock it. "I'll expect your compliance no later than two weeks from tonight."

Two weeks. My burning ears ring as loud as his hanging threat as he and his crew disappear up the stairwell. I'm left alone in the room with a scowling Salvatore, who runs a hand along the side of his slicked hair as he paces, his breath growing heavy. "I told you. Ice don't take kindly to his offers bein' turned down. I tried to tell ya that, but you don't listen!" He grabs the sides of my smarting face, forcing my eyes up to him, his eyebrows knit together with sad anger that bleeds into my skin from his palms—all emotion. "We coulda' picked any Jane, but we chose you, and you *throw* it back in our faces, goin' behind our backs with the syndicate. You ever cross us like that again, I'll have to take you for a ride. And make sure that damn overgrowth don't muck up the entrance again. Pretty little rosebushes or not, it's bad for business!"

He relents his honest grip, whirling toward the stairwell.

"So you're a gardener now," I say under shaky breath. *Just can't help yourself, can you, Rose?*

His hand slams against the doorframe, making me jump. "I ripped out those weeds like they were nothin'! Took 'em apart thorn by thorn"—his jaw lowers his searing gaze toward me—"petal by petal."

The temperature drops to below freezing.

"Oh, and you can keep that singin' bearcat. She's way too much trouble. Almost as much as you."

As soon as the door rattles shut, I run to the back door, throwing it open. Nickels falls all over me asking if I'm okay. I tell him I am, over and over, though my hands are shaking as much as his. We both know I'm not—the redness of my face telling the grim story.

Yet vindication stirs in my heart, lighting my will to carry this thing through. I refuse to live like this. There's no way I'm going to saddle myself to a brute like Icepick, bending to the whim of his sleazy henchmen. Salvatore's not getting anywhere near my petals without encountering serious thorns. Poisonous, if he keeps pushing me. That man better be glad I don't have my abuela's powers; I'd melt his damn brains. But being half bruja doesn't exactly make me weak. I'm resourceful. I'm smart. And I already have a plan. I'm getting the hell out of here to a place where men like Ice can't touch me.

A bitter taste crosses my palate, metallic and earthy like the smell of ground-up scorpion tails in one of my abuela's potions. I almost don't notice it if not for the crisp scent of dandelion that follows, filling me with memories of Mama Sunday on a summer afternoon as she called on the river spirits during a ritual long ago. This doesn't taste like charm. Doesn't feel like it either. It *could* be magic—maybe the last cry of protection spells as the plants in the parking lot wither away. *Maybe.* I chalk it up to nerves.

Nicky's tree trunk of an arm leads me out of the building to the safety of my car, insisting that he follow me home, and I remember I've got more things to worry about than the weird taste in my mouth. The sting on my cheek is a fierce reminder to focus everything I've got on planning our escape from the goons of the underworld. *I'll find a way.*

In the meantime, if Doris can take a few black eyes, so can I.

7

Welcome to the syndicate.
Signed, Tom

The office bustles around me in its usual way, my boss acknowledging anyone wearing a tie, which is good for me because none of them notice my stupefied face as I'm holding a card that was just hand-delivered to my desk by a messenger. Turning the card over, I smirk at the photograph of a familiar building down on Main Street where the Democratic club goes to smoke their big cigars and stroke their big egos. My office may not notice me. But Pendergast certainly does. I haven't decided yet if that's a good thing.

I'm just glad he didn't send his office liaison this time. Having Salvatore delivering my welcome card would have been . . . awkward. He doesn't want me in their club, but the former city councilman doesn't seem to mind. Although, I hardly consider Pendergast's welcome to be a warm one; my mama told me all about his brand of corruption. One thing I've learned about these guys is that almost anything is a warning. These bigwigs are always trying to let me know who they are and what they're capable of. My night life is seeping into what's supposed to be the regular life I created, and it's been a great cover—a single woman making her way in the city. But now the underground knows where I work, where I live. *Some cover.* In any case, I just need to be diligent about keeping all these parts of myself as separate as possible. I'm anything but new to compartmentalizing my life. What's one more split? My day life has always been a kind of hideaway for me, and now it's a part of the juggle, but I can handle it. It'll be fine. Should be. As long as they all stay the hell away from Luna.

This is getting complicated . . .

"Rose Lane, where have you *been*, you busy bee?"

I slide the note under my typewriter, looking up to see the office snoop still hanging around the abandoned workstations. The flower in her belled straw hat is as prominent as her green eyes, which seem far too entertained by my annoyance at her interruption. I smooth my hair in front of my left cheek, thankful that the length has reached beneath my chin. The extra powder I've used all week to cover up Salvatore's red hand mark has been working so far, but I don't want to risk questions. Not that I'm the first lady to walk into the newsroom with a shiner. If I were married, no one would think twice.

"Oh, Margaret," I say, pecking away at the weighted buttons, "just burying myself in this story."

"Well"—Margaret's sage skirt hits the top of my metal desk, her pointy hips jutting my typewriter to the side—"since you can't seem to make any of the meetings I've called, I will just catch you up on the office gossip in person."

"Can you give me the summary? I'm already working late as it is."

"Oh, Rose, you're hilarious," she says with a light giggle, her long legs dangling to the floor. "I called the office ladies together to announce my engagement. I'm getting *married*, you silly goose!"

Another perfectly capable woman gone insane.

I allow my head to tilt to the side, my eyebrows pinching together. "You're what?"

"I know," she gushes. "We've only been dating a month, but he's just everything!"

I resist my favorite pastime of bursting her bubbly joy, although her sappiness is spewing all over my desk. I should probably just congratulate her and move on. "That's great, Margaret," I say, upgrading her smile to face-splitting. "Glad you're insured. Now, let's see that handcuff."

"I'm not even going to comment on your awful vernacular. Just look," she says, throwing her fingers forward. Sure enough, the symbol of perpetual ownership encircles her ivory ring finger, the myriad of beaded diamonds shimmering against the golden band. The large stone in the middle peers up at me like an iris, promising to watch our every move. Just like the one Heck is supposed to be picking out for me. *Ugh.* The giddy bride-to-be wriggles her shoulders, sighing, "Isn't it just everything?"

"Yes. You already said that."

"Did I?" Her stretched mouth sinks. "Well, I . . . He's just so . . . We're so very happy."

"Uh-huh." I look up from scrutinizing the diamond. Margaret's lip begins to tremble, her eyes misting like dewdrops against the grass. "Hey, are you all ri—"

"Oh fine, I'll *tell* you!" she wails, her mouth twisting as the rain falls down her pink cheeks. "The rabbit died!" I don't mean to audibly gasp, but the thought of a perfect Jane like her letting anyone near her skirt almost sets me laughing. She doesn't seem to notice as she plunges her hand into my handbag on the desk, stealing my favorite handkerchief to pat her eyes. "But it's fine. I'm thrilled!"

"Margaret."

"My Archibald wants me to have the best. He'll even let me

decorate the house once he picks it—"

"Margaret!" Her body deflates under my unavoidable pin. I'm not enjoying it this time. Her misery is worse than her jubilation, her gaze drifting across time and space as she twirls a button on her sweater. "Margaret, it's going to be okay." I'm not sure what else to say. Of course she's getting married. He pricks her honor, and she gets a brat and a nice white picket prison.

It honestly sounds like a nightmare.

"How can you say that?" she nearly whispers, a single teardrop rolling down to her chin. The door behind me clatters shut, Mr. Roberts's grumbling sigh following.

"'Ey!" he barks. "This ain't a prayer meetin'. Get the hell outta here with that!" Our boss hauls his tan briefcase down the hallway, rolling his eyes. "These broads can't keep it togetha' till they get home?"

Margaret ejects herself from my desk before I can say anything further, shoving my handkerchief back into my handbag and taking off. I pinch the silky corner, lifting it out with a cringe. Just the thought of love and babies calls for a smoke. After a few seconds of blind digging, I tip my bag over, spilling the contents, compact mirror and lip rouge clamoring to the desk. I lift it higher in the air, peering inside with deadening irritation.

Well, isn't this just everything?

That Brooksy stole my cigarettes.

At least the empty space in my handbag leaves room for the ominously friendly note from the town's biggest corruption star. Or so I thought he was. Ice and Salvatore seem to operate independently of him, but maybe Pendergast doesn't know that. Or maybe he doesn't care. I don't really know. I just joined this side of the underground. And as much as I try to avoid making waves, every move I make seems to bring a tsunami back to me.

I trudge down the empty office stairwell, my heels echoing against the tiles like the calm before the storm. Feels like I'm gonna need a raft. Or some more magic. Or at least some more smokes. *Di mi.*

GUS'S PURSING LIPS DISAPPEAR, HIS HEAD SHAKING AS HE HANDS me a creased piece of paper. His frustration seeps into my fingertips during the exchange. I lean against the brick wall outside the storage basement, wagging my own head at the dismal invoice, signed by the pointy face of all pointy faces.

"Can't do it, Rose," he says, running his palms down the sides of his middle part. "They raise my rent any higher and I'm done for. I don't know what else to do, baby."

My brother snatches the paper from my hand, pressing it to my landlord's chest. "Don't let these tontos intimidate you, Miss Rose. You've got a contract and his rent ain't your problem."

"Whaddya, her new torpedo?" Gus wrinkles his oddly shaped nose, slapping Javier's arm away. "Down, boy. The real men are talkin' here."

"Real men don't shake down women."

Gus's neck stretches but it doesn't make him any taller. "I ain't shakin' her down, ya greaser. It might be hard for your chili con carne brain ta unda'stand, but when my rent goes up, so does hers. Otha'wise, we're both done, you get me?"

"Still doesn't sound like her problem."

Geez, can't men keep it together till they get home?

I step in between them, holding my arm in front of my brother's hunched shoulders like a shield, my apprehension rising along with the stakes in this game. I knew the pressure would be on for me. I didn't count on them coming after Giuseppe. He's just another sleazeball minding his own sleazeball business. Except now he's not, because his business is my business, no matter what Javi might want to believe.

"C'mon, fellas. This is stressful enough." I turn to Gio, who's sucking on his Lucky Strike, rolling up his white sleeves as he peers at the invoice over Gus's shoulder. "So, Mr. Cattaneo, any more brilliant ideas?"

A cloud of smoke swirls around his cap, small tufts of charcoal hair sticking out on one side. "Yeah, boss. You're gonna hafta pay Gus the new rent. And in exchange for keepin' him from goin' unda', he makes sure Salvatore thinks we're givin' up."

"Why would I agree to that if she's just gonna leave me with Ice when she skips out?" Giuseppe's mouth nearly disappears in consternation.

"Because," Gio says, "she's not. You help her get outta here, you get to run the gamblin' at her new club. No more mobsta's. No more threats. As long as you behave yourself, and she agrees, that is."

My landlord looks as intrigued as I feel. This doesn't sound as crazy as it might have a few days ago. For one thing, I don't have a trustworthy poker manager picked out yet, and for another, I know exactly the brand of rascality I'm getting with Gus. He's scum, but I guess he's becoming *my* scum.

I let my shrugging nod tell them that it's an acceptable alliance. The gambling club owner gives my brother and Gio a leery look. "Yeah, I could work wit' that."

"Dios. How?" Javier snaps, shooting a warning eye to Gus. "The new rent takes her earnings nearly back to what they were. It'll take forever to save now."

"That's why we gotta stay ahead'a the game, Jav." Gio taps his forehead, a daring glint in his eye. "We've got the hooch, but it's still a pittance to what we could be servin'. I've got access to brandy. Real high-end stuff. Napoleon 1804. I can get it for a hundred and ten."

"A case?" I ask, exchanging a wide-eyed look with my brother.

"No, a bottle."

Gus lets out a short laugh that sounds like a cough. "You can't be serious."

"Rose, listen to me," Gio says, flicking his ashes at the sneering club owner. "Those swells in the city will pay any price you lay down. I guarantee it. I'm guessing one bottle pays your rent and then some. But you're the boss. Tell me what you want."

What I want is a taller order than any of these guys can give. I want a world of equal opportunity. Those of us who get denied often turn to shadowed dealings where the crook with the most gold wins—and I don't exactly hate it. Gold will give me more success and prestige in the underworld than anything reporter Rose could accomplish. Both worlds are a man's game, but this one gives me a leg up just *because* I've got legs. It's still full of bigotry, but the rules are more clear, somehow. I press my hands over my stomach as though holding down my own angst. "All right, but how am I gonna get the swells in here without being too loud about it? I've gotta keep a low profile until Ice calms down."

"His goons'll neva' see it, boss," Gio insists. "I'm talkin' about special deliveries straight to the clients' doors. The last guy I ran for made ten grand his first year."

Having gin delivered to their porches? *Who are these lazy darbs?*

"Why would anyone have their booze delivered when they could go to a juice joint?"

"Two words—*quality* and *company*." My rum-runner lifts both hands like a ringmaster introducing his next set of characters. "Rich fellas are odd like that. They want the juice but not the joint, you get me?"

My look of disbelief only animates Gio further.

"Priests, conservatives, men with tiny pistols," he insists. "Who knows? All I do know is there's a class of men who won't darken the doors of a place that'll taint their reputation. They're loaded with cloudy morals, god complexes, and a lotta green."

Sounds like most men, but something about Gio's plan is making sense. I roll my tongue around in my mouth, recalling the bitter taste of the rust water Salvatore served me at one of Pendergast's own high-end clubs.

My brother twists his lips, tilting his head with an uncertain squint. "Gio, you know I'm for this. I'd give anything to get Miss Rose outta here. But this is sounding more and more risky. Those putas cornered her, for God's sake."

"More dangerous than running this place without a syndicate?" I ask, searching Javier's hardened face until it softens with a light shake of his head. He knows I'm right. We're dancing with devils and it won't stop until we see this all the way. I reach up, squeezing his shoulder. "All I've gotta do is make the wrong policeman mad or miss a payment, and I'm shut down. Icepick is trying to corner the market, and if I weren't a real threat to him, he wouldn't be bothering me. That's gotta mean we're on the right track."

"Don't be so nervous, Javi. We'll run circles around that guy." Gio kicks up a pebble from the gravel with the corner of his brown brogues, catching it with one hand. "Cuz our girl's got somethin' he don't got."

"What's that?"

Pinching his mouth around his cigarette, he waves one hand over his enclosed fist. As his fingers uncurl, a shining nickel lies in his palm where the pebble should have been. "Charm." I squint, the corner of his lips curving with a pursing smile.

"You know what? He's right, baby," Gus pipes up, his beady eyes falling to what I think might be his favorite blouse and trousers. I can't help it if I look good in blue. "You're a smart businesswoman that runs a speakeasy. Lady 'legga's get a leg up on everybody else— Ice included."

"So you're telling me being a woman can help me?"

Gio leans forward with a grin at my deadpan expression. "Now you're on the trolley! You got legs, Lane. Use 'em."

"Yes, well," I say, plucking the dincher from his mouth and pressing it to my lips with a glance at my black strap watch, "I've got a few other qualities that might work in the meantime." I turn from Gio's raised eyebrows to my brother's suppressed smile. "My appointment shouldn't be long. Try not to let the place fall apart while I'm gone."

"Sí, señorita."

"Work those gams, baby."

"Careful out there, boss."

MY STOMACH FLUTTERS AS MY HEELS SINK INTO THE PLUSH PAT-terned carpet of the luxurious lobby. My eyes leap from one great pillar to the next as I follow the owner like a gaping tourist. This is the finest apartment hotel in this district, with its variety of ma-roon and evergreen seating arranged in an assortment of lounging preferences. We pass by a gold-plated piano unlike anything I've ever seen, colorful flowers painted onto the side. Gio would go nuts over that thing. The short man with the spectacles and the expen-sive double-breasted suit gestures to me with a pleased smile as two attendants open a set of mahogany doors.

"Miss Lane," he says, his thinning hair catching in the gust as the doors open, "I am certain you will be pleased with our accom-modations. We've only been open a few years, but we've already established ourselves as KC's most glamorous place to be for upper-class entertainment."

I take my time stepping into the room, drinking in the soft floors and curtained walls of gold and red that surround a shining dance floor. The raised stage is already filled with every imagin-able instrument, polished to perfection, with even more curtains draped above them like suspended clouds. The thick marble pillars in the club stand at attention in front of the second level, where cloth-covered booths curve around small tables for easy dining and chatting, no doubt designed for elite patrons to reserve. I clasp my hands together, imagining tables of fine linen offering up chalices of delicate refreshments at whatever price I decree.

"Mr. Cornwell," I say, bedding down my nervous breath. "At this price, what other accommodations can you provide?"

The wrinkles in his forehead deepen. "Other accommodations?"

I hold his confused gaze with considerable expectancy. The former tenant's dealings are well known in the underworld, his success at running a brothel and bar beneath this club earning him enough to retire—if he hadn't lost it all on a bad gambling night. His loss. My gain.

"Young lady," Mr. Cornwell lectures, adjusting his spectacles, "I'm sure I have no idea—"

"I want the underground accommodations as well."

He stares at me for a torturous amount of time, his eyes flitting over me like a bug that crawled up his newspaper. "A woman running a jazz club is one thing, but really, miss? Taking on the underbelly? Do you even know what wealthy men do down there?"

"I'm well aware of what they want," I say without hesitation, holding my chin high. "And I'm just the woman to provide it. With our agreement, you will make more from my club than you did from your previous tenant—I promise you that."

Mr. Cornwell's snide nose sticks into the air as he waves to the attendants, who shut the large doors with the clang of a closing coffin. "Young lady, let me be perfectly clear: I am only entertaining the notion of renting to you because Mr. Kessler's mother was a dear friend of mine, and he is well respected in our community. Otherwise, I'd give no audience to a woman business owner, especially one from such a seedy part of town." I lock my jaw to keep it from falling open, heat building into my ears as his eyes narrow further. "I know what kind of klucks you serve, not that they can afford our cover charges. And your employees are even worse! Negro jazz bands are expected, but your barlow girls are as colorful as the damn rainbow, not to mention your immigrant bartender. I can't have him serving drinks to councilmen in my hotel, for God's sake.

Do you know who comes to our metropolis for entertainment?"

"I'd like to think they wouldn't care if the juice is good enough, *sir*."

"Well, that shows how much you know, doesn't it?" The club owner reaches out a polite, stiff hand, and I meet his firm grip, zeroing in on any weakness I can read. The first is simple enough: He doesn't respect me. At all. But like every other side-part I come across, he's greedy as hell. He rips his hand away, steering for the exit.

"I'll pay double," I call after him, my heart lighting with panic. I can't lose this. It's my only chance. "Double the rent. Double the kickbacks."

Mr. Cornwell spins back around, his white eyebrows climbing. "I admire your determination. But that would be a forty-thousand-dollar deposit."

"I can give you ten today and spread the rest into my rent until it's paid up." I don't even know what I'm saying anymore. I can hardly breathe.

"That's what our last tenant said." He sighs, pinching his nose beneath his spectacles. "And he was a well-established business-man. We no longer do personal loans. You'll have to go to the bank . . . unless you have a reputable cosigner, of course."

My fingers grasp at the ledge of my dreams as this little old man hangs on my feet. *Reputable cosigner.* A man. The same ingredient I would need if I approached a bank. I hate the thought as much as I hate the taste of Salvatore's mouth. Oh well—champagne and freedom do the trick of cleansing the palate. I suddenly don't care who I have to kiss. I'm getting this place.

"Fine," I say without a hint of doubt, securing my handbag to my shoulder. "I'll have it for you by next week."

The man has the audacity to chuckle, sticking his hands into his wide pockets as he strolls for the doors. "Very good, Miss Lane. But as I said, I require a proper bartender, or at least have someone in charge of him whose name I can pronounce. And no damn Jews, either."

Right. A fair and evenly distributed bigotry.

Lighting up a cigarette helps clear the smell of prejudice that wafts away with him as he huffs out of the room, leaving me in the empty nightclub. I let the silence take me with a slow spin. My confidence begins to peak as I recall my first days in the business, quickly learning the things that drive men's desires—soft skin, no matter the color; foot-stomping music, no matter the players; and stiff drinks, no matter who's serving them. It might take some time, and I'll have to play by the rules for a while, but this place will be brimming with double-breasted suits yearning for my variety of gratification soon enough. When Cornwell gets his kale, he'll stop caring about where it's coming from. And when this becomes *my* club, I'll run it the way I want.

My staff is the best there is, and this city deserves to know it.

"I CAN'T BELIEVE MAMÁ FINALLY LET YOU MOVE OUT OF THE BOX-CAR."

My brother puffs his chest, staring out the passenger window. "I am the man of that boxcar. I deserve respect and privacy."

"She agreed to this?"

"Of course!" he says, deepening his voice . . . before lowering it. "As long as I come home for dinner three times a week, and still do my chores."

My laughter is short-lived, the uneven road rocking the cabin as I listen to Javier chatter on about his new apartment. He's so excited. I've been able to live my life. I'm glad he's getting to live his. I try to hold back the melancholy as he teases me about being a better housekeeper than I am and instead focus on the man he's become. His mustache is growing, though he keeps the hair on his head trimmed nicely, slicked back like Rudolph Valentino. His nails are so impeccable, no one would guess he was a steelworker, other than the callouses on his hands . . . and his dark skin and accent giving him away. He could be in a three-piece from New York City and it wouldn't matter—people would assume he borrowed it from his factory overlord. Mexicans work most of the hard-labor jobs in the West Bottoms—and that's about all they are able to do. Just like Javier's father and every generation after him if my brother ever has kids.

Unless I can make this crazy plan work. Maybe then our family can all find a better way.

Glancing back up at my brother, I think about an old tin photograph of his father that Gloria used to keep hidden back at home. The young man in the frame looks like Javier in another life, other than the dimple in my brother's chin. I remember slipping my hand under my mother's pillow in the early mornings to have a look at that photo. A rugged man would stare back at me with intense brows and serious eyes—the same look I'm getting now.

"Hermanita, you've been quiet all night. I thought you said the meeting went well."

I peer across the tiny cabin of my automobile, thankful that the darkness hides my apprehension. "Everything's fine, Javi. I just get tired of running into jerks."

"Well, you'll be *running* those jerks before long," he says with a yawn as my car slows in front of a tall brick building. As he opens the passenger door, I touch his sleeve, the familiar sooty air breezing into the cabin. "Luna . . . are you going to tell me what's wrong? Did that man do something to you?"

"No," I reply, shutting off the rumbling engine. "I just don't want to ruin a good night. You've got your new apartment. I have a tentative deal with that weasel's hotel—"

"Yeah, what's your plan with that anyway?"

My eyes close with a shake of my head. "I've got a few ideas, but it's going to take compromise . . . for all of us." Javier's silence says enough. I peek over at him, the shadows concealing his expression and giving me courage. "Javi, Mr. Cornwell stipulated that I hire a nonimmigrant head bartender."

As soon as the words leave my mouth, I feel as though I've plunged a dagger into his heart. Pretending we're not related is hard enough. I suddenly want to take it back, but if I do, my chances at the nightclub are lost. Surely, my brother will understand.

"Hm," he mumbles. "You mean *white*."

Of course that's what I mean. I hate that I didn't just come out and say it.

"Hey, he's also not happy about Penny and the other mixed flappers, but I'm not firing them just because he's uncomfortable," I say, staring at the empty street, dotted by a few lampposts. "I'm not firing you, either. Nothing changes, Javi."

"Just me. You want me to take the hit."

"Not really!" I insist, gripping the steering wheel. "I'll have a bar manager, which I'll need for a place that big anyway."

"Right. I just can't be that manager."

"Not right now, but eventually—"

"Bushwa!" Javier waves his hand in the air, his disgust resonating from the way he shoves the door open.

"Javi, you're not hearing me. I hoped you'd understand." I reach for him, my desperation and the lump in my throat climbing, but he leans away. He just doesn't get it. I must be saying it wrong.

Am I wrong?

He ejects himself from the car, his scowling face reappearing as he ducks back down. "I hear you, Luna. I understand that I'll be carrying more boxes, keeping my dark face out of view of your precious customers while some John D gets all the upper-class tips—"

"It won't be like that—"

"I understand that I'll be expected to talk to no one, not that I know English anyway," he spouts, the whites of his eyes growing larger. "Maybe I'll just stay in the underbelly with the rest of your misfits since none of the friends I've made at the River Rose will be able to afford darkening the doors of your new joint." A long rumble stews in the back of my brother's throat as his teeth clench, piercing my heart and burning my nose. I sniffle. He does too. "I work for gringos all day long, hermanita. You want me to polish some manager's shoes at night too? You think I work that club for the beans you pay me?"

No, no, no, no.

"I'll be able to pay more, now, Javi!" My shaking palm brushes across my moist cheek.

"That's not the point."

"You're as much a part of this as I am," I cry. He turns away, his quivering lips pressed together. "How can you not see that this is what we have to do right now? I can't even be myself, Javi!"

"You don't *wanna* be yourself!"

"No, that's not . . . I . . ."

How can I even argue against that statement when he's spot-on?

His accusation thickens the night air, shame heating my face. My brother is my anchor in a shifty world of thugs and liars. All these years, he's let me walk on his back to keep my feet from getting wet, taking the falls and the slurs. We both knew this going in. We were supposed to do this together. But it can't be worth the catch in his throat, let alone the lead in my chest. This doesn't feel like the right thing anymore.

He stands up, leaving me stunned as he leers back at his apartment building. "You better get out of Armourdale. Don't wanna get soot and cow shit on your shoes."

My uncontrolled tears are falling as rapidly as his.

"Thing is, I do understand, hermanita. I really do. And I hate it!"

"I do too!"

"Fine," Javier says, running his sleeve across his nose. "We both hate it. Muy bueno." He takes a long, deep breath. "It's what we gotta do to get you to the top, though, right? And I'll do whatever I can to get you there. But at some point we both know you're gonna end up climbing alone. I'm only allowed to go so far."

"But you don't have to cut the rope, Javi. You don't."

The slamming door makes me jump, stirring my despair and the tears in my eyes. All the dirt in the world can't heal the wounds cast on authentic souls like my brother. The progressive roar of this decade was supposed to spark a new era of opportunity, but it was never intended for everyone. Taskmasters trade their whips for title restrictions and still claim all men are free. But Clip and Penny and Javier tell a different story. I do too, by literally telling a different story than my own.

Dammit. My eyes continue their stinging. That's what hurts so much—I know I'm climbing over these good people, pretending to be what I'm not, because otherwise, some invisible hand would be holding me back too. My gender is already doing that, and there's no changing that. I wouldn't want to—I *like* being a woman. If I were a man, that wouldn't remove me from this caste system I've been playing into. My brother proves that. So I just kept on playing the game because I've never been in the position to change it.

Until now.

My need to climb shifts in my belly, birthing a new motive with the same goal as I head back to the boulevards. Gio was right. I've got advantages most in the underworld don't have. I've got a heart. I've got legs. I've got bruja magic. Now I've just got to learn how to use them all and, more importantly, for the right reasons.

Everything you put your hands to shall prosper.

The memory of my abuela's blessing is as soft and calming as the night wind coming through the front window. She always said it was a promise of the fates, and I'm certain their blessing, if it be true, is for something greater than me reaching a man-made pinnacle of success, especially if I just end up there alone without the ones that really matter. *Javi.*

My brother's wounded face obscures my vision in the form of fresh tears, so much that I have to pull the car over. I wipe my smeared makeup, my cheek still tender from Salvatore's unforgiving hand. I think of Penny and the scars she keeps hidden under her wigs. I think of the dark circles beneath Doris's eye powder because she stays at the club after hours rehearsing her bit. I think of Clip and the stories he just won't tell. And as I look around at the darkened apartment buildings on either side of the soot-filled road, I realize that there's a whole city out there filled with people just like them. Just like me. Just like us.

But I can't change a whole city. I can barely change my family. I can barely change me.

You don't wanna be yourself!

Javier's words from earlier are a heavy sound.

"Yes, I do," I whisper to no one and everything. Once again, the creeping taste of dandelion and scorpion ashes hits my mouth, and once again, I'm a mix of bewildered and emotionally exhausted. It might not be a familiar flavor, but I know magic when I feel it. Is this all the fates can do for me—fill my mouth with bitterness?

With a frustrated scowl, I wipe the wetness from my chin with my sleeve and stick my face toward the front window, stretching my neck toward the star-sprinkled sky. "Yes, I do!" The tears are falling like the words out of my mouth. I don't know who or what's listening and I don't really care. "I just don't know who that is yet. Tell me what to *do*. What do you want from me!"

I don't know how long I've been sitting here yelling at the sky. I nearly exhaust myself too much to drive, and I give serious consideration to lying in my car for a while.

"¿Podemos ayudarte?"

My head jerks to the side, shocked to see not only one man out this time of night, but his entire family, barefoot and wide-eyed in their nightshirts, clinging to each other on the patio in the apartment building behind him.

"I . . . I'm so sorry," I tell the squinting father as he steps closer against his wife's protests. "I didn't mean to wake the neighbor—"

"Strange sound," he whispers, inching closer.

I lean away, even though there's nowhere to go short of driving off. "Look, you never heard a broad lose her marbles before? I'm not even a crier, really."

"No lose. No cry." He all but ignores his wife's strange pleading. "Cantando . . . mucha gente."

The man's strange tone feels like I've been dropped into a ghost story, my arms prickling up to my neck. What he's saying simply isn't possible. Not for me.

"Señor," I say, the denial coming out as jittery as I feel. "Ese no era yo."

Not possible. I don't even sing. Hell, I *can't* sing. It wasn't me he heard.

As his feet hit the circular glow of the streetlamp, he stands up straight with a gasp, his quivering arm raising a pointed finger toward me. "Tus *ojos*. ¡Bruja de tierra!"

"¡Espera!" I try to call after him, telling him that he's got me mixed up with somebody else—that I'd never hurt anyone, but my hoarse voice will no longer carry that far. I dig through my handbag, yanking out my mirror as fast as that family disappears inside their home. The face looking back at me is pale and terrified, gasping and crying for the third time tonight. *Not possible.* The blue in my eyes moves and shifts like water, swallowing up my pupils entirely. No wonder the man ran. I look possessed. *Oh my God.*

Dropping the mirror, I pull the hand brake, squealing the tires as I try to get the hell away from whatever is going on. Nothing terrible has actually happened, but it feels like I'm in danger. It feels like I *am* danger. And as I race up the boulevards, it dawns on me how much danger I've actually put my family and friends in—the mobsters, the syndicate, and now I've sent an entire family running for cover because I don't know how to control my own damn magic.

Ugh, the fates. What are they trying to tell me, if anything? Am I the one doing this? I want to go ask my abuela a million questions, but I also might fall asleep driving. I need to make it home and rest. There will be time to figure out my parlor tricks later. For now, I'm going to have to focus on getting my family out of this mess I made.

8

8

I'M NOT SURE HOW I MADE IT UP MY APARTMENT STEPS SO quickly, my tired soul aching and my eyes blurring with tears. My floral curtains flutter in the moonlight from the open windows airing my apartment with late-night breezes that are unaware of the turmoil around them. My thoughts turn from Javier to our mother's struggles in her own perilous journey, trekking on railroad crews with the love of her life, losing him along the way while trying to keep my brother alive. The promise of a greater future without the barriers of corruption carried them forward, though the price of assimilation would steal away at my own identity, my heritage just a whisper on the breezes like the old folklore that we tell. My mother's recipes and my own native language fade every day that I'm Rose, burying Luna in the earth beneath the riverbeds.

Driven by desperation to cling to something real, I rush through my door, scrambling onto the white countertops of the Hoosier cabinet in the kitchen. My fingers glide along the middle shelf, brushing against the clay canisters gifted to me by my mother. *Harina*. Even if they could understand the label, no one would think to check the flour jar. I'm terrible at baking. I set the lid down on the counter with great care, lifting a small satin satchel from inside. The walk across my wooden floors seems like a slow dream on the way to the balcony door. I find myself bracing against the large pillar, hiding in the shadow of the roof above me as I set the tiny bag on the banister, pulling the drawstrings. My fingers reach inside, pinching a dusting of dreams, letting it sprinkle into my other hand, careful to hold it close so the wind doesn't steal it away. Earth magic is as beautiful as it is frightening.

I wonder. I wasn't even trying earlier and *something* happened. I look up at the cobalt horizon with one last bit of hope.

"Tierra y estrellas," I whisper into the dark morning. The stars answer back with a silent twinkle, the crescent moon sinking away from the dawn. The dirt moistens from the drops falling from my eyes, blackening against my palm. "Río bendito, por favor, ayúdame."

It's a useless prayer, but it's all I have.

Is anyone listening?

The sky treats me to more silence, except for the morning birds that mock my despair. *Figures.* What did I expect, really? My mother's fervent whispers to the earth echo in my mind along with the memory of the tears that stained her pillow when she thought I wasn't awake to hear it. Javier's father, a great rock in the Alvarado family, left her broken since the night she lost him. I wonder if the heavens ever answered her back.

As I rub my palms together, letting the mud roll into small pieces that fall three stories to the pavement below, my elbow nudges the shining satchel. The one possession that I hold dear, a handful of earth from a homeland I've never seen, leaps as though the wind is reaching inside, carrying it away to where it belongs. Away from me. It doesn't know me anymore. I can't even cry after it; I don't even reach.

My emptiness guides me back inside, where I somehow change into my embroidered sleeping tunic and pants, the cotton a minor comfort as I slide beneath my quilt. Like a phantom in the night, a shadowy figure shifts beside me, a blood-curdling scream exploding from my mouth, sending my heart racing. The phantom screams back, eliciting another shriek from me, which incites its wail yet again.

"Rose!" the phantom gasps, the whites of its eyes barely visible in the dark. "Are you *trying* to startle me to death?"

The overly dramatic, offended voice floods my clammy skin with relief and irritation as I cover the neckline of my gown with my sheet. "Startle *you*? Heck Kessler, what are you doing in my bed!"

I nearly feel his indignation and straightened back as the covers tug away from me. "Well, I've been waiting to talk to you since you got back from Bellerive. And I don't appreciate your tone, as I've had to care for your plants while having quite a personal crisis, wandering around all evening like a lost poet for hours. Then you took Javi to his new place. No one invited *me* along, so I thought I'd wait for you here."

"I'm sorry you weren't able to intrude on my time with my brother," I hiss. "And waiting for me here—that didn't seem odd or inappropriate to you?"

"Well, it's not as though I meant to end up here. I was lounging on your davenport, trying to stay awake by reading your column, which had the opposite effect—"

"All right—"

"So, yes, I came to lie down here for a short reprieve because davenports make me think of . . . *him*."

"But why couldn't you do this all in *your own* apartment?"

"Because of him!" Heck's voice cracks in that way that makes me think he's about to start his bawling. He does. "It's just not fair, Rose, the way they treat me. Making me think I'm something special, but this one ended like all the others—with me feeling used and unwanted. I couldn't go home, Rose! I was too sad . . . and I may have used your bath soap. I didn't want to smell his cologne!"

"Wait," I say, pressing my fingers to my forehead. "What exactly are you wearing right now?"

Heck lifts the covers, my eyes adjusting to the darkness enough to make out his bare chest. "My mauve boxer shorts, of course. Aren't they trendy? I couldn't very well put my suit back on. It smells like *him*."

"Aw geez!"

"Oh please," he says with a sniff. "I'm more dressed than most men you've had in here."

"That's not the point."

"Fine! I'll go!" Heck throws his side of the quilt on top of me, forcing my eyes to roll as I reach out, grabbing his wrist, which leaks of heavy sorrow and confusion.

"Wait," I say, my tone softening. "I'm sorry. I've had a crisis too. It looks like it's been a rough night for the both of us."

He sniffles again. "Oh, Rose. How selfish of me. I didn't even ask how you were doing. You did seem grummy." I pat the pillow beside me and he settles back down on his side, concern etching across his shadowed face.

"Cornwell wants me to demote Javi, and I need to come up with thirty grand by next week."

"Well, that's a mouthful," Heck says. "You know I gave you what I could, unless . . . we run away for the weekend. It would be the most deliciously scandalous marriage."

I shake my head. "Oh no, mister. There's gotta be another way."

"There's nothing wrong with asking for help."

"So people tell me," I grumble.

"Which is why I'm going to help you get a loan."

Where did the earth grow such a man? No wonder Heck's kind heart is always being broken. "No need. Gio's special shipments are giving me a head start. As for the rest, I've got a plan."

"I'm sure you do," Heck says. "But you must promise to come to me if it doesn't work out. We're both bound by others and their expectations. At least one of us can be free. Plus, it would be a hell of a lot of fun helping you take those slimy men down." My smile squints my rolling eyes. "I'm serious. Promise me, Rose."

"Ugh. Fine. I promise, though I'm not sure why you even want to be my friend," I chuckle, tucking my pillow under my cheek. "I'm a terrible one."

"That, you are." Heck sighs, slipping his hand between us, his fingers over mine. "But you're real. And I . . . I can be real with you." The small tap of a tear hits the sheet beneath him. I don't even need to read his skin.

"So," I say, squeezing his palm, "what's this ritzy burg's name?"

"Dr. Henry Chapman."

"Ugh. I hate Henrys. Too bookish."

"Yes! I *know*." Heck's perfect teeth glow as he smiles.

"But doctors are even worse."

"I don't know—surgeons are rather good with their hands."

I let out a jealous gasp. "You dated a surgeon?"

"Of course I have. I'm Heck Kessler."

"Oh geez." We share a light laugh, my heart warming as Heck's mood and thoughts relax. I give him a mischievous smirk. "Well, I dated two lawyers. At the same time."

"Isn't that the frog's eyebrows?" he remarks. "Almost as impressive as a city councilman. St. Louis."

I lift a challenging eyebrow. "Priest."

"Detective."

"Carpenter. Huge muscles."

"Men's boutique owner in Paris. I *still* get a discount."

I bury a snort into my pillow. "Okay, um . . . accountant?"

"Ew."

"I know."

Heck's eyes fall to our hands, his melancholy drifting into my palm. "Did you love any of them?"

"No," I say. "Not a single one. I don't really have that option with my . . . gift."

"Damn." Heck's hand floats away as he lies on his back, his muscles defined under the last of the moonlight from the small window. "I loved them all."

"Di mi, sweetheart."

"What?" He laughs.

"That's your problem. You're a damn monog."

"And?"

"And so that makes you the only man on earth who really wants to commit." I have him laughing again, his arm slinging over his eyes. "I'm serious! You have to stop with that expectation. They wanna have fun with you? Fine. Let 'em. Have fun right back. It's not like you can marry those potatoes anyway."

"My God," Heck says, rubbing his face. "Most of them *are* married."

"Even better. Less of a chance of them getting attached."

"How can you be that way with intimacy?"

My chortle escapes my lips yet again. "Not everyone needs intimacy to be intimate."

"You're sure you're into guys?"

"Absolutely. Every last disgusting one of them."

"I'd drink to that." His hearty chuckle continues, his arms stretching above his head as he yawns before sitting up, the bed wriggling beneath us. "I know you have to work in a few hours, so I'll stop bothering you."

Aside from my brother, I can't remember the last time I felt so safe around a man. I give a playful tug to Heck's arm, forcing him back to his pillow. "Oh, stay. You're already dressed for bed, and I can't have a mostly nude man leaving my apartment at this hour."

"Wait till morning so they can truly appreciate what you've accomplished?"

"Exactly."

"Well, good night then, Miss Lane."

"Good night, Mr. Kessler."

HECK BEING SUCH A LATE SLEEPER WOULD NORMALLY ANNOY ME, but I don't need anyone asking me questions today. After leaving him a note by the stove, I make my way downtown, parking in front of an orange brick building. As soon as I enter the foreboding door, I want to run home, though I'm not sure to which one. Neither will welcome all of me, demanding that I cut away half of myself. But I have business to tend to. Pushing aside the hesitation, I chase my dreams as they scuttle down the office hallway, pulling me deeper into the Pendergast den of lions, where the man who contributed to my very life waits in a windowless room with a frosted glass door. *Mr. Hawkins, Attorney at Law*—the nameplate on the front already has me sneering. My heart is in my throat as a secretary with a drab pleated skirt opens the door with a curt smile.

Like all the other Pendergast puppets, my biological father wears the uniform of a roomy suit cut from the shoulders, with flashy cuff links, his derby hanging on the coat rack behind him. His blue eyes scan the papers in front of him like determined marbles, his stiff hair a shining helmet of graying chestnut brown without a strand out of place. I wait for his acknowledgment, but since he remains transfixed on his task, I seat myself in an upholstered chair, leaving my hat in place. I don't plan to stay long. Were we better friends, I would request a beverage.

The distinguished man's golden fountain pen scrapes across another paper in a very lawyerly fashion. "And what brings you here, Miss Lane?"

My lungs expand in a low inhale as heated ice surges through my arms. I didn't realize how difficult it would be to hear his voice. "I thought you might be interested in an investment," I say, keeping my tone cool.

"Investment? Is that what you youngsters call blackmail these days?"

The document on his desk must be from the president himself, the lawyer's eyes scanning after his pen. I let heat seep into my throat. "A woman asking her father for help is hardly blackmail, sir."

"The fact that you threaten to acknowledge me as such tells me that it is," he says in the logical manner of a man who sees everything in black and white—or brown and white, as it is right now. The pen clatters against the wood as he squares his shoulders. My seething eyes are ready for him when he finally looks up. "Miss Lane, you can't know how disappointed I am that you've had to come to me. Can Gloria no longer care for you?"

How dare he? My lips part, my eyes narrowing. "I was quite well cared for, sir."

"And so you've turned to a life of crime."

"I turn to opportunity . . . just like you do."

I want to rinse my tongue for saying it, but men like him speak only in ego. Even at my club, I'd know to keep my mouth shut. Yes, the man owes me. But I can't afford to have him show me the door—not before I at least try to make him an offer.

"Yes," he says, shuffling more paperwork, "one of many underground businesses in this city. I'm not sure what's supposed to make yours so much more appealing to me than what I've already invested in. You've barely been running that dump for two years."

He knows . . . Interesting.

My hands fold around the fabric arms of my chair. "And I've been made offers already."

"Good," he quips. "Then you don't need help. You won't mind seeing yourself out? I'm terribly busy."

No, no. He's not even listening.

"If you know all of that, then you know I'm moving to the Bellerive." I can feel myself losing. "I'm going to make my investors a lot of money, Mr. Hawkins."

"That I don't doubt. I just can't be one of those investors."

"But—"

"I simply can*not*." For the first time in this conversation, he really seems to look at me, his warning gaze saying so much more that I wish I could hear. I don't know why I thought this could work. I never should have come here. I lift from my chair with Heck-style indignation, straightening my spine as though I were tall, and spin for the door as the lawyer mutters, "You should have taken the deal."

I freeze, my hands gripping the white doorpost. It's easier if we don't look at each other. "Selling my soul and body to Frank Moretti is no deal," I snap. "It's a prison."

"No one forced you into this business."

"No one saved me from it either."

"Then walk away, Miss Lane. Live a normal life. He'll come after you if you don't."

The ivory walls of this office offer me the same answers and inspiration as this man in the high-end suit. Nothing. I whirl around, my jaw set. "This is the life I've made—without your help."

"It's cute that you assume that, young lady," the lawyer says, his smooth expression aloof as ever. "Especially since you came here for exactly that help. But you keep on lying to yourself. Now, if you'll excuse me, I've real business ventures that don't include the flighty whims of some starry-eyed woman who thinks I owe her something."

I storm to his desk, barely raising his eyebrows as I extend a parting hand. If I can read a motive, a thought, anything, maybe I can tug on his heartstrings. "Well, thank you for your time anyhow."

His eyes flicker to my hand. "There's a reason I have nothing to do with your kind. Good day, miss."

I hate that he's this smart. I hate that some of what makes me smart might come from him. I loathe that I'm even here to begin with.

Stupid, Rose. Stupid.

With a begrudging pause, I let my hand fall to my side before making my way out into the welcoming sunshine, all of my hopes and dreams dashed by another man.

HEAVY CHAIRS SCRAPE ACROSS THE DISTRESSED FLOORS AS MY staff readies the club for another humid night, the back entrance already propped open by Clip's saxophone case. The atmosphere is less than jubilant, some shooting me scowling glances after my weighty announcement that I plan to move our operations downtown even as the newer employees and the band grab each other's shoulders in excitement, launching into plans of future entertainment. Penny bites her lower lip, twisting the curls of her yellow wig around her finger as she peers at Javier through smoky eyes. My brother's behind the bar, stocking shelves and lining up tumblers like he does every night. Like a head bartender should.

With a squeezing stomach, I slide onto a barstool.

"Hey there," I say, twisting my fingers on the black countertops.

My brother glances up. "Hey."

"Look, Javi—"

His towel lands next to my arms; a pair of dark hands grab mine. "Miss Rose, it's okay. I'm okay." He ducks down, capturing my gaze, forcing it upward into his sad eyes. "We're all going to be okay."

I'm doing a terrible job of holding myself together. I press his white towel to my face as though the damp air is getting to me. "I used to think that," I sniffle, "but now I'm not so sure." A set of tickling nails runs across my shoulder blades and up to the nape of my neck. Normally, I'd tell Penny to back off, but I appreciate her attempt at comfort.

"Miss Rose," she says in her soothing, crackly voice. "I can't say that I'm not nervous about what they're gonna think of me and the other girls. But you've always been our champion. And we'll follow you, even if it means leavin' all this behind." I look up, swallowing the lump in my throat and sniffing back the burn in my nose. Penny's bronze forehead wrinkles with worry and affection. "It's gonna be hard, that's for sure—all these rules on how to act around the darbs, settlin' into a new place. This is our home, for most of us, at least. But it's our home because'a you."

I let her throw her arms around me, my body stiffening like it always does when people are friendly without motive. I let out a playful sigh, giving her a big squeeze back before she lets me go with a giggle, setting off to bark orders at the new waitresses. My brother grabs the towel, wiping a stray tear from my cheek, giving me a smile that makes me smile back. As Javier's grin widens, I follow his gaze across the room to where Heck strolls out of the flappers' changing room like a parading peacock. The ladies slide by him, kissing his cheek and straightening his tie with an accompanying greeting of praise.

"You were right, Mr. Kessler. This slip is wonderful."

"Isn't silk divine, kitten?" he rumbles.

A manicured hand cups his smooth cheek. "I've never thought to wear green."

"And now you shall wear nothing else as long as I'm dressing you."

"Will you paint my lips, Kessie?" another whines, sticking out her pouty lips.

"As long as I get to taste them first."

I press my mouth together to suppress an erupting smile, turning away from their robust embrace to find my brother with his head down and his shoulders shaking.

"There you are, sweetheart," Heck says. "Now go finish primping. It's almost showtime." His voice is growing closer as I pull my golden cigarette case from my handbag. "Oh, Rose, I didn't see you there. I hope I haven't upset you too terribly."

The bubbling laughter in my mouth bursts out with a puff of smoke that turns a few heads. Heck tilts his chin, his eyes glittering as he sits next to me. I regather my composure, matching his challenging smirk. "Kiss whoever you want, Mr. Kessler."

My piano player and rum-running partner saunters from the stage, rounding the counter to collect a few drinks for the band for rehearsal. Gio takes his time, his eyes flitting between Heck and me as Javier fills the small glasses with an amber liquor.

"That is mighty gracious of you, my dear," Heck says loudly, reaching down to run his thumb along my chin. I resist slapping his hand away as another chuckle shoots from my nose. Several passing staff members slow their walks, leaning into each other with entertained whispers. "After such a silly night together, I was hoping it wouldn't affect our working relationship too much. One last mug for old time's sake?"

"Now hold on a minute—" His mouth hits mine, his apology ringing across my lips like a town crier's bell, announcing his supposed regret about this performance. He's also very satisfied with himself. At least he tastes good. With my allure bedded down out of the danger zone, I deliver a message of my own onto his tongue amid the room's whistles and jeers.

You are nuts!

Heck breaks our comical osculation, leaning around to my ear. "Just go with it. We've got to look hot and heavy if I'm going to ask you to marry me. Besides, this is great for my reputation."

"What about *my* reputation?"

He laughs as though I've said something terribly funny. "Rose, you are *so* clever! I'm glad we can be friends after all of this." Heck's walk is a grand performance itself, leaving me staring as he drapes his arms around two shimmering ladies. Gio sidles up to me, giving me a smile like I've been caught sneaking out my window at night.

I throw him a flat stare. "If I told you it's not what it sounds like, would you believe me?"

His sable eyes peer over at Heck, an amused smirk crossing his face. "Actually, yeah. I would. But is it what it looks like?"

"No. For one thing, I don't fraternize with employees."

"Good to know."

"Not that it's your business."

"You're the one who brought it up," Gio says, gathering the small tumblers into his hands. "I don't like the guy's bravado, but if you want him, have at it." He winks at my annoyed growl as he heads back to the stage. As the first customers of the night begin to filter into the club, Clip's floor-thumping band starts to play. The waitresses skip around me with wide smiles and trays full of sweet rums and dry whiskeys, all selling out so quickly that Nickels has to carry in three more crates to keep our shelves stocked after a few hours. My former doubts about Doris melt beneath her enchanting voice, which is a sensation, as my crew knew it would be, our patrons ogling and clapping after each song, hailing Clip for such a find. Gio's fingers fly over ivory keys while Heck kicks around the dance floor, making my brother laugh from behind the counter. Penny's stockings are stuffed full of dollars as she collects for the other girls, slapping away hands and filling drinks with her own witty banter.

My head flapper was right. This is our home. The thought of leaving this glorious, filthy place brings a mist to my eyes. At least we're all going together, embarking on a new journey into the raging night. Since I struck out with my father dearest, the choices I have left are taking Moretti's hand or Heck's. I hate that I'll have to follow through on my promise to let Heck help me, but we're bound together in this crazy world. His need for love and acceptance is as old as time itself, ingrained in all of us . . . even me. *But probably not Icepick.*

As much as I hate the idea of needing a man, I'm starting to think that getting help from a friend is quite a bit different, all of my gender biases aside. In fact, I've *been* getting help when I step back and look—my brother carrying boxes all night before his day job. My abuela blessing river dirt. Gio bringing the syndicate to my doorstep when he could have moved on . . .

I really haven't been going it alone, no matter how much I like to say I have. And maybe I'm not supposed to. Truth is, I haven't had a friend who wasn't family in a long time. Maybe forever. Or better yet, maybe Heck is being added to a crew that has been my family this whole time and I'm just now realizing it.

I sip at a warm beer, twirling the glass in my hand as I overlook the kingdom that built me.

There's no way I'm giving up now.

MY EXHAUSTED BODY HITS MY QUILTED MATTRESS, MY THIN BRAS-siere and bloomers acting as nightwear once again. At least I don't have to contend with Heck's sheet thievery all night, though I do miss the company. His sly eye told me all I needed to know as he instructed me not to wait up for him at the end of the night. *Good for you, Mr. Kessler.* One of us should end the evening on a high note.

A loud thump at my door elicits more than a small tick of worry as I roll out of bed, stumbling to the front room. Salvatore's recent stalking has ruined the previous pleasure I used to get with a late-night rap on my door. And it's too early for Heck to be back from his jaunt, although I hope it is him now, all sad and annoyed that his night didn't go well. I'm half asleep enough to lie to myself enough to bed down my nerves a little. *It's gotta be him.*

I flick on a nearby lamp, shielding my eyes and wondering if I'd heard anything at all. Before I reach the knob, my bare foot crunches over a thick envelope. After a solid stare at my mail slot, I snatch it from the floor and seat myself beneath the lamp's glow on my prized couch. My fumbling fingers dig at the corners, tearing it open with the fervency of a small child at Christmas. The accompanying note is less than thrilling, but the contents speak volumes. It's almost enough to cover my deposit. Almost. I'll only have to borrow ten grand. *Maybe less.* With the projected earnings, I can have that paid off in months, only owing kickbacks and rent to legitimize the operation. I'll be as free and clear as one can be in less than a year.

It's as close to owning a club as I'm going to get.

Damn. This is really happening.

I scan the note again, bouncing on the balls of my feet. *Miss Lane*, it reads. *Tell Gloria this is the last she'll get from me.*

I'm not sure how long I've been standing there, gazing at that stack of money, but my senses finally come to, sending me running back to the door. As I fling it open, my wide eyes meet a heated couple whose hands and mouths are so busy, they don't notice my gaping appearance. It's not that I've never seen two men in a passionate tangle; I've just never seen them in such good lighting—or right outside my door. While it's well after midnight, they're being anything but careful.

My clearing throat rips them apart, ties hanging as they try to catch their breath, mumbling odd explanations about checking each other's pulse because one is a doctor I recognize and the other is . . . well, Heck. They both give me a curious once-over, rounding my eyes further as my scrawny arms cross over my undergarments in a futile attempt to cover myself. "I was just, um, checking the mail"—I peer down at my partially nude body—"and doing laundry."

"You know, it's getting late," the doctor says, his face flushing as much as mine. "I have patients in the morning."

"It's okay," I assure him, backing through my doorway. "I'm going to bed—"

Heck rolls his eyes, taking the man's hand. "Oh, this is my

neighbor I was telling you about."

The doctor looks to me again, his face calming with a slight grin. "Oh. Her."

They ignore my squint as their arms wrap around each other again. "My God, Rose," Heck says as the man tugs his giggling frame into his apartment. "Can't you answer the door in anything decent?"

I don't know whose door shuts first, but the man has me laughing. It's wonderful to see Heck this happy. And his joke about my current undress is all the more funny because, honestly, it's not the first time I've been caught in my knickers.

9

MY ADMIRING FRIEND FLASHES A SHINING SMILE, SMOOTHING HIS golden hair, though it's perfectly slicked to the side. He's quite taken with himself, his striped red-and-blue jacket over stark white slacks—a breathtaking high roller without an ounce of modesty. Even for this uppity wedding we're attending, the man is a billboard, his navy vest and tie completing his flashy look. The floral-and-gold ballroom seems built and decorated around him. I lift the arms of my baggy frock, which isn't even close to a flattering color, its pleats and waistline drowning my best features.

"So, what poor heart do you plan on breaking tonight?" I whisper, giving Heck a playful squint as I take his arm.

He purses his lips with a pleased smile, his hands folding in his lap. "*Well*, a doe-eyed doorman has been dropping pins all afternoon, though I prefer to play a more . . . *receptive* role in our twilight aristocracy."

"Uh-huh."

"I don't make the rules, my dear," he says, leaning close to my ear. "And try to smile. Confidence is key."

My stomach flutters at what this night could hold for me. With Heck by my side, I'm less nervous about meeting a new class of men with deeper pockets, his connections giving me an edge to secure some real prospective clientele. I need to make a name for myself if I'm going to have a successful opening night.

I suppose the wedding is important too, but I can hardly pretend to be happy about another lamb to the slaughter.

So are these men, I determine. Gripping Heck's soft hand, I'm treated to the excited thoughts bouncing around his palm in hyper phrases of more names than I can remember and the occasional wardrobe judgment. Pushing the corners of my lips into a plastered smile, I let him lead me through the crowd of conservative tailored suits and gowns that reach the calves, much like mine. He's obviously in his element, spouting warm greetings and polite laughter to the dullest jokes. His magnetic charm smooths over my mumbling salutations, leaving me wondering which of us has actual magic.

I rattle off my practiced greeting with each kiss of my hand. "It's so wonderful to meet you."

"Yes," Heck follows up with a winning smile at whatever broker, judge, or councilman we're talking to at the moment. "And as I said, Rose and I would be honored for your attendance at our private opening. Just a small party, but quite exclusive."

"Mr. Kessler," the current suit and his Brooksy reply as though they were Heck's closest friends. "We wouldn't miss it. You must be heart-strung over this one."

My suitor's loving gaze lingers on mine, and I try not to giggle as he says, "Anything for my kitten." Linking arms, we stroll around the room like gallant lovers, juice glasses clinking around us amid the conversational hum and light laughter. The hotel reception room holds the well-bred, upper-crust men within its painted walls of clouds floating over blue skies, offering cloth-covered tables of fine delicacies. My mood lifts even further as several gentlemen offer me a variety of cigarettes along the way. I select the most popular brand, allowing one to light the Philip Morris English Blend against my holder. As I pinch the thin golden tube between my fingers, a small commotion of startled voices sounds behind us. I look to Heck with a knowing glance, my chest tightening with annoyance.

"Hey! I told ya I got an invitation," a husky voice declares, her sultry tone a dead giveaway. Wrenching her arm away from a tuxedoed staff member, the blond woman with a face almost as red as her lips begins to argue with an attendant, slinging insults and smoothing her lace dress. "And keep your hands off'a me, ya creep. I'm a respectable woman, and from the looks'a your suit, you ain't got the green to make me your biscuit—"

The shocked gasps and light tittering around us cover Heck's low grumble. "Nothing like being two hours late. Some star I'm supposed to promote here."

"Yeah, well, she's promoting herself at the moment, and not quite how I'd like," I hiss, cringing as she waves her fingers at us from the arched doorway. "I thought you talked to her."

Heck clears his throat, pasting on an amiable expression. "I did. She doesn't exactly listen."

Several gentlemen shoot subtle leers at her rocking hips as she struts over to us with a scowl. "Hey, I don't like the way these bug-eyed Bettys are lookin' at me."

"Well," Heck says with a squinting smile, "if your mouth matched the sophistication of the ensemble I've given you, we wouldn't have to endure their scrutinization, Miss Fenton."

"You can talk as fancy as ya want, *Mista' Kessla'*." Doris slides her hands to her waist, her lips pushing out with an impressive amount of attitude. "That don't make you betta' than me."

"That remains to be seen."

"How 'bout you take ya fashion advice and—"

My eyes flick to the glittering chandeliers as I grip Heck's arm.

"Doris, this night is about *all* of us, and Mr. Kessler is Penny's assistant and, therefore, your superior on the job. You asked for a chance, and I'm giving you one." I level my eyes to make my point. "*One*. Tonight we're introducing society to Doris. Not Bearcat. If you can't handle that, we can part ways here and now."

The challenging gaze leaves my lofty friend, her expression softening as her teeth pull the corner of her lip. "Aw, I'm sorry, Miss Rose. On my word—you won't see no more tempa' from me tonight. I just don't like bein' treated a certain way."

"Well, you're in good company then," Heck says, taking her hand and lifting her knuckles to his lips. Her disdain melts further, her penciled eyebrows rising. "Because there will always be those who will never see who we truly are. But if we waste our energies punishing their ignorance, we will drown in our own bitterness." He lets her hand down, her eyes shining back at him in confused wonderment. "Miss Fenton, will you let them steal your chance at happiness?"

Peering around the room with a wrinkled brow, Doris straightens her back with a deep breath. "No, Mista' Kessla', I will not. They've stole enough."

"Good. Now, how badly do you want this?"

"More then anythin'."

Heck leans in with an arched eyebrow and a curved lip. "Then behave yourself."

To my shock, Doris laughs, a sound as wonderful as her singing voice, her celebrity-level smile sparking Heck's, and I find myself standing between two blazing suns that attract a fair amount of admiring eyes, including a blushing bride and her pointy-eared groom, whose gaze skims over us like he's wondering why we're still here. I press my lips around my cigarette holder. My suitor saves us all, his returned grip on my hand recharging me with his buoyancy as he leans over to kiss the cheek of the newlywed in the white dress. "Margaret Grove, I don't think I've seen a lovelier bride!"

"Oh!" she giggles, waving her hand in front of her flushed face. "Mr. Kessler, how kind. I didn't even know you knew who I was! But it's Margaret Swinson now."

Heck lets out a gasp of feigned offense. "Now, now, don't be so coy. Rose has told me all about you and what great friends you are."

I brace at that look in Margaret's glittering eyes as she gushes, my body stiffening for the impending hug. Her capped veil and breath near my ear tickle, enough of her cheek brushing mine to share her small panic through our skin. Of course, she's not the first bride to be nervous, I'm sure. Marriage is a big, gross commitment.

But if she'd linger—with her, it always feels like there's something else . . .

"I *knew* you were up to something!" She laughs, throwing back her head. I grunt as her arms tighten around me, smoke sputtering from my mouth. "How long have you been Heck Kessler's blue serge? What a catch, Rose! Really!"

"I'm the lucky one, I think," he says, pulling me from her arms with a suave spin, his hand cupping my cheek. "It's catching *her* that's the challenge. She won't give me an answer."

Margaret's squeal turns more heads than I'd like. "Rose, you are *terrible*." Her groom clears his throat, the tips of his ears reddening. "Oh, where are my manners? Archie, this is my coworker I always mention, and her new beau, Heck Kessler, whom you've surely heard of, and . . ." Her smile falters as she touches her fingers to her pale lips, looking to my newest employee, who's squinting a shadowed eye at the couple. She offers them a ginger handshake.

"Doris Fenton," Heck explains with a sweeping arm. "A phenomenal jazz singer we've hired for our new club. You two *must* come by when we open."

"It's *Archibald*," he says to Heck, correcting Margaret, who now looks mortified at having used his nickname. *Seems like a hopping time you've got on your hands, Margaret.* "And much appreciated,

Mr. Kessler," he continues, taking back his hand. He glances at Doris and me with a subtle wrinkle of his nose. "But my wife and I must decline such an invitation. A jazz club is no place for a woman in good standing." Before my nose can flare, he excuses himself to meet up with his family, leaving us with a nervously smiling bride.

"Oh, he's so conservative," Margaret laughs, tucking a few orange strands back beneath her Juliet cap. "He doesn't even like me to wear makeup, but I convinced him to let me do this smoking eye."

Doris crosses her lace-sleeved arms. "It's a smoky eye. And it's runnin'."

"Oh dear."

"No worries, Miss Margaret," Heck says, whipping out a silk handkerchief. "Just a minor mishap. The trick is to add enough charcoal to your Vaseline. It gives you a much more defined line. And those cheekbones are simply amazing." My coworker's head tilts with curiosity as he dabs the corners of her eyes. I'm certain she's not used to such compliments, but she really is quite beautiful in her flowing beaded dress, her pink cheeks glowing. Her husband is clearly a fool if he would deny her such affirmation.

Like most other women, she's locked into Heck's enchantment until that same awful husband calls to her. "It was great meeting you all," she says, giving me a knowing grin. "I expect to hear all about this when I return to the office." Her long veil flips behind her as she bounds away.

I stare after her, Doris sidling to my side. "What a gimlet, Miss Rose."

"Yeah, he's something, all right."

"He's an even worse cuddla'."

Heck's eyes are as wide as mine as we slowly turn to the primping blonde, her head cocking as she gazes into her compact mirror. "Doris," I say with an inflection of warning. "What do you mean?"

"Oh, that burg's ordered my cocktail at the Chesterfield Club more times than Mista' Kessla's played checka's," she says, snapping her mirror closed. For the first time tonight, Heck's confidence wavers, his lips parting at her insinuation.

"I . . . I think you have the wrong idea," he stammers.

"Aw, you ain't hidin' nothin' from me. I seen it all, sweetie." Doris's hand intertwines around his, her lips curving into a sincere smile that smooths his furrowed brow. "Between you and me, I bet we know all the secrets in this room."

I glance around at the chuckling businessmen with their proper postures and pearl-draped wives, and then add myself—and my magic—into the mix.

She ain't wrong.

"Enough to take down the damn city," Heck whispers, his eyes locked on hers.

"I'm up for that." Doris's smirk widens. "So, you gonna introduce me to all these stuffed-shirts, or what?"

The heir to a land-development fortune leans down, pressing his lips to my cheek. "Spread out and mingle, my flower. Miss Fenton is in need of a cigarette."

IF BY MINGLING, HECK MEANS TO ISOLATE MYSELF ON THE THIRD-floor balcony to have my way with a smoldering Camel, then I'm following his advice to the letter. My preferred tobacco is earthy, a toasted burn that beds down my angst, lying to me for a few gratifying moments. The wind picks up, the moist air provoking the glow of the smoking cherry between my fingers, my holder long since abandoned. In the distance, a slow rumble accompanies a brief flash, the stars blanketed by floating gray clouds against the black sky.

"Ah, Miss Lane, it appears you are still here."

I whirl around to the snide voice, pursing my lips at the man who accompanies it. "What can I do for you, Oswald?"

His narrowed eyes flood me with vindictive satisfaction. "It's *Archibald*." A smoky exhale is my only response, lifting my chin with an innocent shrug. He waves his hand with a rather dramatic cough. "Would you mind putting that out? I came out here to breathe. It's like a damn gambling club in there. I don't know how smoking became so fashionable."

A snort beats against the back of my nose as I try to picture a bore like this man taking in a floor show, ordering Doris's company. "Well, I came out here to be alone, so it looks like we're both gonna have to deal with it."

"Look," Archibald says, his jaw tightening under the darkening moonlight as the clouds thicken. "I realize a simple woman like my wife may have needed whatever friends she could acquire, but now that she's mine, I don't see a need for exposing herself to such a four-flusher."

Damn darbs. Blood simmers in my veins, though I shouldn't be shocked at the way this joker sees me. "Hey, I earned everything I have, mister. I'm no mooch."

"No?" He steps closer, his disdain flashing in his eyes. "Margaret might not know who you are, but I'm well aware of your other ventures, and of all the men you've had to tease to *earn* your spot on the boulevards. Your awful column isn't what's paying your rent, now is it?"

"This *city* pays my rent, and it sure doesn't seem to mind." I seethe, taking a big drag, igniting his eyes even more.

"This city is a perpetrator of pleasure and sin and nothing more."

White smoke swirls around us. "Are you saying that because you're worried about the soul of Kansas City or because you're having trouble keeping your own hands clean?"

"I *beg* your pardon?"

"Hm, Doris said you like begging."

If it weren't so dark, I'm sure I could see the scarlet in the tips

of his ears as he stutters with insistence, "Th-that harlot is a devilish siren who . . . who uses men's weaknesses against them!"

"Yes," I say, examining the glowing end of my cigarette with an
aloof expression. "A man walking into a joint with nude women and
tonic water is there with the best intentions."

Margaret's horrendous husband sputters like a teakettle just
before the whistle. "I don't need to explain myself to some trash
snake charmer!" His pointed finger stops inches from my nose,
raising my eyebrow. "And don't go fooling yourself into thinking
Kessler has any interest in you. He drops women faster than Hol-
lywood, Miss Lane. You're nothing special."

"Heck and I have a fine understanding."

"Well, men of our station all go lallygagging once in a while."

"Hey," I say, my own ears burning, "just because you got yourself saddled to someone you didn't want, doesn't mean you have to
take it out on the rest of us." I try to ignore the vein popping in this
jerk's forehead, but it seems to want to say something itself. I nearly
fail at suppressing a chuckle.

"She told you."

I shake my head with an incredulous smile, sucking on the end
of my cigarette as a drop lands on my nose from the billowing sky.
"Like you said, she doesn't have any real friends, and her husband's
a smooth bell polisher pretending to have morals, so who's she got
to talk to?"

"Listen here!" Archibald growls, gripping my forearm with a
hard shake that ices my chest. The read begins immediately. This
man's lack of inner compassion and warmth is bordering on fright-
ful. He's as cold and dark as an empty casket. Still, he's full of vile
words that he spews out almost faster than I can read them. "I take
business clients to that club because men require a certain atmosphere to loosen up. A dirty smoke-eater like you should know that.
I'm a powerful man in my circle, and if you weren't with Kessler,
I'd show you just how much I don't appreciate your mouth." His

grip tightens like a dentist's clamp, fanning the heat to my clenched teeth. "That said, you *will* stay the hell away from Margaret. She doesn't need your kind making her think women can act this way. Your very presence here offends me."

The cool drips on my face and hands do nothing to quench the sweltering fire that escapes my mouth in a hiss. "Take your hands off me or I'll march right in there and tell her about your nightly business in Chesterfield's brothel."

"She won't believe you," Archibald says, a loud crack announcing a brilliant flash of light across the sky; a heart-shaking rumble curls his sneer. "And even if she did, the scene you would cause would kill any interest in your new business. Kessler's not the only man in there with influence. Salvatore happens to be a good friend of mine."

"How surprising. Now," I say, wrenching my arm away, "let me go!" I lift my cigarette to my lips.

"I said put that out, you horrid bitch!" He grabs my wrist, yanking the burning Camel from my mouth, but I hold tight, twisting my arm. Men grab me all the time, and I often let them because it activates my power. But I've already read this guy, and there's no way he's gonna get away from me without a split lip if he doesn't let go. And there's no way this weasel's taking my smoke.

His fingers begin to bend mine in the flailing. I think he'd break them if he had the nerve. The lingering taste of smoke in my mouth becomes bitter—earthy. Dangerous. Light rain taps around us, the brilliant illuminations in the clouds lighting our hands as the orange ember smashes between them, fading in the dampened tobacco.

My anger crescendos with the raging sky, the ice of retribution reaching my fingertips as I tighten my grip, uttering my abuela's favored rebuke. "May you reap what you sow!"

Through the soaked brown leaves between our palms, his skin signals me to brace myself for his flying hand; my eyes squeeze shut . . .

It never lands.

With even the sky halting its howling, I peel a slow eyelid at his hitching breath, my forehead wrinkling. "Aw, Oswald, it's just an ember—"

"I . . . I think I'm not well." Archibald snatches back his quivering hand, his face paling as he dusts the tobacco onto his vest. "Weddings are a stressful time. Good evening, Miss Lane."

The vengeful wind sends stinging pellets crashing to the wooden balcony, and me huddling under the small awning in wonder. I don't know what the hell I just did, if anything at all. No, that's not true: *Something* happened. Again. Mama Sunday will know, and I can't let this go much further without talking to her.

The tickle of my hair lifting into a frizzy curl rolls my eyes as another shadow darkens the patio doorway from the glowing party inside. "Rose, *there* you are. I've been looking for you for ages."

I throw my wry smile over my shrugging shoulder, lifting the golden case from my bag. "Well, you found me, Mr. Kessler."

"Yes," he says, "but what am I going to do with you now? You're a mess. I swear, I can't take you anywhere." Heck's grin makes me grin as he leans down, lighting my cigarette. "This party's a dud anyway. The groom has vomited on his own wedding cake. Clearly, his constitution can't handle one toast."

"Probably so," I agree, rubbing my shivering arms that have turned bumpy beneath my sleeves. Figures a rat like him can't stand up to the scrutiny of a single woman like me, much less an entire room of suits. Margaret could take his wiry frame down easy if she had the gumption to fight back. "Who cares? We've got real villains at our heels."

"Indeed."

"Oh," a sultry voice sounds from the doorway, "that Archie just needs a good spoonin'. Turns him into a koala."

Heck claps his hands together. "Well, that's my cue to get you two out of here. It's nearly midnight. Don't want your carriages turning into pumpkins, now do we?"

"Hey!" Doris whines, digging for her own cigarette, "I was pretty classy in there."

"That you were, darling. You were wonderful."

The lounge singer beams as he holds a lighter to her smoke.

These two orchids have me chuckling as we make our way out of the swanky hotel, their witty banter and honest company warming the chill in my bones. I'm used to confrontations from guys like Archibald, ruler of all balconies. But his particular brand of contempt has shaken me up more than usual. Beneath the layers of cotton button-downs and fluttering skirts, Margaret has a lot to offer, though her obnoxious husband will never know it. Men like him don't give anyone a chance to shine . . . or smoke, apparently.

I still can't believe he just ran off like that. I usually have to charm a guy who gets that bunched up, although there was zero chance of those rubbery lips touching mine.

I stretch out on Heck's back seat, kicking my shoes off in the white interior of his prized Chrysler as he and Doris trade stories about so-called gentlemen, lulling me into daydreams of high-society bowing at the feet of my Bellerive overture. I'm right on my way to a place without emotional mobsters and self-righteous clowns who disguise themselves as protective husbands. I'm still figuring out what I really need to get where I'm going. But one thing's clear: I don't need any of that.

10

"TO THE STRANGEST GROUP OF TOMCATS I EVER SAW," I AN-
nounce, leaning on the distressed countertop. Gio's grin radiates
behind his lifted tumbler, my other two partners in crime following
suit as they swig my most expensive commodity like it isn't worth
more than they make in a month combined. The sweet cherry-
soaked brandy tastes like spiced summer with a sharp splash of
coveted vodka. I haven't had anything like it since I was a girl, before men decided to outlaw everything enjoyable. But while laws
and regulations shift with the generational tide, the desires of humanity continue on, unchanged and unrepentant. Like water or air,
what I have to offer has always been in demand and always will be,
leaving the world for the taking. My dreams are firmly gripped in
my hand in the form of a shot glass.

Javier slings an arm around my shoulders, giving me a light kiss
on the temple. "I'm proud of you, Miss Rose, signing on at the Bellerive. You're tough as hell." I giggle as he plants another kiss on my
temple before strolling away for the nightly lockup from Monday's

inventory.

"You sure you won't go dancing with me?" Heck pleads, stretching his arm over the counter to grab my hand. His adorable eyes flutter, chipping at my resistance as his palm asks me to come along to help him seek out prospective suitors.

I want to help, but I want my bed more. "I'm worn out with crowds, Mr. Kessler."

"Fine," he says, lifting my hand to his mouth before dropping it in a very ungentlemanly fashion, his back straightening with a gasp. "Ooh! Maybe Javi will go!" Gripping his herringbone jacket, he sails out the door in search of my poor brother, who will likely get dragged into Heck's carousing. At least our friend will have a safe ride home. I shake my head after him with a smile, turning back to put away the cordial and clean up the glasses while my stubble-chinned piano player spins his tumbler in his hand. I glance up as the small glass lifts in the air, balancing on his finger like a miniature cyclone, glinting in the light of the wall sconces.

"So," he says, keeping a cool eye on his performance. "You and Javi seem pretty friendly."

I lay the glasses in the black cast-iron sink, turning my lips down with a shrug. "We've known each other for a long time, since I started this business. He's like a brother to me."

Gio tosses the glass up and catches it with his other finger. It spins to a stop, suspending in the air between us. "I wouldn't judge you, doll. No one here would."

It's a nice sentiment, and nice to know a man outside of Heck and my brother doesn't seem off-put by race. Personally, I love the adventure of variety, my first heartbreaks ending with Javier lecturing me about kissing boys by the railroad tracks. He wasn't as keen as I was on the trinkets I brought home, courtesy of whatever starry-eyed boy I'd managed to charm. It's not like I knew what the hell I was doing at the time. By secondary school, they had caught on to my allure, avoiding me altogether. *Not that I cared.*

I shoot Gio a playfully sarcastic nod, turning the knob for the waterspout. "Thanks for the approval, but it's really not like that between Javi and me, and it's never gonna be." I hold my hand out, furrowing my brow at him. "I need to wash that glass, sir."

"Yeah, well, when it ain't there, it ain't there, I guess," Gio says, slipping his hand over mine, sparking my magic's reception. "Plus, I forgot you don't date guys you work with." He bends my pointing finger upward, giving the tumbler another spin on my fingertip. Holding my wrist steady, his hand tingles with a measure of disappointment he's trying to swallow, accompanied by a small jolt of jealousy that raises my eyebrows, though I am quite mesmerized by his brand of magic tricks.

"Gets too complicated when it doesn't work out," I reply, using the whirling glass as my excuse to scan the odd elephant and the flaming swords on his forearms. His soft hands and scrutinizing thoughts distract my curiosity; he thinks I'm a little jaded.

Well, that's an understatement.

The balancing act meets its end as the glass wobbles. Gio snags it before it falls, pressing it into my hand with an unreadable expression in his sable eyes. "Well, you just ain't met the right guy."

I force my flirty smile back to where it belongs, far away from Gio and this little fire we're kindling as I scrub the tumblers out with the care of a heart surgeon. *Not this one, Luna.* I can't have my rum-running partner mixed up in my voodoo, even if I do like him. Which I don't. There's no time for that applesauce right now.

I don't date my employees. I'm annoyed that I have to remind myself about a hard-and-fast rule that's never been an issue until now.

"Listen," I say, avoiding his eye. "I don't do the love thing—some guy stealing everything I've worked for, especially after I've changed my name for him. Most men will say whatever they need to get in my skirt; I'm guessing that goes double to get in my purse."

Gio nods, reaching over to toss me a white hand towel. "Ah,

now that I unda'stand." His finger taps his forehead, stealing back my grin. "I walk the lonely road myself. It's easy'a this way."

Right. That's not exactly what I read earlier, but I appreciate his attempt to seem less wanting. It looks like he got the message—we can't get tangled up, emotions or otherwise.

I dry the last of the glasses, trying to set them in rows the way my brother prefers as Gio's fingernail scratches a bit of chipping paint on the countertop, his hair falling into his eyes like a curtain of silky coal.

"So you and Heck's ruse seems ta be holdin' up, I guess." He glances up, rubbing the back of his pink neck. "Javi think he's handsy, though."

I toss my towel to the counter, grabbing my hips. "Well, we kind of have to be if it's gonna sell on Main Street. High society needs to think we're together. What do I care if he touches my hip or pecks my lips? Really, Gio, what do *you* care?"

Of course, he doesn't know that I'm aware of his feelings, and it's all just so aggravating to deal with right now. This is why I don't do love. The only thing I want clinging to me is a silk blouse.

"Okay, *jeepa's,*" my frowning piano player says with an irritated laugh, raising his hands in defense. "I'm just lookin' out for ya, boss. Anyways, there's somethin' else I wanted to tell ya tonight—I booked the Bennie Moten Orchestra for opening night."

Di mi!

I resist any urge for propriety, letting my mouth and eyes hang open as I bounce on the balls of my feet. Any irritation I had at Gio fizzles in the excitement. "You didn't!"

"I didn't wanna tell ya till I knew we was official." Gio grins, slapping the counter. "Clip's band'll open for 'em, and my Chicago contacts are ready to send invites wherever you want 'em. Word is, Capone's already got wind of it, which I wasn't even expectin'. This is gettin' huge!" I squeal with my hand over my mouth like a silly schoolgirl, running around the counter to throw my arms around my laughing bootlegger, sending us both stumbling. "Whoa there, Lane. It ain't happened yet!"

"It's okay," I gush, trying to catch my breath in his tight hold. "This is all just so amazing. Feels so real!" My dreams solidify around me like a fortress. The Bellerive. Capone. A real club, with real booze and a real orchestra—all run by me.

Gio's heart beats against my cheek. With a shy laugh, I push him away before I can read him anymore, his disappointed eyes telling me all I need to know. *So real.* His hands take my wrists from his shoulders, confirming the desire in his face. But I can't do this to Gio. Or myself.

Even with his mouth so dangerously close to mine . . .

"We should check on Javi," I blurt out, wincing at the dashed hope in his palms. I force myself to meet his eyes. I've hurt him. *Damn.* I feel . . . bad. *Get back on the trolley, Rose. Get back to business.* What the hell is wrong with me? I can't go around feeling bad about this kind of bushwa. And that's all it is—bushwa. Gio's no different than any other fella. Just another sexy smile with sharp wit and strong arms I'd like to use for balance . . .

No attachments!

"It's just that he should be done by now."

Gio steps back with a curt nod, his cheeks flushing. "Right. No, you're right. We should . . . I should . . ."

"Gio—"

"I'll check around back." Turning on his heel, he bolts for the rear door, leaving me stewing in heavy regret.

Where the hell did I put that cordial?

MY LIPS ALWAYS FEEL A LITTLE BIT NUMB WHEN I'VE HAD MORE than one drink. The accompanying warmth that rolls down my shoulders eases my earlier trepidation over Gio's almost kiss.

That fella! He's my employee, for God's sake. *What was he think-*

ing?

What was I thinking? My conscience has the audacity to lecture me.

I answer back with a final nip from the bottle. *Unbelievable.*

I slip from the wooden stool, twisting the lid back onto the bottle of cherried cordial, leaving it on the counter for tomorrow. The idea of putting it away makes me almost as tired as knowing I have to drive myself home. I may have to wait a while. Maybe Heck and Javi will keep me company now that I've scared Gio off for the night. He's been gone for a good fifteen minutes. Come to think of it, none of my associates have returned in quite some time, leaving me sipping on sweet brandy and wondering what Gio's mouth tastes like. *Such silliness.*

I veer across the wooden floor, stifling a giggle. "Geez, you guys," I mumble to the back door, fumbling with the knob. "I apparently can't be trusted with that upper-crust liquor—" Throwing the door open with a stupid grin, I freeze, my amusement tumbling to my feet. Javier's hand grips my elbow, pushing me between the holes that once held bushes and shutting the door.

"Stay behind me, Rose," he whispers. Heck and Gio stand silent beside him, their gazes traveling across the nebulous parking lot to where three men stare back at us like ghosts, with the hoods to match. A half-moon gives their white robes a murky illumination between the passing clouds, their eyes darkened by the cutout holes and the shadows. Moisture beads across my skin, the hair on my neck prickling.

"Wh-what do you want?" I ask, unable to mask the trembling in my voice and hands.

My brother juts his arm across my body like a shield. "Don't talk to them, Rose."

"Is that how you talk to your betters, boy?" the ghost to the right sneers in a grated drawl. "I believe your manager asked us a question. You're gonna wanna keep quiet if you wanna walk outta here with that dirty immigrant tongue, ya hear?"

Javier's terrified rage echoes through my hand as I push his arm down and step forward, ignoring the silent protest he's sending me. Heck's hand squeezes my shoulder, his fingers sliding to the nape of my neck. He wants me to stand down and let him handle this, speaking before I can summon the courage.

"I beg your pardon, gentlemen," he says, "but you're frightening my fiancée and her staff. What is this about?"

"So you are serious about her," the middle phantom says. I squint in the darkness at his clean, learned dialect, blinking away the muddledness of my tipsy mind. I've heard that voice . . . I think. "Mr. Kessler, you are on a very tight rope with us as it is. Your surname is the only thing that has kept us from turning you in for your debauchery—that and our compassion toward your and Miss Lane's predicament."

Heck's panic lights the back of my neck, his fingertips growing sweaty. "I can't know what you even mean by that, *sir*."

"Which is even more disappointing—to be unable to see that you've enabled each other's misdeeds. But you don't know any better. You don't know the influence you've been under. And if you value your inheritance, you'll pay attention." The man cocks his head, the hem of his white fabric tousling in the humid breeze. "We came to speak to *her*."

My mouth goes dry, those black eyeholes aiming at me. Gio walks past me, his hand raised. "Hey, anything you wanna say to her, you can say to us. We're her business team, and I ain't neva' seen Kessla' in any kinda debauchery. These two are always togetha', for God's sake—" The quiet ghost on the left arcs his arm from behind his back, a large shotgun lifting in front of him. As the double barrel points at Gio's rounded eyes, he takes a small step backward, moving in front of me. "Look, just take it easy."

"Miss Lane," the articulate man says, offering his hand, "won't you come out from behind that wall of lies and deceit you've surrounded yourself with? Your friends need not escalate the situation. We only wish to speak with you."

No! Heck's hand screams into my neck. *Don't you dare.* I'd answer back, but he can't hear me without my lips, not that I can get my thoughts together enough to use impartation anyway. *Maybe booze should be illegal.*

That would have made any of the Roses laugh any other time—except for Luna. She hasn't done much of that lately. It's an odd thought to have at the present moment. I lift my chin, marching from Heck's hold, pushing past Gio as I head for the ghost's pale hand. As soon as my fingers clamp around it, the heavy regret returns with a vengeance. His dark thoughts ice over my veins, flooding my palms with cold contempt aimed at the men behind me, my club, my trousers, and . . . himself. He wants to hurt Heck and, strangely, do other things to him that make me cringe. The brand of hate is a familiar flavor. I can't quite place where I've sensed it before, but it's definitely not new.

"Well?" I lift what I hope is a confident eyebrow, trying to shake away his intention toward my friends if this meeting doesn't go well. As if a run-in with the Ku Klux Klan ever goes well. Despite that, I've got to keep everyone calm—somehow.

"Look at you," he says, tightening his grip. "A poor white woman from north of the river comes to the big city to experience the metropolitan life and gets ensnared by one devil after another. You fall in love with a wealthy man who promises to make your dreams come true—your way out of this sewer of a life. But you find out he's not what he seems."

I lower my chin, my jaw hardening. "Most of us aren't. But he's one'a the only men I've found who's actu'lly *better* than I first thought. You obvi'sly don't know him."

My words might be a little sloshy, but he seems to get the point. Disdain boils beneath this specter's contempt. "Tell me, Miss Lane," he says, his voice seething, "when you find him trading favors with other men in private booths at opera houses, will your fine raiment of silk be worth the sale of your soul? How far into Hell are you willing to let him drag you?"

"His life is his own an' no bus'ness of yours," I shoot back, the thumping in my chest growing louder than this man's awful thoughts. "Our souls aren't your bus'ness either. In case you didn't notice, I chose this life. Every part of it. I'm not sure why you're so intr'ested in it."

My human manacle peers over my head like a demonic watchtower. "Sober up, Miss Lane! You're surrounded by the lowest society has to offer—a criminal bootlegger with a record that stretches to the East Coast, a filthy Mexican bartender whose new apartment is barely an upgrade from his riverside boxcar, and a sodomite for a fiancé who would already be in jail if his great-uncle hadn't been so influential in our city." He yanks me forward, leering down at me with his burning eyes, his indignation rising. "Don't tell me you've chosen this life of sin. You are bewitched by the devil himself, as is Mr. Kessler. Jews, Negros, Catholic mobsters, foreigners—they're using your skills and influence to further infect our wholesome city with their shame. It's what they want!"

"Maybe it is, maybe it isn't." I'm amazed at how well I'm following this conversation. I might be floating, but the booze is giving me boldness I might not have otherwise had. I'm way too drunk to figure out if that's a good thing. "But if I've got the right to vote now, then I've got the right to decide my own life, too."

"More devilry. Women's suffrage is an anathema to the Christian laws of this country. God said women should serve their husbands." He wants to spit, and only his ridiculous mask with its pointed hood is keeping him from doing so.

Calm. It's the only thing my drunken mind can muster.

"Well, I don't 'ave a husband," I slur, "but I do have a fiancé. And according to what you say, shouldn't I be listn'ing to him rather than you?"

"Not if he's possessed by the devil!"

I'm done with this. I was never one for theology anyway—and I'm sure this self-proclaimed holy man's got a quote for any response I'd give. I summon a softer reply, which isn't hard to do since my body feels like heavy tingling. "I'm tired. We're all tired. I'm guessing you're tired too—it's pretty late to be out an' about, as you so keenly note. I'm sorry if you don't like Mr. Kessler, but I do. That's *my* choice, not the devil's, and cert'nly not yours."

"Open your eyes, stupid girl," he rasps, "and see the curse over this city. It breaks federal law openly without recourse. It's absolute witchery! And we aim to stop it, starting with this club."

His intentions mingle with my own alarm, the sour tobacco chew on his breath repelling me backward, but he holds fast to my hand. If I'm bewitched, then he's the one truly possessed, his desires raging against his conscience, disorienting my blurred thoughts as I choke out my response. "Is *that* what this is? You want me to shut down?"

"We want *all* the clubs to shut down, even Pendergast's."

They truly do want to dance with the devil. They better be ready to Charleston all night long. "Good luck with that."

"We'll get it done," he says with the confidence of a zealot—whether to religion or whiteness, it's not clear, but at this point, it doesn't matter. "Never you mind. This was just a warning. We're cleaning up the dirty jazz district and its Negro bands and brothels, starting with you. And don't even think about opening that new place of yours, bringing that scum to the boulevards. If you refuse to comply, you'll find yourself on a difficult road. Kessler's name, Pendergast's influence—they only go so far. With enough chaos, the people of this city will plead for order and family values once again. Do be careful to stay on the right side of this conflict, Miss Lane." Throwing my arm back to me, he and his two specters snicker before floating back into the night. Soon, their crunching footsteps fade down a darkened alleyway.

"Mierda," Javier gasps, bracing his hands on his knees. "The damn *Klan*."

Gio swears, rubbing his chin. "I thought they got pushed to the outskirts."

Heck nods. "Yes, well, they're back, and they know *way* too much about us. Something must have gotten their attention."

"Or someone," I say, my eyes misting. "Like a snake charmer bringing Capone to town."

The term used to be a badge of honor, a woman running a bootlegging operation. But now the label I've earned is a screaming accusation of all I've brought down on myself and my family.

Heck's arm hooks around my waist, pulling me toward his black sedan. Despair shakes my insides, threatening to pour from my eyes, burning my nose. "Rose, come on. I'm getting you home."

"That's a good idea," Gio says. "I'll take Javi. I don't trust those cretins—startin' a damn turf war. Betch'a Ice'll flip. Lemme run and lock up inside so they don't get any ideas. Then we'll get the hell outta here."

As he sprints into the bar, my brother whirls around. "What's he planning, Luna?"

"I couldn't hear it all," I insist, raking my fingers through my hair. "He's got this self-loathing over his own desires. He thinks if he can get the city cleaned up, he won't be so tempted to indulge."

"What desires?" Heck asks, letting me lean on him.

"I don't know. It was all a jumble." My swirling head falls to his shoulder as I try to slow my breath. "All I know is, they're planning to sweep Eighteenth and Vine, and the man is seriously conflicted. So much of his attention was on you. He loathes you . . . and he's attracted to you."

Heck's body jilts. "He's . . . *what*?"

Gio bursts out of the joint like he's being chased by goblins, slamming and locking the back door. "A'right, you crooks, let's go. Those guys gimme the heebies!"

With a solemn warning from my brother to be careful—which I reply in turn—I slide across Heck's leather seats as he shuts the passenger door. His headlights shine over the newly paved boulevards, my head on his shoulder, our fingers intertwined. I squeeze his hand tighter. *I shouldn't leave him alone.* He's pretty shaken up. He could use a hand to hold tonight.

Sure, yeah, he's the only one.

"Will you stay with me?" I ask, just above a whisper.

"Of course I will."

"I'VE TOLD YOU THIS BEFORE AND I'M TELLING YOU AGAIN," MY now faux-fiancé says, cocking his fedora with a perfectly arched eyebrow. "No one would blame you if you backed out. I'll still marry you."

"Heck Kessler," I reply, taking his suave arm to hide the rock on my finger that's already weighing me down, "I'm not backing out, and I'm not marrying you, especially after you announced our engagement in front of the Klan."

"Which you played into."

"So they wouldn't shoot us!"

"As direct as ever, Miss Lane. That is why I love you so."

I glance down at my knee-length dress, its shimmering beads scratching against the underside of my bare arms. It's not quite flapper, but it is a splendid nod against conservatism. "If you love me so, then why make me wear this frock?"

"Because your legs are divine and such a pair deserves to be seen with my new suit." His eyes sparkle with mischief as two attendants in evergreen vests open the mahogany double doors in front of us. Heck's mouth nears my ear. "Darling, try not to break my heart until after we've acquired our nightclub, won't you?"

"*My* nightclub, dear," I say, allowing him to kiss my nose before leading me into the gold-and-red ballroom. Waiting on the oak dance floor, a balding man pushes up his spectacles, checking his pocket watch.

"Mr. Kessler," he announces at our approach, his indifferent gaze lingering on me like a drifter who snuck into his precious hotel. "You're actually following through with this, I see."

Heck pinches two cool fingers in the air, looking down at him with a decent measure of conceit. "How do you mean, sir?"

Mr. Cornwell snaps his attention back to Heck. "Er, um, the purchase of this club, of course."

"Naturally."

"Yes, well, why don't we review the details of your loan—"

"My fiancée has filled me in quite well enough," Heck says, peering around the room before sliding his arm across my shoulders. "It's going to take a lot of improvement, darling, but it could work."

I tighten my mouth to hold in a bubble of laughter, nodding. This place is more beautiful than I could have ever dreamed. The owner seems less entertained by the snide assessment, sputtering, "I beg your pardon? We have only been open a couple of years—"

"Yes," Heck replies, waving a dismissive hand, his eyes traveling the room. "So my Rose has told me. Show us the underbelly. Let's see if it's worth this ungodly price you're demanding."

Mr. Cornwell's scalp reddens beneath his white wisps as he shifts on his oxfords, but he knows his place in the pecking order of privilege and so gives a compliant bow before spinning away. Heck squeezes encouragement into my hand as we follow our miffed guide across the plush carpet toward the long bar, stopping in front of an oversized cabinet with intricate carvings of winged cherubs. Shooting my fiancé a curious glance, I stand on my tiptoes as the old highbrow inserts a long silver key into the side of the door. His withered fingers give a light pull to the curved metal knob, my eyes widening as the entire cabinet pulls away from the wall. *Jeepers.* As if plucked from my childhood storybooks, a stone staircase awaits our descent into its cavernous belly.

Heck clutches my palm, his heart alight with adventure. "Don't be frightened, darling." He flicks his comical eyebrows up at my flat look as our guide pushes a small white button on a golden plate set into the slated stone. Glowing with our anticipation and the bronze wall sconces, we follow Mr. Cornwell down the winding stairs, my excitement buzzing as much as Heck's as we reach the carpeted landing.

"Mr. Kessler." He presses another white switch on the wall, igniting several small chandeliers. "I pray you find these accommodations more acceptable."

Heck's gentle tug pulls me away from my annoyance at being ignored and into the provocative speakeasy. Its very essence turns my fiancé's thoughts to revelry as his mind shares snippets of staff placements and costume designs. In keeping with the upstairs color theme, the ruby red and shining golds adorn this vast tavern as well, though the ambiance is more rustic. Dark mahogany chairs surround several matching tables, each with a set of poker chips and golden ashtrays. Opposite the black marble bar, a raised stage is cut into walls layered with crimson curtains.

"All right, well, is this it?" he asks the huffing club owner. "We plan to hold the private preopening here in the Drawing Room."

"The Drawing Room, sir?"

Heck's eyebrow lifts, his proud eyes beaming down at me. "Yes, my Rose chose the name for the downstairs club. She's going to make this underbelly quite something."

"Your fiancée chose the name for a *gentleman's* area?"

"That is correct." Heck grabs my hand, his subtle eye warning me of our game plan. He's had a lifetime of training on how to negotiate with high-class idiots like Cornwell, and I have a feeling my attitude could muck this up if we're not careful. Many deals have been lost to a bruised ego.

It's a dance, my faux-fiancé silently explains to my hand as he gazes around with scrutiny, ignoring the hotel manager's incredulous stare. *One must know how to be rude, my dear.*

"Mr. Kessler, I surely assumed she came to me on your behalf. I've known many husbands to grant far too many liberties."

I grit my teeth and attempt to appear pleasant. *Of course* the upper crust will assume this isn't really my venture—that my fiancé will take over my accounts as soon as we're married. All I need to do is keep quiet so they don't figure out it's never going to happen.

Heck's head snaps back to the scowling man, pulling me closer to his side. "Mr. Cornwell, I am truly here on her behalf as a cosigner and I hardly need to explain. My kitten's ideas were keen enough for you to call us back here." Entertainment and challenge flicker in Heck's eyes. "Now, are *these* the only accommodations?"

The old manager flushes. "Aside from what you see here, Mr. Kessler, there are two dressing rooms, two washrooms, and ten private rooms that can be rented out at whatever price you decide."

"And their furnishings?"

"Complete." Mr. Cornwell's dignified arms fold behind his back. "Chaises, gramophones, and armoires to keep certain supplies as well as a small liquor cabinet."

The man has yet to acknowledge me. He doesn't really care that I made the decision—he only cares about the money . . . and keeping the place as white as possible. But Heck is honestly doing a fine job at moving this along as they discuss all the details I previously coached *him* to ask about.

"I see," my fiancé says, lifting his chin. "We'll complete the tour on our own and meet you upstairs to sign the documents in twenty minutes."

"Very good, sir." It never stops amazing me how obsequious men without money can be to men *with* the lettuce. With another cordial bow, the hotel owner trickles from the room, leaving us jumping up and down in gleeful silence as soon as the heavy door clicks upstairs.

My heels leave the floor, Heck's arms lifting me into his embrace. I hold tight to his neck, joining his laugh as he spins me around. "You made it, Rose! If I weren't an opera-house-slumming gonsil, I'd take you into one of those private rooms to celebrate."

"Keep teasin' me, big-timer," I say with a coy grin as he lets me down. "I might make you follow through one day." He rears with feigned fright, making me laugh harder. "Gee, thanks."

"Oh, my darling flower, what did I ever do without you?"

"You took lonely tours of cities."

"That, I did. I'm much happier now." He chuckles with a shake of his head, taking my hands. "In just over a month, I've become engaged to the elusive Rose Lane, dabbled in magic that will cure my ills, and invested in a jazz club . . . which, by the way, the main club upstairs needs a name for the general public. Have you thought of one yet?"

Taking a deep breath, I drink in the possibilities, settling on the one name that encapsulates what this means to me. "The Casbah Lounge." The words drip from my mouth, sealing the evening.

"Ah, fortress," Heck says, pinching my chin with a wink. "Sounds just right."

"Thank you." My satisfied smile reflects the notion as we comb the remaining rooms with stuffy judgments and glee. My club will be impenetrable with the syndicate as my moat, and devoid of heavy-handed mobsters who want to take advantage of my divine legs. They're *my* damn legs. This is *my* damn castle. And no one's going to take either from me.

11

SETTLING INTO THE STIFF WOODEN CHAIR OF A BREAK ROOM DE-
signed to quench all inspiration, I pull a crisp novel from my handbag with the earnestness of a small girl receiving a treasured toy.
An uttered grumble simmers in the back of my throat as the break
room door flies open. My irritation turns to silent wonder at the
flattened bill of my coworker's hat over her eyes, her hair smashing
against her wet cheeks in tufts of orange. "Rose, I . . . didn't think
anyone would be in here." I squint up at Margaret's avoiding gaze as
she turns her head, wiping her nose with a handkerchief and adjusting her hair forward. "I know it's terrible to call in sick on a Friday.
I'm just running in to turn in final prints. I best be off, though, in
case what I have is catching."

"Hold on there, Margaret," I say, my book lying forgotten as
I stand, taking a few tentative steps toward her. She freezes, her
hand playing at the doorknob as a tear drops from her eye. Friendly
touching isn't exactly my wheelhouse, but the woman looks like she
could use a comforting hand on her shoulder. If I'm being honest,

though, I feel like I'm reaching out to pet a strange animal. "There now, Margaret. Why don't you tell me what's wrong?"

"I told you, I'm sick," she utters through her stuffy pink nose. Amazed with my own kind concern, I slip a careful hand beneath her jaw, tilting her tearstained face toward me. Her eyes close, sending more rain down her cheeks that reverberate with despair into my fingertips as I gently push back her hair, revealing a sizable black bruise at the corner of her bloodshot eye. "He didn't mean it, and he gestures so wildly." She says it so quickly.

I level my worried eyes. "This isn't normal, honey."

Margaret's sweatered shoulders broaden, her hand gripping the door. "Well, what would *you* know?"

"I know the man I'm engaged to wouldn't put a hand on me."

She leaves me in the wake of her furious huff. I could chase after her, but it would only draw further attention to her humiliation. The last thing she needs is to become the center of office gossip and criticism, even if she is usually the one doing the gossiping. The women are often more vicious than the men, who will go about their day, pretending their office assistant didn't just barrel out of here with a shiner. It doesn't help that she's married to a prominent lawyer with strong political ties. I lean on the doorpost with a long sigh. No one, especially not Margaret, will say a word.

"Rose," a scowling secretary snips with her hands on her pleated hips. I turn halfway, giving her just as much attention, deepening the lines around her frowning mouth. "You're wanted on the phone at your desk. It's rang twice since you've been God knows where."

"You mean on my break?"

She storms off, probably working on a comeback that she'll share with the rest of the girls later. I can't even begin to care. Smirking at her curt exit, I saunter to the desk that I share with Margaret, who takes calls for our boss. He'll assume I'm on a personal call if he catches me—not that I've ever been docked for it, but I don't feel like being yelled at today. *Maybe tomorrow.* Glancing back toward his office, I press the earpiece to my ear, holding the speaker stand to my mouth. "Good afternoon. This is Rose Lane of the *Kansas City Star.* How can I—"

"Boss, we got a little bit'a trouble here."

My rounded eyes dart around the room, my voice lowering. "Gio? Why are you calling me here?"

"Look, Rose, I got no one else to call. Javi ain't home durin' the day and Heck's probably at a luncheon or some sh— Look, I'm gonna need you ta come down to the police station, all right?"

"The *what*?" I hiss. I knew better than to trust a criminal. I don't have time for hot water. "What did you do?"

"*Really*, boss? Use that head'a yours. Or betta' yet, get down here!"

Rearing back at the loud click in my ear, I put the receiver back in the holder, snatching my handbag as the realization of the situation dawns. Gio's a bootlegger. He's in jail because of me.

"WOULD YOU CARE FOR A DRINK, MISS?"

Cops have a certain way of dressing. A certain way of speaking— this one taking the time to straighten his brown tie and jacket before gesturing to the grimy chair next to him. The hanging bulb from the ceiling is the only light in this brick-walled room, highlighting the scratches and bloodstains in the grooves of the coarse table that holds two tin tumblers. I flinch at the metal squeal of the slamming door behind me. "Really, Miss Lane, why don't you have a seat?"

With my white knuckles gripping my handbag, I lower myself into the chair, unease drifting through me like electricity. I've done everything in my power to avoid the law. Kansas City makes it easy . . . usually. Men even easier. I've just got to figure out what this one wants. "I came inquiring about Gio Cattaneo. I don't know why your secretary brought me in here, Detective . . ." I lower an expectant chin, drawing the word out as his crooked teeth flash through an eerie grin.

"Higgs. Detective Higgs," he replies, crossing one lanky leg over the other. Reaching into his breast pocket, he pulls out a large leather flask and pinches the lid. Every instinct tells me to run, but that would be stupid. Where would I go in a city jail? I swallow a lump of nerves as he pours a light brown liquid into both cups, sliding one over to me. "Your associate has been arrested in every major city from here to New York, Miss Lane. I was just curious why a woman like you would be interested in his well-being."

I keep my eyes fixed on his amused gaze. "He's a friend of mine."

"Do you normally run with friends of his nature?"

"What nature, sir?"

"Oh, smoking, drinking, disregard for chastity laws."

"I can't see how that matters."

"Ah," Higgs says, tipping his cup into his mouth with a loud slurp. "You're going to be a challenge for me, then?" My eyes narrow as I start to respond, but he shoves my cup closer to me. "Have a drink. You'll feel better."

"No, thank you."

He tilts his head with mocking concern. "No? Don't tell me you're worried about prohibition laws, now. Or do you not partake when you're working the River Rose?" My courage collapses to my toes, my skin dampening. He lets out a light laugh, lifting his cup once again. "Come on, baby. Lighten up. Not a single person's been arrested in this city for selling liquor. As far as I'm concerned, the federal government can go take a ride."

"Then why are you holding me here?"

"Who said anyone's holding you? I just wanted to talk to you."

I let out a snorting scoff, pushing my chair back. "Look, I've been waiting for over four hours, so just tell me how much the bail is."

His grin widens. "I'm trying to, sweetheart, but you're not listening." The electricity is back in my veins, my arms cramping from holding myself so tightly. This room is too small. "We don't care about your little henchmen or your ventures with your dashing fiancé."

"Then what do you and the rest of Pendergast's machine want?"

"Now *that* is the perfect question," he says, his eyes outlining the neckline of my blouse. "We want peace, Miss Lane." His smile fades as he leans forward with a sneer. "Now *drink*."

I reach out a slow hand, curling my fingers around the tin handle. *Rats. That's really full.* The unmistakable burn hits my nose before I even taste the rank piss water. As the cup hits the table, he fills it again with a commanding nod. I'm barely five three in my heels, almost a buck thirty. This stuff will go right through me, but I'm not swimming in choices. I've got to find Gio.

"Good girl." Higgs smiles as I swallow with another cringe. "You seem to have the ability to comply, so listen up. Our city runs on stalemate policies, unwritten but very much respected. Italians run crime. Jews run politics. Hell, even the Irish mafia have their operations without making too many waves. It's an . . . *understanding* that we all have."

"So what's that got to do with me?" My damn cup is refilled to the brim, my lips already tingling.

The detective slaps the table, making me jump. "Everybody makes money. Everybody's happy. Unless someone messes with the rules. *You* are shaking the stalemate, Miss Lane!"

"What? How did I—"

"The Klan's crawling out of the woods, Ice is pissed, and Capone's syndicate is trying to stake a presence here—all because of the little skirt who wants a piece of the pie."

My mouth falls open, my tongue thickening with my thoughts. "*Whose* syndicate?"

"Holy hell, I should've known a woman wouldn't know what

was going on around her." Higgs sighs, tilting the bottom of my mug. As it pours down my throat, my stomach almost sends it back up. "That tattooed runner has you enlisted with mobsters bigger than Ice could ever hope to be, and it's shaking everything up. Don't you know that's who Cattaneo worked for back in Chicago? Do you know anything about your partners?"

Gio worked for him? "Al C'pone," I mumble. I should have eaten today.

"All right, that's probably enough of that." The detective's hand swipes my tin cup, the outline of his fingers swirling. I blink hard, shaking my head to no avail. "Miss Lane, not only are you gonna stop making waves, but you're going to tell us what Moretti wants from you."

"He . . . wants to invest'n my club."

"Yeah, we know that, baby. For what reason?"

"Cuz he likes me. I don't know."

"This is *not* the time to get cute!"

"Can'a help it. I'm cute."

A rough fist pounds the metal door. Swearing, the flushed detective bolts from his chair. "*What?* I'm in an interrogation!"

The door swings open; a man in a double-breasted suit stands beside a wide-eyed Gio, both of their noses flaring as the detective crosses his arms.

"Rose!" Gio's arm hooks around me as he lifts me from my seat, my heavy head falling forward. He pushes the hair from my eyes. His pinched eyebrows tilt with the room, his palm warm against my cheek, but I can't read anything right now. I can barely think. "Doll, are you okay?"

"What in the hell is happening, Counselor?" Higgs snaps.

The suited man clears his throat, the papers in his hand shuffling. "That's what I should be asking *you*, Detective. You have no grounds to hold Miss Lane, and your superiors have released Mr. Cattaneo. I am here representing them both on behalf of my client Heck Kessler. You'll kindly step aside now, sir."

"This is an outrage—"

"Finding my client drunk in an interrogation room without counsel is an outrage."

"What? I . . . I—"

"Shall I pursue it further? Perhaps with the Treasury Department?"

Higgs's clicking footsteps storm out of the dim room. My head feels like a bowling ball as Gio folds me into a cradle hold. "Everything's all right now, boss. I'm takin' you home."

"But I hafta work t'night."

"Oh, no, you don't."

"But—"

"That's enough, Rose. Just rest for a while, huh?"

I'm too weighed down by drunken exhaustion to argue. It's kind of strange being carried, like being on a human boat, a little relaxing and concerning at the same time. I cling tight to fight the nausea as Gio floats me away to safety, far away from the sinister clutches of the political underworld.

THE BACK OF MY SPINNING HEAD BOUNCES AGAINST MY SOFT quilt, a snorting giggle escaping my nose.

"Aw, sorry, boss. Little rough on the landin'."

I grip Gio's shoulders as he starts to pull away, nuzzling his white shirt to inhale his outdoorsy scent. "You smell good."

"That's what the guy in the jail cell said," he says with a sideways grin. My horrified face twists, deepening his small smile. "Kidding." His laughing eyes seem to study me as he untangles my fingers from his shirt. "Anyway, you get some rest. It's been a day."

"Wait." My hands cling to his arm like he's a life raft, the uncharacteristic desperation furrowing his brow. If only I could get a grip on my wherewithal, but my eyes are jerking around like a skipping gramophone. I try to read his hands, but all I hear is his steady breathing. Damn piss water.

"What's the matta', doll? You gotta go to the washroom or somethin'?"

"No, I just . . . Where's Heck?"

Gio's amused smile fades as he slides his arm from my grip. "He got called to an emergency meetin' with his trustees in St. Louis. I guess he's gotta schmooze things ova' with this whole jazz-club thing—and marryin' you, of course. He came to the Riva' Rose afta' I got arrested and called the lawya' when Penny and Clip told him what happened. Barely made his train, but he saved our necks, huh?" His cheeks redden as he stands, running his hand through his dark hair. "He'll be back in a couple'a days."

"A couple of days?" I whine, pushing myself up, the flowers of my wallpaper dancing around me.

Gio's gentle arms push my shoulders. "C'mon, boss. You gotta lay down."

"I can't. He doesn't like me being alone at night."

"Uh-huh," Gio says, jostling the mattress as he sits. His hand lifts the back of my head, lowering it again onto my pillow. "So, he stays with you?"

"Only when he's upset," I slur, pointing my finger in the air. "But don't get the wrong idea, mister. I ain't that kinda girl." Another snorting laugh erupts from my lips. "Well, I am, but not with him."

"Yeah? Not with your flashy fiancé? With who, then?"

My hand waves around like a lead glove. "Oh, not anyone for a while. Usually some joker who wants me to worship the ground he walks on *just* because he's a man. I wouldn't mess with them at all if they weren't so damn handsome."

"So that's what you like? Joka's with pretty faces?"

"No, that's the problem. They like *me*." My fingers tease the stubble on his chin, my voice hardening. "'Oh, Rose, you're all I ever wanted. I'll do anything for you—even leave my wife.'" My laugh meets Gio's sad face, his furrowed brow crinkling his cute little scars. "'Well, isn't that awful sweet of you, Mr. Pretty-Face? How can I say no to that?' So I give you all what you really want—a good mug with no commitment."

He grabs my hand, his sincerity registering through the fog. "That ain't all we want."

"Well, what *do* you want?" I ask, intertwining my fingers through his.

He lays my hand over my chest. "I want you to rest."

"Yeah? Well, it's very ungentlemanly of you to leave me here like this."

"Ah, so a real gentleman would lay in bed with you while your fiancé's away?"

"Precisely."

Gio's mouth breaks into a chuckling grin, his face blushing as he rubs his eyes with his hand. "All right. You're the boss." I smile as he ignores all my flirty touches, handing my hand back to me every time as he settles in beside me. His eyes shine while I regale him with stories of my early adulthood, working at juice joints to save a few bucks before meeting Giuseppe. Gio's full-belly laugh has me laughing too as I tell him about the slimy kiss we shared.

"Ah no, doll! Tell me you didn't!"

"He was cheating at cards!"

"You musta' been losin' a lotta money, baby!"

"I was," I insist, shoving him in the shoulder.

"Did you win in the end?"

"Of course I did."

"Oh God!" Gio falls into more laughter, his inked arms over his eyes. "No wonda' he's so obsessed with you." His giggling stops before mine, his face turning wistful. "Rose . . . back at the jailhouse . . . Greaseball cops'll do anything to get information—threats, booze, whateva'. But you don't gotta listen and you don't gotta talk. Don't you eva' do something like that for me again. I'd ratha' rot in that cage."

My own humor melts, my ears heating. "Yeah, well, you don't know what women have to do to get ahead in this world. All you have to do is walk into a room with a confident smile and that pistol between your legs. So I think the word you're searching for is *thank you*."

"And I think the word *you're* searchin' for is *rifle*," he says. My eyebrows knit together with a confused squint at his smirk. "Or *cannon*. Anythin' but *pistol*."

I roll my eyes with a laughing groan, my mouth twitching beneath the fatigue. As I shift on my pillow, my eyelids close, only fluttering to the softness of Gio's lips on my forehead.

12

THE SMELL OF TOASTING BREAD ROUSES ME FROM A DREAMLESS sleep. I jolt upright, my head searing with eye-stabbing pain. Heck is up way too early, and he never cooks, but maybe he got the inkling. Long shadows stretch across my bedroom floor, the squalid taste on my dry tongue wafting up to my nose. *What time is it?* Hell, I'm not sure what day it is. I push my disoriented frame from the tangled sheets, stumbling to my bathroom, small snippets of last night's dreadful adventure poking through my consciousness. Margaret's face. Gio was arrested. The office had no coffee. *Wait . . .*

Gio!

Pushing past the nausea, I strip down, running warm water into my claw-foot tub. Though the soaking scrub does little to ease my headache, the botanical oils I rub into my skin make the rest of me feel better. I give my mouth a thorough scour with tooth powder, running the brush over my tongue as well before sneaking back across the hall with a towel over my body. My hair is still wet when I trudge into the tiny kitchen, a silk bathrobe covering my cotton house frock. Besides Heck and my brother, Gio may be the first man to ever see me so casually, but I don't have the energy to doll up for anyone right now.

Still in his black trousers and white shirt from last night, my bustling hustler of a pianist works around the white cabinets like a professional chef, lifting the iron coffeepot from the burner with an oven mitt. His suspenders hang down the sides of his legs as he pours the steaming drink into two mugs, singing a soft jazz tune about the mischief one can get into when left with too many idle hours. His gritty baritone voice warms my belly and sends ripples across my arms, making me want to stand there and watch him open the top cabinet of the oven, scooping out crisping bread with a spatula. He nearly drops it as he turns around, his serenade halting as well.

"Hey there," he says with a cheerful smile. "You didn't have hardly no food, so I did what I could. No flour, even."

My laugh makes my head hurt, so I settle for a small grin, folding my arms. "Yeah, I usually get a sandwich during the day. Not a big breakfast eater."

"I can see that." Gio slides the bread onto two glass plates, carrying them to the table. I feel like I should help in some way, so I grab the coffee mugs before sitting down next to him. He taps the tabletop. "Thanks, boss. Nice furniture, by the way. Solid craftsmanship."

"It's oak," I say, blowing steam from my mug. I love coffee but hardly have the patience to brew it anymore. "My brother made it."

"Oh, nice. Didn't know you had any family around here."

My lips freeze against the teal rim, my head pounding. "I don't. I haven't seen them in a while."

"Yeah, I hear that," Gio says, biting into his toast. "I'd offa' you some suga' for that coffee, but—" He peers over his shoulder with a comical shrug at my perfectly lined canisters.

I manage a light chuckle. "Well, that's the secret to having a pristine kitchen. Never use it."

He sits back in his chair with a short laugh through the nose, his eyes sobering. My cheeks heat under his silent scrutiny. *What's he staring at?* I know I'm no movie star in this getup.

"I never seen you like this," he says.

"What?" I snort, staring into my drink. "A mess?"

"Was gonna say relaxed. Vulnerable, even." He tosses his half-eaten toast onto his plate, wiping his lip with his hand. "I don't mean that in a bad way. Just a different side'a you is all I'm sayin'."

The heat climbs into my neck as I pick at the rough corner of my bread. "Most people wouldn't like me if they really got to know me."

"Try me."

"What do you mean?"

"I don't know, um, tell me how you ended up in a place like this."

"I started working for Gus."

Gio shakes his head, folding his hands on the table as he sits up. "Nah, I mean before that. What made you want this life? Does your family know where you're at? Why the hell is there so much blue in your apartment?"

My giggle makes my head throb. "Oh no, Mr. Cattaneo. Just because you made it into my bed and toasted some bread doesn't mean I'm gonna give you the interview."

"Damn," he says, picking up his mug. "Guess I'm gonna hafta get you corked again to get you to talk to me."

Oh no. "What did I say?"

Gio's eyes twinkle like sable sequins. "Oh, nothin' really. Just how I'm the only guy for you, and how you been waitin' your whole life for a joka' like me."

"Aw geez." I laugh, cringing. "I'd never say anything like that. Not to anybody."

"That's right. You don't do the love thing."

"Ooh, I said that?"

"Implied—unfortunately for the rest of us." His warm smile assaults my iced heart, provoking my nerves. This guy can't take a hint.

Unless the problem isn't him. Maybe I can't take my own hint.

"Well, it's true," I say, pushing myself up from the table. "And don't take this the wrong way—I appreciate everything you've done to help me, but you seem like the kind of guy who wants more than I can give you, and I just don't want you wasting your time."

Gio rears back, his dark brows lowering. "Hey, that ain't fair. All I did was carry you away from some goon and make you breakfast. I ain't neva' got handsy with you, aside from that awkward night I nearly kissed you, which you made *very* clear—"

"Yeah, that's what I mean," I insist, heading toward the door with him on my heels. "If you just wanted up my skirt, it'd be different, but you don't. So it's not. Tucking me in, kissing my forehead—"

He lets out a laughing grunt, throwing his hands up. "Whoa there, Rose! You don't know me at all. I ain't never been accused of bein' a decent guy. I'm just not an animal like that jerk-face Salvatore. If all you want's a good time, just let me know, 'cause I sure ain't used to hearin' classy broads talk that way. I gotta say, it's doin' a lot for me right now."

"You're something else, you know that?" I stick my hands on my hips with a grumbling sigh that pounds my head. "Thing is, I kinda like you. But the other thing is, that's always when things go south."

"When you *kinda* like someone?"

"When it gets more complicated than that."

"No problem, boss," Gio says, snagging his cap from my coatrack. "I got a few irons in the fire myself." A giggle escapes my lips before I can stop it, picturing this edgy pianist making ladies swoon. "Oh, you thought that was funny."

"*Kinda.*" I attempt a more serious expression. "Who is it?"

"Jealous?"

"Hardly." A twinge of irritation flashes across my chest. *Of course not!* It flashes again.

Am I?

Gio leans back on the door, his arms crossing. "I was thinkin' of askin' out Penny. This city's gettin' lonely, if you get me."

I lower my chin, rolling my eyes. "She's not just a manager, Gio. Penny's asked to work the underbelly on the third shift."

He shrugs, raising an eyebrow. "It ain't my job to tell a lady how to make her money."

"How progressive of you." I laugh, my hands shooting to my head. "But nobody dates Penny. It's not her style. You don't have to lie to me. I won't judge you."

My pianist's melancholy returns, his eyes suddenly lost. "You know, you're right. I *don't* have to lie to you, which is kinda new to me." My frown follows his forlorn gaze to the sunlight that spills across the rug in the living room. "Rose . . . I'm not just Italian." He turns away, raking his hand through his hair. "I'm . . . half Jew. My name used to be Gabriel."

"Gio," I say, reaching for his shoulder. "You don't have to tell me anything. First off, you know I don't care about—"

"Please. Just listen this time." I hug my middle, biting the inside of my lip as he shifts on his feet, staring at the floor. I don't care about his criminal past, but the pain in his eyes is quite bothersome. Maybe that's not what he's trying to tell me. "My motha'—she got shut out from her family when she moved to America and married a workin'-class Jewish man. But not just any Jew—a political loudmouth. Got in a lot of arguments with a group'a immigrant Germans, debatin' about their new nationalist party in their homeland or some shit. My parents got killed durin' a hit in Philadelphia when I was nineteen. Said it was the wrong place, wrong time, but I know they was targeted. Got told I should watch my draft-dodgin' capitalist back if I stayed. Took my motha's Sicilian name, ended up in Chicago, and ran odd jobs to make it. It's been seven years. A damn lifetime ago."

Gio's shoulders hunch as he picks at his nails, his cheeks flushed. I lay my hand over his, reading his mild panic. "You're safe here, Gio."

With a slow nod, he looks up. "I wanna believe that. I know the different factions all have their problems here, but Kansas City's got somethin' goin' on that I haven't seen anywhere else."

As much as I hate to admit it, he's right. Amid the high-handed bigotry, Pendergast's loose laws and crime-boosting councils make it possible for all these groups to work together and, in some strange way, make it safer for people like us.

"I get it," I say, "but you don't have to be ashamed of who you are—not with me."

He gives my hand a pat. "I know. I'm really not. But havin' my own family targeted is hard to forget—and even harder to forgive."

His knuckles tell my palms of a young man weeping over his mother's body. *Oh, Gio.* "I'm so sorry. Really."

"I'm all right. I just . . ." His head turns to hide his blush as he drops his hands to his suspenders, pulling them to his shoulders. "I guess I mention all that shit to say that I know I don't got a real reason to dislike Heck."

"Other than association," I say, the realization as heavy as Gio's expression.

"Yeah, which I know ain't fair." His thumbs slide across his chest, tucking beneath his arms as he looks everywhere but at me. "And who knows? You puttin' this team togetha' might just be savin' me from some bitta'ness. He's a nice guy. I can see why you like 'im."

My surprise gives way to a sympathetic smile. Heck truly is anything but threatening—Gio obviously sees that now. But we all battle prejudice at some point in our lives.

And it takes real guts to admit it.

I must be looking starry-eyed because Gio is looking far too amused by my silence.

"So . . . you still like me or what?"

"Even more now, I think."

"Well"—his back straightens as he grabs onto his hips—"all right then. Back to the part of the story that actually helps our business. I ended up on one of Capone's teams in Chicago while he was still right hand to Johnny Torrio. After the North Side Gang shot Johnny back in January, Capone took ova' and I moved here."

"So I've heard," I say with a wry squint. "I had a real live gangster in my bed."

"And you wasted the opportunity." He smiles at my snort, pushing away from the wall. "But seriously. I was a nobody then, and I'm a nobody now. I just run shipments. Hell, I just help make those connections. But I think you can see how those connections can make a difference for Heck's club."

"*My* club."

A wicked smirk crosses his lips. "Thought you'd like that. Here's another one for ya—this city's love for jazz and juice is gettin' all kinds of attention, and Capone's definitely got his sights set on opening weekend. The Sunday lineup."

"For real?" I breathe, my excitement wavering beneath my tender nerves.

"For real. Confirmed yesta'day."

"Wait. Is that safe? Are *we* safe?"

Gio grins, rolling his eyes. "Rose, you run an entertainment venue. And you're buying *his* booze. As long as he's getting his cut, you ain't gotta worry.

"What's more, that mob boss brings big names. That's why all these factions are so shook up, 'cause when he gets here, you're gonna have the biggest benefactor there is. No one'll mess with you anymore."

I clap my hand over my mouth, my eyes widening. "Gio! Do you know what that would do for my club?"

Pressing his hat down over his messy hair, he pulls the door handle and tosses a grin over his shoulder. "Everything you ever wished for, boss."

THE TOAST IS COLD AND DRY, BUT I EAT IT ANYWAY AFTER HE leaves. It's not Gio's fault I don't have any butter in my refrigerator. Heck's the only reason I had rye in the first place, treating me with occasional delicacies from around the city. Otherwise, I live on apples, cheese, and olives. Washing my breakfast down with the remainder of Gio's tepid coffee, I pick up last week's Sunday paper from the oval coffee table. This day is going to be spent with my legs propped up and the sun warming my living room.

So when a determined knock sounds at my door, my jaw twists, my head rolling back onto the couch. *What now?* Wiping my mouth with a hand towel, I force myself from the firm cushions to the front door, half expecting to see Heck's playful smile, the carefree heir home early from his trust fund interrogation.

My spoiled mood thickens at the lanky ginger wringing her hands in my doorway. "Margaret?"

She peers down, giving me an idle once-over before squeezing past me into the living room. "Honestly, Rose, it's nearly eight in the morning. Just because you're blessed with natural beauty, doesn't mean you shouldn't try." My flat expression is my only response as she skitters across the patterned rug with a jolly gasp. "Is that a *davenport*? Just look at those clawed feet! Is it cherrywood? And that floral print is so modern." While I'm thrown by her unannounced visit, I disguise my horror with a tight-lipped shrug as she ogles my furniture like she plans to stay. Another tiny squeal chirps from her mouth. "You have the matching chair! Rose Lane, I didn't know you were so urbane."

"Oh. Okay, thanks," I say, shutting my door like I've let a fly in. Since I told her husband we were friends, I try to treat her as such, offering her a seat on my prized couch. Margaret's checkered suit dress and jacket aren't exactly hugging her curves, but they look smart with her short string of pearls and wavy curls like the first lady. My arms cross, my knees locking together as she bounces down next to me. "You're looking well. For a moment there I thought Grace Coolidge was at my door."

"Oh, Rose!" she giggles, wrinkling her nose. "Archie just hates this dress. He thinks it's too brassy for a girl of my station." Her smile fades like it's been doing so often lately, her eyes falling to her twisting fingers. "I'm really lucky to have a man who wants me to be better than I am."

"Uh-huh."

"I'm not here to ramble on about the pitfalls of new love, though. You'll find out soon enough, one day." Margaret's back straightens as she clears her throat. "But as my friend, I thought you should be one of the first to know—after my mother, of course."

My tightened shoulders relax, my eyebrows knitting. "Know what? Are you all right?"

Her normal vibrancy diminishes beneath her downcast countenance, though she seems to be trying desperately to maintain her composure this time. "I lost the baby."

"Oh no," I breathe. "I'm so sorry."

"Well, the doctor says it happens sometimes." Her eyes shut as she balls her hands up in her lap.

All of the pain I've encountered with my friends and family lately has me feeling both helpless and determined. I know I must do something to help. *But how?*

I reach out a tentative hand, laying my palm over her fist, nearly flinching at her miserable contemplations. But as I tighten my fingers around her knuckles, a familiar sensation flutters behind my eyes, much like my wrestling match on the balcony with her precious Archie but without the rage. In an instant, my mouth is filled with a flavor I definitely recognize—a potion I often stirred for my abuela. The mixture of rose petals, tea, and bog water isn't exactly unpleasant, although it's all certainly shocking. I have no time to discern much else. The snippets of thoughts in Margaret's mind turn to a scene like a moving picture, and far more disturbing, her voice isn't the only one I hear. Her husband's shouts echo through my ears, listing her faults before his fist sinks into her abdomen. He drags her through the house by her hair that he hates. She cries a thousand apologies. The horrible scene is faded and hard to hold on to, especially since I've never read this far before on anyone. Ever.

Now I can *see* it.

Even though I'm doing all I can to suppress the urge to shudder, I want to keep exploring—maybe find something else about that son of a bitch I can use to help her. Testing the presence of my magic that has remained steady so far, I take a step further into her memory, following Margaret's kicking feet to where her husband throws her to the floor like a burglar in her own home. Her emotions are so powerful, they send my own nose stinging before she takes a loud breath beside me.

"He and Archie talked it over outside my hospital room," she says, her voice yanking me back to the couch. "And they decided I'm under too much stress. The best thing to do now is to take it easy at home until we can try again."

I blink, shaking my head to refocus on the present. This feels different than the other recent times my power decided to take over. I've never felt any of this before, and it keeps shifting inside me. I definitely need to find time to talk to my abuela.

Margaret's words finally hit me as I realize what she just said. "Wait—at home? As in, quit your job?"

"Yes, it's for the best."

"But you love your job."

"I was going to have to leave it eventually," she explains as though reciting a practiced confession. "For the baby."

My hands cup around her fists, which weep hopelessness into my palms. "What if it happens again?"

"No." She shakes her head. "Archie promises to take extra care of me next time. You should have seen how despairing he was. And the doctor seems sure I can carry to term."

"Oh, I'm sure he was despairing. What I'm wondering is, what if Archie hits you again?"

Margaret's head shoots up, her mouth dropping as she snatches her hands away. "What would make you say that? He would never. I can't—"

"Hey," I say, leveling my eyes. "Like I told another friend this morning, you don't have to hide anything from me."

She looks at me for a full minute, her teeth pinching her trembling bottom lip before she peers around my apartment, waving her hand. "Someone was here before me *this* early on a Saturday? You're not even dressed for company."

I wiggle my eyebrow. "Depends on the company."

"Oh gee!" she suddenly laughs, swiping a darting tear from her eye. "Aren't you progressive? I could never live that way."

I press my lips together with a dramatic squint. "What way, exactly?"

The forlorn look in her watering eyes darkens, a long gasp signaling the deluge that pours down her cheeks, her mouth twisting. "Free."

She grabs the hand towel from the coffee table, burying her face as her sobs sputter out like a dying engine, her breath catching the harder she tries to hold it in. Even with my arms around her, she continues, her shoulders shaking and her head in her lap.

"That isn't true, honey," I insist, rubbing her back. "I say drop that pilot."

"Aw!" she wails into her knees. "I can't divorce him, Rose. I'll go back to having nothing!"

My eyes roll. "It's better than being with a guy who treats you like *you're* nothing. Besides, you've got our friendship. Not that that's saying much, but I'll listen. And I'll *never* hit you." Her long frame rises up with hopeful rounded eyes, her freckled face red and blotchy. "I'm not as bad as I seem. Just ask Heck."

"Oh!" she squeaks, dabbing her nose. "I heard he was opening a new club. What a scandalous consort to an engagement announcement."

I should let her gab, let her come to her own conclusions. But as she pours out her advice on bridal announcement photos, giving my arm the occasional tap, I read nothing but sincerity. Her trust in our camaraderie is warming with subtle affection. She's come to me for advice. Shared her secrets, even if unwillingly at first. An office gossip knows better than to divulge those to anybody they don't trust. She doesn't think me her friend. She *is* my friend.

Which is something new for me. *I'll give it a go.*

"Well, technically, the club is mine," I interject with an absent air.

"*What?*"

My lips curl at her awe. "Margaret, he cosigned for me to purchase the jazz club. I'm starting a new business."

Her mouth falls open. "You're kidding! You tawdry rascal. How venturesome! Next thing you'll be telling me it's a cover for a speakeasy." She collapses into delighted laughter that gives way to light chuckles at my pursed lips. "Rose . . . for crying out loud, don't tell me you're a bootlegger."

Talking to such a prim woman about the underworld is strange. And kind of fun. I kick my bare feet up on the coffee table with a small shrug. "I've been running one on my own for two years in the jazz district."

"Jeepers." She shakes her head with an impressed smile. "Wait, you and Heck—you're not in love, are you?"

"Was love ever a requirement for marriage?"

"I knew there was more to you than meets the eye!"

"I could say the same about you." I give her an earnest smile as wonder etches across her face. "You're smart. And beautiful. Strong as hell. And if you want to write articles, write them. If you don't want to be married, don't be. I know a good lawyer, and I can find you a place to stay until you get your own apartment again." Her motionless face stays locked in my direction. *Is she in shock?* "Margaret?"

Dropping the towel to the floor, she bends forward, pressing her pale mouth against mine. My eyes shoot open at her sudden advance and the hefty amount of allure that loads at my lips, ready to deploy at its whim as if my magic knows how long it's been since I've kissed anyone. These few seconds explain a whole hell of a lot. I'm not the first girl she's kissed. And it started long before she married that bigot.

The scent of roses tells me not to linger.

With a sharp gasp through the nose, I slant back, holding her shoulders with a firm grip. I don't mean to be so abrupt, but I can't risk charming Margaret. Her situation is complicated enough. She's starting to take my alarmed expression the wrong way, bumbling about being on medicine for dizzy spells, her face as red as my favorite rouge.

"The doctor says I'm still not well—"

"Wait, honey. It's okay."

"I know Archie will be waiting for me. I'll call on you soon!" She ignores my assurance as she bolts from my apartment like the building is on fire.

"Great catching up," I grumble to the door, throwing myself back onto the best couch in the entire world. I've known women like her my whole life—beaten down until there's nothing left of them but a fake smile and a string of pearls. The real rub here is that she was beaten down long before Oswald the Terrible came along. She'll never be able to be who she says she is as long as she lets people like him *tell* her who she is. It seems like she wants that cycle to stop, but like the rest of us, doesn't exactly know how. Society has been telling her what to be since she was born.

It's just not *fair*. It's not right.

And even though it's not my problem, I find myself dressed with my phone receiver in my hand, spinning the numbers on the rotary for Margaret's favorite weekend beauty parlor.

"Yes, it's for Mrs. Swinson," I snip back to the curt debutant on the other line who reads my message back to me. "That's right—the grocery at Eighteenth and Vine. Just tell her that's where she can find me."

The rude bird hangs up before I can say anything else. *Right back at'cha, lady.* I don't know if Margaret will ever show up. But at least she'll know it's a safe place she can go. The clanking ringer in my hand sounds off, the startling volume sending my heart racing. I take a deep, irritated breath, unhooking the earpiece.

"Hello?"

"Luna, I've been trying to call you for five minutes."

My frayed nerves have my hands shaking at the dread in my brother's voice. "Javi, what's happening?"

"Everyone's okay. But you're gonna need to meet me at the boxcar. Family meeting."

I leave my phone on the floor, my arm dangling off the side of the couch. *Damn you, Saturday. Damn you.*

JAVIER IS WAITING FOR ME BY THE SLIDING DOOR. AS I STEP INTO the entryway of our childhood home, the tension in his face tightens my chest, my mother's heels pacing the wood planks. Gloria's graying raven hair is set in its perfect crown, her sharp eyebrows neatly pointed as she reaches the corner of the tiny kitchen counter, turning back toward the living area. She lays her hand on the cinched waist of her polka-dot dress with a stern purse of her lips.

"Niño," she says to my brother in her lectury voice. "I don't need my children worrying themselves over these things. Your abuela and I will take care of this."

Javier's wild hair curls after he's showered if he doesn't comb it right away, so clearly he's been rushed; I raise my eyebrows at the clean white T-shirt that hangs over the waistband of his pants. He didn't even take the time to attach his suspenders before leaving his apartment. "Javi, what's going on?"

He turns to me, pulling a folded yellow envelope from his back pocket. "This is what's going on. Mamá started having her mail sent to my place, which I bring over every Saturday—"

"To save me from having to go to the post office!" Gloria yells, her indignant finger in the air. "Not so my only son can snoop into my business!" She throws her hands up, stalking behind the couch where my abuela sits on the burnt-orange cushions, knitting a colorful blanket in the sunlight that spills from the small windows. "Aye, aye, aye! Mamá, tell your grandson to go back home if he's here to admonish his elders!"

The old woman's wrinkled brown hands continue pushing the long needles through the tangled holes, working their way from red to yellow. Her floral dress brushes against her ankles where her stockings bunch as she shifts to peer at my mother as though realizing there are people in the room.

"Oh," she says with a toothless smile. "You upset yourself too much."

At my mother's dramatic groan, I seat myself on the oak coffee table, eyeing Javier with a shrug. Typical family argument: everyone wants me on their side, and I don't even know what's going on. "So . . . what are we upset about, exactly?"

"Nothing, hija." My mother flaps her hand around, smoothing her dress. "Let me get you some food, eh? You haven't had a decent meal in—"

"Hermanita—"

"Don't you dare, niño!"

My brother claps his hands together, his intense brow lowering. I've never seen Gloria shut her mouth so quickly. I've also never seen Javier's determined look directed at her, either. "Mamá. Por favor. You've cared for us. Luna and I have cared for you. And that doesn't stop just because we don't live here anymore. Through the years, I've promised father's ghost I wouldn't abandon you. Countless times, I've spoken to the sky on your behalf. Countless times, I've worked late hours so you can have the extras for your baking. So Luna could continue schooling. So we don't live in filth. And I won't be talked over as if my voice holds no weight in this family. Does my sacrifice deserve any respect?"

Gloria taps her long fingers on the top of the couch, her chin lifting as she circles around, lowering herself next to our abuela. Javier grips the edge of the floral upholstery with both hands, his shoulders deflating with a long sigh.

"Luna," he continues, his tone softening, "I received Mamá's tax bill. The city is condemning the boxcar community to make room for new projects. I guess the steel corp is going to start ramping up production."

My heart twists at my mother's dejected face, her rigid back almost slumped next to my humming abuela. "How can they do that?" I ask. "Where's everyone supposed to go?"

"This area's been zoned industrial for a while now," Javier says, laying a gentle hand on our mother's shoulder. "Hell, even the Serbian church is movin' out. *Everybody's* movin' out. It was only a matter of time."

She pats his knuckles, her spine erect once again. "Watch that language, niño. You may be a grown man, but I am still your mother."

"Sí, señora," he says with a small smile as he leans down to kiss her forehead. "That brings us to our next item of business." She groans, her head dropping forward. "Mamá, I know you hate the idea of having an apartment—"

"Hijo, I have already looked, and the closest apartment that we can afford is in Argentine, Kansas."

Might as well be Argentina. I can't stand the thought of them being farther away. "What about that house in Westside near the Guadalupe Center?"

Gloria points her hand. "We have enough for the deposit or the tax bill. Not both."

"It's a nice place," Mama Sunday interjects before returning to her light humming.

Javier's fuzzy hair frizzes under his raking hand. "I'm sure it is, Abuela, but it's too expensive for now. Maybe if you stayed with me for a while—or Luna."

My eyes narrow with mild panic. "Javi, I'm in the middle of an acquisition."

"Oh, you can sneak in your midnight visitors, but you can't hide a couple of old ladies?"

"*Excuse* me?"

Our mother clears her throat. "Perdón, but I am not old."

"You know what?" Javier presses me with a snorting scowl. "Just tell people you've hired some poor immigrants to clean your apartment!"

"My goodness, Javi," I say, my ears lighting. "Where is this coming from?"

He shakes his head, his fiery eyes cooling as he leans his forearms on the couch between the matriarchs. "I don't know, hermanita. I just . . . Sometimes I'm not sure where you stand on things, and I need to know that we're together—with the club, with this family. With *everything.*"

Like a dagger through my soul, a burning exhale falls from my open mouth, my nose tightening with the threat of tears. "How can you be saying this to me? I've only ever done what was expected of me—what Mamá trained me to do. My success. My achievements.

This was what *she* wanted. It's what you all wanted."

But is it what I want? I swallow the large lump in my throat, sniffing back the burn. Before I may have doubted it. Now, however, the answer is a wholehearted *yes*. I have a chance to own something, to have something that's mine, that I did for me. To say I'm abandoning the family, though?

Al Diablo con eso.

"This family is my whole heart. I would face anything for it." The words I choke out lower my brother's eyes. And I *would* face anything—my entire life spent being trained to bust out of the box-car barriers, plowing a place for us all when I reach my destination. But the closer I get to my ambitions, the further away my heritage sails on this teeming ocean of unmarked cultural waters, fighting the deluge of every torrential pitfall imaginable. As big as that is, I never thought I'd be untethered from the three people in this room, and being accused of that practically destroys me. Teardrops make their way down to my chin, feeding my words. "The mafia wants to control me, the Klan wants to shut me down, every man I know is trying to push me around, and now the one safe place I have in this world acts like it doesn't even recognize me."

"Luna," my brother says, his voice softer than it's ever been, "I am for you, not against you. I'm sorry you've ever felt anything different."

I keep my tired eyes on our abuela's knotted hands as they continue to work. "Yeah, me too."

The cool air from the windows mingles with the aroma of the mole—a chocolate chili sauce from my childhood—that's simmering on the burner in the corner. It mocks me with memories of a girl named Luna, asking me what Rose is doing here. The old bruja's humming ceases, her face turning in my direction in a slow lag, the glittering dust particles in the sunlight freezing in the air. My mother and brother stare at different planks of the floor, their hopelessness suspended in time. With a sluggish blink, I tilt my head at Mama Sunday's soft smile.

"So much doubt, niña," she says, her ethereal voice tingling like ancient bells. The brown in her eyes begins swirling like willow trees beneath a calm wind. "Such despair."

"Abuela . . . something's been happening to me."

"New taste? Curious spells—diente de león."

"Yes!" I was going to wait until later when we could talk in private, but having my brother's judgments frozen in time outside this bubble that my abuela created is just fine with me. "I've tasted dandelions, and something bitter, and I apparently scared a family with my singing, and I may have made some jerk vomit."

"Your branches thirst. They long to grow."

I shake my head, the angst of my run-in with the fates pouring out of me. "I walked around in someone's mind this morning, Abuela. I don't know what I'm doing. What if I'm dangerous? What if—"

A long exhale escapes my abuela's lips like a ghost stretching from a century-long sleep. The willows in her eyes rock back and forth across her pupils. "Where is faith?"

Ask my brother that, I want to say bitterly. Instead a tear creeps down my cheek. "If I knew what faith was, then I might be able to find it, Abuela."

"Faith made of hope. Evidence of what we no see."

"Hope?" My lip quivers. "I don't think I have that anymore."

The old witch's smile deepens, her irises like swinging trees on a stormy night. "Faith is gift. You lack faith? Ask for more."

"But, Abuela, how—"

"The deposit on that house is more than I would ever ask of you," Gloria insists as my brother hands her a colorful hand towel to dab her eyes. I blink again, my eyelids fluttering fast and hard as my abuela hums, her tongue between her gums as she concentrates on her knitting needles. Tucking my magic and identity crisis away for another time, I turn my attention to problems I can actually solve.

"Well," Javier says, "I can cover about a third." He steps around the couch, handing me the tax bill with my mother's notes at the bottom. She's right. The rental deposit is expensive, but she could walk to the bakery if she needed to. I'll have just enough after Heck and I cash in on the loan. I was going to use it to cover anything else that might come up with the club, but my mother has given me everything. It's the least I can do.

"I'll pay the rest, Mamá."

"Luna, you can't! I won't let you."

My brother eyes me with an accepting nod. "We're doing it, Mamá. I'll set the table. That mole isn't gonna eat itself."

I wiggle my eyebrows at him, turning back to our mother. "¡Su hijo es muy mandón!"

"I'm not bossy. I'm hungry, hermanita."

"Luna! English!"

And like that, we're family once more.

13

"SOCIETY LADIES AND GENTLEMEN, WDAF IS THE FIRST TO AN-nounce news from the distinguished Hyde Park area in downtown, straight off the presses . . ."

I shush the excited squeals of my staff, turning back to pinching my thumbnail between my teeth. In the center of the crimson room of my new club, we huddle around the modern radio box, its fancy gold plates and superior reception a vast improvement to the one at the River Rose. "The esteemed Heck Kessler, great-nephew of our city's beloved George Kessler, has acquired the ballroom at Hotel Bellerive. The Casbah Lounge opens next Friday, May thirtieth, to host the Bennie Moten Orchestra. Come out for jazz, dancing, and a kippy good time. Floor seats are three dollars, VIP will cost ya five. You're not gonna wanna miss Bennie Moten's hard-swinging ragtime style. Come down to the Bellerive to land your seat today!"

The muffled broadcaster continues to list ballroom and music events around the city, but I'm not listening, my own excitement splitting my face into a grin as I whirl around, throwing my arms over Heck's taut shoulders. My brother turns the black knobs on the wooden box as the signal starts to crackle, the remaining staff embracing around the rustic tables as Gio calls for a celebratory shot of gin.

"Not too much, girls!" Penny calls out, adjusting the turquoise feather in her dark hair. The deep blue sings on her bronze skin. "You all gotta work tonight! We're gonna show these darbs what we got!"

Amid the happy cheers, my fiancé skips around, shoving shot glasses into everyone's hands. As Javier fills them, he throws back witty comments to those who call out a playful assessment of Heck's boldly printed suit of green-and-brown herringbone. I take it all in, their joy and mine, before my raised hand silences the room. The sparkling dancers and waitresses wriggle with eager smiles.

"All right," I say, "let's review the protocol before the guests arrive."

Penny clutches my arm. "You're gonna do amazing, Rose!"

"Yeah!" one of the guys hollers from the band's brass section. "Especially in that getup!" I look down at the plunging neckline of my silver beaded dress with a slight flush, jutting out my hip in response to the appreciative whistles.

"You're *all* going to do amazing," I reply. The musicians, dudded up in fine, crisp shirts and slacks, tilt their fedoras around the tables while Clip rolls his brown eyes at their silliness. My brother's elbow digs into Heck's side with subtle laughter at something the showy aristocrat is saying in his ear. Javier's bartender uniform and apron are always impeccable, but his black hair has an extra sheen tonight, his clean yet rugged looks capturing more than a few wandering eyes in the joint. The jovial faces around me lift my chin, moistening my own eyes. This is my other family, and although we're in a new house, the resonance of home electrifies the atmosphere with adventure instead of worry. We'll succeed or fail together. Either way, we'll be together. Emotion gathers at the bridge of my nose with its irritating sting as I force composure to the rest of my face.

"I want everyone to know," I start with a clear of my throat, "how proud I am of all your efforts in preparing for this private opening. While this place is several times larger than the River Rose, we will operate the underbelly of the Casbah Lounge in much the same way. The ballroom upstairs opens next week, so tonight should give us some good practice serving patrons from a different part of town than we're used to—"

"Yeah," our curvy lead singer teases from her barstool. "Brook-sys and dappa's."

"Hey now, Doris." I point a playful finger, joining the chuckling in the room. "Yes, they're well-off, but they're not all old. I've seen the list."

Nickels's muscular frame steps beside her as he holds his arms out with a side grin. "'Ey, I'll be patrollin' around the gamblin' area if you need me. You know I'll take care'a ya if some darb tries ta lay a hand on ya."

"Yeah, well, I can take care'a myself," Doris shoots back, piping a cigarette through her jade holder. Her matching eyes ice over at the resident bodyguard, whose innocent brows shoot up while he fumbles in his pocket for a lighter.

"You don't gotta be mean about it, Bearcat," he whines. His nervous shifting and flushing cheeks give away his darting gaze as he tries to avoid looking down her crimson dress.

With an eye-rolling grunt, she crosses her legs, white smoke leaking from her lips before her face softens. "Oh, heel, Nicky. I'm just nervous. I ain't sang in front of a crowd this big."

"That's completely normal, Doris," I say. "We've never been here before, none of us, but we're going to run this place just like our last one—just a little more polished. In fact, let's review the schedule one more time."

I nod to Gio, who looks a little anxious himself, fastening the shirt buttons around his wrists. With me and Heck hobnobbing, I won't be able to coordinate between the leadership staff like I usually do. All the big shots are coming to tonight's private opening in the Drawing Room. If we're a hit, next weekend's grand opening will be a knockout. I barely had the green to shell out for a second piano player to trade shifts with him, but I have to use people I trust.

"All right, team. Clip's got the music covered, hoppin' tunes ta keep 'em gamblin'." He salutes our fearless band leader, a stubbed cigar hanging from Charlie's dark lips. "Like usual, all waitresses will report to Javi regardin' anythin' on this menu." In his hand, the black-and-white framed card shimmers with a golden border, listing the underbelly's delicacies with the title *Underwood Baking Company*. "Chiffon is gin, pineapple cake is whiskey, cherry gelatin is cordial, and so forth. Your tips are split with him, same as the Riva' Rose. Any questions about private rooms go to Penny."

Our staff's head of red-lighting sashays forward, her turquoise lace sashaying with her. "Yeah, well, it's the same as it's always been, except you got better rooms, with cheese and fruit, and those suits'll pay twice as much. You treat these dewdroppers like the kings they think they are, and they'll leave here with empty pockets and thank us for it." The glittering ladies cheer and push out their red lips at each other, my own mouth curving. Penny's always to the point and damn proud of her job. Sex is a business just like anything else, and I'm blessed to have her on my team. "With that bein' said, if any of my girls needs a break for a while, I'll move your shifts to the ballroom upstairs when it opens next week. No questions asked. I get it. I been there. Until then, let's work these gams. Heck didn't have us buff our legs for nothin'!"

My fiancé's honored bow lights the room once again with laughter as I dismiss our first downtown staff meeting, the excited scurries of two-toned loafers and sparkling shoes clunking across the floors. My heart stings more than a little when I catch Javier's forlorn eye behind the bar. His last night coordinating the drink orders before opening weekend has made him more stoic than usual, our flirty waitresses fawning over his slicked-back hair barely evoking a smile. I need him more than the few potted ferns we were able to bring into the club. I don't think I can stomach hiring anyone else, even though I know I have to.

It's my place, but it's not my town, so I don't make all the rules. *Not yet anyway.*

As the band settles onto the stage opposite the bar, Gio's fingers pinch my elbow. I glance down at his shirtsleeves. "I see you made an effort tonight."

"Yeah, well, since we slept togetha', I thought I should thank you in *some* way." He shakes his head at my flat stare, the scars in his eyebrow crinkling. "C'mon, Rose. I'm just razzin' ya. I know we're friends and that's all we're gonna be. And that ain't nothin'. It means a lot to me, your trust. This business. I don't wanna mess that up."

"You haven't," I say with a soft smile. The worry in his fingers subsides, sending relief to my elbow. As Charlie's low, grumbling voice beckons Gio from the stage, my juice supplier gives a soft pinch to my chin before sidling off with a wink.

Now that that's settled . . .

I straighten the sleeveless band of my dress, squaring my shoulders as my brother jogs to the service side of the black marble, Nickels taking his place by the entrance. The metal knuckles around his hand gleam as his fingers ready around the iron handle. I'm glad I was able to get my abuela to bless a few ferns and hazel twigs to increase protection in this place since my others were smashed into oblivion. I wish I had a couple of cactuses, and I'd pay serious money for the good luck that blessed fennel brings, but the few potted plants will have to do. Mama Sunday can only do so much in her older age. I tell myself that it's going to be a great night, throwing silent prayers toward the ferns. My courage comes with a deep breath through the nose.

"This is it," Heck's tickling voice whispers through my hair, his arm sliding around my waist. "Rose Lane and her scarlet sanctuary."

"Indeed," I reply. The charged thrill courses through my limbs. "Open the doors, Mr. Ibina."

I COULDN'T HAVE ASKED FOR A BETTER PRIVATE OPENING. THE Drawing Room's gold-trimmed walls and ashtrays offer the underbelly club a rustic decadence fit for modern royalty. Toasted tobacco smoke drifts around a variety of wavy bobs and slicked hair tonic as my flappers present our venue's finest spirited delicacies courtesy of the man from Chicago. Clip's saxophone belts around us, Doris's husky voice and the saucy jazz numbers he chose for the night doing their job as double-breasted dappers whisper in their waitresses' ears before being led off to the private rooms. Nicky settles a dispute near Giuseppe's spinning roulette wheel in the gambling corner with a warning look. The patrons tip their genteel wide-brimmed hats with apology. I send him an approving nod, too nervous to allow myself the comfort of contentment just yet. Things are going so well.

Too well.

Halting my rolling eyes at my own negativity, I tighten my grip around Heck's arm as he mercifully blabs on with the highest-rolling craps table. My eyes follow the rolling golden dice with relief as they bounce along the green felt, landing on numbers that make half the table groan, the other half cheering and raising their amber-filled glasses. This is the last of our rounds. My aching feet yearn for a respite by the bar. Most men want to talk with Heck anyway, treating me like his trophy with flirty winks, clapping him on the shoulder. I'm the damn owner, but this isn't the time to challenge their chauvinism. Not while I need their money.

The table's dealer clears his throat, smoothing his evergreen vest to signal the start of a new game. The other players toss wooden coins as Penny saunters off with the assistant to the city alderman. Heck's lips hit mine in a quick kiss while I'm still smirking after our head flapper, my insides jolting. My allure seems dormant amid my apprehension, but I know better. He should be more careful. I widen a fake smile at his questioning look, knowing we have to play up our relationship in front of these darbs.

"Darling," he says, his teeth shining back at me, "will you be all right without my company for a while? It appears our waitresses are left without their manager."

"Of course." *Finally.* "I'll see how Mr. Alvarado is getting on."

I want to limp, the straps of my new shoes biting into my ankles, but I maintain a light stroll as I make my way to the long bar along the wall. A tall ritzy drink of water sits with his hands around a small glass, his side-slicked hair and white suit gleaming beneath the bronze wall sconces. As if serenading the moment, Clip's lower-toned sax belts a smooth, slow melody, the stand-up bass and light cymbals joining the sultry story. The man lifts his deep-set hazel eyes that beckon with interest at my approach as the rim of his glass hits the cupid's bow of his lip. Continuing his leisurely appraisal, he straightens his back—a rivaling posture to Heck's with more subtle conceit.

"Miss Lane," he says, his voice as smooth as his angular jaw. "May I buy you a drink?" I peer over my bare shoulder toward the stage, the dressing room doors swinging on either side. "Unless your fiancé wouldn't approve, of course."

My head snaps back around, my hands hitting my waist. "I don't need approval from anyone to have a drink in my own club."

"The fact that he allows you to own one says a lot about him," he quips, sizzling the tips of my ears. At my stern scowl, his deep-throated laugh rings through his immaculate teeth. "It was meant to be a positive assertion. I don't think for a minute that anyone controls you. Especially Kessler."

I lift my chin, sliding onto the padded stool next to this cake-eater who thinks he's the cat's meow—my favored fare. The silver beads of my dress shimmy, tickling my lower thigh as I let the hem shift with my crossing legs. Javier sets a long-stemmed cocktail glass on a napkin in front of me with a knowing glance. Tending to my dreams has left certain needs of mine feeling pretty damn neglected, my only prospect at physical satisfaction lately lying somewhere between a conflicted mobster and a lovesick musician. I need some normalcy, emptying myself of my worries in a game without rules or commitment. I want my old self back again. And this libation is just the man to give it to me.

The costly vermouth mixture glides down my throat, the dry vodka balancing out the spices. My brother sure knows how to make a martini. "What do you mean by that?" I ask lightly, lowering the coned top of my glass. "'Especially Kessler'?"

Another laugh escapes this suitor's mouth, his expression growing wolfish like a clever storybook character lurking in the shadows behind Little Red Riding Hood. "I suppose that wasn't the most polite way to begin a conversation with a lady. Please, allow me to introduce myself." His hand extends to mine, lifting my knuckles to a heart-shaped mouth that confesses his enticing intentions to my receptive skin. "I'm Stuart Kensington."

I let my hand linger, shoring up his pride as I read his cunning perception. He's spent most of the evening sizing up the room, waiting for my fiancé and me to separate. My approach was a pleasing happenstance he now wants to take full advantage of . . . not that I mind.

"Pleased to meet you, Mr. Kensington," I say, taking my hand back. "I don't think I've seen your name on the list. What part of the city are you from?"

"St. Louis, actually. I'm only here on business with a few colleagues, who were dragged to the private rooms hours ago." He lifts a copper eyebrow, provocation glinting in his eyes.

I suppress a smile as his tongue flicks over his bottom lip, warming my chest along with my vermouth mixer. "St. Louis, hm? So you know Heck?"

"Quite well," Stuart admits, his gaze drifting across the room to the waitresses who keep flagging my debonair fiancé down for his attention. He nods in our direction, blowing me a kiss and sending a short wave to the glossy man next to me. Stuart's wolfish smile deepens as he leans closer to me. "In fact, we boarded two summers in the same finishing school. I see he's still consorting in odd circles."

My heart skips. *Uh-oh.* My palms grow clammy, our cover on the fringe of discovery. The suitor's ice clinks as he tilts his glass before wiping his lip with his thumb. "Please forgive my crude observation. His lifestyle is none of my business. I only meant to provoke a real smile from you, although I understand your apprehension about discussing this in such a public setting. We can always go somewhere else to talk."

I squint at Stuart's coltish challenge. "Do you normally pursue taken women?"

"Sometimes," he admits without batting an eye. "But you're not taken aback . . . or dismissing me . . . *are* you?"

My eyes fall to his unbelievably kissable mouth, my brother's clearing throat a mile away. Leaning on the bar, I lay my chin in my hand with a satisfied smile. "What a rude question, Mr. Kensington. I hardly know you."

"What would you like to know?"

"Everything."

"MISS LANE," A STERN VOICE SAYS FROM BEHIND US, STARTLING me as much as the halting music. Spinning around on my padded stool, I shoot an apologetic glance to Stuart before standing to my aching feet. My blond husband-to-be bolts from the dressing room at the non-commotion, adopting his most indignant walk across the wooden floors toward the bar area. The way he weaves around the tables and a thick crowd of suits makes his approach less dramatic than he likely intended.

In the entryway, Mr. Cornwell's wispy white hair glows over his reddening scalp, his nervous finger pushing up his rounded spectacles. Two men in plain suits breeze into the club after him, their police badges gleaming under the sconces. A medium-statured man trails after them, his narrowed nose and hawk eyes pointed at me with embittered accusation. The hotel owner stammers, straightening his tie like it's going to make him taller, but my accuser continues walking past him in my direction.

I definitely needed those damn cactuses.

"Well, it looks like we finally found the place," Salvatore says, shoving his hands into the pockets of his baggy slacks. "Ice was beginnin' to think he wasn't invited to such a prestigious preopening. An oversight like that could make a guy feel unappreciated."

A prickle of irritation beds down my angst, a chafe against my dormant temperament. I'm tired of making men feel appreciated. My head cocks to the side, my nostrils flaring. "It wasn't an oversight, Mr. Salvatore, and you know it."

His narrow neck spots with pink. "See now, baby, that hurts my feelings."

"Is this guy bothering you, Miss Lane?" Stuart interjects, reaching my side at the same time Heck does. A low murmur hums through the room, a few chairs shifting near the roulette wheel.

"Who's this?" Salvatore snaps, sticking a cigarette between his lips with an upward sneer. "Your new belle?"

Stuart's mouth is pretty, even when it's turned down. "*Excuse* me? Who do you think—"

"¡Basta ya!" I recognize my brother's insistent command before I can whirl back around, instant panic climbing up my arms like heated nerves. One of the policemen has his hand deep inside the cash register, the other meeting Javier's darkening eyes in a silent threat. Their ill-mannered thievery doesn't stop my brother's mouth as he continues his protest. "Fifty dollars? Get a real job, you blottos."

"Dirty bindle punk," the scowling officer hisses, forcing him back with a menacing step. His partner lets out a snorting laugh, filling his pocket with a tip of his brown hat. "Attaboy. Now get back to serving drinks to your betters."

Somewhere around panic and boiling, my fingers tighten into fists. If we can just get through next weekend, I'll be a famous club owner with enough clout to pay off my own cops. And the first thing I'll do is make sure no one will ever talk to Javier like that again. But this night's already going to hell, and I might not have that chance.

We might not even *make* it to next weekend.

Clip's band begins a moody number with a brush-tapped snare, the saxophone bleating like a sneaky criminal avoiding his captors in the shadows.

"Betters?" my brother asks, heat seeping into his voice. His ears redden, my own face lighting. *Come on, Javi. Not here. Not now.* As Rose, I had to learn fast how these games are played. I know when to shut up for my own good. On the other hand, I also want to give these jerk cops a piece of my mind. Then there's Luna—the side of me whose thoughts are dark as a midnight river dance right now. *If those men lay a hand on my brother . . .*

As a bouquet of flavors scales across my tongue, I realize that letting Luna have her say could be more devastating to my opening night than anything Javier could do. More alarmingly, someone could accidentally get hurt. I've got to defuse the situation, but my brother's hardening face is already melting the officers' smirks.

"There's nothing about you that's better than me," he says, looking one of the cops dead in the eyes.

The murmuring in the room grows to harsh whispers and shocked chuckles as smoke streams from Salvatore's nose, which points right at me. "Tell your bean-eatin' bartender to shut the hell up if he knows what's good for him. I've already gotta put up with your mouth. I ain't takin' lip from some dirty immigrant, too."

My mouth boils in a botanical stew. For the hundredth time tonight, I wish I could control Luna a little better. *I'd let her have you, Salvatore.*

His head lifts in a signal to his henchmen with badges, his eyes darting to the dashing visitor beside me. "I expect a better reception next time I come calling. And lose the ginger, huh?"

The crooked cops grab a few potted ferns before the door drifts shut behind them, sending my searing eyes into an aggravated squint. Salvatore obviously still feels that my plants are a sign of my noncompliance at the River Rose. Guys like him can't handle the loss of control—over what club I buy, and even over the ferns. If I weren't seething, I'd be more entertained by how offended he is by them.

Stuart furrows his brow at Salvatore's quick exit. "What did that goon just call me?"

"I'm so sorry Mr. Kensington," I say, wiping my damp palms on my dress. At least that's over. "He's my old landlord and he's just sore our contract is ending."

"He took your foliage."

"He does that." *Dammit, Salvatore.* Those plants are what keeps him from doing more; he just doesn't know it. And they're damn hard to come by. My abuela slept for days after preparing new dirt for those planters.

The spectacled hotel owner stands dumbfounded, his flabbergasted animations coming back to life like a rosy-cheeked marionette. "Mr. Kessler, we've been over this. Your bartender is to have a white supervisor. This employee obviously does not know his place."

I hold up a subtle hand to shut my brother's opening mouth. "Mr. Cornwell, *I* am the club manager down here. I'm supervising him."

"I will not buy into that, Miss Lane. Neither women nor owners are appropriate supervisors to waitstaff." His nose sniffs as he lifts it higher in the air. "Your ignorance is astounding."

"My *ignorance*—"

Heck squares his boldly printed shoulders. "My fiancée is the brightest, most capable—"

"Keep your hand off my fanny, you creep!" All heads crane to the stage, where our lead singer stomps up the small steps, her crimson fringe flying around her legs as she points a painted finger into the audience. "I ain't for sale!"

"Ease up, baby," the flushing patron calls out, tossing her a coin. "It was barely a pet."

Her ivory cheeks turn nearly the same color as her dress among the tittering room as she bats away the flying piece of copper. "Yeah, well, I'll give ya somethin' to pinch, you goon!"

"Make it hot, sweetheart!"

Nickels bolts toward the hecklers at the center of the room, the guffawing patrons silencing at his clenched shoulders. "Don't you talk to my Bearcat that way!"

"*Your* Bearcat?" Doris shrieks.

"Don't none'a you clowns *eva'* touch her!"

Heck lifts his hands to regain the attention of the taunting gentlemen, but the room has joined the rowdy group. Deeper pockets don't buy manners when drunken men are riled by a beautiful woman. Their unruliness puts my old club to shame as two men leap over the poker table, tearing at each other's suits and swearing. The surrounding company tosses money into a hat to bet on the winner. The house band swings into a hard and fast thumper. Heck's palm hits his forehead.

"We can't have this chaos going on upstairs, Mr. Kessler!"

•

Cornwell shouts over the turbulence. "Get a handle on your whores and your staff or I'll end this for breach of contract!"

My brother tears his white apron from his waist. "You know what? Don't bother, pinche wedo." His thick lower lip pinches beneath his teeth in a sharp whistle over my pleading protest for him to calm down. "Gio! I'm taking a cab."

The tinkling piano stops and starts again, the band carrying on.

"I'm sure I beg your pardon." Cornwell's mouth drops open, and he turns back to me as Javier storms from the room. "This is why you don't hire these people."

My panic and resentment start fighting each other again, the hotel manager leading himself back upstairs with his nose to the ceiling. The higher-class underground has gone from a roaring success to a resounding disaster.

Gio rushes to us, smashing his taxicab hat over his dewy hair. "Miss Lane, I'll go after 'im. Heck can settle this down if you wanna come with."

"Nonsense," Stuart insists, slipping his arm around my shoulders like Heck isn't there. "It's hardly appropriate for you to chase around your employees." He tips his hat to my tight-faced fiancé. "Mr. Kessler, I'd be obliged to have my driver take her home while you wrap things up. It's nearly closing time anyway. And don't be too discouraged. Private events are often difficult."

Gio narrows his suspicious eyes at this new hero. "Is that what you wanna do, Rose?"

My stomach sinks at his melancholy. Surely, he can't expect me to climb into cars with them in a place like this. "Yes. I think it's best that Mr. Alvarado have some space, so I need you to close out the bar and send the staff home with a complimentary shot."

"Well, there you have it, then." Stuart gathers his jacket and hat, offering me his arm with a nod to my piano player. "Nifty playing earlier tonight."

Gio lets out a small grunt, his mouth pressed into a thin line before grabbing up Javier's apron. Geez! Just what I need. Like many men, he doesn't mind taking orders . . . until he doesn't agree.

With a loud sigh, Heck leans over the counter. "Where's that damn pineapple cake?"

"Oh, come on," Stuart says, clapping him on the back. "Our colleagues didn't look too dismayed. Private tours in silk rooms. The finest rum we've had in ages. A little bit of danger with some lively music. You've certainly given us something to talk about—and that's what makes money."

I lift an eyebrow at Heck, who returns the gesture. I was going to send this new darb on his way with an allure-filled kiss to remember this good night. Honestly, I expected nothing more of this evening besides hope until this moment. As Nickels finally calms the quarreling patrons and coaxes them back to laughing and drinking, I give Stuart's arm a squeeze. "You really think this place has potential, Mr. Kensington?"

He gives my knuckles a subtle brush. "Oceans of it."

And his hands tell me that he means it. He loved the atmosphere and wild events of the evening to tell about in other cities. To his high-end friends. In high-end places. This man is good for business.

My fiancé's mouth rises into my favorite smirk as he wags his head like he's impressed with himself. "Indeed." He lifts a crystal decanter toward the happy but raucous crowd, Clip piping a bluesy tune to end the evening. "To high-end revelry."

"Cheers to that, Mr. Kessler."

Heck gives my bare shoulder a squeeze as he takes a small swig before kissing my temple. "I could be late, darling."

Ah. He's met someone. *Perfect.* Pressing my cheek to his in farewell, I whisper, "To high-end revelry." I follow Stuart's strong lead, throwing a wink over my shoulder. I'll have a mess to clean up tomorrow, but at least I know how to forget about it for one night.

"SO, YOU LIVE IN HOTELS?" THE HANGING CHANDELIER SHINES across the ceiling moldings of nude angels with mermaid tails. I crane my head up, running my hand over the fabric footboard of the giant sleigh bed, examining the intricate carvings and mythological creatures. Stuart's fingers slide over the back of my neck to the front of my chin, commanding my eyes to him.

"About half of the year, yes," he says, his darkening eyes and fingertips igniting my lower belly with his ravenous thoughts. I almost don't even need to read him.

"Sounds adventurous." My heels sink into the thick carpeting as I step back, circling around to the side of the bed. Examining the baroque wallpaper with feigned interest, I drop my handbag to the oak nightstand. Stuart removes his jacket, smirking at my coy delay. "So, how is the Bellerive treating you, Mr. Kensington?"

"Very well. But it was missing something."

"Oh?" I ask, turning away like I'm half listening. "What's that?"

A light gasp hits the back of my throat as his deft fingers tug at the zipper between my shoulder blades, the dress gathering around my ankles as it hits the floor. That mouth I'd been dying to taste all night teases the spot beneath my ear, sending shivers across my skin. His breath tickles my neck. "A woman with chestnut hair that hits just below her chin, where her adorable dimple deepens with an earth-shattering smile."

"I don't think those normally come with the hotel rooms."

Stuart's hands slide beneath my ivory slip, lifting me to the bronze coverlet. "Oh, they do. I like mine tangled in silk sheets, calling out my name."

I grip his black tie, staring at his wolfish mouth. He's a shark. A hunter. But so am I. "You're not a subtle man, are you?"

"There's no point in wasting time when it's clear what we both want." He sits up on his knees, unfastening the buttons of his black vest, his fingers attacking his dress shirt. Stuart's chest soon greets me in all its splendor, carved like the ceilings above me. I've missed this distraction, taking what I want from nightly creatures who do the same to me.

I drop his tie, crawling backward toward the stack of brown pillows near the headboard. "And what is that?"

"Your games are cute." His warm muscles and full lips hover over me, his eyes lit with desire. "Let's play another one."

His mouth and hands abandon all propriety, sharing his wanton desire to take from me. To make me his. No sweet nothings or proposals. Just selfish need, burning at each other for not being enough. It's been a long time since I've felt such control of my enchantments. A carnal confidence consumes what's left of my anxiety from the evening, my decadent branch of magic reaching my skin in thrilling reception as his hands glide over me. It reads his emptiness and doesn't care. Anger smolders alongside my allure as it awakens from its dormancy in the pit of my stomach and climbs higher, arming my lips with the potency of a broken spirit. My brother's hurt eyes, Gio's insistence for something I can't give him, my family's expectations clashing with this city's foul standards all boil like an incantation, ready to sentence Stuart to an acrimonious dance, scorching him with hostility. The magic even tastes different as it pushes into his decadent lips in a venomous arrest. Its typical sweet playfulness gives way to a nearly vengeful rush. We both tear at each other, animalistic and primal, like enemies rather than lovers. I want to mess up his hair. I want to mess up his heart.

The curved headboard hits the wall one last time, my head falling onto his sticky bare chest.

"My God," he gasps. "What was that?"

I push away from him, grabbing his gold cigarette case from the nightstand with a shrug. "Did you not enjoy it?"

His eyes are wide with hazel glitter. I nearly roll my eyes at the impending proposal. "Rose . . . you are the most enjoyable woman I've ever had." Still nothing new. He reaches for his metal lighter, holding out a yellow flame. "But that was a lot more hellcat than I was expecting. It felt like you were punishing me for something."

He doesn't mean it as an insult, and I don't take it as one—I definitely feel on fire right now. Scooting off the bed, I then shimmy my dress over my slip, adjusting my silk stockings. "Maybe I was."

"Well, I'd like you to do it again sometime," he says. "If you're not too busy conquering the underworld, that is." I snap open the lid to my hand mirror, securing the slender strap of my handbag over my shoulder. As I check my lips, my eyes catch his lovely form stretching out on the sheets. "I'm serious, Rose. I'll be between our cities for the next several months."

My nose wrinkles at the idea. "I thought you weren't interested in permanent situations."

"No, nothing like that." He laughs. "I was offering a steady arrangement. No commitment. I have connections in this venture, you know."

"So does Heck."

"Yes, but Mr. Kessler has a conscience, baby." Stuart's wicked smile spreads his cupid's bow. "Men with real connections don't have those."

Hitching up the hem of my dress, I saunter over to his side of the bed, pressing the cigarette between my lips before blowing out a slow plume of smoke. "So you're a bad man?"

"Very," he admits, tucking his hands beneath his copper hair. "But isn't that relieving to know? Neither of us expects loyalty. We're here for the pleasure and when that dies down, as it most definitely will, then we'll walk away with whatever we could get out of each other. Unlawful expectations without the drama."

I lean down, letting our detestable thoughts and tongues mingle. "Sounds perfect. Though I doubt you'll ever tire of *me*."

His laugh is almost as satisfying as his gasp through the nose when I kiss him again—sultry and hard. His breath picks up speed, my allure racing through my lips with his heart, untamed and haughty. He grabs the sides of my face, shaking his head. "Most women walk out when I word it like that."

"Most women think they need someone like you."

His lips part, his awe soaking into my cheeks from his palms. I give him an extra rock of my hips as I walk away, throwing him one last smirk as he settles back down on his plush pillows.

"Thanks for playing, Miss Lane."

I roll my eyes once more. Darbs always think they're the ones playing me. Except this time I don't feel like I won anything. My walk down hotel hallways is usually a triumphant one. The emptiness that builds inside me by the time I reach the stairwell grinds against my conquest. This game was supposed to bring me back—Rose Lane, an underworld contender full of grace and confidence. But all I can think about is my brother's bitter tears in my car. I miss Heck's company. Gio's parlor tricks. I bet he'd love to see some real magic.

My face falls further as it hits the humid air in the marbled lobby. I can't let anyone that close. I don't know how to fill the void just yet, but something tells me the answers aren't in the beds of guys like Stuart.

14

THE FINAL NIGHT AT THE RIVER ROSE IS BITTERSWEET, THE
scuffed floors filling with toasting patrons, many throwing their
arms around me in sincere hugs. A few guys hang around the bar
with my moody brother, their faces staring into the chilled mugs
of beer Gio brought in as a special farewell. The scene wraps me in
nostalgia. Even with Giuseppe running a few impromptu gambling
tables, the mood is still a little subdued. My old patrons are going
to miss me as much as I'm going to miss these warped floorboards.
This must be what apprehensive brides feel like on the night before
the wedding—weepy with the violent urge to run the hell away.

It's just been a rocky week. I tell myself that and a few other
excuses, filling my belly with warm lager to coax away my crip-
pling world. Heck's steady arm circles my waist, his body humid
like the night air that blows through the open back door, ushering
in another round of wet sprinkles, a cool respite in the swampy
atmosphere of this old club. I look over to the door when the room
throws a few whistles, watching as a tall woman stumbles into the

room with a newspaper held over her windblown hair. Her pale lips blow an orange strand from her face, widening with a smile at my dropped jaw.

"Margaret! You made it!"

"Of course I did!" She flushes at a few flirty calls from the raucous tables, waving at the smoky haze in vain. "I really must adore you—driving to the jazz district this late at night. And that wind! Isn't this cozy, though? Still wearing those slacks, I see."

Heck jogs to her side, taking her felt hat and trench jacket. "Welcome to our lair, Miss Swinson. What a lovely frock. May I get you a drink?"

Margaret's blush deepens as she smooths the front of her tan cardigan, mumbling about the expense of her pleated skirt. Pinching her chin, Heck sidles off to the bar, leaving me nearly spitting out my beer at her mirth before my fiancé returns, shoving a foaming glass into her trembling hands. She leans down as she slurps the foamy drink. "Wow. Archie would have a conniption if he saw me drinking this."

"Like we tell all our patrons," a sultry voice says from behind us, "have a few more of those and you won't care what your husband thinks."

Margaret ducks her head to hide her laughter, her gaze avoiding Penny's ruby-red wig cut into a waved pixie. "Geez."

"Penny," I say, "this is my good friend Margaret, and she could use some cheering up."

Margaret laughs again. "Oh, I've just been a little blue."

"Tell ya what," my head flapper says with a flick of her hand, "a good makeover will put a smile on any woman's face. Bet your last dollar."

"Really?" Margaret nearly bounces with glee. "You'll let me wear a flapper dress?"

Penny's getting a real kick out of this. "I won't let you do anything. It's all up to you, sugar."

"Then yes! Yes!"

My head flapper's shadowed eyes give Margaret a quick once-over, her bronze hands on her curvy hips. "Well, aren't you suburban? How do the fellas find your bubs in that getup, anyway?" My coworker's hand claps over her mouth. "Yeah, that's what I thought. Don't worry. We'll find 'em." Margaret's rounded eyes grow wider, her mouth stammering as Penny drags her off toward the ladies' washroom.

I saunter over to the wooden stools, nudging a downcast man who gives me a side smile. "Aw, come on," I say. "This is supposed to be a celebration. Jav, get this man another drink, huh?"

A tall mug slams down in front of the man, making me jump. My brother ignores my narrowed eyes, turning back to wiping the clean counter. The gloomy man shrugs his dejected shoulders, his suspenders hanging.

"Come on, darlin'," I say, ignoring my brother right back, "you can always come visit us at the Bellerive."

"Nobody here can afford those cover charges, baby."

"Well, maybe I'll run a special, just for River Rose fellas." My encouraging smile fades at my brother's loud snort, hardening my jaw. "All right, what's your problem, Javi?"

"Me?" he shouts over a trombone blast, leaning over the counter when a few heads turn in our direction. "People been telling you all night, Rose. This new thing you're doing—it's leaving most of us in the cold. So forgive us if we're not exactly excited to be treated like the dirty blue-collars we are!"

My fiancé slides off his seat at the end of the bar. "Javier, that's not fair."

"Stay out of this, Heck," my brother says as he pinches the bridge of his nose with a heavy sigh. "Please."

"What are you talking about, Javi?" The burn of tears and shame hit my face. "You were a part of this."

"And now I'm not."

"Wait . . . what? What are you *saying*?"

I thought we were okay. I thought we were working it out.

His thick brows even out, his hard eyes brimming. I'm barely keeping it together myself. If my brother cries, the flood behind my eyes is going to burst. "Look, I wasn't gonna say anything until later, but . . . I've gone as far as I can go."

"Don't do this, Javi."

"You know I'm right, Miss Lane," he says, tossing his towel to the marble counter like his composure could break any moment. "You know that swanky part of town ain't for me."

My throat shoves my climbing emotions back down. "But . . . I need you."

"And you know where to find me. But you don't need me at that bar."

Gus's nervous hand taps the counter, his mouth twisting. "Look, uh . . . why don't you two lemme finish the drinks for the last hour? Your personal shit's eating the profits right now."

"Javi, wait," I plead as he unties his apron. He lifts his hands up, avoiding my eyes as he backs toward the exit with a compliant nod. A long, wistful intro sweeps around the club, sending Heck's bottom lip between his teeth, his somber eyes staring after the open door.

"Rose . . . I'd like to offer him a ride home," he mumbles. "Maybe I can talk to him."

I sniff back the burning in my nose. "Thank you. You can try, but this has been a long time coming."

After a quick kiss to my temple, Heck sails from the room. At least I have my own car this time. Several patrons offer their apologies over my lost bartender while congratulating me on the new nightclub. Penny bursts from the dressing room, dragging a glittering Margaret to the center of the dance floor, igniting loud cheers at her long ivory legs and the emerald dress that matches her eyes. The makeover is worth a hundred bucks. Her face powder does its best to hide her blushing cheeks as the dancing flappers pull her into a spontaneous sensual waltz that splits her rouged lips with laughter. I feign a light chuckle for her sake. Peering back at the lonely bar where Gus stands in my brother's place, I am robbed of any joy, the evening whirling around me in a dull blur.

"GIO, YOU'RE SURE ABOUT THESE NUMBERS? THE PRIVATE OPEN-ing was kind of a disaster."

"I'm sure," he says, lining up a variety of unmarked bottles by the cast-iron sink. "And no, it wasn't. We got enough to pay for the orchestra *and* some extra green for Clip's band."

A toasted burn hits my lungs before drifting from my parted lips as I hunch over the marble counter, squinting at an opened led-ger. *So Stuart was right after all.* My brand of high-end revelry was greeted very well by his companion's pocketbooks. The earnings were through the roof for such a small crowd. "They went through two crates of cream soda?"

"Yep. Darbs like their rum."

"Well, that's relieving." Leaving the River Rose isn't easy, but these numbers mean this can actually work. It means we'll be out from under Ice's thumb. Not that Mr. Cornwell's a dream landlord, but he's safe enough in comparison.

"Mm-hmm." Gio's short answers lift my head, my cigarette lowering to the wooden ashtray. What the hell is his problem? The last thing I need right now is another man in my life angry with me about things I can't control. I aim to tell him so, but he gets right down to it, leaning forward on his hands with a scowl. "So did Mr. Pretty-Face get you home okay, seein' how he was so worried about your *reputation*?"

My mouth peppers with annoyance, pinching together. "Oh, he was a dandy umbrella."

"Really?" Gio attempts a laugh, his eyes hardening in sable

angst. "Because I think you can do betta' than some bimbo who treats you like an open buffet. At least Kessla' keeps his playmates unda' the table."

"Look who's being discreet, Mr. Jealousy." My arms cross at Gio's lifted eyebrows. "I happen to have a degree in discretion."

"C'mon, Rose," he says, tossing his raven hair from his eyes. "This ain't about jealousy. Your new boyfriend caught onto your ruse real quick, and that's dangerous for all of us. Try to think about that before you go ridin' off into the sunset with flashy dappa's. You ain't supposed to be available."

My annoyance upgrades to riled, an incensed snort rushing from the back of my throat. "Oh, I see. I'm supposed to paint my face and smile while everybody else gets their wheels greased?"

"That's not what I'm sayin'. It's just bad timin', boss."

"When *would* be a good time for you to see me with someone?"

He can deny it all day long, but his green-eyed monster is absolutely what this is about. And I don't have time for anybody's jealousy, especially from one of my employees. This is way too messy already.

The silence of the empty club builds, Gio's eyes icing over. "I told you, that's not what I'm sayin'."

"Maybe not out *loud*. If you've got feelings to deal with—"

"Aw geez. I'm talkin' about business!"

"I don't think you know the difference!"

"That's a helluva thing for *you* to say!"

The clattering of smashing glass jerks both our heads toward the stairwell entrance. Gio's questioning eyes dart to me before a second crash sounds. Then another. I've stopped counting by the time he leaps over the counter. Snatching my building keys from my handbag, I toss them to him, springing from the barstool. He flings open the door, yellow and orange flames flickering from the top of the stairs where two silhouettes rear back with fiery bottles in their hands. Gio's strong arms lift me from the floor as he spins, slamming me against the wall beside the doorframe. The burning projectiles fly past us, crashing like angry fireworks into several wooden crates at the foot of the bar.

"Shit, Rose! Run!"

My legs push me through billowing black smoke, my lungs raging as much as the fire that swallows the floorboards. Heated vapors assault my skin through my clothes. Tables keep running into me. Squeezing my burning eyes open, I careen beside Gio through the back door. The cool night air after a rain betrays the horrors behind us in our scramble over the gravel to my Model T. My trembling hands work the levers and throttle, his shadow flailing in the headlights as he twists the crank until the engine catches. He yanks open the passenger door, sliding across the seats. "Go, Rose!"

Exploding glass pops and shatters from the basement doorway. Ducking, I shove the hand brake into idle, tearing up the dark alleyway like bank robbers on a heist. Gio's arms brace against the broadcloth, our bodies thrusting as I spin onto the street. The front headlight scrapes against a white Chrysler. *Damn.* My breath hitches. *Wait!* Stomping my foot on the brake pedal, we lurch to a stop beside it.

"What the hell, Rose! We gotta go!"

"No!" I shriek, the terror gripping my insides as I rip myself from the front seat. Gio's protests stop short, the realization dawning on his face as we reach the familiar prized vehicle. The muffled screeching from inside chills my limbs, a harsh thumping rattling the passenger door like a hellish creature trying to escape its cage.

"Oh my God." Gio's hand rips open the gleaming door. "Oh my God!"

I push past him, climbing over the gasping man whose tearstained face twists as he tries to speak over the cloth gag in his mouth. Sweat pours around Heck's wide eyes, his wrists writhing against the metal handcuffs that have him bound to the inside door handle.

"Move, Rose! I can get those open!" Gio starts to climb beside me, my fumbling fingers pulling the knot behind Heck's head, releasing his mouth from the tied fabric.

"There's no time!" he screams, shoving me back with his feet. "Javi's inside, dammit! *Javi's inside!*"

Gio whirls around, bounding for the burning building, my feet twisting over Heck's as I stumble from the vehicle to the damp street. My hands land in a thick puddle, my fingers sinking into a muddied clump of dandelions. Righting myself, I start for the grocery store, flames pouring from the large windows. Heck pleads after me as I charge the inferno with no clue of what I plan to do when I get inside. *If* I can get inside. I don't have to strategize long. Gio bursts through the billowing smoke that pours from the entrance, holding up my wavering brother, their arms slung around each other's shoulders.

I reach Javier's side as his knees buckle. Gio leans, taking most of the weight as we drag my brother to the Chrysler, laying him in the back seat. My Model T abandoned, soon the inflamed building becomes a flickering light in the distance as Gio zooms toward the city hospital. Heck's hardened gaze stays fixed on my brother, his spotted face as red as his chafed wrists. Ire makes its way down my cheeks in hot, wet indignation, my mud-dried fingers stroking my brother's singed hair. Blood from his swollen face soaks my cream blouse, his rolling eyes fluttering as he groans and coughs.

"It's okay," I whisper, my lips quivering as I press them to his forehead. Dreadful memories plague his mind as he slips in and out of consciousness. Curses. Blessings. Healing. I stopped reaching for them long ago. But Javier needs me. He's always needed me . . . and I need him. I begin with the branch I know, charm, forming a thought and imparting it into the sorrowful ridges above his brow. Hibiscus floats from my mouth to my nose. *You're safe now.*

With my heart skipping with shock like the coils buzzing on Heck's Chrysler, my impartation sparks a new fire deep in my bones. But Javier's moaning response threatens to drag my hope from me. I reach for it as I slip my hand beneath his collar, spreading the drying mud across his heaving chest.

"From dust you came, to dust you shall return," I sob in hiccupping gasps. Like the squealing brakes of a train, my brother's breath continues to hitch. Heck leans his face against the door with shaking shoulders. I should have known better than to hope. I'm just not a healer. "What kind of people would do this?"

If I had any hope left, I'd direct it right at those monsters. I hope they get everything that's coming to them. I hope their pride becomes their downfall. I hope the earth swallows them up. With my trembling hands stained with yellow pollen and dark earth, I cling to Javier, weeping the useless prayer I whispered on my balcony. "Ayúdame, ayúdame, ayúdame . . ."

I've only ever felt this shifting when my abuela has spoken in a way that only she and I can feel, like the air around me is transforming into cool liquid. In the upholstered cabin, the earth and sky draw closer, a home that's been waiting for me. My brother's breathing stills, the rumbling engine of our car crawling to a sputter. Blurred boulevards become a shuttering photograph before freezing outside the window. Like a dormant seed, my magic springs forth inside me as a white oak sapling with tender leaves. Shooting through their slender branches, the leaflets plead for nourishment from the sky. Retribution feeds the roots. My abuela was right. My branches are growing. I can only pray to the wind that I know what I'm doing now. Mind tricks are one thing. Curses on my enemies are quite another. Not that I can even stop myself.

I don't know why the fates chose to lead me into this vengeful spell instead of showing me one for healing. Perhaps they know that my brother is going to make it. I hope that's the case. Perhaps the spell was ignited by my fury mixed with the dandelions on our bodies. The powdery flower can arouse the most potent curses, though I've never seen it in action. Until now.

The magic grips my emotions as much as I grip its chaos, and all I can do is let it take me. As I lift my eyes to the roof of the car, the metal gives way to the starry heavens that await my announcement. "Que la tierra trague a nuestros enemigos si nos tocan de nuevo."

Stillness and every sound that's ever been made collide at once, my roots trembling and shaking my bones as they let out a burst of unshackled fearlessness. And all at once the heavens close again, the breath leaving my body depleted and relieved. Javier's wheezing snaps me back into the cabin, Gio's occasional swear peppering the atmosphere as we roll on. Exhaustion weighs down my eyelids and arms, my thoughts drifting along with my bobbing head. I don't know how I know it—the end of our pain, righteousness pushing through the grime that threatens to bury us. But . . . I know it.

THE GENERAL HOSPITAL'S WHITE FLOORS AND TILED WALLS MAKE even the basement wing seem cosmopolitan with its state-of-the-art electric elevators and in-house drugstore. The early Renaissance architecture would normally set my journalistic juices flowing for a good fluff piece, but the argument between Heck and a stern-faced nurse sends my dirty thumbnail between my teeth.

"What do you mean you're sending him away? He can hardly breathe!"

"Sir, Mr. Alvarado is unable to pay his accident room treatment," she explains, folding her hands in front of her white pinafore. "Why don't you try Wheatley Provident? They offer municipally funded care for non-whites."

The way she says "non-whites" sets my teeth on edge, but it's really steaming Heck, whose indignant finger points to the marble floors. "He is not leaving this hospital until he's well. I'll pay for it myself!"

Gio's sooty hand finds mine, giving it an encouraging squeeze while his thoughts inundate my palms with a hefty amount of uncertainty. With all we're pouring into the club, Heck's monthly trust allowance isn't enough to cover a hospital stay. We'll have to dip into our opening night funds, which makes it all the tighter if things don't pan out right away.

But what choice do we have? I'm not forcing my brother to wait even longer in the lines of another general hospital. He needs help now.

"Sir, you should let me take you back to have your injuries tended to—"

"*I'm* fine. Go help him!"

The nurse purses her lips before huffing down the shining halls, leaving us in the crowded waiting area overflowing with moaning patients and their families. A few folks exchange sympathetic frowns with me as I lean against a hard wall, Heck's suit jacket around my shivering arms. The coldness is deep in my bones even though the room is stuffy, a foul smell wafting around every so often. Heck's shoulders touch mine, his disheveled head hanging as he crosses his arms with a loud sigh.

"She's right," I say. "I didn't know you were bleeding that badly."

His fingers tap the back of the crimson-soaked hair that falls over his forehead. He winces. "I suppose I hadn't noticed until now myself. But it's Javi I'm worried about. I'll get help as soon as he does."

"What the hell happened back there?" Gio asks, his voice lowering.

"Hell came after us, I guess." Heck chews his bottom lip with a shake of his head, his eyes squeezing shut with a grimace. "After I left the club, I found him about a block away, and we decided to take a long walk to help him cool down. We toured the entire jazz district a few times over—even stopped in a lounge to grab a drink. I was just trying to cheer him up. We weren't doing anything . . ."

His voice cracks with a stuttering gasp through his reddening nose.

My heart twists as a trail of tears makes its way down to his quivering chin. "No one said you were, honey."

"But someone thought you were," Gio says, his mouth pressing into a hard line. "Didn't they?"

Heck's lips tighten as he nods, the trapped sob escaping his nose. "We were . . . walking to my Chrysler since the clubs were all closed down when this car comes barreling down the street from behind us. No headlights. Javi tried to get me to run. Then something hit me over the head. It was dark."

My hand has found its way to my mouth, my own tears scattering over the cracked mud on my knuckles. Gio swears, reaching behind my neck to grab Heck's shaking shoulder.

"How did you end up in your car?" I ask through chattering teeth. "Did you get a look at them?"

"No, I . . . When I woke up, they had those demon hoods on. No robes this time. My head was pounding and this guy was handcuffing my wrists. I thought it was a nightmare." Heck straightens his back, rubbing his face with his hands. "They started saying all these nasty things, accusing Javi of— It was my fault."

"No, honey—"

"It *was*," Heck insists, throwing his hands down. "They tied him up and dragged him inside after making me watch them beat the soup out of him."

My fiancé's raging eyes fade to a sea of cerulean hopelessness, my own dismay building at the thought of my brother being beaten. Nearly murdered. *What have we gotten ourselves into?* Every step I take to get us away from dangerous bigots lands us right into the lap of another disgusting entourage of corruption. I never suspected there was anything fair about this life, but this is too much. This is too far.

"Mr. Kessler?" A somber doctor beckons from the exam rooms. We follow Heck as he pushes away from the wall, extending his hand with knitted brows. "It appears your friend was pulled from the building before major damage was sustained to his bronchial tubes. We're not seeing any signs of internal burns, though the noxious gases from the smoke itself have made him very sick. He'll recover, but it's going to take some time."

We breathe a collective sigh of relief, more tears flowing as Heck's jacket smashes around me, his and Gio's hugs lifting me to my toes. The doctor moves on to other waiting families, a light tap near my heels pulling us apart.

"My dear, you've dropped something," Heck says, retrieving a folded piece of paper from the floor. "Or rather, I have. It came from my pocket." His curious face falls as he reads, his chest rising with my apprehension.

"What is it?"

He jams the note into my palm, his red-rimmed eyes alight with wild recompense. "It's them."

Unfolding the crinkled corners, I scan the hasty writing:

> *Mr. Kessler, we took care of that bindle punk bartender who made a show of himself at your private opening. You may not understand this now, but his kind are responsible for the curse on this city. While we don't approve of your vices, we won't put up with anti-Americans making a fool of successful white men. Know, however, that the lawless world you've found yourself in is no place for a man of your standing, even if you're too enamored by the life to see it. Perhaps the absence of that disrespectful immigrant's devilry will bring you to the right conclusion about your life choices. At least you won't have that cesspool of a club to run back to when the Bellerive fails. Consider this a step toward your salvation.*

"You see?" Heck runs his sleeve across his nose. "It's my fault."

"They did this, not you, Kess," Gio says, reading over my shoulder. "And every damn one of them are cowards—wearin' their hoods, hidin' their faces. And real men don't send out anonymous scare tactics like this one."

"Well, it's working."

I can't help but agree. *Scare tactic?* It's way more than that. Yes, they came after Javi and Heck—I've got the proof in cursive. But the Klan destroyed Moretti's property—mob territory. Our attackers had to know that. *How are* they *not afraid?* That question only scares me more. They're either not worried about reprisals from Moretti or they bit off more than they can chew. I hope it's the latter. I hope they're not so powerful that they can just burn their way through mob territory. But then again, Moretti's been too busy wanting to be the new Pendergast, and he's making it big enough that cops are sniffing around after *him.* Everyone's making waves around me. But I'm not the real target—the city itself is.

The city itself. Idly picking at the dried mud between my fingers, I study the tile floors like they hold all of my answers. This city is full of enemies of my enemies. And if I can turn them all toward each other and away from me, we might just make it through this. More than make it.

I'm done being pushed around.

My hand clamps around the dastardly note, vengeance filling my veins. "Fear kills magic." I meet Heck's darting glance before turning to my squinting piano player. "Gio, move forward with the extras. We're gonna make it work. These guys don't get to win."

"You got it, boss."

"And, Heck?"

His perfect nose sniffles. "Yes, darling?"

"Let's get Javi home."

15

GOLDEN LIGHT STABS ME IN THE EYE, BLANKETING THE SPLIN-
tered walls and oak dressers with morning sun through the open
windows. Even though Javier and I no longer live in our childhood
home, four beds fill the remaining space in the room. The hearty
smell of my mother's huevos rancheros filters through the door
from the adjoining boxcar, lifting my nose as I arch my back into a
groaning stretch. Blinking away the brightness, I lift my head, my
heart warming and sinking at the same time. A weathered arm lays
across my brother, dried mud caked to his skin from the dark hand
on his bruised chest. Though his trimmed mustache is split by the
cut on his upper lip, he looks peaceful—like the boy I used to annoy, running after him on the riverbanks. His facial hair and our
abuela's snores usually make me giggle. But right now her ashen
coloring has my eyes brimming.

"Luna." Javier lifts his sluggish eyelids with a raspy cough, his
voice harsh and broken. Bolting upright, I reach down, pushing his
hair from his purple eye. He scrunches his face, licking his lip with

a grunt. "We're alive. How did I get here? Where's Heck?"

"Everyone's okay, Javi. Heck and I got you to Mama Sunday last night." We peer at our sleeping abuela, who inhales like a spinning auto coil, flipping over in the mess of cotton sheets. "Your wheezing is already sounding better."

"She doesn't look so good."

"This one really took it out of her."

My brother's head drifts back to me, his brows lowering over his watery espresso eyes. "Hermanita . . . I'm so sorry."

"No," I cry, a deluge of regret pouring down my cheeks as I grab his hand. "My own selfishness got us here. I should have just stayed at the River Rose. I should have never left home—"

Javier's hand touches my mouth, his head shaking. "I never should have left you."

"Javi, I'm gonna fix this. I swear it."

"Listen to me, Luna," he says, his hoarse voice just above a whisper. "I know things haven't been easy for either of us. I've only ever wanted to take care of you and this family. And the truth is, I was kind of jealous when you started doing so well. But I look at you now and all I feel is pride for the person you've become. I realize now, I *was* a part of that. Neither one of us should be ashamed of who we are."

I let out a long exhale, a small tear pushing beneath my closing eyes. "Who we are."

Who am I?

My brother's palm warms mine with earnest affection, my face twisting in silent sorrow. His quiet sigh has the sound of a smile. "My sister is an earth bruja—Weaver of Thoughts. Conjurer of Spells." I open my eyes; his mouth is turned up, as I suspected. "Healer of Hearts."

"I can't do any of those things."

"No?" His smile widens. "You didn't speak to the stars last night?" My lips part at the ornery twinkle in his eyes. "Aye, aye, aye.

I've been around earth magic my whole life. I know when the fates are being called, even in my sleep."

I slap my hand against my forehead. "I don't even know what I did!"

"Oh, you probably summoned a legion of frogs or something like that." With a comical grimace, his dimple deepens. "You're even dressed for the part."

His chesty laugh makes me laugh as I smooth the front of my borrowed nightdress, running my thumbs over the colorful hand stitching. "Yes, well, all the brujas are wearing these."

Our mirth mends my trepidation, filling me with renewed hope. *We really are going to be okay.* Falling into more giggles at our abuela's smacking gums, we hardly notice the light knock on the doorframe.

"Oh good! You're awake—and looking so well, Javi. Your grandmother is an angel," Heck says, sticking his hands on the waist of his baggy trousers. A snort shoots through my nose at the cropped-sleeve shirt I recognize from my brother's wardrobe, the casual style an odd pairing with his slicked hair and cocky grin. "Rose, I've washed and pressed your clothes, and I do hope you're hungry. Gloria has made a hearty breakfast that smells divine—some kind of red sausage. But you better get a move on if you want me to get you to work on time."

Tapping his finger to his shimmering watch, he glides from the room as quickly as he appeared. Javier's wrinkled forehead smooths out, his eyes squinting. "We should keep him."

"I'll let the fates know."

"Luna, one more thing before we join the others."

"Anything, Javi."

He crosses his arms with a grimace. "I want you to hire a bar manager."

"Well, anything but that."

"I mean it," he says, his decisive nod making my lips purse. "I know you don't have the funds to pay Cornwell's extortion. And I don't want to hear any arguing from you."

He has the audacity to smile at my frustrated sigh. "Fine."

"Good. Now, speaking of funds, I heard what you guys did for me at the hospital. And I'm thankful, but . . ." My brother's dimpled chin lifts toward the kitchen, where Heck's laughter rings out. "How will you make up for the shortfall?"

"Well," I say, leaning back on my hands. "We tried borrowing again after I paid for Mamá's deposit. But investors won't risk it until they see that this club pays off."

"And you're sure you won't marry him?"

"I've put the people I care about in enough danger." Hell, our friend nearly got killed just being engaged to me. If Heck had any smarts, he'd run for the nearest train station.

Javier taps the cut on his lip in deep consternation. "What about the syndicate? Could they help?"

"And let them know we don't have the funds to pay them for all of our orders?" I close my eyes with a groan. "We haven't even opened yet. They're more likely to take over the damn thing, and we don't need more irons in the fire."

"But—"

"Javi," I say, pushing the covers with my feet, "I'll figure something out. You know I will."

My brother throws his comical eyes to the ceiling. "Yeah, well, that's what I'm worried about."

With a tender kiss to my brother's tousled hair, I roll out of bed, a hunger for life, love, and breakfast reviving my soul.

"SO YOUR BOYFRIEND DIDN'T GET A GOOD LOOK AT THEM, YOU say?"

A heated grumble simmers across the back of my throat, pinching my boss's eyebrows together like fluffy gray cymbals. "Mr. Roberts, Heck is my fiancé. And no, he didn't see their faces. They were wearing hoods."

"Hoods?" The chief editor's protruding belly rests on his folded hands, the wooden chair beneath him creaking as he leans away from his desk. "Hell's bells, Rosie. Why didn't you say so?"

"Well, it just happened—"

"Margie!"

My sweater-clad coworker flies through the open door of the office, shooting me a professional nod before turning her lightly reddening face to her uncle. "Yes, sir?"

"Get Banks in here. We got a hot one! I want it front page of next Sunday's paper." He tosses his spectacles onto the sea of papers that cover his oak desk. "The Klan attacks the great-nephew of George Kessler outside a grocery store, and the *Star*'s the first one to report it. Got his girl here as an eyewitness."

"Yes, sir."

My jaw twists amid Margaret's note-taking, her pencil scribbling across her tiny notebook as she avoids my eye. I was too distracted the other night at my joint to discuss our encounter with her, but she really has nothing to worry about; it's not the first time I've been kissed by a beautiful woman. I'd reassure her now, but the bigotry in this office is heating the tips of my ears. The editor's typical drive for a juicy story adds to the hilarity of his wooly hair sticking straight up, but my dreams being run over for the hundredth day in a row has my patience on a short fuse. "Excuse me, sir, but why can't Margaret write the story?"

Margaret's pencil freezes, our boss's head falling backward in a long sigh. "Not this again. You birds! Are you tryin' to put me six feet under? I got enough to deal with around here."

"Look, Mr. Roberts," I say, squaring my shoulders, "just give her a chance. She's a good writer."

"Listen, kid"—Mr. Roberts directs a bossy finger in my direction—"you girls want more responsibility? Fine! Edit the damn thing. I'll even give her a thirty-word quote. That's it! Now get the hell out before I change my mind!"

Margaret and I scuttle from the room, covering our mouths with muffled laughter, breaking the awkward air between us as we exchange knowing looks. Banks is a dud of a writer whose arrogance keeps him from noticing the heavy edits his pieces often need. This is my friend's chance—her shot to put her own personal flair into a real story. She deserves it after all she's been through.

"So," I say with a clearing of my throat as I pull our boss's door shut behind us. Her flush returns as her thumbnail hits her teeth. "The club was so busy the other night, I. . . . We didn't get a chance to talk—"

My fidgeting friend laughs in a snorting kind of way, waving her hand near her eye roll. "Oh, Rose, I can't tell you the pressure I've been under. I mean, I considered quitting the paper right away, but this is the only place I feel normal. And . . . you're my only friend . . . and . . . I'm really sorry—"

"Hey," I say, scraping my chair across the carpet, "nothing to apologize about, okay? I'm serious."

Her big eyes peek in my direction, her face turning away as she takes a deep breath. "Okay."

"Good." I set myself to work, rescuing her from having to say anything further.

"So I guess Archie was right," she whispers, settling at our shared desk in front of our typewriter. "Those clubs are a dangerous place. Not that I told him I went."

"Oh, Margaret, the world is a dangerous place." Feeding a fresh sheet of paper into the setter, she makes a few adjustments, a sly smile crossing her lips. I lean over her flying fingers, the buttons ticking with fervor. "Um, Margaret? What are you doing?"

Her mouth presses together, but it doesn't hide the grinning glow in her eyes. "Writing the article. Banks will drink himself silly and think that he wrote it. Let the men have their fun while we take over the world."

I think I'm starting to like this new Margaret.

MY OLD CLUB IS A CHARRED SHELL OF WHAT IT ONCE WAS, THE songs and dancing a ghostly memory inside the condemned building of soot and ash. The only evidence of the gambling club next door is the stubbed legs of an old poker table that Gus left behind in the move to the Bellerive. If I didn't know there used to be a store full of hats and hosiery above Gus's old place, I wouldn't guess it now. My determined gaze takes in the blackened bricks of the conjoined buildings. Several scorched beams curve inward like the skeleton of a great creature that couldn't be tamed. I slide my metal lighter into the pocket of my trousers, a hand over my heart. *Still beating.* The creature lives.

As a stream of smooth smoke leaves my mouth, the rumble of a Rolls-Royce ricochets off the pavement of the alleyway, its covered wheels crunching over the gravel. I lean back against the door of my automobile like the Spirit of Ecstasy hood ornament coming to stop beside me isn't sending chills down my spine. The flying woman clothed in silver clouds remains blissfully unaware of the steel-toed shoes that step out of the back seat. *Steady, Rose.*

Frank Moretti's stacks of golden rings gleam in the twilight as he fastens the herringbone jacket of his double-breasted suit. I've seen predatory men before, their weighing eyes searching for any weakness in their prey. The trick is to make them think they've got me. He ignores my extended hand with a tip of his hat's wide brim.

"You keep surprising me, Miss Lane," he says in his sneering, scratchy voice. "Going around my liaison I've provided to call on me directly?"

I set my arms into a nonchalant shrug. "Salvatore seems to want more from me than you do."

And it's true. I never should have let that slimy goon kiss me.

I wonder if Moretti even knows about half the times his sidekick has shown up in my personal space lately. I'm sure the mob boss doesn't care. But it was worth the risk in cutting out his middleman to get a real negotiation going.

"After our phone call, I didn't expect you to show. And alone at that."

"I'm not looking for anyone to save me."

His crooked nose puckers with an eerie smile. "I can believe that. But you *do* understand the stipulations to the offer you've made me? I don't accept late payments. Ever. Your tip on the Klan doesn't give you any more favor with me, although I do appreciate it."

"And I appreciate your willingness to compromise."

"It was a good offer, Miss Lane," he says. "Why have my hand in the candy dish at the River Rose when I can stake a claim to the Bellerive? I was going to start breaking the fingers and legs of your precious crew, but you saved me the trouble."

"I have the protection of the syndicate."

"As long as you've secured a bootlegging business that feeds their payroll—a business you didn't quite have in your hand until now." His patronizing stare makes my teeth clench. "Miss Lane, don't tell me you came here to squabble about the details."

I can feel my face tighten. I have no intention of letting Moretti have his hand in my business for long. And I can't wait to pay him off just so I can see the look on his face when I'm finally able to call on the syndicate if he threatens me again.

My enemy might be the dumbest place to go for help. But then again, it's damn brilliant. Ice thinks I'm giving in under the guise of a loan just to save face—or at least that's how I presented it.

"I understand." My lips press around my cigarette, pulling in the serene courage of burning tobacco. Moretti is the last person on earth I want to enter into any kind of contract with, but the expenses for my opening weekend are racking up. I can't lose it all now. Not while I'm this close. It's not a huge loan anyway. I can have him paid off in less than a year, but my club won't make it that far without this green.

I extend my hand once again with an expectant eyebrow pointed at the mobster's carnivorous grin. My chest thumps with adventure and jittery unease as he pulls a white envelope from his breast pocket. "Well, at least you're decisive. Careful that it doesn't get you into trouble."

"What? Knowing what I want?"

"Wanting it this badly."

The demonic alabaster vehicle rolls away in hellish luxury, my mind and conscience wrestling for attention. The way back is lost, my interest payments accruing the moment I touched that white envelope. I should be awash with fear, a statue of uncertainty. But as my rounded toe snuffs out the glowing cherry of my burning stub into the gravel, my stomach fortifies with the will to climb. Higher this time, but not afraid. And certainly not powerless.

16

MY HEART LEAPS LIKE A BULLFROG ON A RIVERBANK AS CLIP gives a halfway bow after the final number of our band's performance, waving to the crowd of white-vested tuxedos and cocktail dresses whose applause turns to a roar. *They love him.* I knew they would. While black musicians aren't allowed to play in many cities across America, the Casbah Lounge welcomes him with the appreciation he deserves. The thrill of success dizzies my head as pearl-draped ladies compliment my bold sapphire dress. Its trendy cut rivals the satin drop-waists with hanky hems around me, their calves showing skin that only a place like this gets to see. We're all somebody else on nights like these.

Nothing new for me, though. *I'm someone else every night.*

A sea of gentlemen in satin striped vests and top hats chat with Heck amid white tablecloths and flickering candles, leaving me happily alone at our table. Though I'm giddy with the joy of the evening, I swallow an inward sigh as a shadow stops by my elbow. I turn to the white glove reaching for my hand. Relief floods my annoyance as Gio's sable eye winks, his smooth chin brushing my fingers with a light kiss over my knuckles. "You mind if I join you?"

He takes the seat next to me with a surprising amount of breeze, his back straight and his dark hair parted and slicked back around his ears. *Goodness.* If not for the tiny scars on his eyebrow and the ink poking out beneath his cuff links, he could pass for a gander himself.

With a light laugh at my stunned expression, he hands me a Lucky Strike that I promptly tuck into the end of my holder, leaning in as he flicks his lighter. The long drag and his company calm my overstimulated nerves. His continued chuckle is carried away by the loud applause as the overhead chandeliers dim, a beaming spotlight hitting the center of the dance floor where my fiancé's hat tilts down over his eyes.

Hushed excitement skips around the room like stones across water. Now that our band has the room warmed up for the main event, a ritzy group of gentlemen takes the stage with suits and hats that tell us they're somebodies. My own arms shiver with a good amount of glee. Bennie Moten's orchestra is highly acclaimed for one thing: Bennie and his amazing skills on the ivory keys.

"Ladies and gentlemen," the orchestra leader soon announces into the circular microphone. "Please welcome your host for the evening—Heck Kessler and his barlow girls!"

Bennie Moten spins back to the gold-plated piano, his band's trumpets belting in syncopation with the crashing cymbals. The spotlight on Heck grows larger with each beat, illuminating the jeweled beads on our flappers' knee-length dresses, the feather boas around their necks glowing like an array of colorful clouds. The room is alight with encouraging calls and delighted gasps as the floor show grips our patrons for the next several minutes. My fiancé's feet effortlessly fly around the dance floor, his ladies spinning through his arms. Pulling him in different directions, they steal his hat, making the crowd roar with laughter. Sealing their final pose with a brilliant grin, the barlow team bows, the room leaping to its feet in whistling applause.

Gio and I join in the happy cheers as Penny's bronze hand leads the string of dancers from the wooden floor, the ladies waving on their way to the elusive Drawing Room. Heck skips up to the stage, blowing kisses into the adoring crowd as a set of rocking hips in a snow-white dress sashays up beside him.

"Di mi, they were born for this," Gio mumbles, blowing a stream of smoke away from me. I exchange a head-shaking grin with him, the oak barrel of our house gin catching the back of my tongue in a smooth burn as our resident billboards finish their comical show. My belly churns with expectation. *It's working.* I could have Icepick paid off in just a matter of months. Hell, my brother could come on board full-time, ending his backbreaking job at the steel factory. My dreams settle in front of me like the clinking ice in the bottom of my glass, my fingers gripped tightly around it.

The slower swing from the stage is bringing out the corn shredders—upper-crust couples waltzing around the dance floor as Doris's husky tone belts out a melodic story about finding satisfaction in the arms of another until the real thing comes along. A pointy-eared man saunters by our table, stopping to untangle his doe-eyed wife from his arm. "Really, Margaret, we're in public for God's sake. I swear you've been odd all evening."

Taking Gio's hand, I stand with him to greet the posh couple, exchanging small grins at her swimming gaze. She poses with a hand on her laced hips, patting her silk headscarf.

"My, my," I gush, grabbing her hands. Her thoughts are a messy jumble. She's definitely been lapping. "Don't you look nice?" Archibald's grunting eye roll tilts my head. "And how do you do, Oswald?"

A snorting laugh spits through Margaret's nose, her face freezing at his stern glare, which turns back to me. "Splendid, now that we're leaving," he sneers. "Your balcony seating is far too close to the rowdy vagrants on the bottom floor."

Gio shoves his hands into his trouser pockets with a shrug. "Well, it ain't like folks gotta work tomorrow. They're just havin' a good time."

"Yes," my coworker agrees with a heavy nod. "But I for one am looking forward to Monday. The *Star* is my only window to the outside world these days."

"Don't be so melodramatic, Margie." Her scowling husband peers at his watch. "I should have never agreed to let you finish out the month."

My eyes narrow as I drop her confusing hands. "What do you mean? You really are quitting?"

"Of course she is. That liberal newspaper office is a biased window, I assure you," Archibald insists. "Maybe it'll cure her of this face powder kick as well. This society's not healthy for a woman's welfare."

"Which is why you brought her here?"

"I'm not one to visit places that mock the laws of the land, but one can't change the city council's mind about this debauchery unless one makes an appearance every now and again." I hold his hostile gaze as he steps closer. "But don't expect to see us here often."

"You're breaking my heart."

A loud slurp snaps his head to the side. "Margie!" The snooty businessman snatches an amber-filled glass from his giggling wife's hand. "That is *not* a cola. My God, are you that dimwitted?" Her shoulders clench in an innocent shrug. "I'll find you some water. Don't touch anything until I get back!"

My smirking friend turns a wagging head to me, her smile growing. "I've already had four. He's got the perception of a carrot."

"Now don't go giving root vegetables a bad name," I say as Gio offers her my seat to rest until her elvish knight comes back.

After I help her onto the cushioned wood, she clutches my arm, the honeyed rum wafting from her painted mouth. "What was that you said about finding me a place?"

"Um . . . well, I know Penny offered, but we shouldn't discuss it here."

Her eyes glitter up at me with her warm smile. "Okay."

Glancing across the room, I purse my lips. Archibald heads back in our direction with a determined stride, collecting his wife before I can give her a final farewell.

"Welp," Gio says, pinching his lips, "while we're up, might as well dance."

I level my best deadpan look at his rotten smile. "You know I don't dance, Gio."

"Neitha' do I. But we're two inches from the dance floor and about twelve jerks are sizin' me up right now." His hand tugs my arm, pulling me into the harrowing sea of goofy couples.

"Aw geez." I clap my hand into his, amusement and delight buzzing from his palm as his other hand slides over my waist. His shoulders are more square when he's not hunched over a piano, and definitely a solid place to hold on to. I let him lead since he's got the gift of rhythm, keeping us moving without too much incident.

"You're doin' great," he says, my eyes flicking to the ceiling. "No, really. I mean it. All of this. You really hit on all sixes tonight."

I shake my head with a shy chuckle. "Yeah? I couldn't have done it without you, Gio."

"Truer words ain't neva' been spoken!" His gritty laugh sends his scars crinkling. "Listen, I hate to talk business, but I heard back from St. Louie just before our set. Coon-Sanders Novelty Orchestra wants to play here tomorrow!"

Applesauce! My mouth drops open, the thrill of the evening rejuvenating my tired bones. The renowned jazz band brings in fifteen dollars a plate. They're on the damn radio. "What? Gio, how are they going to get here in time? What do I need to do?"

"All you gotta say is yes!" He laughs at my bouncing toes.

"Yes! Yes!"

A few heads turn in our direction, casting their silent judgments among the swaying patrons. The atmosphere glows with possibilities. Tinkling glasses and light laughter surround our slow frolic as Gio's teasing smile returns. "Great, I'll make the call as soon as you get your claws outta me."

"Geez, you were almost a gentleman tonight," I say with a light slap to his shoulder. "You can't leave a woman on the dance floor in the middle of a song."

"Hey, I ain't a total savage." Gio clears his throat, avoiding my eyes. "So, uh, your new Brooksy—he treatin' you good?"

"Yeah!" I say, my face warming. "Stuart's been great. Easy to deal with."

"Good. You deserve to relax. I mean that." Gio's fingers pinch my chin. "But if he eva' gets sideways with you, you know where to find me—not that you need my help. I seen how you deal with greaseballs." We share another laugh before his grin falls, his eyes hardening over my shoulder. "Speakin' a which."

Following his glare, I draw a steadying breath into my lungs. The glowering gangster behind me crosses the arms of his pinstriped suit, his sharp nose turned up at my piano player. "My turn." Gio's solid stare has the intruder's beady eyes flipping backward, his permanent sneer curling up his birdlike face. "C'mon, what am I gonna do to her here? Beat it, hero."

Gio leans forward with a slight conceding bow, the fire of challenge sparking in his eyes. "You're kind of a desperate little thing, ain't you?"

"Yeah, she don't want you, either. I said take a hike."

In all this, no one asks me what I want. Typical.

My new dance partner careens me toward the center of the floor, cursing at a few couples to get them to move. His awkward sway is saved by the start of a simpler tune, the brassy trombone bleating a long, sensual solo. With my newest heels on, he's forced to meet my eyes, no longer at the advantage. Reading an unsuspecting jerk might be my favorite charm ability, the impartation and allure skills fighting for second place. My reception readies itself as his damp palm shares his discomfort with my hand.

"Isn't there a puppy somewhere that needs kicking, Mr. Salvatore?"

The mobster in training shakes his head, clicking his tongue. "Always so formal with me, Rose—treatin' me like we ain't been through nothin' while you lay down for these rich klucks. Marryin' a damn fluke. Hell, you barneymuggin' the musician, too?" My ears are sweltering as I try to pull away, but his grip tightens on my hand, his fingers digging into my hip. Like being forced to kiss a great-aunt with a hairy mole, he pulls me closer, his eyes dropping to my mouth. "I really admire you, you know that? Goin' over my head. Makin' deals with my boss."

I figured that would burn him. In fact, I was hoping it would. Salvatore has made it clear that he doesn't give a rat's behind about my club or Moretti's interest. He's just sore that he doesn't get to harass me anymore now that his boss is satiated for the time being. From the sound of his thoughts, I've downright humiliated him . . . and there's not a damn thing he can do about it.

I jerk my head to the side. "Get to the point."

"I have, but you ain't listenin'," he says, his anger building into my palm. The bitterness my reception captures reverberates up my wrist and scales higher. Jealousy and liquor marry in a seething torment that seeps through his skin, emanating from his hissing mouth. "Everyone else gets in on the action, but I get left in the dust? Moretti gets his green, you get yours, and even that tall-dark-and-handsome you're seein' gets a piece too? You know he don't care about you."

"And I suppose you do?"

"Can't you see we're both afta' the same things? I'm goin' places, and I wanna take you with me." Salvatore's grudge against my constant rejections reaches his eyes with an annoying amount of ardor. *Great.* Another heart-strung sap homing in on my action. "Oh please. We're not after the same thing. I want my club, and you wanna lay me down in the back seat of Moretti's Rolls-Royce." "Every damn night, Rose. But at least I'm honest about it."

I knew my success would draw the best and worst kind of attention, but this guy really takes the cake. "You think I've been lying to you?" I ask. "Leading you on? I don't know how many ways you want me to say it—I don't need you."

His vise grip refuses to free my twisting arm, his teeth clenching as his whiskey-soaked breath hits my ear. "You're a real vamp, you know that? I don't know why I even mess with you." The embittered gangster turns on his heel, pushing back through the crowd as Gio slides past him with a furrowed brow. I rub my elbows, trying to wipe away the hostility still hanging onto the raised hairs on my arm.

"Boss," he says, scanning the crowd, "have you seen Heck floatin' around here anywhere? He's supposed to close the night."

My tan wristwatch ticks toward midnight, the orchestra readying its grand finale. "Maybe he got caught up in the Drawing Room. Have Doris give the farewell and meet me downstairs in ten."

"You got it."

THE UNDERBELLY OF MY PACKED BALLROOM HAS HALF THE amount of seating but seems twice as full, the previously suave gentlemen shedding their princely dinner jackets and gloves around the dark tables. Clip's band draws out hoppers of every variety to the dance floor with our flappers, a certain adorable darb missing from the feet-kicking action. *Where is he?*

My brother edges next to me behind the bar, setting down a dried mug. Between him and the bar manager upstairs, the two of them are barely keeping the glasses full. But we've been working our whole lives for that kind of problem. Sunday is sure to be a record night. The growing absence of my fiancé before closing time beds down my excitement, though, my neck stretching to examine every shiny head of blond in the house.

"Could've sworn he was down here thirty minutes ago, but I lost sight of him in the crowd," Javier says.

My heart sinks further as Gio appears at my side with a confused frown. "No sign of him yet?"

"No." My teeth tug at the inside of my lower lip. "He always tells me where he's going, and he didn't finish his show."

Gio peers around with an apprehensive nod. "Yeah, he talked to a lot of people tonight. He could've met someone and lost track of time."

"Maybe," my brother says, his brow ridging. We're all trying to stay positive, but the image of Heck bound and gagged in his back seat won't shake from my mind. The tense look on Javier's face matches the sentiment. "I should have been paying attention."

I lay my hand on his shoulder. "Don't do that to yourself, Javi. He's a grown man, and you had your hands full. We'll find him."

"Hey, hey." Gio taps his knuckles against my arm. "The dressing rooms. We didn't check there." Whipping my head around, I push my palms against the marble counter to lift myself higher. Through the shifting dancers, the closed door stares back at us with an ominous prediction. The sinking in my gut turns to a plummet as I follow our storming bartender across the club. We barrel past the thundering stage, the music fading to a muffled roar as Gio shuts the dressing room door behind us. "Heck! You in here?"

The array of shimmering gowns along the walls answers back in silence, the walk-in wardrobes revealing silk stockings and gaudy jewelry . . . but no Heck. In one dawning moment, our eyes turn to the storage room beyond the row of white vanities, their oval mirrors reflecting our horrified faces. *No, no, no, no.*

My pounding heart nearly drowns out Gio's swears as we clamber for the door, my brother throwing it open. "Kess, dammit, where are you?"

A glowering lawyer jerks his head toward us, straightening his back and his bow tie as he smooths his hair above his oddly edged ears. The air thick with disgust, I swallow hard at Heck's stiffened posture against the stone wall, his defeated blank expression staring past us. Not a moment too soon. The twist in my stomach heats to a boiling rage I can barely contain as the pompous intruder lifts his nose into a sneer.

"What the hell's that gink doing down here, Heck?" Gio snaps, his eyes locked onto the lawyer's. "I thought he took his wife home a half hour ago."

Archibald sputters, his eyes widening. "I'd beg your pardon, but this is a private business conversation to which the likes of you are not invited." He fastens a hanging cuff link, giving a quick nod to my stony fiancé, whose cerulean eyes deaden further. "I look forward to picking this back up over lunch soon, Mr. Kessler."

"Of course," Heck says, his gaze following the man to the door as he shoves past the suspicious scowls of our crew. Archibald has some nerve. My brother's tightening jaw loads with menace. Heck's shivering hand grabs Javier's arm to keep him from storming after the offender. "Please don't. It's not worth it, Javi."

My brother's fists clench, his nose reddening. The turbulence in his eyes declares a helplessness that fastens to my chest, suffocating my ability to reason.

"Sweetheart," I plead, "we should go to the police."

"And tell them what? That I'm a sailor and so's Archibald? It won't help." Heck snaps his crimson face toward the tower of boxes and crates as he adjusts his tuxedo jacket. "Swinson is friends with the commissioner and he let me know it. Just drop it. It's damn humiliating enough."

Gio looks out to the dressing room, his lips pressed together. "At least tell us how he got in here so we can tighten security. This is gettin' nuts."

Adopting a confident posture, Heck raises his lifeless gaze back to the open door. "I was looking for my show fedora before our last act. I didn't know he followed me until I was locked in. Said he'd start yelling for help, telling people I assaulted him if I didn't . . . if I didn't. But then you guys showed up."

"Hijo de *puta*," my brother hisses, his teeth clenching behind his trembling lip. "Lemme find him, Rose. I'm not afraid of him."

"I said no!" Heck insists, his face twisting with his watering eyes. "Everyone will know what happened. I'll lose the rest of my inheritance. This club will be abandoned, but *he'll* go on ruling the world because I'm the one who tempted him."

"Is that what he told you?"

Heck's growling sob pierces my heart, his palms covering the flood of tears. "I don't want everyone to know . . . all right?"

"Maybe they need to know," Javi says, his tone softening. "Animals like that don't deserve to hide."

"*I'm* the one who's hiding!" My sobbing fiancé throws his hands down, his eyes burning. "*I'm* the one who ends up taking the fall! You think this is the first time this has happened to me? This is the price we pay, Javi!"

"Listen to me, Kess." My brother's patient hands lift in the air like a shield to Heck's self-loathing. "This is not normal. That man is sick in the head and so is anyone else who's done this to you."

With his chest rising and falling, Heck stares straight ahead until his furious expression melts into agony, his gasping sobs catching in short spasms. "No, my . . . father was . . . right."

"Kess—"

"I never fight them, Javi!" His forearms hide his face once again, his body smashing against the wall like a child hiding from his monsters.

My brother loops his fingers behind his neck with a sigh, wiping his damp eyes with his sleeve. "Guys, we close in ten minutes. You stay with him while I help Penny wrap things up in the Drawing Room."

"No," Heck gasps, burying his face into his own shoulder as he reaches for my brother's arm. "Don't leave me."

Easing my fiancé against his chest, Javier wipes his stormy eyes that search the desperate hand clutching his sleeve. I stay with them, stroking Heck's hair while Gio volunteers to lock up, sending the crew home. We can always clean up tomorrow. But the brutal tarnish on souls like Heck's won't scrub away so easily.

Is this how things are now? Our crew has already paid a heavy price for pressing against social norms and standing up for ourselves. Yet we're still paying.

Is every night going to end in disaster?

17

"GOD, I CAN'T HARDLY STAND BEIN' IN THIS ROOM RIGHT NOW." Gio shoves the last of our Saturday shipment against a stone wall, one of his brown suspenders falling as the glasses clink together inside the boxes. The hanging bulb in the ceiling chases away most of the harrowing shadows from the night before, but I'm still on heightened alert, having hired three more men for Nickels's team. I always thought our security was protecting us from hardened mobsters. Real criminals. But the greatest threat so far has come from smooth-faced gentlemen in tailored suits.

"Yeah," I say, wrapping my arms around my body, "I tried to phone Margaret this morning, but he answered, so I hung up."

Gio wipes his beaded brow with his sleeve, smashing his taxicab hat back down over his rumpled hair. "That's okay. She's gotta know he's nuts. How's our boy doin'?"

"He says he's okay, but Javi doesn't believe him." The rough wall scratches against the soft fabric of my blouse as I lean back, my head dropping. "I don't know, Gio. This is all getting so . . . *so.*"

It's not *tough* I'm thinking about here. I can deal with *tough*. I knew it would be *tough*.

No, there are no words for the burning vitriol stewing in my stomach, its arms reaching into my limbs like angry tree branches. I want to attack our enemies' hypocritical bigotry head-on. I want to cast a spell.

I want to drink until I can't feel anymore.

One of these things I can act on, and I'm about to head out to the bar when Gio's earnest hand lifts my chin, his predictable affection leaking into my jawline. "They don't get to win, boss. We won't let 'em—not Archibald, not Salvatore, not nobody. You're sellin' for the syndicate, rememba'? Now that you're done with Ice, I can call hellfire and brimstone for you."

Aye. My eyebrows slowly lift, my face freezing into a tight-lipped smile.

"Right?" he asks, tilting his head with a skeptical squint. "You *are* out from unda' that rat, ain't you?"

"We will be soon, Gio—"

"Whoa, hold on. Whaddya mean *soon*?"

"I mean that I found a way to keep him off our backs for a while *and* got the kale we needed."

"Jesus, Rose! A loan? Do you even know what friends *are*?"

"Yes! Which is why I did it."

"Gah!" His fingers pinch around the bridge of his nose as he paces near the doorway. "You told us you got more money from your fatha'. You lied to us!"

"I had to," I hiss, pulling him away from the opened door. "Besides, it's temporary."

"You think Moretti thinks of it as temporary?" His jaw stiffens, the tiny stubble forming an indistinct shadow. "How much?"

"You can't tell the others."

"How much, Rose?"

I let out a huffing growl. "Just . . . a thousand."

"A *what*?" Gio shrieks, his wide eyes darting at the doorway before leaning closer. "What's goin' through your head, boss?"

My long sigh accompanies my shaking head. I know I did the right thing—for my business, for the crew. Yet I can't look him in the eye. "I did what I had to do and now we're up and running. If we keep earning what we did last night, I'll have him paid off in a few months."

"You should'a told me. I would'a done it for you."

"You have a thousand clams?"

"I would have figured it out."

"Yeah, well, I wouldn't have let you."

He wags his head like he's tasting his thoughts to see if they're worth saying before leaning closer. "Of course you wouldn't . . . not a big, strong businesswoman like you. You'd rather deal with a respectable mobster than a dirty criminal."

"You're *way* out of line."

"No, you're outta line," he snaps. "But go ahead and fire me if you wanna. Hell, get rid of all of us since you don't need nobody."

He's not understanding. I did this for all of us.

"I never said—"

"Yeah, you did. The moment you took that money from Ice." Gio straightens his back, raking his hair away from his face as I fix a sullen gaze on his collar button. True or not—and they're not; I *know* what I'm doing—his words sting. "Rose . . . when are you gonna look around and see it, huh?"

"See *what*?"

"You're not alone." My supplier's troubled sigh follows the sting in my nose. For a second I wonder if he's going to hug me, but he shoves his hands into his pockets instead. "This ain't about my feelin's this time. Ice don't loan money 'cause he wants to be paid back. He does it for control."

He's talking to me like I haven't weighed this out. It won't matter why Moretti does what he does—not after I'm putting the final check in his hand. Raising my indignant eyebrows at Gio's button only animates him more.

"You think this is gonna be over the moment you pay him back?" He taps his palms to his chest like he can't believe what he's hearing. "I didn't think you was that naive, Rose. He might just try to steamroll ya' head this time, or come at you anotha' way. He's scum, and scum don't care about people—hell, they don't even see us as people."

I raise my brimming eyes up to his, our firm gazes battling in the light bustle floating in from the dressing room. He's the one who breaks away first, but I don't feel like I've won this argument with his flaring nose and pursed lips.

"Hey, Gio," I say as he starts for the doorway, "no one needs to know about this right now. They've got enough to worry about."

I can already imagine my brother's lecture if Gio's reacting this way. Of course, his concerns make complete sense to someone who doesn't know what I've been through, obstacles I've had to overcome. To him, I'm just a dame with a dream too big for the sleazy world she wants to be a part of. And maybe I'm not the master criminal he is, with connections to the big man in the Windy City, but I made it this far on my own, and while this may be the riskiest decision I've made so far, it was *my* decision, and one I can live with.

I've been indebted to greedy jerks my whole life. I've never been in debt to my friends, and I'm not about to start now.

Gio finally gives his head one last frustrated shake, his jaw as hard as his eyes. "You're the boss."

Damn right.

His quick exit tightens my chest, but we can't really continue anyway, the adjoining dressing room filling with hip-jutting dancers laying out their garments for rehearsal. Heck flutters around the room like a mother hen, lecturing the ladies on posture and proper nail care while Penny gives out tips on the subtleties of enticement. Slipping around the jovial coop, I duck out of there before anyone decides to engage me in their merriment.

No danger of that. I might as well be invisible with the way my staff frolics around me, laughing at inside jokes and asking about each other's families. My slow walk toward the bar goes unnoticed by Giuseppe, who practices a dice throw at his table, the band's trombones and cymbals clattering around the stage behind me. My brother raises an encouraging fist pump to another one of Nickels's failed attempts to woo Doris as I round the marble counter. We should be going over the night's menu, but Javier's having too much fun and Gio's left me to do it alone.

Of course he did.

I *should* fire him. But then who would be honest with me? He might have a knack for telling me things I already know, but his motive comes from a good place—a protective place. *So does mine.* This is why going solo is so much easier.

I saunter to the wine cabinet in search of an elixir to cure the growing hole inside me. It won't really fix anything.

But it sure won't hurt, either.

IF THE WORLD EVER WANTS TO SEE A DAZZLING ENTERTAINMENT cast during rehearsals, they should frequent a speakeasy at midmorning or so. After working all night, they show up ready to work themselves to perfection, swearing and sweating and cheering each other on. The rest of us behind the scenes leave them to it, setting up for a post-opening-night staff meeting to work out the wrinkles from the night before.

The gambling corner of the underbelly is, by far, my favorite feature, with its U-shaped poker tables of green felt and extra padded seats to keep the patrons drinking comfortably all night long. As the last of the entertainment crew strolls away up the stairwell after their final run-through, my smaller group of partners in crime gather around my brother, who deals a mean hand. Most of us fold in the second round, resorting to sipping on the cheaper gin and smoking a full hope chest between us.

"Now *this* is how you do staff meetin's," Gio mumbles with a dincher between his lips. Smoke drifts around his gaze that twinkles across the table at our head of security, who scratches the sandy hair under his cap with a wrinkled forehead. "What'chu got, Nick? It's you and me, baby."

The chair beneath Nickels creaks as he leans his elbows on the table. "Aw, Gio, all I gots is a full house." He slaps his cards down, his triumphant smirk revealing the gap in his front teeth. "Magic your way outta that one!"

"You know, I think I will." Gio's straight flush makes all of us groan as his arms cradle the pile of wooden chips in the center of the table. Reaching across Heck, he taps his ashes into another shining tray. "I neva' thought I'd be snuffin' out a dinch in a plate'a gold. Javi's fancy menus are workin'. Penny and Heck's girls are gettin' hot on that dance floor—"

The crew's laughter barely lifts my sour mood. In fact, the way Gio's lording over the table is making it worse. His lectures play in my head over the jokes he's telling, my team's morale shining in ways I've never been able to muster out of them. *Oh please.* Just because he's more likable doesn't make him a better leader. I'm the one who's had to make the hard decisions. *I made this happen.* I force down another sip, the juniper tones of the gin leaping over my tongue like everything's okay when it's not. The liquor isn't high-end, but it's damn good with a cigarette.

Heck throws his head back, setting his tumbler down next to mine with a loud swallow. I've got to get this crew back on track before we all get too sauced.

"All right," I say, my smoke cloud forcing my fiancé to rear back in his seat, "we should probably discuss more productive ways to make our second night run smoothly. Has anyone heard from Charlie?"

Gio presses what's left of his cigarette to his mouth with a squint. "Clip told me to take notes. He ain't interested in anythin' that ain't his area—especially Nicky's drama."

The table snickers at the security guard's open mouth. "Drama?"

"Yeah." Gio smirks. "You can't keep shakin' down guys who look down Doris's dress."

"That's what the unda'belly girls are for. They don't got a right to look at her."

Penny tosses her head, her long curls hitting Nickels in the eye as she smashes the end of her cigarette into a tray. "Bearcat's a choice bit of calico with a loud mouth. You might try getting used to a woman being who she is without tryin' to change her."

I give Gio the eye at Penny's words, but he ignores me a little too efficiently. *You better take notes too, Mr. Cattaneo.*

He has to know I'm right.

"Beauty's a curse, really." Heck sighs, leaning his cheek into his hand. We all stare at the green felt, my heart squeezing. I can only imagine how he feels, bitterness swirling inside me at the thought. If it weren't for my charm, the same thing would have happened to me . . . a few times. I think back to the detective pouring drinks down my throat. *Sometimes even the charm isn't enough.*

"Kess . . . you know you can take the night off," my brother says, leaning his hands on the edge of the table. "Let Doris do the solo show."

"Sitting at home contemplating my miserable existence just isn't my game."

Gio nudges his fist into my fiancé's hunched shoulder, giving him a slight shake. "Then let's get you warmed up, huh? Jav!"

As he leaps from his seat, I turn a curious eye to our bartender, who holds his hands up like an innocent man at a crime scene. "This was not my idea."

"Come on, Jav," Gio calls out, jogging to the stage. "You gotta show 'em what you showed me. Everybody get out here. This is golden."

I should bring the business meeting back around, establish my position and all that. But I'd give anything to see Heck's genuine smile again. And I'm downright curious to see what in God's name my brother is blushing about. We could all use the distraction. With a groan that's half performance, he trudges to the dance floor, the rest of us following with the interest of a tourist in Paris. Javier hates being the center of attention as much as I do, his neck reddening up to his shy smile. He isn't quite resisting, either.

He's changing. These people have been his coworkers for a long time, and he's always regarded them warmly. But now, with our collective tragedies and victories bringing us together, our crew is clearly pulling him out of his shell. Something about seeing my brother open up pinches me with longing. Sure, they've seen Rose— the reporter and club owner—with all of her snark and savvy wiles. But they've never truly seen all of me.

They've never seen Luna.

"Okay," Javier says, rubbing the smooth space above his lip where his mustache used to be. "I happened to mention to Gio that my father was a mariachi player, and we started messin' around with this song—"

Penny gasps, grabbing onto his sleeve. "I haven't seen you dance in ages, Javi."

"I haven't seen him dance at all," Heck says, his eyes widening with his grin.

My own delight hits my toes, bouncing my heels against the shining planks. Javier is a phenomenal dancer, though only a few have seen his carefree side. With the right amount of whiskey, Clip used to get my brother's feet moving back at the River Rose at cleanup time. Nearly everyone in our small crew has let their hair down during our former late-night encores, but this is different. This feels . . . special.

The gap in Nickels's teeth is forever showing as he crosses his arms, his muscles bulging through his cropped sleeves. "I can't wait to see this."

"Aye, aye, aye," my brother groans, covering his eyes with his hand. "This is stupid."

We all collectively encourage him, pulling him back as he tries to walk away. The tinkling piano covers his protest, the notes riding with crescendos that remind me of a Latin hero seducing his evasive lover. Gio's gritty voice grabs the melody, snapping my head to the stage at a serenade I've never heard before. The fusion between his bluesy hook and Javier's added flair have my own shoulders wriggling before I realize it.

My brother grabs Penny's hand, pulling her hips close, his other hand on her waist. "Now, the key is to let your feet take turns with your hips for the beat." He counts with Gio's dancing fingers, strutting forward and back again until his partner steps into rhythm with him. Her silver dress shimmies against her bronze skin as he gives her a quick twirl, tugging her back toward him like a magnet. Circling around the dizzying couple, Heck cups his chin with interest, turning his piqued eyes on me.

"Oh no, sir. Not me—"

His determined arms lift me from my escape, spinning me around before throwing my arm over his shoulder. My trouser heels are just tall enough to keep my feet on the floor, my sweating hand gripping his in a slight panic, though his thoughts guide me through a few awkward steps. If only his thoughts could help my coordination. Nickels's laugh rings across the club, his hands encircled around his mouth. "Switch partna's! Kess is dyin' over here!"

With another whirl, my stumbling frame runs right into Penny's buoyant chest, her arms keeping me from falling. "Geez, Penny. Sorry about that."

"Not a problem, Miss Rose," she says, chuckling at my continued fraying. "But, uh, why don't you let me lead?"

"I thought I was."

We're both giggling as she has mercy on me, leading me into a few easier steps while my brother roars with a throaty laugh that even I don't get to see that often. Heck has latched onto this dance like he invented it, spinning and clutching Javier's hips with an exaggerated sneer that has us all guffawing until a sharp knock raps at the door. The piano ceases, our heads craning around to the huffing hotel manager with the rounded spectacles.

"We approved your morning rehearsals, Mr. Kessler," he lectures, his hands folded behind his back. "But my guests will not be forced to endure such lascivious racket during the day. I don't want to hear another tittle until you open this evening. Am I clear?"

Heck's mouth pinches together, the rest of us turning to hide our smiles. "Yes, Mr. Cornwell. I greatly apologize."

"Very well. Good day!"

The bravado of the man's exit has my spitting snort spraying all over Penny's shoulder as we hold each other up. I can't remember the last time I laughed this hard, my joy almost drowning the dread of the risks I've taken to get us all to the final destination. My rushed decisions. The lies I've told. My happy crew wouldn't be so happy if they knew the danger I've put us all in. The thought only reinforces my desire to keep my worries from them—because I *am* going to get us out of it.

The other option is admitting this is a sinking ship and I'm the only one who knows the sharks are circling. I've got to keep us above water.

I will. I promise.

Somewhere deep inside my chest, where my retribution and passion collide, I feel a rush that reaches my fingertips and the flavor of a summer bouquet hits my lips. It's nice to sense Luna's agreement. The harmony is both comforting and unexpected.

Sending my loved ones to their lunch break, I wave at their grins and teasing quips as they make their way up the stone stair-

well. I wish every day was like this for them.
One day it will be.

18

I NEVER CAN EAT WHEN I'M ANXIOUS. A BURNING CAMEL SATU-rates my nerves with dishonest serenity as I wait on the Drawing Room dance floor, examining the intricate flowers painted along the clawed feet of Gio's piano. The intimacy of the stage reminds me of the River Rose. *Simpler times.* As several sets of heavy foot-steps sound behind me in the stairwell, a cloud of bitterness sur-rounds me like the smoke seeping from my mouth. Greed itself is coming for me. But I'm not afraid anymore. I'll do what I have to do to find freedom for all of my friends in this forsaken underworld. And if I had to do it over again, I wouldn't change a damn thing. The soft breath and shuffling shoes of my debtors approach, their shadows growing around me.

Making my first payment after opening night was an odd stip-ulation in my contract with Moretti even if I did rake in enough green last night to more than cover it. Having to endure another exchange with his sidekick only makes my nerves worse. At least I'm in a fairly public venue. Meeting beneath the hotel has its benefits—if things go south, at least someone can hear me scream.

"The money's on the counter, Salvatore," I say, pressing the filter to my lip. "Now get the hell out."

"And he said you were charming."

A gasp chokes the back of my throat as I whirl around to a raspy voice I wasn't expecting, a pair of predatory eyes I've come to loathe glaring back at me. His crooked nose wrinkles into a sneer as two henchmen snicker beside him, adjusting their tweed jackets. The way their eyes trail down my body provokes a churn in my stomach that increases with their wicked grins, the white envelope lying untouched on the marble bar.

"Mr. Moretti . . . I thought your assistant was collecting payments."

"I was in the neighborhood." His expression cools as he slides his ring-draped hands into his pockets, strolling around the tables. The gangster's nod sends his thugs to a seat near the dance floor, my angst turning to dread. Clicking across the hardwood, his steel toes gleam under the lighting. My body tenses as he passes, making his way to the gramophone on the edge of the stage. Moretti grips the outside handle, slowly winding it around, my nerves winding with it. I attempt a direct approach.

"Look, there's no need to bring your goons in here," I say, steadying my voice. "I'm hardly dangerous."

His smile flares his crooked nose. Still winding. "I tend to disagree, Miss Lane." The rasp of his voice chills me, though my palms are damp. "You see, you and your team were still under contract the night my club burned down."

My face freezes like the dawning of a nightmare. "We were attacked. I told you that, and told you who did it."

"Yes, what you've admitted to me is, because you insist on provoking people, the Klan destroyed *my* property." Moretti's fierce eyes fall back to the gramophone, the needle hovering above the black record. "Your defiance has cost me over ten grand, and as far as I see it, you owe me. That envelope won't cover it."

Ten thousand? There's no way I can get that many clams. The envelope was just a taste of the thousand I already owed him.

They don't even see us as people . . .

Gio was right. I'm a fool. Sweetened bitterness coats my tongue as though Luna's disagreement is just as flavorful as her contentiousness. Of course Ice is playing a hidden card, insisting that I fold. He's crooked.

And I'm a witch.

He doesn't know me at all.

"So ten thousand. Fine. Add it to my balance."

Moretti shakes his head with a shark's grin. "Oh, we'll get the money. But I'm here about the inconvenience fee."

With clenched teeth, I narrow my gaze. I've been here before—the lewd looks on his henchmen's faces, the way they smooth their hair. "Say what it is you want, then. I have places to be."

"You really are spunky," the mobster teases, letting the needle fall. "Let's hope that's good for you." The crackling horns of jazz music fill the thick air as he turns to his snickering men. "The price today is simple. Please my associates. When they're ready to leave, we leave."

I should be frightened. These two clearly aren't here for my dazzling wit. I know what they want—what Ice wants—the same thing the detective wanted. The same thing so many other men have tried to get from me. My charm knows what to do, although it usually takes some focus and time. Unfortunately, Ice doesn't look like the patient type. And he's wanting me to tend to his greasy goons, not him.

I normally don't like this game, but we're a long way from the newsroom, and after his nasty trick, anything goes at this point. Plus, I'm too fed up to act *professional.* So now Rose turns to Luna, who has been waiting for this since Salvatore first laid his filthy hands on me.

Your branches thirst.

Mama Sunday was giving me the way out before I ever needed it. My eyes narrow at the smirking henchmen on the upholstered stools. *Diente de león.* I might not have time, but dammit, I can focus. And I can already taste lavender. As I let my mind empty itself of whatever fear I should be feeling about the two men and their psycho boss, the familiarity of raging balconies and my brother's coughing gasps come back to me like an old friend. Its shadow grows like the passion in my heart. Shielding me from the hail and torment these men would have me endure, the thick branches of my magic reach over me, strengthening my arms. Strengthening my lips. The roots find their way to dark places. It takes some concentration, but reaching for my power at will doesn't seem as impossible as it used to be. In fact, as the mobsters' greedy eyes scale down my body, it's not difficult at all.

I *should* be afraid, but I'm not.

I'm angry.

Luna is angry.

I am Luna.

"And if I don't?" I ask, letting the disgust register on my face.

Moretti's sneer falls, his gaze deadening. "Then you and your friends will learn how I got my name."

My eyes close, Javier's words reminding me of who I am. I add a few titles of my own. *Render of Thoughts. Breaker of Hearts. Seductress of Souls.* These crooks think me their victim; the earthy tobacco smoke in my lungs tells me it's the other way around. Sex and magic are for *my* amusement. They always have been.

Snapping my eyes open, I pinch my cigarette with my lips, lifting my blouse from my waistband. The men's smiles curl as they nudge each other. Moretti settles back on the stage. My hands unfasten each ivory button, one by one before the soft blouse slips off my shoulders. I take slow, purposeful steps forward, my audience's eyebrows rising when my trousers gather by my ankles. Leaning down, I let my hands slide down one man's suspenders, his jutted chin tightening with his smile as my palms brace against his thighs.

"How's this?" I ask his middle part since his bulging eyes are focused on my chest.

His fingers tug at my bloomers. "I think you need to lose these, baby."

"Not yet." Clenching my teeth over my bottom lip, I grab his wrist, turning his slimy thoughts into fuel as his face snaps upward with a curious grin. His buddy elbows him with a stupid giggle. "I can't please a man I haven't even kissed."

"Well, whaddya waitin' for, toots?"

I could fill him with his greatest fears if I really concentrate, but having these guys run out of here in a sweaty panic would be too suspect under Moretti's watchful eye. I'll give these goons a heart instead. A sharp gasp shoots through his nose as my mouth hits his, unloading a heavy amount of allure mixed with weighty concern for my well-being. *Ice is always playing power games. I've got better things to do.* I push the impartations through his lips in a barrage of confusion that quenches his desire, his hands cupping my face. The laughter in his eyes melts into twinkling adoration. "Toots . . . your mouth's like a spring mornin' after a rain."

The man next to him sniffs his long nose, gripping my arm and pulling me into his lap. "Lemme get a taste'a that." His crude mind is even more pliable than his friend's, bending to every manipulation I push into his filthy mouth. As I stand up, the curves of their homburg hats are in their hands, their forlorn faces turning to the squinting gangster sitting on the stage.

"Ice," the middle-part says, standing to his feet, "you were right. She's somethin' else, but I think we're done here."

Moretti's intrigued eyes scan my body, glaring back at his men before he does something unexpected.

He smiles.

"Very good, Miss Lane. Even better than I expected."

Huh? *Why is he looking at me like that?*

Readying a few choice thoughts at my lips, I push away the heaviness in my eyelids. He'll wish he never laid his mouth on me. I lift my chin like I do this for a living. "So are you wanting a kiss too? I've got a business to run."

"No—I got precisely what I came for," he says as he saunters to the bar, sliding the envelope into his breast pocket before heading to the stairwell. "Until next time."

Long-Nose's empty gaze locks onto me, his friend dragging him from the room. *Until next time.* I snatch my clothes from the floor, my chest burning. Next time, I'll make them beg.

ANGER AND DISGUST FINALLY FIND THEIR WAY TO MY EYES, DRIVing me to the last place I felt powerful. Darting a burning tear from my cheek, I twist the hotel key into the lock and swing open the door. My newest distraction is too busy with his newest distraction to notice my crossed arms and tapping foot.

"Oh God, baby. Just like that."

His neck flushes, his eyes rolling back as he braces against the papered wall with a loud grunt. The woman on her knees shrieks as she catches sight of me out of the corner of her eye, scrambling to her feet with her maid's apron over her mouth. Buttoning his pants with one hand, Stuart tucks a wad of bills into her clenched fist, giving me a quick nod. She flies past me, mumbling an apology in Spanish before slamming the door.

Turning my deadpan expression back to my suitor, I shake my head. His deft fingers are already twisting the plug on a crystal decanter by the wet bar, his shirt hanging open.

"It's nice that we can have this kind of arrangement," he says, the amber liquid filling a tumbler. "I can't tell you how dramatic my wife can be over these kinds of things." He glances over at me, sipping the rim. "Wait, are you *crying*? Maybe I spoke too soon."

"Ugh." My eyes flick to the ceiling. His copper eyebrows rise as I storm across the room to steal the drink from his hand. "As disgusting as I often find you, no. You are not the reason I'm upset." The full-bodied bourbon empties into my mouth, the glass tilting with my chin.

Stuart takes back my solution with a laugh. "Whoa there, baby. Before you get too sauced, tell me what happened. Anything I can do to help?"

"Maybe. Depends on those connections of yours." I raise my face to his, the thought of another meaningless kiss threatening to reprise my bourbon. "How bad are you, Mr. Kensington?"

His long lashes flutter, that wolfish smirk crossing his face. "How bad do you want me to be?"

"Bad enough to get Icepick Moretti off my back."

Stuart holds my serious gaze, his smile fading with a shake of his head. "What do you owe him?"

"Money—at least, I *thought*," I say, letting my forehead fall to his bare chest. "But today he wanted me to pay his friends in a striptease."

"And?"

My head shoots up, my eyes narrowing. "And *what*?"

"What's the big deal, baby?" Stuart shrugs, pushing my hair from my face. "It's just a dance. You've done a hell of a lot more for me."

Is he really this dense? "It's always been my choice!"

"So you don't like the price of the underworld all of a sudden?" My predictable potato sneers as I push away, his looming gait following me to the door. "Baby, if I get myself involved in this, you'll have yourself in another mix soon enough, and I don't want those kind of strings. You play the game, you lose sometimes. That's just the way it is."

"Well, maybe what I want's changing."

"That's your prerogative, baby," he says, opening the door for me. "If that's the case, it was nice knowing you."

The snapping of my fortitude sounds in the pit of my stomach like a tree splintering under the weight of a hurricane. I won't be used again unless it's for my own gain. Not by him. Not by anybody. I reach for Stuart's chiseled chin, a beautiful deception. He lowers his brow, curious and unsure as I pull his face to mine, planting my punishment to the tip of his cupid's bow. Dark desire. Deep regret. Debilitating shame with the essence of lavender. All the mistakes he spent so many years guarding behind his numbing wall come crashing forth at my beckoning, misting his eyes with a shudder.

He pushes back my shoulders with a trembling gasp. "I don't know what you are . . . but leave me the hell alone."

"Go home to your wife, Stuart," I say, my own eyes burning. "Sounds like *you're* the one not fit for the underworld."

As I back through the doorway, my lingering exit turns into a dead run, only slowing when I reach the marbled lobby, where my crew is filtering in for our second night. My club opens in an hour. The place where I should be in the most control, the most comfortable.

Where I can be the Rose I want to be.

But I don't know how long it will be before I'll ever feel like myself again.

"LET'S FIRE ALL MEN."

"From what?"

"Everything."

I lift my bobbing head from Heck's shoulder, pushing my heavy lips into a bemused smirk. If only we could. My fingers wrap around another empty tumbler, our second magical night at the Casbah Lounge fuzzing in and out of my musings. Once again my fiancé and Doris stole the show, wetting the club with laughter, easing the skeptical brows of the high-class suits, who were more than willing to spend the rest of their capital gains in the gentlemen's club by the end of the evening.

"To 'nother successful venture," Heck slurs, lifting what's left in his glass. He snorts as I pull his drink to my mouth. I can't even taste it anymore. I can't even feel anymore. At least I have my davenport. The floral upholstery of my prized couch meets my cheek, the fringed fabric brushing the backs of my sweating ankles. The pattern of my rug is phenomenal. "Don'chu fall asleep, dear flower. It's too humid, for one thing, and I must know how you plan to move forward. You can't make them *all* hop the train back ta where they came from in a sea of regret."

"Can't I?"

Beneath my hanging lamp, Heck snorts into his empty cup, slurping the last few drops. "Welp, at least share your magic so that I may use it if this next one doesn't work out."

"Oh yes," I say, craning my head around. "You haven't talked much about this darb."

"That's because he's not a darb. He's different."

"You say that every time."

With a long grunt, my fiancé slides his tumbler onto my coffee table, his unsteady head hanging. "Yes, well, maybe you're right." His downcast form slumps back against the couch. "I shouldn't get my hopes up."

"Aw, honey." My weighted arms push my body back up into what feels like a sitting position. "Don't listen to me. I'm bitter . . . and a lil' tanked."

Heck jerks his head as he flops it to the side, squinting at me. "*You're* bitter? Do ya know my father forced me into insulin shock therapy? Psychol'gists. Priests. We're not even Catholic. Now the trustees have taken it 'pon themselves to withhold my 'heritance as though I could just decide to get better."

"They what?"

I thought we had this ruse in the bag.

"Another 'non'mous letter made its way to my trustees," he says. "They'll 'parently sign when they see a marriage certif'cate, but don'chu worry. We'll figure it out."

My numbing heart sinks. I can't imagine being forced to marry. My problems don't seem to compare, but my agony joins the parade anyway, my own head falling back. "My mother thinks I should go 'head and fall in love. Like it's even optional for someone like me."

"Come now, darling. Not ever?"

I roll my head, flattening my eyes.

"Not even Gio?" Heck asks, perking up. "Really, if you don't impart thoughts, what's the big deal? He'll jus' think you're the best he's ever had. That's hardly a problem. You can't live your whole life without love." His shoulders clench in an eye-rolling snort. "God, both our lives would be so much easier if your allure worked on *me*."

"What do you mean?"

"The times we've kissed."

One of my eyes squints as I recall his strong lips that begged me to stop. "Uhm . . . I didn't use my allure on you."

My fiancé's beaded eyebrows pinch together as they lower, his mouth dropping open. "But . . . you told me you couldn't control it."

"Well, it's more like I can't stop it once it starts," I say with a shrug, my tongue rolling over. "It can come on its own if I'm feeling confident and lost in the moment, but I was flustered both times you kissed me. Distraction makes it really difficult to control. Other times it just loads up on its own. But not with you."

"Neither time?"

"Nope."

"So, wait . . . then it's possible—"

"Heck. No."

"*Rose.*"

"No."

"Fine," he snips, shoving his socked feet into his loafers. "I never ask an'thing of you. And the one thing I want—one night of seeing what it's like—and you deny me a blink of happiness." His lower lip and pouty eyes plead with me in cerulean melancholy, whittling away at my resolve. My swaying logic escapes my throat in a deep sigh that brings out his belly-warming smile. Just one kiss to lift his spirits. The man's been through enough.

"I'll grant'chu feelings," I mumble, pointing my finger in his smirking face. "But thass all you're getting, mister."

"Deal."

My magic's been getting a real workout lately. And my abuela *said* I needed to practice. In the back of my mind, this feels like a really bad idea. But my tongue is tingly. And Heck smells like patchouli and shoe polish—ritzy and clean as a fresh dime. His eyes widen and we both giggle at the touch of our lips, his brandy tongue exploring mine like a shy first date. My allure is difficult to sense through the muddle of alcohol, but as our kiss deepens, the steady jasmine makes its way to my mouth. Heck's breath hitches, his comical thoughts turning to wonder before a familiar greed forces my eyes open. My black dress sticks to my skin, and not because of the damp air that floats through my balcony doorway. I've always wanted to hear him groan like that. I push his shoulders back, his hooded eyes as starry as the night sky behind him. "That's enough. It's done."

"Rose. Please," he moans, sliding his hands up my thighs as his soft mouth tastes the skin below my ear. As much as my arms erupt with goosebumps, I can't let this continue. It's not real. Even if it was, my feelings for him aren't the same as they used to be. Besides, I warned him well enough.

With every ounce of integrity I have left, I grab a fistful of sweaty hair and pull his head back from my neck. "I said that's enough."

Heck's chest pumps beneath his tuxedo shirt, his face determined and set. "You could have let me feel this way *all* this time?"

"No," I plead. "It's temporary."

"No, it's working." He grabs my elbows, giving me a light shake. "You'd really have me go back to being miserable and alone?"

"It's nothing but a lie."

"Everyone in your bed is a lie!"

My mouth drops open as I send him careening backward. "Since you're drunk on gin and magic, I'll let that one go, Heck Kessler. Sleep it off!"

"Oh, well, isn't that convenient?" he growls, stumbling to his feet. "Is it because I'm not a big enough jerk like the rest of those guys or because I'm not Gio?"

Tears spring to my eyes at his flared nose and trembling lip. "You're not thinking straight, honey. Please just go."

"If I wasn't so enamored with you right now, I'd end this sham of a friendship!" my fiancé spews, snatching his dinner jacket from the chair. "Teasing me with the way you look at me, letting me into your bed. Now you've got the chance and you don't want me?"

"Not like this," I cry, wringing my hands. "In fact, not ever. I like what we have. I like who you are, not who you think you need to be."

"Fine!" His wounded face turns away with heavy gusto as he bolts for the door. "Keep spinning those empty wheels, baby. Leave me in the wake with the rest of them."

"It wears off, Heck. I swear it does."

He whirls back around, his hand on the brass doorknob. "It better. Because I can't even *look* at you without my heart breaking."

Crying is the worst. But drunk-crying—it makes me feel like my face is going to explode from agony. Between submitting for Moretti's sport and Stuart's predictable ineptness at integrity, the strength to keep myself from emotional collapse has left me just like the best friend I've ever known—with the slamming of my apartment door. Why would Heck want such a thing of me anyway?

Ugh. Gin was supposed to wash away the emotional bankruptcy of this day. *I really am going to fire all men.* That thought is barely a consolation as my arms wrap around the cold davenport, my tears soaking the fabric as I fall into a restless sleep.

19

I'M GLAD I DECIDED TO SLEEP UNTIL NOON, SKIPPING MORNING rehearsal. My new workouts with bruja magic have me so drained lately; I start falling asleep when someone gets too long-winded. While I'm not a part of the stage show, I've got to be ready to put on a show anyway. Being refreshed tonight is to everyone's benefit. My high-society skills take as much mental energy as a love elixir, and are better spent smiling and offering my hand to handsome passersby while my fiancé commands the crowd with his movie star grin and charisma. Still, I know he's been busy in between our house band's sets, but he hasn't looked at me all night. I choose a corner table by the side of the stage, giving me a perfect view of the upper balcony, where a single booth waits in the center beneath a sparkling chandelier. Patrons who've opted to stand due to the packed house eye the navy fabric of the lonely seating, leaning into each other's ears with curious excitement. As gloomy as yesterday's onslaught of masculinity made me, the thrill of our tardy guest of honor still courses through me.

Rats. It's nearly eight, but there's still time. My sparkling strap watch taunts me as much as the sequins of my scarlet dress. The hem is too scratchy. *It better not snag my stockings.* As Heck announces the Coon-Sanders Novelty Orchestra amid thunderous applause, my heart soars so much I almost don't light another cigarette. Even if Capone doesn't show up, this night will be one for the record books. Just two tables away, Alfred Lunt lifts his prominent brow, offering a lighter to the "Queen of the Movies." Mary Pickford's golden-brown curls flip over her shoulder as she crosses her long legs. The film stars' attendance is almost as impressive as the British ambassador and his wife, seated on the upper balcony, where a tuxedoed waiter pours them each another glass of champagne. It cost me an ungodly amount of capital to provide, but the fifteen-dollar cover charge for the orchestra is more than enough to make up for it.

As the highly acclaimed band begins the brassy hop of the Charleston, a moderate commotion buzzes through the crowd. My lips part as I stretch my neck to see through the variety of bowler hats and colorful feathers. Either the tables near the entrance have brought in a rowdier crowd than usual or someone significant is coming through those double doors. The adoring assembly of gentlemen and ladies who stand to shake hands with the latecomer finally parts, offering me a view of the most infamous bootlegger in the Midwest. His white fedora is a presence itself, with its black stripe above a rim that's curled up on one side in his signature way. I imagine he keeps the other side curved down to shadow the large scar across his cheek, but I think it makes him look like the big cheese he is.

A small entourage accompanies the grinning mobster across the golden ballroom, his big lips stretched over a smoking cigar as his crew makes its way up the side staircase. Every dream I've ever had couldn't fathom the pride of this moment. From the bar, Gio winks at me with a shot glass in his hand. I knew this night was going to turn out great.

Of course, it's not like things could get any worse.

"And now, my esteemed colleagues," Heck announces from the stage, pinching his fingers in the air. "The lovely Doris Fenton."

Polite ovation welcomes our resident singer, the tassels of her silver dress swaying as she shimmies to the microphone stand. A long whistle from the upper deck arches her golden eyebrow. "Well, right back at'cha, fella," she says, igniting a small laugh from the audience, her throaty voice echoing off the walls. "I'd like to thank Mr. and Future Mrs. Kessla' for givin' me a chance to sing. It's always been my dream—"

The center of the VIP section whistles again, followed by a few heckling jeers.

"Forget the song, toots! Show us them gams!"

"Baby, I'll give ya somethin' to dream about!"

My fingers clench the white tablecloth as Doris's nostrils flare, her jade eyes narrowing at the snickering crowd. *Oh no.* Her cheeks flush as crimson as her lips, and before Heck can signal the band to start, she opens her sneering mouth. "Hey, just 'cause you showed up with ya bigwig boss, don't mean you run the place. I wouldn't let you piss on me if I was on fi-ya!"

Nervous chuckles flow through the room like an apprehensive current; the scrawny thug next to Capone leans over the railing, his buddies falling into the booth in boorish howls.

"Sweethawt," he yells through cupped hands, "skip the jazz and give us a real show!"

"I *would*, but I don't think ya motha' knows you're out this late."

"I bought my motha' a house wit' what I earned last month! So she don't got a say!"

Doris tosses her head. "Oh, I didn't know a head-worka' earned that kinda money."

The ballroom rumbles with champagne-spitting laughter, the heckler from the second deck holding his hands up in surrender as he sits back down by his guffawing friends. Doris plants her hands on her hips, turning to the scarred gangster in the striped suit with a scowl that rounds my eyes. *Let it go, Doris. Sing, you ninny.*

"How 'bout you, Snorky?" she snaps. "You got an awful nice getup. Whaddya do for a livin'—besides babysittin' goons who go 'round harassin' lounge singa's in fancy clubs?"

The house spotlight drags across the shocked faces in the crowd, coming to a rest on the glaring mobster. My teeth sink over the end of my thumbnail as Gio jogs across the club to my side, hissing up at the stage, "Bearcat, are you *nuts*?"

Like a slow death to my dreams, Capone pushes his chair back, rising to his feet. A hush falls over the club as he pinches the wide lapels of his husky suit, his smile illuminating under the bright beam. "Baby, all I do is satisfy a public demand."

All heads snap back to the smirking lounge singer.

"Hm," she purrs, fluffing her spiral curls. "So do I." The crowd's applauding laughter widens his grin as he tips his hat before taking his seat.

I could pass out here and now, and I'm eighty percent sure it's not just my nerves. As my heart seeks a steady rhythm, Doris enters into her transitionary song with the guest orchestra, bowing to the cheering crowd at the end of her final number. Standing behind her waving fingers, her handsome cohost casts me a subtle smile with a short nod toward the cupboard behind the bar. My body nearly leaps with my heart as I spring from my seat, gliding along the outer wall toward the Drawing Room's stone entrance. For cordiality's sake, I greet a few more people before my strappy shoes clack down the stairwell and across the underbelly floor in my rush to the empty changing room. The sharp burn behind my nose is like a dam holding back a river as my fiancé bursts through the doorway, his strong arms lifting me from the floor.

"Heck!" I cry, gripping his neck. "It would be miserable. You would wake up every morning knowing it isn't real. I love you too much to let that happen!"

"Oh, kitten." Letting me down, he presses a kiss into my hair that makes me bawl even harder. "Please don't cry. I made a fool of myself. It wasn't your fault. And I love you too."

"Our friendship means the world to me. I can't lose it."

"Never," he says, pulling back. His perfect eyebrows knit together as he pushes the wet strands of hair from my face. "But, Rose, don't close yourself off to other kinds of love. I know it's easier to run, to push others away. Take it from me, though: it's terrifyingly lonely, isn't it?" Heck's cotton handkerchief dabs at my cheeks, making me smile. "There, there. Where's that poker face I always admire? We have big fish to catch tonight."

"You have your eye on someone in particular?" I ask with a sniffle in an attempt to cover a sudden yawn. Heck usually would look at me like I've stuck my thumb up my nose for such appalling manners, but he's as preoccupied as I am tired.

He peers at the bustling club through the doorway, a thoughtful expression spreading across his face. "Let's just say that had you allowed last night to happen, it would have spoiled my chances."

I start to inquire further, but my cryptic fiancé arches out of my reach with a light shake of his head. I blow him a kiss, giving him his space. He'll tell me when he's ready. Pulling an envelope from his breast pocket, he tilts his own fedora with a mischievous twinkle in his eye.

"That splifficated youngster on the upper deck delivered this to me on my way down here." Heck slaps the offering against his palm with a grin before holding it out to me. "Told me to give it to you."

My eyes widen with my gaping mouth as I tear the envelope open, my chest thumping at the words written on the note inside.

While I don't normally get involved in local scraps, seems like you needed a leg up. Ice is a profitable guy, but, kid, you did in one weekend what he couldn't get done in years. If anyone

*asks about your green glorious, just tell them it came from a
businessman who gives the people what they want. And, baby,
they want you.*

Al Capone

"My dear, I'm nearly bursting. What does it say? Is that a *check*?"

My shaking fingers hand the note over as I peer back into the
envelope like a pirate holding a treasure chest, the breath escaping
my lungs. "Heck . . . shut the door."

"Rose," he gushes as the brassy sounds of the club beyond are
cut off. "There. Now tell me. I can't stand it!"

"It's more than enough." My words are just above a whisper,
threading together my fraying parts. It's more than enough to pay
off Moretti's loan. The part I don't tell him has me quivering, all the
tenseness in my body finally letting go. I realize how much I haven't
rested—from the stress, from my fears. And from the magic.

Heck's arms wrap around me from behind, his chin brushing
my temple as he peers down at the small paper in my quivering
hands.

His gasp hits my ear. "Kitten . . . you did it."

I think I tell him I need to sit down. Either way, I'm down. His
concerned face is the last thing I meet before my eyes fold on me.

"I BEEN MEANIN' TA TAKE YA TO GET A DECENT MEAL. YOU BEEN
lookin' kinda puny today, boss."

I fall into step beside Gio, shoving my hands toward my pockets only to be reminded that I'm still in this damn dress. Garments
without pockets are the real tragedy of modern society. "Gee,
thanks."

"Stressed is all I meant." He chuckles as he offers me his arm.

"That's not any better," I say. Nudging him with a squinting smile, I let him lead us away from the bright lights of the theater, its glowing sign displaying the title of the latest moving picture. At Heck's and my brother's demands, I was forced into Gio's care for a proper dinner that turned into an unexpected respite from the excitement of our club. I hadn't realized how much I needed a break until my piano player coerced me into the jubilant atmosphere of a movie house that had us both laughing at Charlie Chaplin's on-screen antics.

Strolling down the sidewalk, Gio tips his cap to the thick crowd of nightlifers, ignoring their judging glances at his forearms. It's another hot night. Frankly, I no longer care if he rolls his sleeves. I hardly notice the drawings on his skin anymore.

But I do enjoy teasing him.

"I could swear you're almost trying to look cosmopolitan," I say as we emerge on the other side of the crowd. "You didn't have to wear that vest outside the club."

He looks down at the checkered pattern before adopting a Heck-style posture. "Well, it goes so well wit' these fancy pants." His eyebrow crinkles at my laugh, his smile turning a bit guilty. "So . . . that check, huh?"

Cocking my jaw to the side, I throw him a heavy I-told-you-so look. Of course I'm upset that he didn't trust my judgment. At the same time, I wouldn't be feeling so victorious had Capone not stepped in tonight. Sure, my magic helped me out of the extortion from Ice that Gio predicted would happen, but I'm too irked by the whole situation to give him the satisfaction of knowing it. I can't get into explaining my witchery anyway. All he needs to know is our tussles with the mob boss are over. *Good riddance, too.*

"I shouldn't'a went off on you like I did. I know I was outta line when I was sayin' it," Gio says, staring down at his feet before looking back up with a shy grin. "I think you're really somethin' anyway. You're a good boss."

As always, his sincerity rings loud and true enough. His hands are a big snitch. The only confession he leaves out is his affection for me gaining momentum in all of this. I let him suffer in his bashful apology for a few seconds longer before ending the awkwardness for the both of us. "Yeah, well, I think it's safe to say we were both coming from a good place."

"Hey, thanks." He swings my arm, shaking his head. "Whaddya gonna do with fifty greens?"

I shut my eyes, breathing in the city air of heated exhaust fumes. "Pay off Ice and my other loans. Then . . . take care of my friends."

"You're good to us, doll. You take care'a you for once. I worry about'cha, you know?" He pulls me to his side, our arms linked around each other's waists.

I let out a long sigh as I lean into him, my fatigue still pulling at me. "I know."

Large-rimmed automobiles line the curbs of the rumbling street as we saunter away from the flood of lampposts and down the long alleyway where I had to park my car. Soon my engine sputters, growling to life in half the time it takes me to do it on my own. It's not so bad having Gio around sometimes.

Using him as an anchor, I step up into the driver's seat, his arm holding open the door. My fingers part along his skin, revealing a slender figure dangling from a rope. I cock my head, my brow furrowing as I lift my palm at the ten-gallon hat near his elbow. A shotgun laugh bursts through my nose at the drawings I never noticed before now.

Is that a circus *tent?*

"See anything you like?" he asks, his teasing smirk returning.

I bite my lower lip to hold in a giggle. "Gio . . . what *is* this?"

"Don't you know all the tough guys in jail get these?"

"Tattoos of the big top?"

His eyes roll at my wonderment, his amusement blaring through his skin. Sliding my hand down to his wrist, he points to the large tent with wide stripes. "They do if they were in the circus for a while."

"*What?*"

"That's right." Gio grins, sweeping his other arm in the air. A flash of a thought tells me he doesn't want to move from under my hand. "Ringling Brotha's and Barnum and Bailey Circus. 'Da greatest show on earth!'"

My hands give him a cheerful clap before settling back onto his wrist. "What in heaven's name did you do in the circus? Magic tricks, I'm guessing."

"Nah. Played music. Saw the craziest things, though—acrobats with gold skin. A ten-foot-tall cowboy with feet the size'a my head."

My eyes trail along the comical ink, landing on a pair of stilts with fishnet stockings. "What are those legs?"

"Well," he says with a slight blush, "there was a woman with mechanical legs . . . she actually drew this one. It was kind of an inside joke between us."

"Was it now?"

His blush deepens as he throws a hand in the air like he's swatting a bug. "All right, she was a lot of fun. That's all I got to say about it."

"Aw, fine," I concede, tugging on his arm. "Tell me about this one, then." I point to a top hat with a wand hovering over it.

"Magicians. Real snake charma's. You name it." The shine in Gio's eyes and the affection from his wrist make me grin. He really loved that place. "There was a guy who swallowed a damn sword. They took an X-ray and everything. It was wild. The clowns were the ones to watch out for. I got a tattoo for every city we visited."

"So they really aren't from jail."

"Boss, the closest I came to jail was the lion's cage."

"And you just let the circus paint you from head to toe?"

"Mostly—plus a couple'a souvenirs just for me."

"Which ones?" I ask, my curiosity exploding as my eyes search, but his skin emanates with embarrassment.

"Well, ah . . ." He rubs the back of his reddening neck. "They're under my clothes, doll." A sly smile crosses his lips. "I mean, if you *wanna* see 'em, I guess I—"

"Oh geez!" I say, clapping my hand over my mouth. I decide to save him. "So you left all that for rum-running in the underbelly of Kansas City?"

My flushed pianist gives me a grateful grin. "Well, I joined Barnum after I left Philly. Got as far as Chicago and then jumped the train. Just wanted a new adventure, I guess . . ." His fading smile floods me with stomach-fluttering intention that his fingers confirm as they slip around my jaw.

I shouldn't encourage him. This can't go anywhere. The flirting is fun, but that's all it can be for me. I'm not responsible for his insistence on getting the wrong idea. And if the man insists on tossing his heart into my chaos, then maybe I ought to lay it on him and let it break. It's not like I haven't warned him. Lifting my chin, I lock onto the fierce earnestness emanating from his eyes, breathing a beckoning response. "Did you find one?"

"Yes," he whispers, leaning forward, his thumb stroking my cheek. My breath trembles as his nose brushes mine, the scent of Lucky Strikes hovering over my lips. "Whaddya so scared of, doll?"

"You waking up tomorrow," I whisper back, "realizing this was a mistake."

"So you're savin' me, is that it?"

"Um . . . yes."

Boy, you don't even know it.

Gio's eyes and fingertips intensify with a heat that has my own breath hitching. "Well, don't."

Reading him intensifies the desire between us, his heart committing to me even though I can't give him the same. Through his skin, his thoughts echo as loud as a train that he doesn't want to stop. He knows I can't give up my independence. And I won't.

The crazy part is that he doesn't care. He doesn't want to take over my club or my life. He just wants me—exactly as I am. The safety of that realization quells my fears and the allure that was trying to creep up with it. Although I'm still unwilling to give too much of that away, it's the first time I've ever felt a man think of me like this. What he perceives as love doesn't feel like the idiot ideals of the other fellas who promise nonsense that belongs in songs and pictures. No, it's much more than that. It's respect.

Fascinating.

My will lets go, clinging to the hope of what could be as our mouths claim each other beneath the ghostly light of the moon. He lets go of the driver's-side door as I turn my body toward him, throwing my legs around his hips and pulling him close. The umbrella top might be down on my car, but it doesn't matter: the blackness of the night blankets the alleyway with enough shadows that anyone passing on the street beyond wouldn't be able to see the animalistic way Gio and I are going at each other. His palms confess his mad desire through my thighs as he tugs on the snaps of my garters. He likes the crimson of my dress. The rouge on my lips. The small rip in my stockings. His carnal thoughts play with mine, but his love weaves through the hunger like a delicious craving. His skin has confessed it to me too many times before now. *Love.*

Our kiss tastes like roses and hibiscus. *Allure.*

A cold shiver runs through my flushing body. The things I'm capable of—the things I can do without meaning to, like sending Margaret's husband home vomiting on his wedding day or when my allure pulled Salvatore's attentions closer instead of pushing him away in that dark parking lot. I'm dangerous. Moretti's goons flash through our raw embrace, their pliable minds bending to my vengeful will. Stuart's terrified eyes. Heck's despair. The things I *meant* to do are even worse. I want him so badly; the piano player's fingers could play a delicious song across my skin. But I can't expose Gio to any of this. I thought I could—I thought I could let him fall and it would be his problem, like all the other Stuarts and Edwards. But this is different somehow. And this needs to stop.

With a heavy breath, I push his shoulders back before my allure spews all over the place like flower petals and heartburn that rises with panic.

Standing between my parted knees, he holds me there for a moment, his eyes cast down to my mouth. "If you kiss me like that again, I'm takin' this all the way."

He's trying to joke like usual, but his smile is gone, his dark eyes pulling at my hunger for something real. I want to heed my own lectures. Pushing him away was the right thing. I need to end this.

Lavender and hibiscus stake their claim on my tongue. I don't *want* to end this.

Once again, our mouths become a bumbling mess of thoughts as his tongue finds mine, drinking in the secret desires that impart with my allure before I can stop their release. *Oh, Gio, I could make love to a guy like you.*

His hard breath wets my mouth as he presses his forehead against mine. "Rose . . . I wanna make love to you."

Dammit, Luna!

"Gio," I say, shaking my head, "we can't."

His desperate hands cup my face, his expression almost angry. "Look, I ain't never said nothin' like that before. I'm turned inside out here. But I don't want you like this. Lemme take you somewhere decent."

With determined resolve, I press my mouth to his, trying to feed his greed back to him as I coax my will in between kisses. "It's okay . . . Flowers and hotels are . . . just a bunch of hooey."

I need to turn this around. No love. Just lust. Want. *Take me!*

He groans with a pleading amount of effort, fighting the impartation. He's got some serious willpower. Probably because he's got some serious feelings, unlike the crowd of potatoes who just wanted something from me. With a gasp, he pulls away, his jaw clenched. "I told ya, it's not how I want it, doll." I can feel the lead-up without reading him. His eyebrows crease at my crossed arms, his lips parting as he steps back. "Is that how you want it, Rose? You want me to throw you down in this alley like a damn cuddl'a?"

I press my lips together, swallowing against the emotion that fills my eyes. "Maybe that's what I am!"

"No," he growls, his own eyes brimming. "No, it's not. You might fool those otha' guys. But I see you, Rose. I really see you."

Bitterness and fear fill my lips as he reaches for me again. It's all I have to give. He doesn't deserve that. "You don't see anything!"

I make him jump back as I slam my car door, sealing the barrier between us. "I take advantage of the moment. It's what I do. It's not my fault you're so charmed by it."

He grabs my wrist as I grip the hand brake. "I don't believe it. Not with the way you kissed me just now—"

"It wasn't real," I snap, my heart shattering along with his. This is for the best. "I can't be what you want. Not now, not ever."

"That's just an excuse—"

"Look, Gio, you're not getting it!" Hot tears march down my cheeks, nearly blinding me from his devastated face. "It gets in the way and ruins everything I've worked for. I'm not even sure it's real! And even if it is, I don't have time for it!"

The thing is, I *know* it is real. Gio's heart tells me so. I hate what I've done to him already, my heart mirroring his own discordant wave of regret and affection, which is so foreign to me that I nearly take back my words. But I can't. I can't be setting up hearts to crash and burn—not just his. Heartbreak is everything I thought it would be.

I feel his insides ripping apart as he swallows that lump in his throat, his misty eyes narrowing. "Well, thanks a lot for that, sweetheart."

The darkness embraces his fleeing silhouette, leaving me

shrouded in shadows, as empty as a man's promise.

20

20

ANOTHER MORNING SPENT IN BED SALVES MY WEARY HEART—this time, avoiding an awkward encounter with a certain pianist who's just a glutton for punishment. As I power through the doors of the Chesterfield Club in my favorite shade of teal, I almost smile at the angsty memory of the last time I was in here. Salvatore's offer to fulfill all of my dreams turned into a damn nightmare, but I've come full circle, holding fast to what they tried to steal from me—my dignity. Dignity and pride. And now some of my money, but this is the last these train robbers are getting from me.

My emotions fall away like a severed limb; I can't afford to be held back by anything anymore. Callouses and scars might keep my spirit from letting anyone in, but they've also kept me from being crushed under the greed of my enemies. The rules in the underground aren't fair. Love and vengeance don't make room for each other. Maybe one day things will be different for me. *But not today.*

Moretti's fierce countenance is like a storm cloud in the empty gentleman's club, its painted walls and fancy tables striving to be as elegant as mine. Though as I stroll past the center floor designed for bare-chested ladies in cellophane aprons, I conclude that elegance is not what this club is going for. The surrounding murals of nude figures dancing in the trees would be a funny contrast to the seriousness of this meeting if the two pairs of eyes in front of me weren't so seething. Stopping in front of the long granite bar like I'm not being shaken down by angry mobsters, I pop a cigarette between my teeth, lighting it before the goon with the hawkish chin can offer.

"C'mon, Rose," he says, his hair shining under the gaudy chandelier. "Don't tell me you're still mad at me."

My ashes float to the floor. "I'm not anything at you, Salvatore. Can't say you've even crossed my mind."

"Why you gotta treat me like that, baby?"

The intensity in his boss's eyes grows as he shoots his sidekick a look that shuts his mouth, intertwining the black gloves that cover his ring-laden fingers. "Mr. Salvatore, surely you two can settle this lovers' quarrel some other time. Miss Lane has called this meeting. Let's give her the respect of our audience."

"Yes, sir," Salvatore says with a bitter whine in his eyes. "Rose, you better have a good reason for callin' a meeting with Ice."

"I do." Pulling a crisp envelope from my handbag, I hold it out to them in triumph. "Almost eleven grand. Enough to cover my debt and the damage to the River Rose."

The henchman's birdlike features narrow even more as he squints, cocking his head. "What? Rose . . . are you *serious*? Where the hell'd you get that kinda—"

"No," the raspy voice next to him interjects. My veins chill and heat at the same time as Salvatore shrinks back beside his boss like a dog who's been told to heel.

The envelope holds the space between us as I lower my chin, trying to keep my Camel going. *This can't fall apart.* I made it. I won. It's over. "Mr. Moretti, that was our deal."

"All I said," the mobster rasps, "was that envelope won't cover it."

"I . . . don't understand."

"You will." His glove slides into his pin-striped pocket as he eyes my pouting admirer. "You see, those two associates I brought to your club—what did you call them? My *goons*? They aren't security like Mr. Salvatore. They're business partners. Partners who were going to buy into your old club before it burned down."

My cigarette freezes by my lips. I'm sure the look on my face wonders what the hell that has to do with me, because the predatory curl on his lip grows as he continues. "Instead of giving them back their capital, I decided to make a bet. I told them if they didn't fall in love with you at our meeting, then they could go ahead and kill you for the trouble you caused."

"Hey, those ghosts burned your club down. Not me."

"And they're still going to pay, but they did me a favor. You might have slipped through my fingers otherwise."

The heated ice burns my veins once again, the confidence I came in with shredding in the vortex of Moretti's storm cloud. I feel exposed like the paintings around me. "What is it you want from me?"

"Do you know why they call Luciano 'Lucky'?" he asks, his face filling with wonder.

Salvatore snorts. "Aw, Ice, not the Brooklyn witch again. Gives me the heebies."

Huh?

Everything freezes from the inside out as cold sweat and panic seize me.

Wait, no. That's not what he said. But he did. The very word. Right in front of me—*witch*.

Oh God . . .

My feet shift, taking the tiniest step back toward the glass entrance. All the blood in my body heads for my feet. This wasn't worth it. He can't be saying what I think he's saying. I shouldn't have come here.

Moretti smiles as if he's the mind reader, and continues. "Luciano knew no one would believe him. Hell, no one listened to his drunken ramblings . . . except me." Moretti takes a slow step around me like a hunter closing in on its prey. "Bullets fly through him, but he somehow survives. Money finds its way to him. Women find their way to him. It took twelve shots of gin, but I got him to talk. I never found the witch—he kept that to himself. But he told me what to look for."

"Come on," Salvatore groans, "she don't know nothin' about Lucky's dirt."

The claws hit my jugular, the storm decimating my only real protection. My cigarette hits the floor just like my secret. The mobster's hissing teeth are suddenly at my ear, his chest at my back. His hand around my neck. My pulse thumps against his leather glove like the heart in my chest as he growls, "Look for the blackberries, he said to me. The cactus. Overgrown rosebushes."

I can't tell if the breath escaping my body is from his hand or my fear. *No, no, no, no.*

"Look for the impossibilities," Moretti continues. "A juke joint full of drunks every night in my district, but no real conflicts." He nods to the envelope. "Look for the money that comes out of nowhere. Said to follow the trail of bread crumbs. Listen for the stories of a woman with lips that smell of roses . . . and watch out for the taste of lavender."

The growing panic lights my chest, my fingers curling between his to loosen his grip as the pieces to the puzzle fly around me in taunting debris. Trail of bread crumbs. I thought I was so careful. *Ice said I should keep my lips off'a you!* Thinking back to Salvatore's words the night of his assaulting kiss by my car, his boss's orders to cut down the hidden shield around my club, that rat stealing my protection ferns—dread crushes me more than the gloved fingers.

Moretti was testing me. He's been testing me this whole time. He *knew* I was going to charm his goons.

The worry etching across Salvatore's face gives me little comfort. He might not have known what his boss was up to, but he helped bring me to this place all the same.

"Hey, wait a second," he says, turning to his boss while keeping his wide eyes on me. "Is that why you had me and my guys cut down those plants at her club that night? Cuz you think they got some kinda magic?"

Moretti's silence is all the answer the room needs.

His sidekick grunts and blinks like he can't wrap his head around it. "You've been havin' us chase *witches*, Ice?"

"You're far too small-minded to grasp the reality of what's been happening," Moretti growls. "And you nearly mucked it up by chasing her skirt."

That's right, Salvatore. You're just another rung in Moretti's ladder. And he'll step on anyone to get what he wants. And he's been climbing to get me this whole time.

The lids of Salvatore's eyes begin to redden as he lifts his chin at his boss's scolding. "I ain't been nothin' but loyal to you and you're losing your damn mind."

"You kissed her . . . didn't you, Leone?"

"You're not hearin' yourself, Ice."

With gritted teeth, Moretti turns his attention back to me. The leather burns against my neck. His breath is hot against my ear. "Tell him."

"I'm not . . . a full bruja," I plead, just above a whisper.

My neck shakes, the grip tightening with my fear. "Now tell us what that means," Moretti demands.

"Charm," I choke out, tears filling my eyes. "I only have charm." It's all I know to say. Other strange things have happened with my powers, but I can't begin to explain what they meant. If anything at all.

"Watch out for the taste of lavender," Salvatore mumbles, reaching out before taking back his hand, eyeing me like Barnum & Bailey's newest exhibit. "No—Ice, this is nuts. I don't believe it."

My pinched throat is dying to swallow, but it's too closed off. *He could kill me.* The tears won't stop coming. These are the bad men I grew up hearing about. And I brought them right to me.

Moretti's chuckle hits my neck. "Of course you're conflicted, Mr. Salvatore. These witches can read you with just one touch. Control you with just one kiss."

"Lavender." The henchman's distrusting eyes slowly harden, his jaw setting. "Is that what you did to me, Rose?"

Moretti's fingers loosen just enough to allow me to cough out an answer. "You've got your weapons . . . and I've got mine."

"Madonna santa." Salvatore presses his quivering lips together, storming to his boss's side before shoving a pointed finger in my face. "I should'a thrown you in that club and watched it burn!"

"Use your head, Leone. She's no good to me dead." Moretti's vise arms spin me around, shaking me by the shoulders as he glowers down at me.

My wheezing breath catches fresh air. "Please . . . I'm just a charmer."

"You're not as charming as you think," Ice spits. "The *spells*, Miss Lane. I want the plants. I want the dirt. I want *it all*."

"I'm telling you," I cry, "I can't *do* blessings."

"Then show me who can." My arms pinching, I wrench away, Salvatore grabbing my elbow to keep me from running. His other hand grabs a fistful of my hair, yanking my head up to face him before his boss shouts, "Don't let her touch you!"

It's too late: My trembling hand locks onto Salvatore's smooth cheek. Except, like a word on the tip of my tongue, my magic won't come to me, Salvatore's terrified face twisting as much as mine. I know it's the fear. My racing heart is a telling witness of my panic. Of the nearing end of everything that I've come to love and everything that I am.

But as one of his tears trails down to my thumb, his anxiousness trickles into my skin. A familiar perception wakes from its frozen slumber. The trickle becomes a rush, turning to a deluge of terror—*his* terror. His breath and my magic pick up speed. Like before, the limbs stretch into new places, tasting of the air, the roots feeling their way through Salvatore's nightmares. His mind is a grisly place . . . and I seize on it with a hibiscus blessing.

A flash of a spiked tool. Shouting swears. A jeweled hand curls around the wooden handle before plunging it into a young man's chest. A boy with a little pointed nose crawls backward across the basement floor in horror.

"Ice, please!" The boy shields his face with his arms as the mobster approaches, dark red drops dotting the concrete from the icepick in his hand. "I told my brotha' to give the money back. I'd neva' double-cross you like Jonathan did, I swear!"

The more youthful Moretti deadens his already empty expression. "Oh, I'm certain of that, young Salvatore. Little pricks like you serve guys like me. And that's just the way it works." He tips his wide-brimmed hat before turning. "Now get this mess cleaned up."

As the youngster pushes himself to his feet, his quivering face turns to dark disdain at the mob boss's back, a silent promise filling his soul. One day he'll be strong enough to take on Moretti. One day . . .

The henchman's pleading gasps snap me out of his memories and back to the present, where his boss watches in fascination. "Tell me what you saw, Miss Lane."

"I . . ."

Salvatore's face pales, his damp chin pleading with my hand.

"The day he lost his brother changed his life," I begin again. The henchman stares, paralyzed at what I might say next. "He thought Jonathan was a fool . . . and wishes he could have done it for you."

As Moretti pulls down my shaking arms, his stunned henchman holds his hands to his chest with a deep sigh. As the expense of such an intense enchantment depletes what energy I have left, the ground becomes unsteady. The stress didn't leave much in reserves in the first place. My heavy eyes fall to the floor that rushes toward me. Pin-striped arms catch my wavering frame, the mob boss's pleased smile shining down at me. "My new secret weapon."

The insinuation is loud and clear, my bleak future of paying raunchy visits to his enemies twinkling in his eyes. And I'll do it too, because the other choice isn't a choice at all. I can never tell him where the dirt comes from. My abuela isn't well enough to produce enough for him anyway. It could kill her. My weighted mouth finds my voice, pushing out the only words I have the energy to say. "There's no more dirt."

The walls spin around me in green and gold. I'm having trouble keeping my head from falling.

"My dear." He grins with a short chuckle, his leather fingers brushing the hair away from my cheek. "This city will soon be mine. And you will do *everything* I ask you to do, including bringing me a bag of blessed dirt from wherever you got it . . . or that boxcar will be burned down by midnight tomorrow—with your family inside it."

I want to scream. To fight. To warn my family.

But my eyes close on me instead.

"ABUELA!" MY TEARS AND PANIC BLIND ME, BUT I DON'T NEED TO see. I've run these damp grounds my entire life, the evening wind whipping my hair around as I bound up the steps. My mother's wrinkled forehead greets me before she slides the door halfway closed behind her.

"Luna," she lectures, her voice low as she glances through the open crack, "Mama Sunday is asleep. What's this about, niña? Is Javi all right?"

"It's not Javi. I need her. Now!"

My mother's calm hands cup the sides of my face, stopping me from going any farther. I finally meet her worried gaze, my chest and sinuses tight with despair. "Mamá, please. I need her to bless dirt just one more time."

It won't be much, but it could buy me a few days with Moretti. Maybe enough to get my family out of here. Several graying strands swirl around my mother's head, her espresso eyes setting. "You know it's too much to ask her right now."

"She *has* to. They're *coming*." My cries sputter out, uncontrolled and wailing like the time I broke my leg chasing my brother down a ravine. Mama Sunday saved me then. She can save us now. The resolute look on my mother's face seals my hopelessness. She must not be hearing me. "Mamá . . ."

"They've come before, niña," she says. "We'll handle it—"

"Mamá, they'll be here tomorrow," I cry, gripping her hands as she tries to shush me. "They have guns. Abuela's a healer. She blesses the sky. But she can't stop guns!"

My head trembles beneath her grip, her chin lifting with the pride I've come to love. "Have some faith, mija." She's not a bruja, but she was raised by one. As a blood moon aligns with a lunar eclipse, so my mother's eyes well with tears—rare and worth paying attention to. "If those men show up the day before we leave, then it is no accident. What will be is what is meant to be."

I haven't spoken to the fates since the night monsters tried to kill my brother and assaulted the best friend I've ever had. I don't know what happened between me and the sky. All I know is, the sky never answered back. My tears give way to helpless staring, the river frogs croaking their enchanting songs with the cicadas like my entire world isn't falling apart. "Mamá . . . how can you believe that?"

"You don't have to be a bruja to walk an imaginary line and have faith that it still holds power," she says, stroking my soaked cheek with her thumb. "I blurred the world's eyes so they could see you for what you're worth, and not for your blood. I have always believed in you, mija. It's time for *you* to believe in you." My mother squares her shoulders with a gentleness in her face that almost makes me wonder if she's right.

"Belief is all we really have, niña." Her prim smile returns, tightening the dimple in her rounded chin as she holds my swirling hair back. "It's something no one can take away from us. Now go. Come back in the morning, and don't fret. Tomorrow has its own troubles."

"But, Mamá—"

"Your new club is celebrating tonight," she says, lifting a silencing hand in the air. "Go. Be with them."

"I'm going to get Javi."

"Sí, do what you must."

I GET A FEW LOOKS FROM THE HOUSE BAND AND A COUPLE OF flappers as I squeeze past them on the stone stairwell. Their jovial smiles greet me on their way up, thanking me for throwing them a private party to show my appreciation for all they've done. It's not nearly enough, and my awkward side hugs don't exactly convey what I mean for them to, but they are the best crew a boss could ask for. If I wasn't so choked with my own apprehension—that this may be the last party I can ever give them—I would tell them so.

"We missed ya tonight, Miss Rose," Penny says, waving her fingers as she skips past me with the bass player. "Everything's all locked up, though."

I give her a weak thanks as I push the heavy door closed before rushing to my brother's side. A wet rag twists in his hands, dripping the last bits of water into the sink while he whistles a low tune.

"Dios. Nice of you to show up to your own party when it's over," he jokes, glancing at me as he lays the rag on the marble counter. "That wind really got ahold of your hair"—with a start, he looks to me again, his eyes squinting in concern—"Miss Rose . . . what happened?"

I try to stop the tears, but they rudely burst from my eyes, my hands flying to cover my twisting face. Everything I've tried to do to protect the people I love has ended up putting them in more danger. All my magic, the ways I've allowed myself to change, all the help I've gotten, and it's all amounted to the same thing: It's a man's world and I'm never going to be enough to carve a place in it. I'm all out of ideas. I can't fix this. And right now I just want my brother. I let him pull me into his sturdy arms, his hand stroking my hair.

"Javi!" I sob into his shirt. "I messed up. I tried to fix it—I thought I could do it. But . . . but I made it worse!"

"Hermanita, hermanita." His soothing voice rumbles through his chest and against my cheek. "I'm right here. We're in this together, remember?" I let out a long exhale, my nose plugged like a dam as he tilts my head up. "Whatever it is, we'll handle it."

After snagging a hanky from his back pocket, he dabs under my eyes with a small smile as he pinches my nose, telling me to blow. Taking another deep breath, I turn to find my piano player sitting on a barstool, his frown thick with concern . . . and confusion. I quickly realize the way I'm clinging to my bartender like this, no matter how long I've known him, might seem a bit off to Gio.

It's time to level with both of them.

"Gio," I say, gesturing toward my patient bartender, "Javi is my brother."

He studies us both for a moment before pushing his lips out with a slow nod, adjusting his taxicab hat. "Okay, well, that makes a lotta sense."

"Yeah, well, hold on to that feeling." I rub my swollen eyes with my fingers to avoid my brother's reaction to my next confession. "Javi . . . I made a deal with Moretti and didn't tell you guys—"

"¿Qué?"

"It was just a small loan that turned into a charge for the damage to the River Rose."

"Aye, aye, aye! Luna," he groans, taking my hands from my face. I was right not to look. He's definitely mad. "How much does he want? We got a fortune from Capone."

"I know. And I tried to pay him, Javi!" My damn tears make their reprise, softening my brother's stern face. "But Moretti wouldn't take the money. He wouldn't take it!"

Gio pushes up from his seat, shaking his head. "Whaddya mean he wouldn't take it? That crook only speaks in dolla's."

"He wouldn't take it," I insist, turning back to my brother. Squeezing his hands, I level my eyes with a knowing look. "He knows who we are."

"Who we—" His head shakes like I'm quizzing him on world geography. "So he don't like Mexican money or what?"

Javi, you're not following. His confusion soaks into my palms. He thinks I mean that we're brother and sister. Gio's eyebrow couldn't get any higher at this exchange, and while he might as well be brought into parts of this, I'm not ready to share everything. Not yet.

"Moretti wants *something else*," I explain to my brother, flicking a glance toward Gio. "Something only Abuela and I can give him." Javi's eyes widen in understanding, and I deliver the last bit of bad news that makes me nauseous just to say it. "And he's threatening to come after our family to get it."

"Aye." Javier steps back, his hands pushing up into his raven hair as his eyes shut. "Luna, Abuela's too sick."

"I know!"

"How much time do we have?"

"Midnight tomorrow."

"¡Mierda!"

"Jav," Gio says, circling around the bar. "If you need somethin', just tell me. Maybe I can get it."

"Not this time, Gio."

"What, is it a Mexican thing?"

My brother and I look at each other before answering, "Yeah."

"Damn."

Javier's arms cross, his lips pressed together as he scans the crimson walls. "I've got an idea, though." He beckons to Gio. "Give me Heck's keys."

Gio smirks at my furrowed brow, digging into his pocket. "We took 'em from him after he lost a drinking game to Nick."

As if the gentlemen's club just materialized in front of me, I finally begin to notice my surroundings, including the adorable blond curled up in a suede corner booth by the craps table. "Javi," I say. "I can go with you if you help me get him home."

My brother catches the golden key Gio has tossed to him. "You're staying here—I'll arrange it. And I'll go get a room across the hall for Gio and Heck. If Nick wasn't half-seas over, I'd call him back here too." He holds up a hand to my protest in a very Gloria-like fashion. "Luna, you're safer in a public place. I don't want anyone traveling home tonight."

I'm far too shook up to be annoyed by his typical bossiness. Besides, he's right.

As Javier weaves around the tables, sliding his arms under our incapacitated friend, Heck begins to stir. "Mmm, Javi, not tonight. I'm too tired."

"Mr. Kessler." My brother clears his throat as he hoists a stupidly grinning Heck into his arms. "I'm taking you to a room to get some rest."

"Nooo," Heck whines into his shoulder. "I don't want you to go."

"I have to go. Gio will stay with you."

My brother avoids my curious eyes as Gio and I exchange a look, my brows lifting at the flush climbing up Javier's cheeks. My piano player shrugs like he's known all along. I suppose I'm not all that surprised, either. They're both great guys who deserve a great guy. Heck's groan breezes past us, his eyelids fluttering. "You're going to make your Kessi sleep alone? I promise not to steal the covers again."

"Heck," my brother says, his tone low as he reaches the door, "we're about to head upstairs. Try to control yourself."

Heck reaches up, running his fingers across Javier's stern chin. "That's not what you were saying last night."

"Kess, for the love of God, stop talking."

"Ooh, I love this game."

"Me too. But you must listen."

"Okay!"

"Good. Now, no more talking and keep your eyes closed." Heck's heavy eyes fall with his hands to his chest, my brother's cheeks blazing like the curtains around us. "He'll be asleep by the time I hit the elevator."

"So, wait," I call after him, my amusement fading. "What's your plan, exactly?"

Turning halfway, he shoots me a solemn look. "The brujas north of the river."

"But . . . they only deal in curses. They're dangerous, Javi."

"Exactly. We've still got a little healing dirt left—maybe enough to make a trade." He nods to Gio, who has returned to furrowing his brow. "And you should probably tell him."

"Everything?" I ask, lowering my chin.

"Everything." With another crisp nod, my brother leaves me alone with the startled piano player.

Aw hell. Here goes.

"WELL, THAT SHUT MY MOUTH."

Gio and I stare after the doorway where my brother just stood with my fiancé in his arms, my lips twitching despite the day's chaos. "Which part?"

"All of it." Which is almost funny, because he hasn't even heard half of it. With a long sigh, he leans his arms onto the counter, his expression a mixture of guarded amusement. "So I'm guessin' you don't share both parents?"

I nod, leaning back against the marble beside him. "Just our mother—Gloria. We lived in the River Bottoms until I grew old enough to move out. She changed my name when I was young to wipe away any traces back to our family . . . to give me a better chance, I guess."

"Did it?"

"I mean, I used to think so. But most of the time I just want to be me."

Whoever the hell that is.

"That's why you won't let anyone close to you?"

Well, one of the reasons. I give him a light shrug.

"Boss," he says, his scars crinkling with his eyebrows. "I've been a real dope lately."

"No, Gio, you've been great. I just can't—"

"I understand," he says, bracing against the counter to stand. "I know it didn't help that I kept pushin' somethin' you didn't want. That kiss, though—it drove me crazy. Made me think things . . . I shouldn't'a let it." His hand slides over my cheek as he plasters on a friendly smile. "I'm glad you told me about the deal with Ice, and now Javi, and tellin' me the truth about how you feel. It ain't your fault I been misreadin' ya about . . . us."

His fingers around my ears bleed with regret. He wants me to be able to move on, thinking the troubles between the two of us have been making things harder on me. Maybe if he understood. Gathering every ounce of courage to drown out my fear, I plunge forward. "Gio . . . what if you didn't misread me?"

The happiness in his face fades to melancholy in his skin. "Please don't play with me, Rose."

"I'm not," I say, my nose burning in a familiar way that's beginning to annoy me. *Dry it up, Rose.* Straightening my back, I take a determined breath. "Gio, I'm a witch."

His head rears back with a frustrated huff, his hands dropping away. "You . . . what? Are you *serious*?"

Explaining that my kisses are armed with a web designed to capture heart-strung victims would crash this train even further, so I settle for a resolved pinch of my lips.

"Okay," he says, clasping his hands together with an annoyed lick of his upper lip. "Let's say I believe that for a second. That's got somethin' to do with what Ice wants from you?"

I ignore his tone and deadpan expression, nodding with a big sigh of relief like I'm making sense. "Dirt, in particular."

"Dirt."

"Yes. Very powerful stuff."

"I'm sure it is." Gio drops his head back, waving a hand in front of him like he's done with this entrée. "Look, whatever contraband you're movin' around—"

"Whatever *what*?"

His hand slices the air again. "You don't gotta tell me the truth. In fact, it's probably best you don't right now. Keeps you safa'. We'll regroup when it's ova'."

"Gio—"

"No, listen. Please." Both of his hands take mine, flooding my palms with doubt. Of course he doesn't believe me—to him, the magic is just a metaphor. Still, he levels his eyes with a sincerity that matches the affection in his skin. "The most important thing right now is keepin' you and your family safe. I'm callin' the syndicate, boss. It's time to get some backup."

"I thought they wouldn't help with Moretti."

Crossing the room to the phone on the wall, he grabs the black earpiece from the holder. "That was when it was about *his* money, Rose. Now they're messin' with Capone's money."

It's a quick conversation, but it floods Gio's face with relief. As bothersome as it is to pour my heart and secrets out to this man only to have him not believe me, I don't blame him—I don't know what I'd do if someone came up to me and said they were a sorcerer. If the syndicate is sending someone to investigate, though, it might mean I'll have a chance to convince him later.

If they get here in time.

As we make our way to the carpeted hallway of the second floor, Gio opens his door with a pause, the space between our rooms like a river of what should have been. "Rose . . . whateva' troubles ya havin' about who you are—just know that I wouldn't change a thing about you." He shakes his head at my slack jaw, a hint of a smile pushing through his sadness. "Rest tonight, boss. We're gonna be fine. You know where I am if you need me."

Across the chasm, his door closes before my heart can reach out again.

21

MY THUMBNAIL IS FAIRLY NONEXISTENT, A TINY STUB WITH NO-where left to chew, so I settle on the padding of my fingertip. The plushness of the carpet is trampled under my thin stockings as I stop my pacing under the glittering chandelier at the foot of the bed with a grunt. It all reminds me too much of my last relationship attempt. The mahogany curve of the sleigh frame mocks me with the promise of eternal loneliness, the matching stand-up mirror in the corner reflecting back a taunting image of my silk slip that no one will have the pleasure of seeing. I need to finish getting ready for bed anyway; I've been in these garters all day.

I wouldn't change a thing about you.

Gio's words soften my apprehension, my reflection crossing her arms. I know he meant it—charm or no charm. Though he doesn't really know what I'm capable of. *I* don't even know. But the more I walk the floors of this exorbitantly large hotel room, the less intimidated I feel in the face of my own magic. Mama Sunday told me not to be afraid. My mother said the same thing. Even Javi, the most

324 ◆ DESIDERIA MESA

protective brother on earth, told me to level with Gio. My family is behind me. So maybe it's time to give myself permission to want this. With him, I almost feel normal. Maybe Heck's right: Perhaps the only risk between me and my persistent admirer is intensified lovemaking doused in charm. He'll respond to my magic. And I'll let my walls down the moment he moans in my ear. A man going to sleep with a giant smile on his face and a full heart—that suddenly doesn't sound so bad, especially in light of the earnest confession he hasn't had the courage to say out loud.

He loves me.

Before I can talk myself out of it, I march across the hall, tapping on his door. His wide eyes and unbuttoned shirt greet me with a long blink as he tries to keep his gaze from falling to the low neckline of my slip. I'd show him the same courtesy except I've never gotten a good look at his chest before, an array of vivid tattoos splayed across his firm muscles. A blushing smirk crosses his lips. "Come back to tell me you're a space alien?"

My huff snaps my head up as I spin back to my door, grabbing the brass handle.

That is the last time I try—

A firm grip on my wrist whirls me back around. Hurt and desire protrude from Gio's dark countenance as much as from his palms, the orneriness in his eyes vanished. His fingers steady my chin, tilting it upward as my heart thumps against my chest like a wild racehorse at his savory—and unsavory—intentions. As the light scent of whiskey approaches with his mouth, a stout amount of allure floods my lips like the flush in my cheeks. I jerk my head to the side with a soft gasp.

His eyes shut with a groan. "Geeeez, Rose. You're killin' me here. What is it—your *magic* again? You got a magic mouth?"

"Yes."

"Hell, I'd believe that." He doesn't. But it's kind of adorable now. His eyebrows pinch together as his knuckles slide up my cheek. "'Cause kissin' you tears apart my insides 'bout as bad as that look on your face when I don't. I swear, you like tormentin' me, but it ain't your lips I'm afta'." My joy normally sinks at this type of confession, his knuckles blaring his devotion loud and clear. He wants my heart. The thing is, as much as I want to refuse him, he already has the damn thing. He's had it for a long time. His eyelashes flutter as he rests his nose next to mine, his warm breath hitting my lips. "So I think I'll just hang out right here. Listen to you breathe. Smell those earthy oils you use on your skin. Makes me wanna take you inside and make love to you proppa'."

Songwriters. Such a poet.

I tuck his charcoal hair behind his ear. "Make love?"

"Yes," he whispers. "See, I got it all worked out. I carry you to your bed with your legs wrapped around me. And then I let you down real slow, takin' time to taste that mouth, losin' myself to it." My heart picks up speed along with his breath as the tickle of his fingers runs down my arm like we're not standing in our skivvies in a public hallway. Hell, the boldness has me even more wound up. "That's when I start to feel it—you're inside my head and I'm inside yours. I wanna rush it, but I make us slow down, slidin' that baby-blue slip off your shoulders with my tongue on your neck. And then—my favorite part. I have you take off your blooma's and garta's, and tell ya to leave the stockin's."

Gio's hazel eyes hide beneath his lids, a small laugh shooting through his nose as I shake his shoulder. "You can't just leave me like that."

"Aw, Rose." In a slow, torturous tease, he leans around me, pressing his mouth to my ear. "You mean like you been leavin' me?"

"Gio—"

"I lay you down on your bed like you're mine," he continues. His lips slide around my ear, shivers rushing down my neck as I dig my fingers into the back of his thick hair, gasping at his trailed kisses before he suddenly stops. His sullen face backs away, the heat between us cooling. "But . . . you don't make love. So I best be on my way."

I let him make it as far as the dark stain of his doorpost. "Gio!" His hands grip the frame, his head hanging like he's on the precipice of a weighty crossroad. If he's trying to torture me, it's working. I guess that's fair play with all I've put him through. With the same determination he left with, he starts back in my direction and lifts me from the ground. I fasten my willing thighs around his waist as he carries me inside, kicking the door closed.

OH GOD. TELL ME NO ONE ELSE CAN HAVE YOU. I NEED YOU, ROSE— you know that? Tell me you're mine.

The memory of my allure igniting my lover's desires into an inferno, dragging his desperate confessions from his gasping mouth, races through my head. My hunger built up with his, wishing the moment to last forever before we both tumbled over the edge, my own thoughts spilling from his mouth.

I love you. Please don't leave me.

"Last night was . . . I ain't never said nothin' like that to nobody," Gio says with cheerful bemusement as I float into his arms, my knees around his hips. Sudsy water sloshes to the edge of the claw-foot tub. The Bellerive's provided soaps aren't half bad either. "Maybe you *are* magic, boss."

He means it as a joke, his happiness flowing from everywhere our skin touches. But my own doubt makes its way to the back of my throat in a panicky lump of despair. We were both so charmed last night; it's hard to know what's real and what's not.

"I understand if you were caught up in the moment," I say, staring down at a few shining bubbles. "Fellas say lots of things—"

His hands break through the glittery surface of the water, lifting my head with an intensity in his face that melts my defenses. "I don't say things I don't mean, Rose."

My eyes ease shut to the sincerity in his thumbs as they stroke my cheeks. The allure can last for hours—a day or two even, for the simpler-minded potatoes. But I've felt this fervor from him before our night together. Before our first kiss. Before the magic. We'll have a long talk about this soon where he'll finally understand what I've already told him, but his heartbeat against mine seems to be enough for now.

"You okay?"

Gio's devotion breaks through my doubt, climbing to my eyes. It feels real. It *is* real.

"Just listening to your heart," I breathe. Leaning forward, our lips meet with similar beckoning, my fingers sliding beneath the water.

"Whoa there, boss, easy with that!" He laughs. His playful mouth on my neck keeps me giggling. "Look at you. Fallin' in love with a felon." With a satisfied sigh, he lays his head back against the white cast iron.

"A downright bootlegging expert."

He flashes a waggish smile, my hands continuing their descent as he sings the only tune I've ever seen make Charlie laugh.

Five foot two, eyes of blue
But oh, what those five foot could do
Has anybody seen my gal?
Turned up nose, turned down hose
Flapper, yessir, one of those

I plunge beneath the foamy suds, treating him to Heck's most favored felony. Gio's muffled voice shrieks with laughter as he grips my shoulders, pulling me to the surface.

"That's it!" he declares, pushing my sopping hair from my face. "Send her up the riva'!"

Our contented morning feels like a dream. I want to get lost in it and stay in this tub of peony bath salts forever. And while the nightmares outside these walls are still raging, the thought doesn't sink me like it used to. Hope keeps popping up in the most unexpected places, carrying my heavy heart through the wilderness. The faith I'm feeling might be just tiny seedlings, but so far, that's been enough.

"ALL RIGHT, WELL, JAVI'S NOT AT HIS APARTMENT YET," I SAY, securing the gold-plated earpiece on a nightstand built for gold-plated telephones.

Gio fastens the last button on his shirt, his forehead wrinkling. "Well, it prolly took all night to pack your family up, not countin' the detour to find whateva' he's lookin' for. Sun's barely up. I'm sure they're leavin' as we speak."

"Maybe . . ." My brother's a resourceful man, and if anyone can get the reclusive witches to the north to curse a bag of dirt, it's Javier Alvarado. My neck shivers at the thought. The Klan isn't the only dangerous presence that side of the river.

The rumpled sheets on the bed warm my heart and my cheeks as the late-morning light filters across the tiny table and chairs beneath the window. I never wanted to be one of those goofy lovesick birds, but our half-eaten breakfast of oats and fruit makes me smile through my angst. Sliding fresh stockings up my legs, I slip my feet into a pair of strappy heels with a cringe at my slinky dress. Though the mauve fabric is vibrant, I hate dressing up in the daytime, but at least our dressing rooms downstairs had plenty of spare clothing for us to change into for our last-minute hotel stay. Standing to adjust my fringe hem, I pause at Gio's silence, turning to catch him staring at me from the wet bar with one eyebrow raised.

"Damn," he says, sticking a Lucky Strike between his teeth like the classy gentleman he is. "I could watch you do that all day."

My eyes roll with my lovely snort. "Well, if we make it through this, I might let you. And since you're so busy, why don't you go see if Heck is finally ready?"

Gio's grin slumps into a stony purse. "Javi said to stay put."

"Yeah, well, you both know I'm not going to," I say. "Javi might be my big brother, but he's not the boss. I understand if you and Heck choose to stay, though."

My exasperated lover plucks the cigarette from his mouth and points it, his other hand on his hip. "Rose, I told ya last night—I ain't leavin'."

I'd giggle at his brooding demeanor, which doesn't quite go with the flashy suit he borrowed from Heck's stage wardrobe, but musicians can be sensitive. I decide on another strategy, letting my eyes travel down the checkered pattern of his slacks. "You're awful kippy when you're irritated."

"Don't gimme that look. I'll abandon my smoke right here and now." His lips twitch, fighting a grin as I throw him a wink, going back to securing my garters. "I swear to God, your gams'll win an argument every time."

Damn right.

A light knock on the door cuts off my plans to make short use of my dress, Gio shooting me a pouty lip as he strolls past the bathroom.

"Tell Heck he's got terrible timing," I call over my shoulder, dabbing my lips with a cream rouge in the mirror.

"Dammit, Rose!"

The spine-tingling click of a cocking gun sounds behind me, my tinted salve falling to the floor with a light thud. In a slow spin, I'm face-to-barrel with shining pistols secured in the grips of two nameless goons who make up Salvatore's entourage. My chest tightens. The aspiring mobster came prepared, he and his team's leather gloves pulled tightly over their hands. His pointed chin lifts at Gio with his steely side grin.

"If you so much as cough too loud," he hisses, pressing the door shut behind him, "I'll paint the wallpaper with your brains, you get me?" He jerks his head toward the window, his thugs obeying his silent command. They continue to back Gio up with the tips of their guns until his legs hit the round tabletop. The obsessed mobster ignores his glare, sauntering across the room to pour himself an amber drink. "Have a seat, Mr. Cattaneo."

"Go fu—"

The butt of a black gun slams into Gio's mouth, his grunting swear twisting my stomach as they hit him again before hoisting him from the floor. My protest goes unacknowledged as they wind thin rope around his legs to secure them to the chair, then lift his limp wrists in the air to bind them as well. With his head hanging, his dark hair sticks to the blood seeping from the corner of his eye where his scars once were.

"Now that *that's* dealt with," Salvatore says, sipping at the rim of his glass.

I force my hand not to fly to my mouth, adopting what I hope is a professional tone. "Mr. Salvatore, he's got nothing to do with this."

Gio's head bobs up, his eyes burning. "Boss, don't tell this rat anything. In fact, scream for help. This idiot don't wanna get caught—"

Salvatore slams his tumbler down. "Gag that son of a bitch, will ya?" Storming to the breakfast nook, he pulls a pistol from his pocket as his men loosen Gio's tie. The silver barrel presses to his temple. "Don't make me shoot you. It took Ice nearly a month to get me outta jail last time, and I ain't in the mood for that kind of paperwork."

"Untie me," Gio growls, his eyes rolling back, "and find out what kinda weasel you really are." The pearl tie shoves past his lips, creasing his cheeks as the goons tighten the knot behind his head.

"Hell, Rose, where'd you dig this he-man up, huh?" Sliding his gun to the table, Salvatore then gives it a disturbing spin, the barrel twirling like the spinner on a roulette table. "Tell ya what. If it lands on your boyfriend here, he'll never play piano again."

"Salvatore, let's just talk. I don't have time—"

He holds up a finger. "Wait, wait, wait for it," he insists as the pistol comes to a stop, pointing at the windowsill. "Damn. I never was much of a gambla'." My stomach flips like Heck's fedora on the dance floor as Salvatore reaches back into his jacket. His glove grips a small wooden handle, its narrow metal spike gleaming as it emerges. "I been wantin' to do this for a long time, you piece of shit. You're gonna wanna bite down, 'cause I'm tellin' ya, if you scream, I gotta kill her. And when the cops get here, I'll blame it on you."

"Wait," I say, my heart raging against my chest. "The gun didn't land on him."

"What can I say, baby? I don't like losin'." With a cool expression, he turns Gio's bound hands, flattening his knuckles against the wood. The two other guns stop me from even thinking about moving forward, my feet planted across the room. My mind draws a blank on curses, thoughts, or otherwise, a frenzied alarm electrifying my limbs with dread that turns to sickening horror as the spike drives through both of Gio's hands, skewering them together.

Something like a shrieking utterance gurgles from Gio's gagged mouth as his forehead pounds against the table, his legs twisting against the rope. My own voice struggles over my tongue, hot tears rushing from my eyes and dropping from my chin. "Salvatore . . . it's not his fault. I . . . I charmed him."

As if startling awake from a bad dream, the squinting mobster starts in my direction, his gun hanging at his side. "Then it's even more your fault. I told you I'm a jealous man, Rose! Then you went and laid up with *him*. Made a damn joke outta me in front of Ice, too. I don't *need* a broad savin' me."

The look on his face tells a different story. But he's too proud to admit it—just like I was. My abuela says pride goes before a fall. And here I am, tumbling off a cliff, far away from my dreams and what I thought I wanted, dragging everyone I love with me. "Leone . . . would you rather I told Ice what I really saw?"

The back of his hand rears above me. I hold fast to his redrimmed eyes. If Gio can take an icepick through his palms, I can take another slap from Salvatore. The blow never lands, though, his lower lip trembling with a hard swallow. "You need to learn your place in this world, baby. I can forgive you. But I gotta take your legs out from under you, you understand? I don't like this any more than you do. Now gimme that dirt and I'll go tell Ice you're with us." His gloved fingers push a few stray strands of hair from my face. "You know I don't like it when we fight."

"There *is* no dirt. I . . . I tried to get it." His furrowed brow thickens as I stammer. "We need more time."

"Aw hell," he growls. My head jerks toward the gasping groans from the breakfast table, a leather glove gripping the back of my neck and my attention. "What are you sayin' to me right now, Rose?"

The conflicted look on Salvatore's face doesn't need a read. This was not how he planned things. Maybe he'll let us go for help. I've read humanity in him before—enough, at least, to know that Ice is truly a monster; it's the only thing I have left to appeal to. I let resolve wrap around the helplessness that escapes down my cheeks. "Do you know what Moretti would do with earth magic if he could?"

"What do I care?" My captor gives a light whistle over his shoulder with his teeth. "Go make the call." Leaving Gio shivering and pale, the two henchmen secure their guns, sidling out of the room.

"I'm talking about bruja luck and protection. Prosperity, even," I plead, laying a gentle hand on his suit sleeve. *If I could just reach his skin* . . . Even now, his eyes are glaring at my touch and I know any attempt to get to his face would be the end of me. Words have to be my way in this time. "He could build a syndicate bigger than Capone's. If he's willing to kill your brother right in front of you without magic, what do you think he'll do when he's impenetrable?"

Salvatore's jaw clenches, my back hitting the wall. I glance at Gio's desperate, seething eyes, his gagging swears pouring from his mouth. He's probably ready to kill this crook, but he's not looking so good.

"Where's the dirt, Rose!" the mobster rages, his fingers digging into my bare shoulders like talons. I cling to his forearms with a wince to stop him from shaking me so hard.

"I told you, I don't have it! And he shouldn't either! ¡Escucha!"

Before he can rear back, I press my damp forehead to his. A hard barrel presses to my temple. My abuela always used to tell me that a million things can happen in an instant. Mistakes are made. Opportunities present themselves. The heavens can even peer down at us, asking us if we need help. And in that half of a second, a bruja like Luna can answer back. Dandelion has never tasted sweeter.

Salvatore tries to speak, but I've got him, frozen to my will. My own infuriation wants to scour his mind, blanketing his consciousness with so many detestable memories that he'd curl up in the corner with his thumb in his mouth. But the weapon against my head tempers my vindication, forcing a cautious step beyond his brimming eyes. I move past his odd feelings for me—a mirky mixture of obsession and what he considers to be love—and his hatred for Gio, settling around an ominous devotion to his boss. He's desperate for me to come through for him. Salvatore's skin is suddenly starting to make sense.

My breath hitches with my widening eyes. "You're not taking the dirt to Moretti?"

"Let me go," he utters.

"If you're gonna use it against him, I can help you."

"I said let me go!" Squeezing his eyes shut, he tries to push away with a whining grunt. He's a strong man, but he's just a man. My power reaches deep into the ground, clamping around Salvatore's childhood fears, his gun falling to his side. His eyes soften, his skin dripping with sweat and regret. "Baby . . . you think I'm a dishonorable man . . . but you think Ice is gonna really give you till midnight?"

My roots pull away like the tide rushing back to the sea, Salvatore's trembling thumb trying to wipe away the tears from my face. Gun or not, I slap down his hand. "Don't."

The sniffling mobster shoots a weak glare at Gio before stumbling from the room. Shaking like dinner plates on a train, I run to the breakfast nook, my hands tugging Gio's wet tie before yanking the knots loose around his ankles.

"I'll be okay, Rose," he groans with a shiver, crimson staining the side of his face. "We need to get to the Riva' Bottoms."

"We need to get you to a hospital."

"I said I'm—"

As I help Gio to his feet, the door bursts open, Heck flying into the room in a disheveled rumple. "Thank God you're all right! Did you know two men just held me in my room at gun—" His fingers fly to his paling mouth as he looks down at Gio's hands. "Is that . . . an icepick . . . in your . . ."

Gio rolls his eyes as a small burp gurgles in the back of Heck's throat. "Hey, latecoma', I'm the one who's skewa'd here! Her family's in trouble, so keep it togetha' and pull her car around back."

Our gagging friend gives a consenting nod before bolting back through the doorway. My own nausea climbs with my trepidation as Gio holds out his dripping hands, squeezing his eyes shut. "C'mon, Rose, we gotta go! Just do it!"

I swallow hard before grabbing the handle, and pull.

22

MY HEART IS IN MY THROAT AS WE SCREECH TO A STOP NEXT TO Heck's Chrysler, kicking up dirt like a swirling cloud in the wind. I hear my mother's wailing from the front porch before I even see her arms around my brother's bloodied body. Short gasps flood my chest as she rocks him back and forth, singing a broken, sputtering limerick. Salvatore was right. Moretti came early.

"No!" I scream, clawing at the door of my vehicle as Heck explodes from the passenger seat, hurtling up the splintered steps. My feet have forgotten how to push forward, so I have to force them, one at a time, stumbling over the dry earth to my lifeless brother. My stomach lurches. His face is gone, his lacerated skin and arms so mangled, I can't even scream. I've never seen so much blood. This can't be happening. This isn't happening.

"It was the Klan. They left him tied to the car." My mother lifts a hopeless gaze to the Chrysler on the dirt road. I hadn't noticed when we pulled up, but there's something awful attached to the car—something that will forever be in my nightmares. My stomach tightens and lurches again. Fastened to the back of the chrome bumper is a thick noose with a bloodied end, cut from where our mother freed him. Her bitter voice barely registers. "They said they found him practicing devilry. Those bastardos are too afraid to confront the north brujas. So they took him as soon as he left."

No, no, no, no. Please!

She strokes the damp hair away from his forehead with a trembling hand as Heck's knees hit the growing pool of blood on the decking. He takes my brother's ashen hand, his face twisted around his sobs.

"Rose," Gio chokes out from the bottom of the steps, his blood-caked hands drawn to his chest.

The wall of comfort and security that was my family and friends crashes down around me in their lamenting and agony. I can't stand the sounds. I can't hardly stand at all. My tears fall on their own as I grab the railing to keep myself upright. "Where's Abuela?"

"Inside. She tried, mija—"

Stumbling backward, I tear my eyes away from the bitter cries and crimson stains of the front porch, my abuela's hunched frame greeting me through the open door. The aging couch seems to fade with her. Her head hangs over a metal bucket, her withered hand sifting the powdery earth within.

"Too dry," she says.

I know she's done all she can, which is more than I can say for myself. My brother's arms would be a welcome place to rest my tears, but our roles have changed. He needs me now. Javier's teasing voice comes back to me like the magic reverberating in my chest. *Weaver of Thoughts.* He's always believed in me. He still does. I've reached into men's souls, poisoned my lover's lips. *Conjurer of Spells.* I've called on the fates before, though I'm not sure where those curses landed. *Healer of Hearts.* Healer. Could I? I've never even tried.

"I . . . I can get water." My voice is a squeak that catches as my humming abuela slowly lifts her head. The rich color in her eyes has turned gray like her frizzing hair, her eyelids fluttering closed. "Abuela."

"I try, niña," she groans. "Can't do both. But your branches have grown. You feel it, yes?"

Collapsing to my abuela's feet, I grab ahold of the bucket in her lap. "Teach me, then!"

"Faith . . . hope . . . love." Her patient eyes glint down at me with a hint of brown. "But greatest of these is love."

"Abuela, I *do* love—I love deeply." I bite my lip, but it doesn't stop the weeping. "I'm just . . . I'm afraid."

"Perfect love casts out fear," she says, sliding the bucket into my hands. "Words are force, like universe. The stars hear you once. The stars hear you again."

Her eyes diminish once more, pushing me to my feet and out the door. My heels leap over divots and snake holes, Gio's voice following after me as the wind shakes the tassels of my dress like dancing dragonflies. *I can do this.* Jagged rocks cut through my stockings as I sink into the riverbed, plunging the bucket of ground-up rattlesnake tails and dry dirt into the cool water. Without a clue as to how to begin, I stir the mud with my fist until it sticks like black tar to my hand, singing the haunting melody I memorized when I was three.

Las ventanas del cielo abren sus portones
Lavan las montañas debajo
La vida de la tierra corre por los valles
Corren los flujos de cristal
Absorben las camas arenosas de la tierra
Vengan, tomen de las corrientes brillas
Acuesten cargas sobre el viento

Mientras canta el rio bendito

I have no idea how long I've been singing. Eternity may have passed and come again, and it's only the burn in my knees and the cold water lapping at the hem of my skirt that bring me back. I see the beginning through the end, wondering why I ever worried about anything in the first place. A small voice comes to me—a whisper on the wind that slows to a breeze in the sudden stillness. The fates have been waiting for me a long while now, finally celebrating my name as it rings through the sky in a myriad of choral bells. The stars dim the light of the sun with a joyful laugh.

Then they tell me to run.

I look to Gio, whose face is frozen like he's worried I've lost my mind, his hair whipping around his head. I didn't realize he had followed me here. "Rose . . . what the hell just happened?"

"Did you see them?"

"I just . . . heard something." He tucks his hands against his stained shirt, peering back at the house. "Said to run."

Javi!

With a gasp, I grab the bucket handle, soaring back toward the boxcar in a race with the wind. I shout to my mother as she and Heck carry my brother inside, laying his stiffening body on the coffee table. I lower myself to the mahogany top beside him as Mama Sunday packs the wet earth over his marred face and into his wounds. Her hands cover the two nearest his heart.

"This good dirt," she says warmly before nodding at the seeping wound in his stomach. "You help, niña. I not bring back this far before. Together, we try."

Her tired eyes close, her lovely wrinkles gained by time and adventure gathering around her mouth as she hums. I join the melody, my love reaching through the mud into my brother's broken body, my soul stretching to the universe above. Not just my love for Javier, but my love for who I'm supposed to be. Who I *am*—a bindle punk bruja whose courage never dies. My battles with the mob and the Klan, unwanted advances, men and racists—all the things that tried to keep me from who I am and who I love—are nothing compared to the excitement of the stars over us in this moment.

The sodden soil flattens beneath my palms as we look to the sky, the roof opening to brilliance, our hearts declaring, "¡Pues polvo eres, y al polvo volverás!"

The draft by the doorway roars through the house, gusting around my brother like a cyclone, my hair and clothes whipping toward our hands. My abuela's song rises as her dark hands begin to fade into tiny particles that join the gale, swirling through the air until only her smiling face remains. Her melody turns to joyous laughter, enchanting the spinning room before her form fades to spinning particles, dark and earthy.

"Abuela!" My voice echoes to the heavens and back. Her wrinkles transform to a youthful, vibrant woman like in an old photo I once saw as her ringing laughter vanishes. Before I can reach into the whirling tempest, the air stills, soft soil floating to her sandaled feet.

"Abuela," I whisper, both awe and despair lifting my hands to my brother's smooth face. Aside from his bloodied clothes, he looks well—sleeping, perhaps. If only he were breathing. My mother grips Heck's shoulder as he sinks to the chair with a hopeless expression, his swollen eyes on Javier's stiffening body. "Oh, Abuela, we tried."

Her aged lids are heavy, her leathered skin as worn as before, but she still manages a smile. How can she be so peaceful? Javier is gone. A sea of confusion and agony envelops me like the mud caking my fingers, the rich dirt at the foot of the couch resting in a peaceful heap among the whimpering in the room. I *felt* the power. It *had* to be enough.

It's just me *who can't do it.* Bitterness consumes what's left of me. The universe cheered too soon.

"Luna!" My brother's gasp sends me careening backward as he

tries to sit up, clutching his abdomen. "¿En donde estuve?"

He cocks an eyebrow at my trembling hands, my mouth dropping open with the same nonsensical uttering my loved ones are making around me. *Javi!* With a bursting cry, I throw my arms around his neck, joining our mother. Heck claps a hand over his mouth, the blue in his eyes floating beneath a new wave of tears. Gio just swears and apologizes over and over.

"Sí, I'm okay. I'm okay," Javier says, kissing our arms. When we finally release him, our mother fusses over the dark ring around his neck, the scar barely visible, but still a sobering reminder—the earth healed him, but dirt always remembers. He peers down at his arms, peeling the caked mud from where his wounds used to be. "Abuela must be exhausted."

"Javi . . ." My own fatigue sets in like a heavy blanket as I lean against him.

The joy in the room vanishes, my brother's relief fading to knowing consternation. His brimming eyes fall to the black dirt on the wooden planks at our abuela's toes before planting another kiss on my arm, pulling me closer. "*You* did this, Luna?"

The old witch on the upholstered sofa hangs her head in a soft chuckle. "Half bruja is still bruja." She lifts eyes to me that look as tired as I feel. "I am released, niña. You must carry now. Put dirt in safe place, sí?"

"What are you saying, Abuela?" I ask in a slurred panic. *Is she dying?* My reasoning is starting to fade, and I'm quite sure my eyes might shut on me when another thought shoots through me like a swerving vehicle on a gravel road. "Wait . . . you've lost your magic?"

She shakes her head. "Not lost. Passed on, dear Luna."

Passed on? I start to argue that this can't be, but the whispering wind floating through the windows tells me otherwise. My abuela gave what power she had left to save my brother. Though he's the one who's been through trauma, he allows our mother and me to cry into his shoulder, his own breath catching as we hold each other in relief until my legs begin cramping against the mahogany.

"Let's get you cleaned up, mijo," Gloria sniffles, planting a kiss on his forehead before standing and smoothing the sides of her hair. "You must be hungry. Or tired, yes? Let me make you something while you and Abuela lie down for a while."

Heck is quick to help her get them to their feet, Javier's hand squeezing his as he offers his lips to our abuela's cheek. "Abuela, you are more powerful now than ever."

"I think so too," our mother says, tightening her arms in another teary sigh. And like the caretaker she is, she sets off to wash, dry, and cook in request of Mama Sunday's favorite meal.

"WOULD YA LOOK AT THESE SCARS? THEY'RE TOUGH AS HELL."

I manage a feeble chuckle, nudging my wide-eyed piano player as I lay my head on his shoulder. Healing spells are even harder than they look, my body draining the longer I tap into the stars. Skin is the last thing to heal. I just couldn't hold on any longer, but Gio didn't seem to mind the evidence of his marred hands stretching across his knuckles. My lengthy nap gave me a little rejuvenation, leaving me feeling like I've been hit by a small truck instead of a train. Between Heck's and Gloria's hovering worry, we filled our bellies with spicy tamales and had our clothes washed and pressed as Gio carried boxes out to the lawn.

The sunny afternoon suddenly looks like any other day, except for the humming bruja who should be knitting inside on the sofa. She'll probably sleep for days. The small mountain of moving boxes by the stoop stirs the heavy feeling. All the wisdom of my abuela seems packed away . . . except for the tan satchel in my hands. The rickety steps where Gio drapes his arm around me will be a memory after today, my childhood home soon to give way to the city builders' whims in the name of progress. But I can't bring myself to despair; whatever I saw in the sky gives me comfort, even if I can't remember all the celestial visions.

Maybe one day. At least I've got my family.

Gio's thumb rubs along my rib cage, my eyes closing to the soft tickle and the light breeze that carries the sweet scent of honeysuckle and clover from the tree line. "Rose, can I ask you somethin'?"

"Mm-hmm."

"Did you eva' charm me? You know, with that allure Heck was talkin' about at lunch?"

I lift my chin to his shoulder with a tired smile. "Not in the way that it sounds. My allure increases affection, and only for a certain amount of time."

The corner of Gio's lip rises. "Magic mouth."

"Yeah," I say, my cheeks heating, "Abuela says it's not really the kissing. And now that I'm learning how to trust myself, I should be able to do it without giving guys the wrong impression."

"Interesting." Gio's gaze travels across the muddy valley as he leans back on his hands. "So, this *increased affection*. It wears off?"

"Yes. After about a day."

"So I still got some left ova' from this mornin'?"

"Theoretically."

"So," he says, turning back to me with a frisky flick of his eyebrow, "I might wake up tomorrow and wonda' what I eva' saw in you?"

I cross my arms with an exaggerated huff before tilting my face up to his. "Well, did you like me before you carried me into my room?"

He leans down in a careful descent, his eyes falling to my mouth. "Not at all."

"How about before you tried to have your way with me in that dark alleyway?"

"Think you got that the otha' way around." Gio's nose brushes mine with a heavy sigh. "I wanted to take you outta that dark alleyway—fightin' all these thoughts. I guess that was you."

At my guilty nod, he softly pinches my chin, pressing his lips to my forehead. A hard stone settles in the pit of my stomach. "Gio . . . I would never manipulate you."

"You kinda already did. But I unda'stand why you didn't tell me."

"Yeah, but that was to *keep* from manipulating you." I grab his hands like he's in danger of flying away. "I was afraid for you . . . and myself."

His fingers curl around mine. "I know that, Rose. And I appreciate it. It's just . . . this is all a little new to me and I gotta get my mind clear." My sinking heart wrenches my hopes back down like it always does, my nose beginning to tighten. As I turn to hide a sniffle, Gio pulls me to his chest. "Aw, it ain't like all that. I'm not leavin'. You said it takes a day to think straight, so I'm takin' a day. A *day*. That's all I'm sayin'."

"A day from *me*."

"Just your lips," he insists, giving a light squeeze to my thigh. "There are other parts of you . . . and this dress'a your mom's is kinda doin' somethin' for me. If you're interested in another nap, just let me know."

"Oh geez."

"I thought you was somethin' before. But come to find out, I'm sleepin' with a real magician."

"Which I *told* you."

"You did. And now I'm hearin' ya." Gio presses a chuckling kiss into my hair. "Not much of a sing'a, though."

His laughter is as warm as his chest, my eyes closing to the steady thumping beneath my ear. Through the doorway behind us, my mother dotes over Heck and lectures my brother, reminding me how much I've needed every one of them.

AS THE LAST MOVING TRUCK HEADS DOWN THE DUSTY ROAD WITH my abuela and my mother, Javier squeezes my hand. The empty boxcar stands watch behind us just like the many down the row beside it, already abandoned, an empty vessel of the joy it once held. But as Gloria has been saying all day, a home is full of wine, healing, and laughter. Wherever we go, we will always have those things.

Donning another one of my brother's outfits, Heck slides his hand into the pocket of his trousers, waving his other arm with a dramatic bow. "Ready when you are, Miss Alvarado-Lane."

Our affectionate troop climbs down the steps together as Gio jogs over from my idling car. "Looks like your movin' crew got lost."

"What do you mean?" I ask, giggling at Heck's antics as he offers me a suave arm.

Gio lifts his eyebrows over his shoulder. "Well, there's a good-sized car headed back this direction in a hurry. Thought it was one'a the trucks, but now I'm not so sure. Looks too fancy to be one of ours."

Craning my neck, I stand to the tips of my toes, my hand pressing down on my hat to block the evening sun. A trail of dust billows out from beneath the curved fenders as the car picks up speed. Even in the distance, the alabaster vehicle tosses the stone back into my stomach, the silver grill heading toward us like gleaming teeth.

"Ooh," Heck gushes. "It's a Rolls-Royce."

"Get back in the house." My family looks to me, their eyes darting at one another. I let out a frustrated growl, pulling my fiancé backward by his sleeve. "It's Moretti! He's coming earlier than we thought. Get back in the house," I repeat. "I can't heal everyone!"

My warning finally sinks in as the speeding automobile rounds a final corner, my family and me scrambling to the wooden porch. The last one in, my brother slams the door, securing the iron bar. "Luna, please tell me you know the protection spells."

My teeth clamp around my fingertip as I peer out the window at Salvatore and the two goons he brought into my club the other night. *So much for his humanity.* The company of henchmen includes the thugs Moretti used to humiliate me in my own club the day he rejected my payment. The entire lawn is filled with men who aren't worth their suit jackets as they circle around to face the boxcar, Moretti at the lead.

"Damn!" I breathe, shaking my head at my brother, who shares the other window with a paling Heck. "And no, Javi, you know I never wasted time learning spells I couldn't do."

"You made the dirt and healed me."

It's difficult to explain when time's running out. Looking back at all the other times that my magic seemed to manifest on its own, I understand now that the fates have been guiding me in the spells I've used, using my emotions and realizations as a segue to teach me what I'm capable of—which is why fear works against it. *I am learning.* But to Javier, I just say, "Yeah, well, we're gonna need more than a healing spell."

He groans, pinching the space between his eyes. "Aye, aye, aye. And the spell books are with our caravan."

The spell books *and* Mama Sunday. But she was in no condition to even know we were in danger, let alone be able to help.

Gio pushes up next to me, easing his head around the window frame. "You brujas got spell books? Anythin' to help with those guns?"

"Probably," I hiss, "but they're in the books!"

From the desolate lawn, the sneering mobster with the crooked nose straightens the wide brim of his hat against the wind, his associates nodding to each other as they raise their pistols in the air.

"Miss Lane!" he calls out, triumph dancing in the grit of his voice. "I won't ask you again. Bring me my dirt!"

Gio's obscene gesture waves from the window. "You're gonna hafta kill us all, you cocksuckin'—"

The whiz of a flying bullet throws us all to the wood planks as its ting hits the side of the boxcar. My brother's protective arms cover Heck's trembling head. Like steel against steel, another deadly projectile lands against the open window, freezing in the air like an invisible shield before falling.

"The plants!" Javier gasps. I didn't know our abuela's protective magic around the house could stop bullets, but I'm all kinds of surprised today. I silently vow to love blackberries more in the future. We're safe—as long as we stay in this boxcar.

"Come on, baby!" Salvatore's detestable voice rings through the air. "We know the vines can be burned—and so can that tinderbox. Don't make us smoke you out!"

My brother's determined eyes drop to the satchel still clutched between my fingers. "Luna."

"No, Javi. It's too powerful."

"Sí, blessed dirt is," he says, reaching into his pocket. "But so is cursed dirt."

All of the breath in my lungs escapes as I examine the cloth pouch in his hand, tied with a string like an ominous offering of tea. Powdered tobacco. Scorpion tails. A carefully selected cocktail of parasitic insects designed for chaos. As my brother moves to stand, all I can picture is his spiritless body in our mother's arms as she wept over him. He's crazy if he thinks I'm letting him deliver it. Shoving Gio away from me, I snatch the pouch, springing to the door before anyone can reach me.

"Luna!"

The satchel goes out ahead of me, lifted in the heavy breeze like a shield in front of my wide-eyed enemies. They don't know that I'm recovering from an intense amount of magic—that I don't know if I have enough in me right now to do anything to them. I just have to make them think I do. If they take the dirt, it'll work its way into their fate on its own.

The shadows of my loved ones cover the steps around me as I make my way down into the den of lions, their guns lowering at my approach.

"That's far enough for the rest of you," Moretti growls, tightening the leather around his wrists. His gleaming eyes land on the tan bag before his glove seizes my forearm, tugging me forward.

"Hey!" my brother shouts. "You got what you wanted! Let her go!"

The gangster's chilling laugh hits my ears as he turns me around, holding my struggling arms in front of me. He's as strong as he looks, his vise grip keeping me from reaching for his face. "Mr. Alvarado, your sister is going to make me a very rich man."

Javier is a cascade of Spanish swearing as he rushes down the steps, Heck and Gio following. Three guns lift in the air, thumbs cocking them into position.

"No!" I scream, my heart racing against the weariness in my bones. "I'll go. I'll go." I'm resourceful—a damn earth bruja. I can find a way out of this on my own if they just stay put. I'm well aware that the resurgence of my confidence comes with guns pointing at my brother's head—a confidence that reaches all the way into the ground and up to the cosmos, where hailstorms and malice are stored.

But my family doesn't listen, their hands raised as they step even closer.

Of course they don't.

My frustration clashes with the helplessness that seeks to settle inside me as the goon with the long nose purses his lips, a bead of sweat trickling from under his homburg hat. "Stay back! Last warning!"

There are times that I need others, and there are times when others need me.

This is the latter.

Stay back. Last warning. Don't go any farther. My family and I have been told that our entire lives. And every time I push back, the world pushes me again. And again.

The sun peers up from its horizon as it sets. *Aren't you angry,*

Luna?

The stars aren't giggling this time.

The thumbnail moon is opaque in the dusk light, fading into view, like my ire against those who just won't stop pushing. My brother takes another step forward.

Let it go, Luna. The moon's tip gleams. It tells me to look to my hand.

I stare at the magic tucked into my curled fingers—magic that I didn't even have to conjure. Like faith and hope, I just have to use it.

Javi's satchel of cursed dirt slides from my palm, falling to the patches of crabgrass below. With a final echo in the swirling air, the shouting halts. The howling wind and my own heart cease their raging.

The mobster at my ear gasps in the sudden silence, the grip on my forearms loosening. "Wha-what did you do?" Turning, I reach for his reddening cheeks, but he backs away, his breath sputtering. "Don't touch— My God, your eyes . . . Look, just give me the dirt and we'll work something out."

I scoop the satin bag from the ground, Moretti's forehead gleaming as he gawks at his frozen associates, their guns pointed at my motionless family. Greed emanates from his shifty body, a vile fear gripping his mind. The two vices were his gifts to others as he clawed his way to success through the years, sympathy and regret drowned out by his cold drive. The bag tilts in my hand, the quiet brushing of rich earth sprinkling into my palm.

"What are you doing? Just hand it over."

Stepping forward, I hold the bag between us. "What you bury always comes back." My abuela's lessons soak through my skin from the wet dirt, watering my soul with an infinite glimpse into the heart of the ground. What this monster has done to so many, the lives he's taken—they number the grains of soil in my hand. And those grains thirst for vengeance. One of them holds the memory of a little boy weeping over his dead brother, skewered through the chest with an icepick.

The cursed dirt pulls from what strength I have left like blood from my veins. I quite like the burn.

"Right," Moretti says warily, easing the pouch from my hand, his tentative glances on my open palm. His eyes round as I lift my hand to my mouth, his face trembling at the rich clump of dirt that has become dry as sand.

"Recogerán lo que siembra." Like a tender breeze, my breath pushes the granules into the air, carrying the screams of past victims as it lands against the gangster's cringing face.

Moretti's glove snags my hand as I sink to the ground, my eyelids threatening to close against the world coming back to full speed.

"Stay back!" the long-nosed goon orders again. "Last warning!"

"Enough of this." The mob boss yanks me to my feet, sending me stumbling into Salvatore's arms. "Get her in the car, then kill her family."

I'm screaming into a pin-striped suit before the blast from Long-Nose's gun rings in my ears. It takes me as long as Moretti does to realize it's one of his associates soaking the ground with his blood and not one of my loved ones, the goon's lifeless eyes staring at nothing. Another shot, and the second man I stripped for falls in a heap. As the mob boss whirls around to his second-in-command, bewilderment stretches across Moretti's face, Salvatore cocking his head and his gun with a wild sneer. The shock wave of the pistol assaults my ears again—this time so much closer. My legs nearly fold under me. His lack of concern is less than subtle. As Salvatore throws me to the ground where his boss's face is smashed into a growing crimson pool, he points a finger down at me.

"That's for helping me get rid of that loon," he says, swinging his pistol in a wide arc at my family to keep them back. "But all this magic is devil shit. I'm Catholic, for God's sake."

His associate crosses himself in agreement—as if that isn't its own kind of magic—before heading to the back seat of the Rolls-Royce. We all watch in horror as he fills his arms with clear bottles full of liquid and paper, the smell of petrol wafting around us. As the flaming bottles fly over our heads, my family scrambles to my side, away from the igniting boxcar. My childhood home is halfway swallowed in an orange blaze by the time the mobsters crank their car engine.

"This don't make us even," Salvatore calls through the open door. "*I'm* in charge now, you got it? Keep your dirt. I want that ten thou by tonight, and you in a dress going forward. You're done disrespectin' me."

Gross.

Truth is, I wish he wanted the magic. The sky is spinning too much for me to cringe at the thought of being that goon's underground concubine. My brother's desperate voice follows the slamming vehicle door, the kicked-up dust flying in my wavering face. I watch the car drive off, its new owner mocking me with echoes inside my head.

Snap out of it. It's over.

For now.

The ground comes for me in a blackening rush.

23

GIO'S SWEARS STARTLE ME AWAKE, HIS RUMPLED SHIRT WET where my mouth laid against his chest. "Are we there yet?" I mumble, lifting my head to see why we're pulled over a few blocks from Javier's street. At least I think we're close to his apartment. It's hard to tell with the sparse street lighting. I'm still so out of it, I'm not even sure I'm awake. "I thought we were headed to Mamá's."

Squinting into the blackness, I can make out my brother's hand gripping the passenger door handle. Gio keeps looking behind us, finally shaking my shoulder. "You're gonna hafta wake up now, boss."

What is going on?

Blinking away the dragging fatigue, I follow Gio's frozen gaze to the driver's-side window. A black paddy wagon with golden wheels and lettering pulls up beside us, blaring its horn, nearly running us off the road before Heck lurches our vehicle to a stop.

"We was headed to your place, Jav," Gio whispers to our crowded front seat. "They don't need to know where we was really goin'."

I give my face a hard rub. "Will someone tell me—"

"We was bein' tailed. Don't say nothin' 'less you have to."

Two men appear outside the door, holding up gleaming badges, their trench jackets pulled back just enough to show us their sidearms. Heck reaches across my lap and grabs my hand, giving the officers a compliant nod.

"How do you do, Miss Lane? Mr. Kessler," one detective says, rain dripping from the wide brim of his hat as he tips it. "We've been investigating Thomas Moretti for quite some time. We'd like you and your bartender to come downtown to answer a few questions about his dealings with you."

My distrusting eyes narrow, giving them both an eye to let them know how I feel about it. These goons want an interview after sundown? Not to mention they've been following us since who knows where. I'm sure not taking a ride with them. I glance over at my brother, the same suspicion dawning in his face.

"How about we meet you in the morning?" I offer, going for nonchalant.

The other cop snorts. "Tell ya what, you do that. But we're taking the bartender now." He jerks his chin at my scowling piano player. "The rum-runner can come with us too. I'm sure both of them can tell us a thing or two."

Heck's arm crosses over the three of us like a railroad barrier as he leans forward. "These men are my employees. You'll do nothing until I call my lawyer."

"Listen, Mr. Fancy Pants," the one with the hat snaps, "we can arrest you for how many times we've seen you neck outside'a that greaser's apartment, so unless you wanna go heels with the law, you'll take your gonsil ass back a few steps." His looming gait grows taller as he leans through the window, sneering down at my seething fiancé. "I'm surprised you got the eggs to look at me like that. Heard you were a submissive little muzzler."

The cerulean fire in Heck's eyes upgrades to blazing as he curls his fingers before slamming his fist into the detective's face.

THE TINY WINDOWS NEAR THE TOP OF THE PADDY WAGON PROvide very little light inside the cabin. I shift in my seat at the ache in my rear from the wooden bench as the bouncing vehicle increases its jarring. Beside me, Gio rubs his wrists beneath the metal handcuffs.

No—Moretti's dead. This should all be over.

"I don't rememba' any gravel roads near the city jail," he mutters. My breath stills as Gio takes my hands, a chilling message flowing through his palms loud and clear. These guys are no upstanding cops. We're obviously not under arrest. This is something else. Gio doesn't know what it is, but we've been in this wagon way too long.

"My God," Heck groans, holding his head in his hands. "My trustees are going to have me admitted again."

I blink at the thought of my darb fiancé getting hauled to jail, though he's anything but subtle. It was only a matter of time. "You've been arrested before?"

"Of course, but I never get charged." It makes sense. The Kesslers are household names in every major city across the country. In the dark, the whites of his eyes glow as he looks to my brother. "Wait. Javi, I'll tell them I forced you to kiss me. Don't say a word to them."

"It's okay, Kessi. We'll figure it out."

"Do you know what they'd *do* to us in prison?"

"They only sterilize for repeat offenses," my brother says, his soothing tone calming the tension in Heck's face. "This is my first time."

"You think that Mexicans get the same break?"

Javier goes silent at that.

Gio clicks his tongue. "Public lewdness—baloney. It's a money grab. That's all it is."

"Then where are we going?" I ask, chewing the inside of my bottom lip to pieces.

"Somewhere private to make sure we get the message."

The rattling seat jolts us forward, the engine giving a final shudder.

"It's about time," Heck huffs. "My lawyer's going to give them an earful when this is over."

He doesn't seem to be picking up on what Gio's sensing. I don't think any of us are going to be talking to lawyers. I wish I had just a pinch of that cursed dirt. But they threw all of us into cuffs before I could grab anything. I've still got magic, though, and I will use the hell out of it if these jerks try anything.

Once I've recharged, anyway.

Languor weighs my eyelids at the thought. I'm tapped out for the time being.

As the metal doors creep open, Gio's fingers intertwine with mine, echoing the heavy dread that shoots across my chest like lightning. *Stay near me, Rose.* "Oh God . . ."

Any other night, chirping crickets and a flowing stream beneath silver moonlight would calm my bones. But the small mob of waiting specters grips me with anything but serenity, my lungs holding back a breath like Gio's holding my arm.

"Come on out now, Miss Lane," the cop with the hat says, reaching up like he's going to help me down. "The grand wizard doesn't want you hurt more than you need to be. We're Christian men, and I can't say we like any of this. You didn't have to push us this far—"

"Detective, just get her out here."

My eyes fall to the extended hand, Gio's grip tightening as he pulls me backward. *This isn't happening.* We escaped the lions only to be thrown into a furnace. This isn't how it's supposed to be.

I try to still my breath, searching for a flicker of magic, but the only taste on my tongue is dryness and metal. I've bitten my lip too hard. I've used powerful incantations. Too much. *How will the fates hear me now?*

Across the cabin, Heck bares his teeth as he leans down. "If you so much as touch the hem of her skirt, I'll kill you myself." A thick wad of spit flies into the officer's face, his outstretched hand gripping a fistful of blond hair before yanking my defender from his seat. I scream after my brother as he vaults through the open doors, Heck's legs flailing in the darkness. In a harrowing rush, several robes invade the cabin, tearing me from Gio's arms as they drag us all deeper into the humid night, the hard ground softening beneath my feet the closer we get to the river. I've always loved the smell—earth and fish mixing with stones and minerals—but the cold ground soaking into my stockings gives me anything but contentment. Familiar voices start drifting away along with my hope.

"Let us go, you animals!"

"Leave her outta this! She didn't do nothin'!"

My jaw trembles with sputtering breaths, the rest of my body following suit as the water hits my ankles. The strong vises around my elbows stop me from going any farther, while the glowing monsters drag my brother out to his waist. Blood drips from his hanging head. A few blows to the stomach send Heck and Gio sloshing to their knees on the muddy rocks beside me, their captors holding their heads up by their hair. A dark purple robe wades into the river, floating between me and my brother.

"Miss Lane," the hooded man says, his polished tone pricking my ear. "I'm sure you find this all quite frightening. Please know that is not my intention." I almost snort at that—terror is exactly how the Klan operates. Unfortunately, it's working. "However, such is often the place our sin brings us."

That voice. I've heard it before, the cosmopolitan inflection—an uncanny dialect that isn't too different from Heck's. This isn't some backwoods farmer. It's someone I know.

But who? He's too far to touch him. A surface read is effortless, and I'd give anything to have enough juice to walk through his mind. Except I'm not sure I need to. The fingers around my arms tell me all I need to know.

"Is this the place your sin has brought *you* to?" I lift a challenging chin, squaring my shoulders. "*Oswald?*"

The ringleader's uncalloused fingers slowly pinch the cone of his plum hood, his pursed lips showing before the hem reaches the tip of his pointed ears. A fresh wave of chills rolls down my back at Archibald's aloof expression.

"Believe it or not," he says, "I fight for our communities, and each one of you represents the kind of dross we're trying to get rid of. I gave you and your fiancé an opportunity to reconcile. Finding yourselves here with thieving felons and gross sodomites is of your own doing." He turns to the two ghosts holding my moaning brother. "We'll start with the baptism of this trash from the River Bottoms. Knock out the Jew when it's over. We need a scapegoat to pin this to."

My cringe at the delight in my captor's hands turns to the same terror that's reflected in Heck's screams as he and Gio writhe against their phantoms. I lunge forward, bitter tears springing to my eyes, my toes digging into the sandy earth beneath the water.

"I'm protected by the syndicate!" I plead. "They'll come after you!"

"They won't need to," Archibald replies, waving a snide hand that he then places on my brother's forehead. "When they find your body raped and murdered by your own criminal crew, perhaps they'll realize how out of control their evil operation really is. The people of this nation need to open their eyes."

"You think Al Capone is going to let someone mess with his money?"

"You think I'm scared of that rum-runner from Chicago?"

You should be. I can tell the man holding me certainly is. But Archibald has the gleaming gaze of a zealot.

If the threat of the greatest mobster in the Midwest doesn't shake him, then no threat of mine is going to make a difference.

I try another angle.

"You're about to murder innocent people!"

The ringleader's purple arm points in my direction. "Your *brand* of innocence corrupts everything you touch! My own wife is leaving me for that brothel manager! A damn woman!" It's too dark to see if his pointy ears have turned crimson, but the scorn in his face is unmistakable. "Did you hear what I said? I'm being replaced by the foulest creature on earth—a Negro bulldagger!"

"Now you're telling the truth, at least," I utter as an angry sob hits my throat.

"And what would a vixen like you know about truth?"

"I know this is all about your wounded pride. You can't find satisfaction with a man, and you can't satisfy a woman."

Archibald shoves through the water, his determined jaw set as he reaches me. On either side of me, a slew of idle threats from my loved ones follows the stinging hand across my cheek. My head rears as I grimace, laying my burning cheek to my shoulder.

"How *dare* you open your slanderous mouth against me? Try to wrap your ignorant mind around our cause," he hisses down at me. "We knew the devil was behind your operation, and finding your bartender seeking out sorcery proves it. Our city bathes in indecency when this immigrant trash is around. When aberrations like Kessler are considered upstanding citizens. For the souls of our children, I'm going to make sure this demon stays dead this time."

"By God, you will not!" Heck bellows, pushing up against the arms that hold him. His wet hands squirm inside his handcuffs at his futile attempt to unbind himself.

Archibald shakes his head in mock sympathy. "We warned you, Mr. Kessler. You chose this path, associating with creatures like him." He leers back at my brother with disgust. "Look at what you've done to yourself—to your esteemed family name. Be glad your miserable life ends here. Maybe it will be enough for God to forgive you."

"The real cops will come looking for him," I say with a gasping, deep shiver chattering my teeth. "You'll all be hanged when this city finds out."

"The only thing the city will find is their beloved floor-flusher on the end of a rope in his own apartment with a note telling us all how he couldn't live with his own depravity any longer!"

Gio's swearing grows to a roar. "You'll neva' get away with this many murda's, you son of a bitch! You're gonna hafta' kill me to shut me up!"

"You know . . . I think you're right."

I barely recognize the raw pleading that scrapes my throat as our sentencer wades back into the river. I could debilitate the men holding me, the simple thoughts in their fingers easy to manipulate, but the twenty or so men in this river would just take their place. Like being stuck in a dream, I watch my brother's body plunge into black water that shimmers with the twinkling lights in the sky. By the hands of his captors, the promised rope cinches around Heck's neck. Gio's twisted face sinks forward into the river, bubbles floating to the surface with his cries.

My toes dig deeper, curling around the pebbles and stones in the mud as my feet settle into the spongy riverbed. Archibald quotes ancient text that feeds his proud sneer, the haunting company chanting the words back to him—company that doesn't believe in magic, yet pays heed to arcane rituals.

The contradiction isn't enough to make this any easier to bear. My own breath chokes me. The shiver in my bones becomes a violent tremble like the water rippling from the struggling bodies around me. Friendship. Self-acceptance. Perfect love. I've finally found my missing pieces, and these ministers of hate wish to rip them from my grasp. I try to think of a spell—any spell to ward off this many enemies. I'm firmly planted. Ready to speak. But the strength and words won't come to me.

Because they already have, dear child of the earth and stars.

My desperate gaze searches the heavens. They tell me the words I have to say have already been spoken.

Que la tierra trague a nuestros enemigos si nos tocan de nuevo.

Realization courses its way through my shaking body. The fire at my old club. The curse I spoke to the sky that night. I scan the empty eyes around me, my breath returning as a heave in my chest. These monsters were the men responsible. And the damn fates know it. My eyes drift to the cloudless sky, the heavens calling to the earth for vengeance.

The earth answers back.

As the moon tells me to sing, I turn to the phantom beside me with a delicate whisper. "Your penalty is coming for you." He tilts his hood with rearing caution, stammering about my eyes as retribution leaves my lips. "Que la tierra trague a nuestros enemigos si nos tocan de nuevo."

My captor tries to get the others' attention, but they're too busy trying to kill my family. He's the first of them to notice. "Hey!" he gasps, peering down at the water, panic in his eyes. "Somethin's got me! Somethin's got me, dammit!"

A thickening root, dark as umber, breaks through the shining surface, wrapping around his leg. The men holding my brother turn in our direction, their eyes widening as the shrieking man next to me tries to drag himself away from the water, but the crackling roots weave up his body until his robe is barely visible beneath the scaly wood. The captor on my other side soon follows. His company joins the chorus of his wailing, shrill and long as the earth's fingers climb up their thighs, twisting around their waists and shooting higher.

"You!" Archibald shrieks at me, leaving Javier's body to drift backward. "Stop this devilry!"

Shoving against the trunk that was once a man, Heck yanks at the rope around his neck with a raw gasp as he charges deeper into the river toward my brother. Gio's gagging cough is at my side by the time Archibald reaches me, pushing himself in front of me with his handcuffed fists in the air. It's a nice gesture.

But the earth already has my back.

Our accuser's horrified face freezes along with his legs as he tries to step forward, his ankle stuck beneath the water. He jerks his other leg, the panic in his breath picking up speed. Breaking through the surface, the roots stretch up to his chest and shoulders until his screams are cut off by the hardening bark. The last of his longest finger succumbs to the encasement, a narrow branch frozen in time as though clawing at the air. By the time my sputtering family makes it back to shore, Gio's arms have lowered my collapsing body to the smooth stones.

"Rose!" His hand taps my cheek. "Talk to me."

My eyes roll beneath my lids. "Javi . . . is he okay? He needs me."

"Heck's got 'im. He's still spewin' up watta', but he's all right."

"Good," I whisper, my heartbeat steadying in the hum of the stars' lullaby. "Then I might . . . shut my eyes for a minute."

Mumbling some kind of worried compliance, Gio loops his arms around me, pulling my head to his chest that shakes with his quiet sniffling. His lips to my forehead bid me good night with the cicadas and bullfrogs that rejoin the night's melody.

"WE'RE GONNA HAFTA CARRY HER."

I'm barely conscious on Gio's shoulder as familiar voices around me ask each other if they're okay. The hush of flowing water trickles around my ankles as I lean back against a thick trunk that scrapes my shoulder blades. The leaves brush each other in the branches above me, groomed by the mild wind.

My voice comes out as a hoarse whisper. "I just need to rest a bit."

"We can't stay here, boss," Gio murmurs. I feel his nervousness everywhere our skin touches.

I don't know. This riverside bank that was once our nightmare is now as serene as a painting, my family nestled within the grove of trees that faces the dark horizon. I'm not sure there's anything to say, and even more sure I don't have the energy to say it. Our heads leaning on each other seems like enough. I'd rather stay in this oasis awhile and let us recover from all the horror.

But Javi clearly disagrees. "Gio's right," my brother says, clearing his throat against the hoarseness in his own voice. "We gotta get Luna somewhere dry until we figure out how we're getting home."

"Yes," Heck says from Javier's shoulder. "If we follow the road we were on earlier, maybe we can flag down a ride."

Gio snorts near my ear. "In these parts? A Mexican and a Jew aren't gonna find a ride from these yokels. Kessla', you're the only one who can make it through this territory alive."

"You're right. I'll see what I can do."

My brother tightens his arms around Heck. "You're not goin' anywhere, Kess." His shackles slide down his wrists as he tilts my fiancé's chin to examine the red burns around his neck. It's a sad scene, but also one that makes me smile just a bit as I wonder if they realize they are a matching pair now. "We'll get out of here together."

Heck lays his hand over Javier's with a slow nod. "Okay."

"Look," Gio says, his soaked pants dripping as he stands, "we take the paddy wagon so there's no risk of bein' pulled ova'. There's bound to be some spare keys in there, and even if there ain't, I been known to get a few cars to start without 'em if you know what I mean."

With a light laugh that turns into a groan of exhaustion, I let my entourage lift me from the river, carrying me to the boxed vehicle, which soon starts with a whirling rumble. The empty pickup wagons parked in the mud around us stand as silent witnesses to their owners' disappearance. We really do have to leave. No one can know we were ever by this riverside.

I rub my sore wrists as I lie down on the metal seat across from my brother, Gio and Heck navigating our trek to the city from the front of the truck. I'm still exhausted, but I manage a smile as Javier slides to the floor beside me in the empty cabin.

"I'm so proud of you, hermanita," he says, sliding his hand over mine. "Not just the magic, but the person you've become. It's who you've always been, really. You just didn't know it about yourself yet. But Abuela knew."

My nose tightens, his own eyes glistening. "Oh, Javi, I wish she was here."

He lifts his head, searching the ceiling. "Well, when we get to my place, you can tell her all about it." A tear slides down my temple as one slides down his cheek. "We've both always known you were gonna do great things."

"But . . . I don't want to do those things alone. Not anymore."

"You're not alone," he says, gripping my hand.

A breath escapes my trembling lips. "Promise?"

"I promise." Javier's wet shirt clings to his body as he wipes his cheek onto his shoulder. "Now, no more despair. We got our family and friends. We've both got love in our lives—ooh, and now that you can tap into that bruja favor—"

"I was wondering when you were going there," I chuckle.

"Hey, a little bit of dirt goes a long way."

"Not unless we have to, Javi. I like earning our way."

He shakes his head with a knowing grin. "Fine. At least I have a famous boyfriend."

"You mean my fiancé?"

"He likes me better."

"You can keep him. He steals the covers."

My brother's laughter soothes what's left of my brokenness as the bumpy ride smooths out. For the first time, I don't just *want* to believe everything is going to be okay. I go ahead and actually believe it. I'm no expert, but I'm starting to understand that the heavens have always been on my side, rooting for me. Sending me love in the strangest places. My family thinks I saved them.

It's truly the other way around.

"All right," Javi says, stretching out on the ridged floor, "no magic unless it's needed, which is fine now that Ice and Archie and the rest of those devils are gone." His arms tuck beneath his head. "You're the one with the big ideas, hermanita. How do you wanna deal with Salvatore?"

I think back to my dreams, expanding them to allow for every beautiful soul in my life, my eyes shining in the moonlight from the tiny window above. "I've got a few ideas."

MY FAVORITE VIEW ON ANY GIVEN MORNING IS THE WAY GIO'S hair splays across the pillow like a raven fan, his arm thrown over his eyes. He pretends to hate the sunlight, but my roving hand across his bare chest coaxes a smile onto his face.

"Watch it, boss," he mumbles. "I got magic'a my own."

"I'm well aware." Shoving his arm aside, I tuck beneath the turquoise quilt, my cheek against a tattoo of an adorned elephant. "Let's just stay like this all day."

"You got it."

"Really?"

His groaning chuckle rumbles the top of my head where he rests his chin. "Hey, if you don't wanna go tonight, I sure as hell ain't gonna make ya."

"Salvatore's expecting me to be there."

After kissing my hair with a sigh, Gio lifts up onto his forearm, his skin and face sharing his concern. "Well, for the record, I ain't comft'able with that rat anywhere near you, but at least it's a public place."

My lover's expression turns a familiar melancholy that would normally smooth out his tiny scars if not for the newest scab from the butt of a gangster's gun. I'll have to heal it for him when I'm better.

The pad of Gio's thumb traces my lips. "I thought you was dead on that ground yesta'day. You didn't move for the longest time."

"Careful," I whisper, puckering against his fingerprint. "You might end up liking me again."

"Yeah, well, I ain't afraid'a your magic." His orneriness sidles up his cheeks as he pushes my arms down beside my head, holding them like human shackles. "Think I'm gonna capture a little bit for myself."

As his lips near mine, I turn away with a teasing smirk. "So I'm guessing it wore off last night?"

"About the time you started snorin', boss. Now get ova' here and make me yours."

BURNING TOBACCO. SWEET RUM. GIO'S FINGERS FLYING OVER THE ivory keys like Heck's feet on the dance floor. I'm surrounded by the best things in life with the people I love. My newly placed ferns and hanging cactus don't look half bad either. Gives the club an exotic feel. The night is so much more relaxed than usual as my crew enjoys their night off from serving patrons so they can dance and sing and drink when they want to. Their moves on the dance floor are a little more crass, and I'm fairly sure a few entertainers will lose their shirts tonight, but I've never seen them so liberated. The libations help. Heck said it'd be good for morale, and I heartily agreed. I needed this night too.

Even Margaret stopped by earlier in the evening to congratulate my crew as we reprise our private celebration of opening weekend. She tried not to seem elated that her husband hasn't returned home, joking that he probably took off with a barmaid. If anyone deserves to inherit an ungodly amount of green, it's her.

After lifting a satisfying glass in the air, toasting to their job well done, I settle on the wooden piano bench next to a flirty musician who can't keep his mouth to himself. As a hopping song ends, our band leader shoots my admirer a classic eye roll to cover the tiny smile behind the lip of his saxophone.

"Have I told ya how crazy that dress is makin' me right now?" Gio asks my neck, his hand teasing the tight roll of the stockings just below my knees. "These too. Even without the shoes."

I lean my head back to the tickle of his breath, my thin line of smoke joining the rest of the hazy air. "Yeah, I think blue is my color. You could use a shave."

His chin stubble scrapes across my shoulder, my laugh exploding as his fingers dig into my rib cage. "You know what you could use?" I stifle a squeal when he spins me around and tosses my legs over his lap.

"Dios!" a handsome swell exclaims, slapping his hand on the top of the piano. "Do I gotta watch you two all night?"

Gio removes his fingers from my thigh, taking my drink. "You don't gotta watch anyone, Jav. We hired a bartender tonight so you wouldn't have to. Kippy look, by the way."

"Bushwa."

"No, really," I say. "He's got great taste."

My brother's blush spreads across his neck in blotches of red as he smooths the front of his vest. "I guess. Herringbone's not really my thing, and I told him I'm not doing the jacket."

"Well, you look sharp anyhow," Gio says. "Now get out there and put that suit to good use."

The iced rum burns through my nose as I swallow a laugh. "I'm sure he's needing to recover after Penny dragged him to the dance floor for the third time."

"You're one to talk, hermanita."

"Jav, have you *seen* Rose dance?"

I shoot Gio a squint, stealing back my glass. "Don't you have a song to play?"

"I would, but our singa's a little busy at the moment." Following his smirk, I lift my tumbler in salute to the necking couple in the corner booth. It's a good thing our crew gets along. The way Doris has her tongue down Nickels's throat, he wouldn't be any help if a fight broke out. Charlie's brassy notes have that effect on people.

My grinning fiancé's film-star smile shines through the dancing crowd, a manicured hand grabbing at his earlobe and arms as he makes his way to the stage. "Darling!" He laughs, glancing back with a wrinkled forehead. "Our flappers are trying to *solicit* me. You *must* do something!"

"I don't know what you expect me to do," I say, slapping away Gio's straying hand. "I think our ruse is up with this lot."

Heck gives a shrugging nod of agreement, avoiding my brother's eyes like he's been doing most of the evening. Stealing a few hugs from Javier over the course of the night let me know all about the small spat those two are having. It's not the felonious relationship that bothers my brother; it's just that no one ever really knows *who* he's dating—man, woman, or otherwise. Heck's clinginess and Javier's extreme privacy are an entertaining mixture, but they're more in love than any couple I've ever read. If *they* can't work it out, the rest of us are done for.

In the awkward silence of the conversation, Gio joins the smooth sax, tinkling lightly on the piano. My brother shifts, shoving his thumbs into his pockets as he meanders to Heck's side. The peripheral of my eye watches to see if he's as much of a train wreck at feelings as I am, but I have to lean a little to hear over the raucous room.

"It's almost midnight." Javi tilts his head to capture my fiancé's eye.

The poor billboard can't help himself, his lips pressing together to suppress a smile. "And?"

"It'll be two months at midnight," Javier says, stepping closer with an intensity I'm not sure *I'm* comfortable with.

Heck's coy smile falters. "Oh. Right."

"What's wrong? I thought that's what you were looking forward to."

"Um . . . I . . . well, I . . ."

My fiancé's stammering halts as Javier's dark hand travels down his pin-striped sleeve, turning more than a few raised eyebrows in their direction when their fingers meet. "Kessie, do you wish to stop loving me?"

Heck has that watery-eyed look, his lips parting as he shakes his head. Whatever sparks are flying between them ignites Javier as he tugs his lover's jacket, their mouths smashing together in a way that rivals the corner booth. Whistles and jeers erupt around them, Gio shouting out a holler of encouragement along with the rest of the underworld. Though my staff is a mixed bag of progressive misfits who don't give a damn, I've never seen my brother so openly affectionate. The blushing couple finally breaks apart, the tips of their noses touching as the nightclub resumes its bustling merriment.

"Good," Javier says with a small smile, "because there's no cure for what we have."

Heck's mouth falls open. "*What?*"

"Kessie, if there was, don't you think I'd'a done it by now?" My brother drops his head in a hearty chuckle at Heck's second bout of speechlessness. "My abuela was just giving you some time to find out—not just to accept who you are, but to embrace the hell out of it."

"Javi . . ."

Cupping a tender hand to his lover's dampening cheek, my brother shakes his head. "Cures are for the ill. There's nothing wrong with you, bonito."

Heck's eyes brim like glittering sapphires as he pushes his fingers into Javier's hair, kissing him until I wonder when they're going to come up for air.

Maybe by the time I go refill my glass.

On my way to the bar, a series of shrieks parts the crowd near the door. My crew's going to have to keep it down before hotel management gets in a lather. I start toward the commotion, my lips pursed, only to be bowled over by flailing arms and skipping legs. *What in the—*

"Rose! They've got guns! Get away from the door!" my brother's voice booms over the heads of the crowd. From the stage, Charlie's brass instrument clatters to the floor with all the others, mayhem ensuing around me. My glass shatters behind me in my dead run, pushing past the sparkling dresses and flying fedoras that scamper to the exit. The three loves of my life form a wall beside me as a scowling mobster with his goons in tow charges into the room, their pistols in the air. Their shoes take their time clicking across the emptying dance floor. Salvatore's snide look is sure to match whatever's about to come out of his mouth.

"Boys," he says like he's holding back a volcano in his throat. "Take these heroes to her brother's place. It's time Rose and I had a talk."

Javier steps forward, his forehead greeted by a henchmen's barrel. "We're not going anywhere."

"Wha'd you die, like, twice now?" Salvatore laughs before his expression hardens again. "You wanna go for three?"

I might still be drained, but I've got enough juice to lay this jerk out. What's more, I'm learning how to use it. I cross my arms like I'm bored, stoking the irritation in my enemy's face.

"No, you guys go. I can handle him."

"Hermanita."

"Go," I say, holding Salvatore's bitter gaze. The room empties with mumbled threats and concerned looks, leaving me and this wishful mobster in a standoff. As I lift my chin, my power stretches beneath the floor like a crawling vine, finding its way to the warmth of the potted plants in the corners. I've never actually felt their protection before now. Maybe it's because I'm the one that blessed them this time. My chin lifts higher, pulling a small envelope from my garter with the confidence of a bruja who knows who she is. He can't hurt me here.

Not in my home.

"Look at you all high and mighty." His hair shines under the warm sconces as he takes a few slow steps forward, snatching the payment from my hand. "Tellin' me when and where to meet. That dress almost makes up for you not showin' up last night."

"I told you we had a run-in with the Klan. I also told you that you don't own me."

"You better believe I do, you bindle punk vamp!"

Searing heat across my cheek takes my breath away, my left eye threatening to explode from its socket. Salvatore's leather glove hurts worse than his hand.

"You listen to me—the Klan, magic, Mexicans, dirty piano players—ain't none of that my problem," he snaps, tearing my hand away from my throbbing face. Holding back burning tears, I clench my teeth, reaching for his smug pointed chin. His other glove intervenes before my fingers can land. "No, no, my girl. You ain't fryin' my brains or anyone else's unless I say so."

My arms twist fruitlessly, chafing against his grip. "Yeah, well, you have to let go sometime."

"See, that's where your rebelliousness stops bein' cute, Rose!" Tightening his jaw, he forces me into a backward run, our arms writhing in the struggle. He swears as much as I do, our angry dance ending with my arms behind my back and my chest against a wall. Sharp fingers dig into my wrist as he lectures over my growling scream. "I don't gotta do anything! *You* are gonna do what *I* say, or so help me, I'll lock you in a room where no one can find you—then pick off your family one by one until you see things my way!"

My power reaches again, pleading to the earth for protection. I don't get it—I felt the plants. *Why isn't it working?* Maybe I missed an ingredient or said the wrong spell. A familiar fear yanks back my earlier confidence along with my roots. I don't feel anything anymore—except this goon's heated breath against my neck. The dirt in the pots is too far away. I go for a curse anyway. The cactus would make a mighty fine answer.

"Recogerán lo que siembra," I hiss across my quivering lips. Salvatore's breath hitches, his silence turning to a venomous chuckle as I continue the phrase in desperate repetition.

"Ohhh, so it don't work when you're afraid," he whispers against my shoulder. "Now we know each other's secrets, don't we?"

Oh God. Why did I tell my family to go?

It wouldn't matter anyway. He'd just come back another time. It's too late for Gio's phone call to the syndicate to make a difference. This will only end when I finish it.

"Let her go, Mr. Salvatore."

Or if the fates want to help, I'm okay with that . . .

With a sharp handful of hair, he pulls me away from the wall, both of us gasping as we spin to face a real mobster, a tilted fedora over his large scar. His suit is worth more than the envelope sticking out of my captor's front pocket.

Wiping his beaded forehead with his sleeve, Salvatore stammers as the mobster's large entourage closes in. "M-Mista' Capone, I got business dealings with this snake charma'. She's got a real respect prob—"

"Are you stealing from me, Salvatore?"

"*What?* No, I would never."

"I gave her that money," Capone says, lighting a cigar between his plump lips. "It's *my* investment. Even Moretti wasn't stupid enough to steal from me." He shrugs between puffs. "Stupid enough to get himself killed, but not stupid enough to steal from me."

The mob king's exhale is long and loud as he levels his eyes at my adversary. "That would be *way* worse."

Salvatore continues his deluge of excuses as the company of outlaws untangles me from his hold, their high-profile leader offering me a handshake and the envelope. As Salvatore's desperate pleas echo down the stairwell, Capone's hand wraps around mine, sending me images that shoot a shudder down my spine. A bullet-ridden body—it's thrown into a deep hole in a cornfield where no one will find it. Or a terrified hand reaching up through the water of the Missouri River as the victim is dragged down by the weight of chains and cement. He hasn't decided yet how he wants to execute Salvatore. I gently pull my hand back so as not to offend. I don't want to know.

"It was a time gettin' here," he says. "You sure got fast trains."

"Thank you, Mr. Capone." I hate the very words. I hate my fickle magic. It forced me to need him. But I made myself a promise to handle Salvatore, and whether it was the call to the syndicate or the fates that came through just now, this is what was offered me. Still, it was one thing owing Moretti, but owing a favor to a king of the underground . . . I'm done for. The disdain in my crossed arms and refusal to look him in the eye is something I simply cannot hide right now.

He throws out a smoke-blowing chuckle. "It ain't like that, Miss Lane. See, I'm the one that owed you." As my head shoots up, he chuckles again with that giant grin of his. "Your club is makin' me a fortune—and makin' KC a lot more fun to play in than those two idiots you were tied up with. Just keep doin' what you're doin', kid, and we got nothing but sunshine—and moonshine—between us."

Staring after the empty stairwell for a full minute, I finally come to my senses, ignoring the bellman at the hotel entrance as I fly to my car.

"LUNA!"

My family's tearful cries make me laugh as my own cheeks soak with gratefulness. Swapping stories of the past nail-biting hour, they settle me down next to my abuela on Javier's duo-fold sofa. The goons who held them at gunpoint were removed by other goons, leaving my loved ones with instructions to wait for me. The cramped apartment is as warm and comforting as their arms around me. I have ten thousand dollars of green glorious in an envelope, but the most wealth I'll ever have is in this room.

Heck offers my mother the chair to calm her nerves while Gio lowers himself next to my brother on the coffee table, his eyes widening as I grab the weathered hand beside me. "Abuela, I'm thankful we're all safe. I really am. I just don't understand why my magic didn't work this time."

"Oh, niña," she says, her gums shining at me, "magic did work." Her hand pats mine like she's explained everything.

Gio's head begins to shake, staring down at his scarred knuckles. "She's right, Rose." As if I could feel any more bewildered. He looks up, wonder etching across his face. "I only called the syndicate late last night. Said they were a three-day train ride from gettin' here. There's no way Capone coulda' made it in time."

What? I squeeze my abuela's hand to steady myself. "Abuela?"

"The earth not always do what we want," she says. "But does what's best."

As a woman who's grown up with magic her entire life, Gloria claps her hands on the knees of her dress, asking everyone if they're hungry and critiquing Javier's walls, saying that they need painting. Her dark eyes scan the room with an accepting nod. "It's an old shade of green, but at least it goes with the antique furniture, yes?"

"Is a couch bed considered an antique?" Heck muses, sharing a laugh with my mother as Javier snorts in response, "Aye, aye, aye."

"No worry, niño." Mama Sunday gazes at my brother's blemished walls with sparkling eyes. Lightly bouncing against the metal springs beneath us, she pinches the binding strip on the long cushion. "Feels like real leather."

I settle back onto the sofa that's supposed to be a bed, or the other way around. I settle my fears. I settle into the family that surrounds me and let hope wrap itself around me again.

24

THROUGH THE SHEER CURTAINS OF MY MOTHER'S WINDOWS, THE neighborhood children skip along the wooden plants of the sidewalk, shouting gleefully at each other in Spanish like my brother and I used to do. The craftsman bungalow is packed with all of our closest friends, with room to spare. Bustling through the archways between the hearth and dining room, my mother fusses over the luncheon appetizers while Mama Sunday regales our crew with harrowing Mexican folktales. Margaret's giddy laughter can be heard above the rest. My smile is as big as hers at the way Penny regards her so tenderly, rubbing her slightly swollen belly and making her put her feet up. She deserves it as much as the fortune she also inherited from her awful late husband. She always wanted to be a mother. She always wanted love. And now she's got it all, including refusing to quit her newspaper job despite her uncle's disapproval. Or maybe because of it. I think I've got a new hero.

I definitely have a true friend.

"Your mom's done a great job with this place," an uncultured voice with the right amount of grit says from behind me. I sigh into the tattooed arms that wrap around my shoulders with comfort like the wallpaper around us, the color of golden sand, designed with an antique texture that my mother says reminds her of home. Under the chandeliers that hang with several tiny lampshades to match the sconces on the walls, Javier's father's photograph sits on the fireplace mantel, next to framed articles announcing my club opening's success.

"Di mi. My girlfriend's turnin' into a real celebrity," Gio says.

"Yeah, I'm sure Heck's trustees are thrilled he's got a bootlegger for a wife."

"Yeah, just keep draggin' that Kessla' name through the mud," he quips with a chuckle, laying his chin on my shoulder. "You know, marryin' him could be consida'd fraud—not that he minds now that he's loaded."

"Just tack it onto my list of felonies."

"Like hirin' more immigrants cuz Cornwell can't say anythin' now or buyin' an entire downtown apartment buildin' and rentin' it out to the miscreants in this room?"

"What, you don't like our apartment?"

"Not as much as I like you." Spinning me around, he smirks down at me, his playfulness turning wistful. "You ruined my heart, you know that?"

I press my fingertip to his waiting lips. "You want it back?"

"No, you keep it. I kinda like the torment."

"Well, that's because I've got you under my spell."

"This whole city's unda' your spell, boss."

As his thumbs tease the band of my trousers, I smack his hand away before my mother sees his shenanigans. While I'm telling him what a gentleman he's not, a commotion from the bedroom gives me a chance to hide my blushing. I swing open the door to see a slightly disheveled Javier trying to disentangle himself from my husband. Gio's snort shoots through his nose as my brother tucks in the loose hem of his work shirt, smoothing his hair beneath his cap.

"You two finally comin' up for air?"

My brother flattens his eyes to fight a smile. "I'm trying to get Mamá's new trimming installed, but he keeps harassing me." I tighten my own mouth as he bats away Heck's flirty hand, his throat clearing. "Can you watch him while I go to work? I've gotta meet the city inspector at two."

"Javier Alvarado," my husband gasps, "don't act like you haven't enjoyed my interruptions. And why can't I go with you? I'm your designer."

He makes a good point. But my brother only broke ground for the new River Rose a few weeks ago. And the mischief in Heck's face tells me he's not interested in business today. His lover's resolute demeanor tends to agree.

"When the walls go up, you can come with me," Javier says, taking Heck's hands to keep them from playing with his buttons. "Otherwise, the only thing you'll be at my construction site is a distraction."

"*Well*, are there any other disdainful words you'd like to hurl at me this afternoon?"

My brother's espresso eyes fly to the ceiling. "Oh, stop being so dramatic, Kessi. Besides, Mamá loves your help with luncheons."

Heck's body wiggles like he's trying to decide whether to be angry or not before his pout turns into a smile. "I do like lunch. But promise me you're all mine when you return." His teeth pinch the corner of his lip as Javier leans in as if his sister—and his lover's wife—isn't standing there.

"I promise," he rumbles against his lover's lips.

As my brother bounds through the entryway, my husband grabs his chest, slumping against the oak doorframe. "That dashing villain. He'll own half the jazz district in less than a year if he's anything like you, kitten."

"Yeah," Gio says, "between the two'a them, they'll own the damn city."

My smile is as big as Javier's was when he announced what he was doing with his share of the money. I figured we all earned that money from Capone in one way or another. Besides, there's so much more where that came from. Family is what's irreplaceable. And my brother deserves every happy thing he's got coming to him. The underground doesn't care that he's brown—not the ones who matter, anyway. He's going to make the best club owner this town has seen—after me, of course.

"How exciting!" Heck perks up, his hands hitting his hips. "So you're going for the Torrean Ballroom, then? I'm thinking a Spanish motif, what with the vaulted ceilings. You have to go big to accommodate two thousand dancers."

As my husband launches into jubilant plans for our future investment, I lean into Gio, the warmth of contentment spreading through me. We still walk a dangerous path, finding our way in the dark, dancing with each other in the light, our hearts knitted together against bigotry in high places. The road ahead isn't easy, full of new enemies who will want to steal our happiness. But the only way to fail is to give up. And that's just not something we do.

As the luncheon is carried away by Heck's singing and Gio playing the piano—a housewarming gift my mother insisted on for this very purpose—I saunter outside to collect this week's paper. I nearly drop the smoke I just lit when I lift the *Star* from the concrete porch. *Margaret, you beautiful fool.* So she *didn't* rewrite that article. She wrote a new one. Mr. Roberts is going to blow a gasket and then some.

Dear readers of our most beloved metropolis,

I have been so inclined to report to you that the banning of pleasure only deepens our murky desires, adding to the frothy mixture of shame and bitterness. Prohibit alcohol. Punish lust. Lower the hemlines. Redefine love in the narrowest way possible and watch the people die a slow death from the inside out as they reach for a standard they can never attain. But we're not built that way. The legislation of morality has only served to force the underground to provide pleasures to the same righteous citizens who used to indulge in said desires before they were outlawed. But nothing has changed, other than the guilt that whips our backs and slaps our hands every time we don't measure up.

Adulterous husbands stay in loveless marriages. Wives powder their bruises. Immigrants shed their heritages and accents in exchange for acceptance. In more states than I care to count, men and women are imprisoned when their bedchambers don't look like yours. Perhaps there is more to us than what you are so eager to see . . .

"You beautiful fool!" I say to the newspaper. The tears dripping around my fingers smear the words. That's a woman who knows who she is. Doubling over with laughter that I don't want to stop, I let her words soak into me like the ink on my hands.

I am Rose Lane, a columnist at the *Kansas City Star*.

I am Rose Lane, an unabashed bootlegger with a boulevard apartment.

I am Luna Alvarado, a powerful bruja descended from powerful Mexican ancestors.

To some, I am a lover of men and gin, an immigrant tramp from the River Bottoms. To others, I am a soft place to fall when the world turns its back—a heart without bias. I am a smoker. I take my coffee with cream and my stockings without garters. My mouth is a dangerous place. And maybe I *was* a misfit, tiptoeing around this life with my head held low so no one could see the pain in my eyes. But I've looked to the sky beyond where men can reach and learned the stars knew my name before I did. I am an imperfect, broken vessel, filled to the brim with compassion. I am a sister, a daughter, a lover, and a friend. I am who I say I am.

ACKNOWLEDGMENTS

Ace Money Millionaire: my Jiminy Cricket

Gilly Suit: interpreter and amazing friend

My-Indi: my sister always

The Richardsons: family forever

My daddy: LUMI

Yo-Bo: my big brother who reads my shit

OshKosh B'Josh & Ashley: my other big brother and his wife, who gave me a safe place

The Dumpster Crew, the Pantheon, and my Twitter fam: you kept me going

My beta readers

Rachel Brooks: my agent, who saw something in me

David Pomerico and Mireya Chiriboga at Harper Voyager: they brought Luna to life

ABOUT THE AUTHOR

DESIDERIA MESA IS OFTEN FOUND GETTING LOST IN A HISTORI-cal, sci-fi, or high-fantasy novel or crafting her own stories, of course. Aside from churning out novels, she enjoys writing songs, poetry, and short stories. Follow @DesideriaMesa on Twitter for writing discussions, slightly inappropriate jokes, and more information on her historical fantasy debut, *Bindle Punk Bruja*.